SHADOWS &
TALL TREES

"Michael Kelly's *Shadows & Tall Trees* is a smart, soulful, illuminating investigation of the many forms and tactics available to those writers involved in one of our moment's most interesting and necessary projects, that of opening up horror literature to every sort of formal interrogation. It is a beautiful and courageous series." —Peter Straub

ALSO BY MICHAEL KELLY

Songs From Dead Singers
Scratching the Surface
Ouroboros (With Carol Weekes)
Apparitions
Undertow & Other Laments
Chilling Tales: Evil Did I Dwell, Lewd I Did Live
Chilling Tales: In Words, Alas, Drown I
Shadows & Tall Trees
Year's Best Weird Fiction, Vol. 1 (With Laird Barron)
Year's Best Weird Fiction, Vol. 2 (With Kathe Koja)
Year's Best Weird Fiction, Vol. 3 (With Simon Strantzas)

ALSO AVAILABLE FROM UNDERTOW PUBLICATIONS

Skein and Bone, by V.H. Leslie
Meet Me in The Middle of The Air, by Eric Schaller
Almost Insentient, Almost Divine, by D.P. Watt
Singing With All My Skin and Bone, by Sunny Moraine

SHADOWS & TALL TREES 7

EDITED BY
MICHAEL KELLY

 UNDERTOW
PUBLICATIONS

CONTENTS

INTRODUCTION

Michael Kelly

O F ALL THE BOOKS I'VE EDITED OR published, the *Shadows & Tall Trees* series is, unabashedly, and unreservedly, my favourite. The first volume was my attempt at an answer to the various mediocre and dreadful (in the worst sense) volumes of horror that I felt were being published. There are still too many bad books being published; as Series Editor for the *Year's Best Weird Fiction* I see them. And that will never change. But since the first volume of *Shadows & Tall Trees* was published there has been a steady increase in the number of quality presses. Presses that value literary quality, and have a unique artistic aesthetic.

Horror and weird fiction has seen a definite upswing in regards to literary quality, and respect among genre readers.

Which brings us to volume 7 of *Shadows & Tall Trees*, which you hold in your hands.

It has been three years since the last volume of *Shadows & Tall Trees*. That volume had many stories reprinted in various 'Year's Best' and 'Best Of' anthologies, and was a finalist for the World Fantasy Award, and the Shirley Jackson Award. All the volumes have been very well received. And all told, of the 55 stories published in the first 6 volumes, 18 have been reprinted in 'Year's Best' volumes. All this to say that I believe this current volume may be the best one yet. That's no disrespect to the previous volumes. The quality of submissions for each successive volume has increased steadily. I've seen several stories that I had to regrettably turn down for this volume get picked up for other publications. There is exemplary material being published in the Weird Horror field. It is a good time to be a reader. And it's a good time to be an editor.

Thank you to all the writers who submitted work. And thank you to the writers who grace the pages herein. As always, you make me look good.

Finally, thank you, dear reader, for supporting this endeavor from day one. Maybe, just maybe . . . there will be an 8th volume of *Shadows & Tall Trees*.

SHADOWS &
TALL TREES

7

LINE OF SIGHT

Brian Evenson

I.

THE SHOOT HAD GONE WELL—ALMOST too well, in fact. So much so that Todd, by the end, was just waiting for something to go wrong: for production to come crashing to a halt, for the union to try to shut them down with some bullshit excuse, for the lead to have his face torn halfway off in a freak accident. The longer things continued to go well, the more strongly he could feel something roiling below the surface, preparing to go badly. And the longer it didn't, the worse he felt.

He was tempted to hurt himself, just to relieve the pressure. Cut off his thumb, maybe. But he knew this wouldn't go over well with the studio. By the time they wrapped, he was jumping at every little thing: he couldn't have lasted another day. But then, suddenly, it was over, the production a wrap, and instead of being relieved he was flustered, unbelieving, still waiting for something to go wrong.

And yet, even in the early stages of post-production, it never did. No issues with sound, no problems with editing, no problems when the footage was processed: nothing wrong. The film came out, so everybody claimed, better than expected. Even though the studio had been a little standoffish with the rushes, they now claimed to love where Todd had gotten to. Unaccountably, nobody had any final notes.

"Really?" said Todd, bracing himself.

"Really," said the studio exec. "It's great just as is."

"And?" said Todd.

"No ands," he said. "No buts."

Todd folded his arms. "So, what do you think needs to be changed?" he asked.

"I don't think you understand," the studio exec said. "We don't want anything changed." And then a moment later, his brow creased. "What's wrong with you? You should be celebrating."

But Todd couldn't celebrate. He was still waiting for something to go wrong.

Nothing wrong, nothing wrong, he told himself, but he still felt like he could feel the exec's eyes on his back all the way to the door, watching him go. He imagined how he would shoot that scene: a quick shot first of the exec's face, then Todd's back as he walked toward the door, then the exec's face again, expression slightly changed. He should be grateful, he knew he should—there was nothing wrong and everything right, the film was a success. But didn't that just mean that something was likely to go hideously wrong for him on a personal level? But he wasn't married, not even with anybody, didn't even own a pet: what could go wrong that hadn't already? Okay, so maybe his next film would be an utter disaster? How could he enjoy this success before he knew how much it would cost him down the line?

He went home. He looked at the wall of his apartment for an hour, maybe more. It grew dark outside, then darker still. Finally, hands shaking, he drove back to the studio.

It was later than he thought. Still, he had no problem talking his way through the gate, or getting himself into the building. He got the night watchman to let him into the editing bay, then queued up the film and began to watch, pretending that he was seeing a movie directed by someone else.

It was good, he grudgingly had to admit. If he considered it objectively, he had to agree with the studio. The camerawork was excellent, startling even, the film saturated with shadow in a way that made the slow mental unraveling of the lead seem as if it were being projected all the way across the screen and even spilling off the sides a little. The effect was panicked and anxious, and he began to think that his own anxieties about the imminent collapse of the project had filtered down to everybody participating in the shoot, but in a way that paradoxically served the film. The lead, when he began to unravel, seemed not only like himself unraveling, but almost like a different person. It had become the kind of film that brought you close to a character and then, once that character was going mad, brought you closer still.

He stared at the empty screen, the film continuing to work inside his head. He should be happy, he told himself. Everybody was right. He should be completely happy, but there was something nagging at him. What was it? The acting was excellent, the blocking and staging and camerawork just as good. Lighting was superb, sound editing was precise. What did he have to complain about?

He sighed, stretched. He should accept that the film was a success, he told himself, go home, go to bed. Instead, he queued the film up and watched it again.

The third time through, he began to sense it, began to realize what the problem was. In the interior scenes, the eye lines were a little off. Not all the interior scenes, just the ones set in the lead's childhood home, before and after he dismembered his parents. Not off by much, just slightly, not enough for anyone to notice consciously, at least not on first viewing. But who knew what it was doing subconsciously? People noticed things, it didn't matter if it was conscious or not. It needed to be fixed.

And yet, he remembered the cameraman lining all that up carefully—he'd fired the script supervisor at the cameraman's request, because the cameraman had insisted he wasn't meticulous enough about just that: eyelines. He had a vivid memory of the cameraman blocking it, and then re-blocking it, making micro-movements of the camera to get it right every time they shot a scene.

He went onto the computer, pulled up the digital files of the rough footage in the editing bay. Was he right? Even staring at a frame of the lead looking next to a frame of what, ostensibly, he was seeing, he could hardly tell. Was he imagining it? At first he thought so, but the longer he stared at it the more he thought, no, the eye lines were off.

Maybe the cameraman had a slight vision problem so that what looked right to him didn't look right to anybody else. Or maybe Todd was the one to have the vision problem and there wasn't anything there.

He toyed and tinkered with a frame a little, seeing, if he cropped and adjusted it, whether the problem could be corrected. But no matter how much he torqued it, it didn't seem to help.

It wasn't until after he had already dialed that he realized how late it was—midnight or one in the morning now. He hung up. He could wait until morning.

But, a few seconds later, his phone began to ring.

"Misdial?" the cameraman asked when he answered.

"Ah," Todd said. "You're awake. No, I meant to call. Sorry to call so late."

The cameraman didn't bother to answer, just waited.

"It's just," said Todd. "I'm . . . the eye lines," he finally managed. "They're wrong."

For a long time, the cameraman was quiet, and Todd thought maybe he'd offended the man.

"Just in the house," Todd added, as if that made it better somehow. "Everywhere else they're fine."

"Where are you?" the cameraman finally said. His voice sounded strangled.

Todd told him. "Are you okay?" he asked.

The man gave a laugh, part of it cut off by static from the connection. "I am now," he said. "Now that somebody else has finally noticed."

2.

"It was awful," Conrad claimed, as he and the director sat over coffee in a deserted diner at two or perhaps three in the morning. "I would set the eye lines, then look and think, yes, that's it exactly, but the whole time another part of me would be thinking, *no, not quite.*" And so I would frame it again, would check everything again. Each time I would think when I looked through the viewfinder, *yes, perfect,* and then, a moment later, *but . . .* "

It had been like that through the whole shoot. Most days he just thought it had something to do with the feel of the shoot as a whole, the tension present on the set for some reason. *You felt it too,* said Conrad to the director. *I could tell.* But at night, back at home, lying in bed, Conrad kept thinking back through the shots, wondering why the eye lines still didn't feel right.

"I've never felt that way," said Conrad. "I've been in the business for two decades and I have never felt that way."

As the shoot went on, it became not better but worse. Not outside, not in the other locations, just at the house. Conrad began to think of the house as a living thing, expanding and contracting, breathing, shifting ever so slightly. As he told this to the director he believed from the look on the man's face that he felt it too. Being in the house was like being in the belly of something. It was like they'd been swallowed, and that the house, seemingly inert, was not inert at all. It was always shifting ever so slightly, so that even in the time it took to go from a shot of a face looking at something to setting up a shot to reveal where that face was looking, everything was already slightly wrong, slightly off.

"It sounds crazy," said the director.

"Yes," Conrad agreed. "It sounds crazy. But you felt it, too."

And it was even worse than that, Conrad claimed. For when he had stared, really stared, it seemed like something was beginning to open up, like if he stood just right he could see a seam where reality had been imperfectly fused. He had stood there on the balls of his feet, swaying slightly, not caring what the crew around him might think. And then, for an instant, he even managed to see it just right, not so much a threadlike seam as a narrow opening, as well as a someone—or something rather— gazing out.

"Why didn't you tell me?" asked the director.

Conrad shrugged. "You've said it yourself," he said. "It sounded crazy. And you didn't say anything either. The film editor didn't notice it at all. But then, he wasn't on the set, was he?"

The director hesitated, then nodded. Both men sat in silence and sipped their coffee. Finally the director said, "What was it?"

"Excuse me?" asked Conrad.

"Gazing out," said the director. "What was it?"

Conrad shook his head. "I don't know for certain what it was," he said. "All I know is what it looked like."

"And what did it look like?" the director asked, but you could tell from the look on his face that he didn't want to know.

You had to understand, Conrad claimed, that what it looked like was probably not what it was. That if he had to guess, it was the sort of thing that took on aspects of other things that came close to it, a kind of mimic of anything it could manage to approach. In a house like that, in a place where the seam of the fabric of reality was wrongly annealed, it would take on the appearance of whatever it had the chance to observe, to study through the gap in the seam. "At first I thought I was wrong," said Conrad, "that I was seeing some sort of odd reflection or refraction, that I couldn't be seeing two things that looked the same. But when they each moved they moved in a way that couldn't be seen as either the same or as mirroring one another. No, even though they looked identical, they were anything but the same."

The director struck the tabletop hard with his open palm. "Goddamit," he said, "what did it look like?"

Conrad looked surprised. How was it the director hadn't guessed? "Why, the lead, of course."

3.

The whole production Steven Calder (née Amos Smith) had had the feeling that something was wrong. Not with him, not with his acting, no, that was good. As good as it had ever been in fact, for reasons that he wasn't sure he could understand. Not with the director either, though the man was an odd one, jumpy as fuck. Cameraman was okay, too, if a bit anal, and so were the rest of the crew. No, nothing visibly wrong anywhere, nothing he could place the blame on. Just a feeling.

He shrugged it off and kept going, acting like everything was fine. Or, rather, acting like he was losing his mind, which was what the film was about, him losing his mind, his character losing his mind, but when the camera wasn't rolling yes, then, acting like everything was fine, even racking his brains for stupid jokes he'd heard back in high school—or rather, things that the Amos Smith he'd used to be had heard back in high school—things he could throw out to lighten the mood, things meant to demonstrate that he was at ease and nothing was wrong.

But he certainly was not at ease. And something *was* wrong, he was sure of it. In the house meant to represent his parents' house especially. Meant to represent his *character's* parents' house, he meant. Outside, no, he didn't feel it—nor, strangely enough, did he feel it in the other indoor locations, but in the house, yes, there he felt it. It made him feel seasick, as though the floor was shifting slightly under his feet, but that was crazy, houses didn't act like that.

But that was how this house acted. At least for him. Was he the only one who could feel something was wrong?

Steven was most sure something was wrong at those moments when he stood at his mark in the house meant to represent his parents' house—meant to represent his *character's* parents' house—and waited for the scene to be shot. The lighting was adjusted, the camera positioned, and the whole time he just stood there. Soon, he would think, maybe even as early as his next film, someone else would stand on his mark for him, a body double, but for now it was him. This was his big break, but until the break had broken it would be him standing in for himself.

At those moments, standing on his mark, sometimes he felt he could see, there beside him, a flickering, a strangeness in the air. But if he turned his head to look straight at it, he couldn't see it anymore. And then the cameraman would scold him mildly, coax him back to looking in the direction he had originally been meant to look, and the flicker would begin again. What was it? The rapid oscillation of the ceiling lights, maybe? Something wrong with his brain? He couldn't say. He didn't think it was something with his brain, but if it wasn't, why didn't anyone else seem to see it?

It happened about three quarters of the way through shooting, right in the middle of the murder scene. There he was, the dismembered bodies of what were meant to be his parents at his feet. He was still breathing hard, hyperventilating slightly, his vision fading a little, spattered in what would pass on film for blood, and he saw what he'd come to think of as a flicker. Only this time it was more than a flicker, more like a rip in the air, like an animal had torn the air open with its teeth. The cameraman was seeing something too. There was a strange expression on his face, and he was looking at the air just beside Steven's head with a sort of mute wonder. *Don't move*, something inside him said, and he could feel the hair rising on the back of his neck. He held still, very still indeed.

There was a smell like ozone, bitter and deep in his throat, the sound of something unfurling, and then he could feel breath hot on his neck. In front of him, the cameraman moved abnormally slowly, as if walking underwater. And then, suddenly, he was jerked, hard and fast, off his feet, the air knocked out of him.

By the time he had pulled himself up, just seconds later, the room was empty. The camera was gone, the entire crew as well, the room deserted. How was that possible?

"Hello?" Steven called, but there was no answer.

He got up and walked around the room. No sign, as far as he could see, of where they had gone. No sign, if he was to be honest with himself, which he was not sure he wanted to be, that the production team had ever been here: camera gone, lighting gone, none of the cables or other apparatus of a shoot. *What the hell?* he thought.

He walked around the room another time, and then again, growing more and more anxious. He tried the other rooms, but found them just as deserted, just as silent. He called out and listened for a response, but there was no response. Finally, he went through the front door and left the house.

Or at least he would have, if there'd been anything to go out into. There was nothing outside of the house, the door opening onto nothing at all.

How long had be been there? How many days? A long time, it

felt like, though in another sense it felt like almost no time at all. He had tried all the doors and windows. It was always the same: there was nothing outside the house. He wasn't hungry, which confused him. He wasn't sure how he could still be alive. Assuming he actually was.

He sat with his back to the wall, watching, waiting. Looking down at the backs of his hands he could see through them the ebb and flow of his blood. How strange. Had he been able to see that before? It was as if his skin was becoming transparent. He got up and paced, back and forth, back and forth, then sat down again. He slept for a while, woke, slept again, woke, went back to sleep.

He was just stretching, getting up again, when he caught a glimpse of it—that same flickering he had seen before. Immediately he was on his feet and looking for it, searching for it in the air. He swept his fingers back and forth but found nothing: there was nothing there. And yet, when he turned away, there it was, in the corner of his vision, flickering, again.

He moved toward it slowly, not looking directly at it so as not to startle it. He followed it as best he could, backing toward it, head down.

And then, from one moment to the next, his vision shifted, the flicker becoming a line of light, a line that opened until it became a slit and he could see something through it.

He was looking at the house, at another version of the house. This one had the production crew in it. The camera was rolling, and there he was as well, axe trailing from one hand, breathing heavily, his shirt spattered with blood. He watched the scene come to an end, watched as he, his character, killed both his parents, watched until the director said cut.

Only then did the figure that was meant to be him relax and glance his way, looking right at him, straight through the narrow gap. For a moment, they both just regarded one another and then the other him smiled in a way that bared his teeth, and Steven realized that what he was seeing not only wasn't him after all, but wasn't even human.

Through the slit he'd watched the film wrap, watched them pack all the equipment up, watched whatever it was that had taken his place genially shake hands with everybody and then head out the door, out to live his life. The rest of the crew went too. When the last crewmember had turned off the light, the opening faded.

There followed a long period in which nothing happened, where it was just he himself alone. His body grew longer, leaner. He didn't sleep anymore, though he sometimes lay down and pretended to sleep. He was hungry all the time but not for food exactly—for what he didn't exactly know. The flicker maybe, or what it led to. He wandered the house, looking again for that flicker, but it just wasn't there. Maybe it was still there, but if it was, he couldn't find it.

Or couldn't anyway, until something changed. There it was, suddenly, the flickering, and there he was, slowly moving toward it while trying to give the impression of moving away, until, finally, he had found the slit again. There it was, he could see it, the twin of the house he was now trapped in, dimly lit by the beams of two flashlights flickering their way through the dark space.

"It's got to be around here somewhere," said a voice, one he was pretty sure he recognized.

"Are you sure it's a good idea?" asked the other voice, also familiar.

He wasn't the one being asked, he knew, but he was sure it was a good idea. Maybe not for these two men, but definitely for him. Whoever *he* was, now. He could already feel his body changing, becoming more and more like whichever of the two men he looked at the most.

"Even if we do find it, how are we going to get through it?" asked the second voice.

Steven had an answer for this question too. He waited patiently for them to find the slit. When they did, well, they'd have no problem getting through it, because he would help them in. Would help one of them anyway, and in the process swap places and make his own way back out. The problem for that one would not be getting in, as he knew from experience, but getting out again.

EVERYTHING BEAUTIFUL IS TERRIFYING

M. Rickert

"But we, when moved by deep feeling, evaporate."—*Rainer Maria Rilke*

THE STRANGOS COME ALL YEAR, identifiable by the clothes they wear, the giggling behind open hands, the wide-eyed pretense of innocence; like belled cats they give their trespass away. I ignore them—for the most part—though recently the baristas have begun giving directions to Laurel's tree. They think this is funny, apparently, even if they never witness the punch line. Strangos standing in the middle of Wenkel's cornfield clutching their little purses. Strangos in the Piggly Wiggly parking lot next to the dumpsters, noses squinched against the stench. Strangos in front of my house—not funny at all—so close to each other the heels of their black shoes touch. I found them early on Christmas morning, standing beneath the streetlamp, upturned faces dotted with flakes of snow, matching pea coats frosted with ice, knees trembling above soggy ankle socks and black shoes.

They arrive all year, undeterred by the season. July and August bring a few carrying guidebooks and taking selfies (which no legitimate Strango would ever do) things get more serious in September, but October is Strango high season. In October the scent of wood smoke mingles with the beeswax candles perfuming my home with honey. Give me that and a blood moon casting everything in a mortal glow. Give me that and the ghost the Strangos seek, though I am not one of them, but an original.

She was buried, they say, in an unmarked grave at her mother's request. It was generally understood this was done in the usual manner, but after that movie came out with its silly premise that Laurel's weary ghost haunts the mysterious location of her body's interment the Strangos arrived with their earnest obsession. I, myself, seeking answers, once stood on Laurel's porch until her mother threatened me with a kettle of boiled water.

"Forgive me?" the Strangos murmur as they pass. It's just coincidence. The Strangos murmur their forgiveness request because in the movie that's how it's done. I stand in white ankle socks and black shoes, clutching the little purse with the clasp that clicks open and shut. Laurel stands beside me, dressed to match; though it's not really us, of course, but actresses portraying me and her ghost. When I whisper, "forgive me?" she doesn't say anything. The camera pulls back until we are in a circle of light surrounded by black; then a dot, then nothing at all.

I resisted watching for quite some time until one dreary night, while clicking mindlessly through cooking shows, women-buying-wedding-dresses shows, and fertile-family shows I stopped, stunned, as though experiencing a sudden change in altitude. There she was—Laurel—in her black shoes and white socks, wearing a dress I'd never seen; spinning beneath a bright arc of autumn leaves.

That particular scene comes quite close to the end—as you may know—but it was one of those stations that plays the same movie repeatedly. I can truthfully say that by the third viewing I was eating popcorn again; less enchanted by the Laurel look alike and more annoyed by what they got wrong, which was almost everything.

Though accused and found not guilty, my innocence was never restored. The Strangos (and the screenplay writer) are convinced I am a murderer but the truth is so much more benign. Ask the

Strangos and they will whisper, in sibilant tones, "forgive me?" over and over again until the reporter, either irritated by their petulance, or thrilled to have gotten a good clip for the weird news story gives up trying for more while the photographer waits for that moment when the Strangos open and close their purses making a sound like click beetles.

I am disinclined towards empathy with Strangos, but must confess I understand. Reporters are so annoyingly persistent in asking the wrong questions (as are parents, detectives, attorneys and everyone) that sometimes a person can find no response more perfect than the defiant sound of purse latch. I did not do it to be annoying or frightening though the movie portrays me as both. I was a child then, accused of murder. I was terrified, not terrifying.

The tree isn't hard to find, if one knows where to look as, of course, I do. And, while I hate to attribute anything of value to that movie, I must admit after watching it several times I, too, became obsessed with the old oak as a potential location for Laurel's ghost. I did not, to be clear, think her mother would have her buried there. I believe she was cremated; her ashes now in Florida.

But her ghost? It seemed possible the tree would make a perfect host. (Like the Caribbean Lagarou tree where people have reported seeing, from a distance, flickering orbs of lights in its branches which, I know, is meant to sound ominous but I find reassuring.) Thus began my October quest through the backyards of my youth to that small hidden field we discovered all those years ago.

When the seasons turned to Halloween we, best friends forever, chose to be twins. The movie would have you believe we dressed alike for years, but in truth it was only a single month, and not even all of that.

When October comes I close the windows, happy to sever any tie with murmuring Strangos. I take out the old photographs: Laurel and me in our bathing suits (not matching) eating popsicles (and in the left corner, beneath the azalea bush the toes of my father's shoes. He used to like to play that game of spying on us.) Laurel and me on her swing set (there was a time when I was a welcomed guest). Laurel and me in sleeping bags, wide awake, Laurel giving the finger, and me frozen in shock by her bold gesture. I remember how my brother ran to report what she had done and how my mother (still innocent in her own way then) laughed. The last photograph has been widely duplicated—I'm sure you've seen it in some fashion or other—Laurel and me in the matching cotton dresses that Mrs. Sheer made in a single weekend. She had extra time on her hands, my mother said, since Laurel was an only child. We are standing in front of my house in those dresses, ankle socks, and white Keds spray painted black. I can't remember why we did that. Sometimes too much is made of the casual choices of the young.

My mother found the purses at the dime store and splurged, buying both. I think she felt a little competitive with Mrs. Sheer, though this is pure speculation on my part and, as one who has suffered by what people assume, I try not to guess the motivation of others. My mother bought the purses. They were red. Matching white hairbands completed the look.

I suspect that arranging photographs of Laurel on the mantel might seem macabre to others. I can't be sure about what "normal" people think; they got everything so wrong with me that I have never adjusted to their ways. Halloween has, by necessity, evolved over the years into my own manner of celebration. Not for me the freedom of cheap costumes and pillowcases full of candy. That was lost with Laurel's death; first to my grief, then to my shame, and finally to my compromised life. While others were content with false ghosts, I hoped for the real thing. To be forgiven. Not for a murder I never committed, but for leaving her where she was later found with dirt and skin beneath her fingernails.

It is true that, as they said, the skin was mine. So much was made of this! We had a fight. About what, I can't remember. There was dirt on my dress and shoes and socks. We ran through backyards and fields to get to our tree. Dirt is not blood, or criminal in any way, but try telling that to folks set on vengeance, or any of the Strangos who think they know so much.

When October comes I decorate with photographs of the dead: Laurel and me as already mentioned, my parents, and my bother whose suicide is not a part of this story. Also my cats, Batman and Robin, each found with strings around their necks and, I believe, victims of my notoriety. I arrange the photographs in a display of fake autumn leaves ever since trying to use real ones which brought bugs into the house, an infestation I do not want to repeat, appropriate as it may be to the occasion.

Sadly, no one begs treats from me; a pattern I ignored for years, stocking up on candy bars, popcorn balls, and fairly expensive caramel apples which I ate throughout winter, solidifying the caramel flavor of loneliness, the apple bite of regret. While others dress as someone else, I dress as myself (or the girl I once was) in yellow gingham, white socks, black shoes, headband; waiting until dark before I sneak through the backyards, everyone so distracted I make an easy passage to the tree where I wait. The first time I did this I panicked when I realized how, without awareness, I had so thoroughly become Laurel's last moments, or what we know of them, before she was murdered, but no one came to reenact the crime. I just sat shivering, in the dark.

We had gone trick or treating with strict instructions to return home by ten but, if you haven't picked up on this by now, Laurel was cheeky and I, her happy co-conspirator.

"Heyo," she said, (using our twin language) "Let's go-o to our-o tree-o."

Why? Oh, I don't remember though I suspect it seemed just enough of a transgression to deliver a delicious thrill, running through moonlight on that night inhabited by the occult. It was meant to be fun! We giggled and whispered, lugging pillowcases heavy with loot.

The paper reported candy wrappers littered amongst the leaves. I suppose this is right. We probably delighted in our feast, drunk on sugar. We fought. About what, I don't remember. She scratched me and I ran home, though to this day I can hear her cries. "Come-o back-o," she called. "I'm-o afraid-o of the Strangos." A false laugh, and then, "Don't go-o-o."

Later, the policeman handed me a cider doughnut and said, "I often think what I would say if I had one more day with my friend who died. Heck, I bet you know what that's like, don't you?"

Click-click.

"Go ahead. Close your eyes. Picture Laurel."

Click.

"Say it."

"Forgive me."

"Who but the guilty ask forgiveness?" The prosecutor intoned over and over again. In my youth I thought this was compelling, but as a grownup I am shocked that adults fell for this false equivalency. Though I was guilty to be sure, it was not of the crime I was charged with. In the end, I was just a bad friend. No danger of repeating that mortal error again. Who would want to be friends with me? I can tell you the answer is no one. Not even a ghost.

Yet, I persist. In spite of the solemnity of the season I have come to enjoy my celebration which begins, as I have said, with the altar of dead and so forth until the great night arrives when I turn off all my lights and—dressed as myself all those years ago—sneak away from streets teeming with Strangos of all shapes and sizes; generations of Strangos with no connection to Laurel or her life to stand beneath our tree where I beg her to forgive me, jump when a leaf falls (briefly seeing too much meaning in it) and look at my hands. So large, though once they were so small. I shiver in the cold. Walk home alone, shoes and socks dampened by frost.

The next morning I pack photographs, dress, headband, purse and the rest. I toss out the caramel apple sticks and pumpkin tea wrappers. I stand at the closed window noting how the tree limbs scratch the gray sky, the fallen leaves decomposed of color.

November is the worst month, that brutal time after they found her body and my own mother began the wandering which defined her final years. She paced at all hours; locking doors, sprinkling sugar on the floor ("It will mark his footprints," she said) and cut up tablecloths which she insisted made perfect fabric for new dresses, though I never saw any sewn. Perhaps I outgrew them in that time between the charge and my acquittal. My father found solace in fantasies of revenge, which he described in our new ritual of bedtime stories. "First, I'll tear off his fingernails," he said and so forth, seeding my sleep with nightmares from which I often woke to find my brother weeping in a dark corner.

I was arrested in December so it would not be unreasonable to assume the month ruined for me but I have recovered the season; enlivened by the tradition of Christmas ghosts. Laurel loved the holiday; it made sense she would use the occasion to make a grand entrance. In spite of what that movie inferred she never would have become zombified with an appetite for blood; even dead she would remain a life force. I know she wasn't always sweet, or even good but she could make me laugh when no one else did. She told Petal Mearlot and Tina Schubert to stop throwing stones at me, and the day after Christmas—that last year—she pretended to be impressed by my meager haul then brought me to her house (it smelled of peppermint and evergreen) where she dumped the contents of a giant stocking on her bed, dividing it between us because, she said, Santa meant for me to have an equal share. "We're just so alike. Sometimes he gets us confused."

So it came to be that I made the error of inviting the Strangos I found standing beneath the streetlamp into my house. They looked cold and forlorn and, I admit, I was curious. Why would they choose to be Strangos when they could be daughters; loved and loving on early Christmas morn?

"Why are you here?" I asked, as I hung their wet coats in

the downstairs shower where they dropped chips of ice on the linoleum.

"We came to see Laurel's tree. Did you cut it down?" they asked. "Did you save the wood? 'Cause it's haunted."

"Here." I offered the blue willow cup and saucer my mother once loved, trembling with excitement at my first Christmas guests, ever. "Do you take lemon, cream or sugar?"

"Oh, I don't drink tea," said the first Strango, frowning into the cup.

"Me neither," said the other. "What else you got?"

They reminded me of Laurel. She would have sounded bossy, just like them. It put a smile on my face, it really did.

"I have Coke, and milk. There might be juice."

"What about eggnog?"

I shook my head, no. "My mother said it is dangerous because of the eggs."

"There are no eggs in eggnog," said Strango One, frowning into her cup.

"What about cocoa?" asked Strango Two. "But it must have whipped cream. I hate marshmallows."

"Laurel hates marshmallows too," I blurted.

"We know," the Strangos said in unison.

An uncomfortable silence settled over us. I wondered how they knew this about her. Was it buried somewhere in the movie; in the early scene when we met in kindergarten, perhaps? Or maybe noted in the companion volume, which I never purchased though I did page through it once, in the library, hunkered between shelves like a voyeur, my worn copy of Rilke temporarily abandoned?

"What's it like?" Strango One asked. "To live in her house?"

"Whose house?"

"The murderer."

I knew how Christmas was supposed to be and, while I had never entertained visitors, I had an idea how they were supposed to behave. I decided to rise above my guest's poor manners. "Would you like toast? I can cut it in the shape of a star, or a boot."

The Strangos, sitting side-by-side on the couch in their matching dresses with knocked knees and wet socks, looked at each other, wide-eyed then clapped their hands; three quick claps.

"Goody," said one.

"Yes, please," said the other. "With cinnamon."

Laurel liked cinnamon too. It made me sad to remember, though it did make the toast glitter pleasantly. I wished I had cocoa, but the Strangos didn't seem to mind the Coke and one of them even commented favorably on the combination, saying she planned to make it a tradition. I'm not sure if she was serious. It is very difficult for me to differentiate between mockery and affection.

After the Strangos finished their snack we sat and stared at each other. I studied them closely for clues on how to proceed but when Strango One began picking her dress with long fingernails as though harvesting fleas, I began to fear my little party was in trouble. "Would you like to play charades?"

"How about hide-and-seek?" Strango One replied.

Personally, I never liked the game and didn't see what it had to do with the holiday but in the spirit of being a good hostess, I agreed.

"You hide," Strango One said.

I thought it unkind, to send me off alone while they counted to a thousand and five, yet they were guests and, as such, should be graciously accommodated. How strange it was, then, to be alone again in this new fashion; knowing there were those nearby who shared companionship while I had none. Even though they were Strangos, it made me lonely in a way I hadn't been for a long time. Hearing their voices count together brought to mind the sound of Laurel and me reciting "The Night Before Christmas" which we learned in its entirety in second grade. The memory only made me want to create more distance between me and the Strangos. I crept up the stairs; careful to skip the third from the top. The sound of their counting became a murmur that reminded me of waking in my bedroom when I was young, listening to the sounds my parents made.

What had I been thinking? Why had I invited Strangos into my house?

Before then it had never occurred to me to enter the forbidden attic, but it offered a perfect hiding place; its narrow door blended neatly with the paneled wood and the small hole that once housed a doorknob appeared to be a whorl. It was off limits when I was a child, the occasional source of strange noises my father attributed to ghosts, though I had seen him take my brother up there and knew the moans belonged to him. I stood at the bottom of the jagged staircase, looking up the dark portal with the odd feeling of assessing a giant jigsaw piece, memorizing it before pulling the door shut and slowly walking up the stairs, imagining all sorts of frightening things like mice and bats, spiders and the like.

The attic was surprisingly small and, once I adjusted, cozy in a way. As a child I often "played mole," rolling up in a blanket and hiding in my bedroom closet; it made sense that I enjoyed the confined space with its low slanted ceiling jutted at odd angles over inviting corners. There wasn't much up there—an old bed, broken lamps, boxes filled with tools—but it was surprisingly warm. I sat, leaning against the wall and felt something like happiness, or what I remembered of it. "See dad," I whispered. "I always knew it was you," which led to tears that surprised me with their sudden, inexplicable arrival.

The single, old window offered a patch of bruised sky I stared at; finally hypnotized into a slumber until revived by a luminescence that filled the room with a holy glow. "Laurel?" I whispered, but did not wait for a flicker of acknowledgment; instead, I turned away, curled into the reassuring crook of my elbow. For some, hope is an annihilation; a greater loss than the loss from which it is born.

I don't know how long I slept, but when I awoke the attic was consumed by darkness, there was an uncomfortable crick in my neck and my knees ached as I carefully unwound myself. I bumped my shin on my way across the room, maneuvered carefully down the stairs, suspecting the Strangos were long gone;

if I fell and hit my head I would likely die and be decomposed before anyone even noticed I was missing.

What a mess the Strangos made! The house was in chaos; furniture moved, lamps unplugged, cupboards left open. What, I wondered, did the Strangos think I had shrunk myself small as a pin—the refrigerator drawers drawn full to reveal a pale head of lettuce, carrots and eggs thrown to the floor—before I accepted they had not been guests, but invaders. I closed the drawers, tidied up as one does, returned each thing that could be returned to its rightful place and tossed what was ruined; when my eyes fell to an errant orange, an orb of brilliance I plucked from its shadowed corner and peeled, getting skin beneath my nails as the bright spiral fell against the white porcelain. I wiped my tears with orange scented fingertips, finally understanding the answer I had been given: the sweet taste, the holy glow, the great loss and widening absence; to be robbed day-after-day, month-after-month, year-after-year; left to fall deeper into the void, find an orange there, and destroy it.

SHELL BABY

V.H. Leslie

THE CROFT-HOUSE STOOD STARK WHITE in the diminishing light, dark waves breaking against the shore in the distance. Elspeth looked past Donal toward the churning waters. It was desolate at this Northern edge, even the seagulls crooned melancholically as they soared overhead.

"You have to be crazy to move here," Donal said, handing over the keys.

Elspeth nodded and pulled up the collar of her coat. The wind blustered past, obscuring what Donal said next.

"Pardon?"

"Would you like me to help with your things?" he repeated louder, looking toward the car. Elspeth had brought a ridiculous amount of provisions; the back seats full with food, the boot already overloaded with suitcases and clothing. She'd brought as much as she could physically carry. She was loath to make the journey across on the ferry to the supermarket on the Orkney mainland more than was absolutely necessary. She was ready to hunker down and forget all about the rest of the world.

"I'll be fine," she said, shaking Donal's hand and

walking decisively toward the front door. Though it would take her longer on her own to unload the car, she was reluctant for Donal to enter what was now her space. Though technically he owned the croft-house, it was hers for the foreseeable future and she wanted to ensure it remained untainted by others.

She heard the sound of a car door slam behind her as she placed the keys in the lock, followed by the rumble of the engine. She took her time with the keys and waited until Donal was back on the road before she opened the door.

The croft-house looked much the same as the photos on the tourist website. It was traditionally furnished, slightly out-dated in parts with chintz ornaments and horseshoes nailed to the beams. But it was the view that had drawn her, as it did now. Sitting on a small window seat beside the hearth, she could see the sea, girded by a stretch of shingle beach. It was the sea, vast and inexhaustible, combined with the knowledge that there were no other homesteads for miles and miles that restored a peace within her. She was finally on her own.

She'd craved being on her own for such a long time. Over the years, she'd become increasingly frustrated with people, with the relentless noise they made. Even in the relative quiet of her flower shop, noise persisted, her customers' verbal out-pourings stifling her roses and lilacs, their inane conversations drawing all the air out of the room and leaving her gasping. She could only spend so long in the little side alley, among the rotting vegetal remains before having to return to serve another patron, the shrill ringing of the doorbell summoning her back to the fray.

She didn't have to serve anyone now but herself. She watched the waves continue their unyielding assault against the shore and thought of the life she'd left behind. It was more than just an idle fancy, this quest for isolation. She'd felt a change over the last year, as though she had misplaced a part of herself somewhere, in the way she would lose her scissors beneath the debris of leaves and stalks on the counter or under the copious buds of hydrangeas or delphiniums.

She called it a kind of quiet madness, this descent, this slip-
page in herself. She was aware of how far she could plunge if
she left it unchecked. She had imagined herself shouting at her
customers, yelling profanities, striking vases, flowers tumbling
about the room. Or worse, she would recede into herself, losing
her grasp of reality entirely and begin talking to the azaleas and
orchids.

She knew she had to go away. Somewhere where she would be
alone. Where there was no one to witness her decline.

It would have been different if she'd had a child, someone to
look after her in her old age, to accommodate this change in her.
A daughter would have been best. Daughters are always better
than sons at caring for their ailing parents. Elspeth wondered
why that was. Were men only able to satisfy one woman in their
lives? Maybe women were just more compassionate, dutiful.

She knew she was unusual; she'd never wanted a partner—a
mate. Sex was a fleeting appetite that reared its head from time
to time, not enough of a motivation to consider a life-long com-
mitment to another person. But she craved a child.

The sea was disappearing into the encroaching darkness but
she could still hear the reassuring hiss of the waves against the
shore. And she thought of her former fantasies about discovering
a foundling; a gurgling baby nestled amongst her blooms or left
in a terracotta pot in lieu of a crib, as if it had grown overnight
from the rich soil.

It took her well into the night to finish unpacking. It took her
longer because every few minutes she was drawn seaward. Nestled on the window seat, she'd scrutinise the grey surface, waiting
for something to disrupt the steady to and fro of the waves—
perhaps the appearance of a seal, a trawler in the distance—but
the waters remained unchanged, vacant.

Night fell early on the island and as Elspeth made the journey
to and from the car, she was struck by the absolute black of the
sky. Laden with bags, she could still smell the salt reek of the

sea. It was on the last trip to the car that she noticed the green shimmer and placing the bags back down, she leant against the bonnet of the car, realising what it was she was looking at.

In the supermarket earlier that day she'd told the curious cashier that it was the Northern Lights that had brought her to the islands. People don't typically head to the edge of the world in winter, when the days are short and harsh. It was why she'd got such a good deal on the croft-house. She needed a ready excuse and it seemed the most plausible. But the Northern Lights held no more appeal than the orcas and porpoises that inhabited the waters in the summer months. Yet now, looking up at the strange green spectacle, Elspeth felt a twisting, sinking sensation in her stomach, a giddy trepidation that made her short of breath.

She made her way down to the shore, the swelling green sky lighting her way. She needed to be close to the sea, to see the cosmic light dance off the black water. She felt the crunch of shingle underfoot and wondered briefly when the beach had last been walked upon. But she didn't look down. She couldn't take her eyes away from the eerie luminosity.

It was loud at the sea's edge. Not the lazy lapping of the waves as she'd imagined but the violent crash of water against rock. And then there was the wind, whipping past her, drowning out even the sound of the sea, pushing her toward the surf. She was aware at some point that her feet were wet, that the water had crept up on her without her realising. Though her feet were cold, it wasn't unwelcome. In fact, despite being deep midwinter, with the wind buffeting her with icy gusts, she felt strangely unaffected by the temperature. She'd left her coat indoors and now considered recklessly casting off the remainder of her clothes, struck by an overwhelming desire to feel the icy bite of the water on her skin.

It was the kind of crazy behaviour she'd never indulge back home, but here at the edge of the world she could do as she pleased. She removed her clothes hastily, in case she changed her mind and, pausing to glance up at the green sky once more, she stepped out into the sea.

Elspeth rolled over in bed, stretching her limbs as if she were underwater. The memory of the sea forced her upright and into wakefulness and she realised that she was naked. Pulling the bed-clothes tighter, she felt the shame of her younger self; of the times she'd woken unclothed beside a stranger, barely recalling much of the night before. There was no one beside her now, though her memories of the previous evening had the same vague quality about them. When she closed her eyes, a green haze filled her mind, interrupted by brief, half-formed recollections.

She remembered the initial shock of the ocean but later a curious, comforting warmth, as if the water was charged with the aurora's energy. And then there were the strange darting motions in the water, phosphorescence perhaps, snaking through the current towards her: potent rays of light seeking her out in the darkness.

Elspeth pulled the covers aside, looking around for her clothes. She couldn't remember anything beyond swimming. She must have stumbled back to the croft-house at some point, making her way, naked and wet, to her bed; her clothes still cast down on the beach or else washed away by the tide.

She rose and made her way downstairs. Though she wanted to head straight for the beach, to confront the strange experience of the night before, she delayed, putting on the coffee machine, stirring porridge slowly in a pan. What she needed right now was some semblance of normality. After she washed and dressed, slipping her coat on this time and a scarf for good measure, she made her way down to the shore.

She didn't expect her clothes to still be there. She'd imag-ined them drifting away upon salt waters. But there they were in the distance, heaped like a cairn. She hadn't seen much of the beach the night before, only what the green light permitted. It had seemed a mystical place then, of light and shadows, the sea shimmering—primordial. In the daylight, it looked much like any other shoreline. The shingle underfoot was unremarkable, interspersed with driftwood; the hull of a rowboat stood rotting in the distance, while the ocean was flat and grey, the same bleak colour as the sky.

The magic had gone. She watched the horizon for a few moments longer before stooping to retrieve her clothes. They were wet and heavy from the sand and surf. Her shawl had separated itself from the bundle and lay stretched upon the shore. Lifting it, Elspeth was aware of a sticky residue coating the fibres and then she saw what was underneath.

It looked like some kind of membrane, gelatinous and almost translucent but for a pinkish tinge in the middle. Perhaps it was some kind of jellyfish, though there were no tentacles or muscular parts. It was just an empty sac, like a deflated balloon. It put her in mind of a caul.

Elspeth thought briefly about casting it into the sea but she didn't want to touch it. So heaping up the clothes in her arms, she made her way back to the croft-house.

Life on her lonely promontory suited her. She'd walk most days, skirting her way along the beach, or drifting further along the headland. She'd head back in the early afternoon, aware that the dark was creeping in. The days were short here, brief interludes in the drawn-out nights. She read old stories by the fireside—the bookshelves crammed with texts on local folklore and mythology, left by enthusiastic holidaymakers—while she listened to the familiar creaking of the wind through the house. Her memories of the flower shop were an ocean away.

She hadn't thought much more about the night in the water, about the cold lure of the sea. She was unwilling to seek an explanation for her behaviour any more than that she would try to understand the strange phenomenon that made the sky glow. But later, as she walked along the shore, keeping her eyes downcast to avoid the assault of the wind, she happened to glance upon the strange caul-like form in the surf.

It was larger now, if indeed it was the same thing, and pinker.

In its centre a curious growth had appeared, a rose-coloured pro-tuberance that almost resembled a starfish, though it had only four limbs. Elspeth knelt beside it and reached out a tentative finger. The membrane was slimy with sea-foam and salt. The pink swelling in the middle undulated with the movement of the tide or perhaps from some kind of internal pulsation. Was it alive?

Elspeth took a step back. She didn't know what to make of it. The thing didn't resemble any marine life she was familiar with. But then she didn't know what strange creatures thrived in these cold waters. For all she knew, this was a common organism in these parts. Again she wondered whether she should push it back into the open water but something stopped her from doing so, and turning slowly from the sea, she made her way homeward.

The next day it was even bigger. The membrane was now taut and the fleshy star had accrued a halo of seaweed, which appeared to be enmeshed in the translucent bubble that surrounded it. It was certainly alive; Elspeth could see pink darting rays coursing along the body of the creature like blood through an artery.

She thought about calling Donal and telling him about the thing she'd found on the shore. Perhaps it was an endangered species, an aquatic wonder particular to these shores. But she didn't want anyone to disrupt the peaceful silence of her new life, the dark, embryonic stillness of her world. She'd rejoiced at news on the radio that the ferry connecting the island to the Orkney mainland would most likely be cancelled due to inclement weather. The idea of being completely cut off, utterly inacces-sible, gave her the same giddying feeling she'd experienced the night she saw the green lights in the sky. She felt empowered at the idea of her solitude and at the same time, utterly dependent on forces she didn't fully understand.

Elspeth knew something was wrong as soon as she set foot on

the shore. She was becoming accustomed to the sounds of the island; the whistling of the wind, the roar of the surf, the croon of the gannets flying overhead but this was something she hadn't heard before. It sounded like a series of high-pitched cries, a multitudinous screeching and wailing, carrying with it a sense of frenzy and desperation. Elspeth walked faster toward the din, breaking into a run when she saw the host of seagulls ahead, converging on one spot, fighting against each other to get at the thing in the surf.

Elspeth raced toward them, waving her arms wildly and shouting loudly to compete with their noise. As she drew closer, they took slowly to the air, squawking irritably at being denied their meal.

The thing in the surf looked pitiful. The torn remains of the membrane curled about its pink flesh, red in parts from the seagulls' assault. Elspeth knelt beside it and looked over its injuries, seeping red from exposed, raw tissue.

"There, there," she said, gently touching the creature's centre, its texture mollusc-like and slimy. She felt it recoil at her touch. She gathered seawater in her palms instead and gently poured it onto the creature, washing its wounds, hoping that the salt-water would restore it.

She could hear the seagulls encircling above. She picked up a stone and threw it into the air. Then shrieking loudly as she went, she walked toward what remained of the old rowboat, and began to drag it across the shoreline, stopping intermittently to scream at opportunistic gulls swooping low, or to fling another stone skyward.

The sea-battered hull was the perfect enclosure. She lowered it over the creature, sad that she would be denying it the light, though it would mean its survival. And she thought of her own existence, the absence of light in these long dark days that marked her time on the island, and how much she had thrived.

The creature healed well within the dark interior of the boat.

It acquired a carapace of shell and shingle; seaweed adhered to the parts that had been most exposed by the seagulls' attack, compensating for the flesh it had lost. Though it didn't resemble any amphibious life Elspeth was aware of, it looked strangely appropriate on the shore, like a mollusc beneath its shell amid a net of kelp.

It grew in size too. About the length of a newborn now, it squirmed in the surf in much the same way. Elspeth made her way down to the shore at first light each morning and would gently lift the driftwood from the creature so it could see the sky, though it had no discernable eyes. Often she'd take a blanket to sit upon, sometimes a flask and her breakfast so she could stay beside it as long as she pleased. She wondered as she watched the pink flesh stir whether it needed to be fed too, or if it absorbed the nutrients it required from the surf. She tried dangling a variety of food in front of it, but with no recognisable mouth, it was hard to know how it would feed if indeed it possessed an appetite.

She thought often of milk, of how most mammals are weaned by their mothers. She tried splashing it with a little cow's milk but it just ran off its surface and into the spume. She didn't suppose she had anything to worry about. The creature was growing in size each day and though it didn't appear similar to any established form of life she knew, it looked healthy and strong in its own way. But she wanted to exert some kind of influence on its growth.

She began to tell it stories. First the stories she knew from her childhood, fairy tales with moral instructions, then the stories she read in the evenings beside the fire—stories from the island. Tales of creatures that appeared human, living in vast underwater kingdoms and monstrous creatures that inhabited the land: giants and trows, water horses that drowned their riders. She wanted the creature to know the stories of the land it was being born into.

One time after talking of the impious trows—dwarf-like mischievous sprites, who crept into houses after dark to torment the inhabitants—she placed her finger against the soft pink belly of the creature and stroked it softly until it began to purr.

"This island breeds monsters," she whispered, wondering if it possessed enough sentience to recognise her voice.

And just as she was about to withdraw her hand, she felt a sharp stab of pain and looking down saw the beading of blood on her fingertip.

Elspeth stood by the window watching the man beside the boat. She could almost fancy he was a sailor, presumed lost, the wreckage of his vessel at his feet. Or else, one of the Finfolk from her stories, returned from the sea, dressed in a magical sealskin coat.

In the half-light, it certainly looked like a man. She'd fashioned him from driftwood and twine and dressed him in her oilskins. From a distance you wouldn't know that the figure was actually her mediocre attempt at constructing a scarecrow.

It seemed a good idea to create a sentinel. She couldn't watch the creature day and night and she worried about predators lurking nearby. She hoped it would be enough of a deterrent, though its purpose was perhaps to pacify her mind more than anything else.

Elspeth closed the curtains and sat beside the hearth. She thought of what she had told the creature. That islands like this one breed monsters. Maybe it was because things were more extreme here, the climate harsher, more severe, the land constantly besieged by the sea. After all, who knew what dark forces the sea harboured, perhaps from time to time spitting out these peculiarities to accumulate on the shore like flotsam.

Strange things thrived in the darkness, wasn't that right? So this was the perfect place to raise them. It was on a windswept island, much the same as this one, that Victor Frankenstein in Mary Shelley's novel retired to build his second creation. A female this time, at the behest of his first creature. Why did he choose such a lonely place to bring her into being? And what did he create her from anyway, far from the mortuaries and grave-yards he'd plundered back in Ingolstadt to build his first monster piecemeal? Was she made from the shingle and spume like the creature on the shore?

Maybe it was something to do with femininity and wild places. Frankenstein's monster was the product of the civilised world, but the female, she could only be engendered in the wilderness.

Elspeth made her way back toward the window and peered out from behind the curtain. It was darker now, but she could still see the scarecrow's silhouette and the dark outline of the boat. She could imagine the creature within, pink and engorged, sleeping softly to the sound of the surf and she knew then, with a strange certainty, that the half-formed thing was more like her than she'd realised. The creature was female.

She'd always wanted a girl and here she was, brought in with the tide. The goddess Aphrodite had been born of the sea, formed on the foam after her father's castrated genitals were flung into the surf. It was an odd parentage; Aphrodite's existence was dependent on her father's emasculation, and her mother, according to this genealogy—was the sea.

The sea. Elspeth thought of that night in the luminous green water. Of the energy she felt charging through the current.

She would name her child Aphrodite.

Elspeth smiled and returned to her place by the fire. After all, it's a fine line between monsters and gods, a vague boundary like the shoreline itself where neither the land nor the sea hold dominion.

The next day Aphrodite began to crawl. She was now the size of a baby seal and moved in a similar lumbering way, pulling herself up on her fleshy stumps. Elspeth stood next to the driftwood man and clapped feverishly. Proud parents.

"Well done, Aphrodite. Well done," she called.

And Aphrodite basked at the applause, though Elspeth could only surmise as much from the quickening of her movements, the excited writhing of her form. She still had no perceptible features; she was just a mass of pink flesh, like an oversized starfish, though the two lower limbs were less developed. When Aphrodite rested, reclining against the rocks, she almost resembled a human torso. Lying in the surf, dotted with sand and shingle, she gave the impression of a drowned person brought in by the tide. The only discernable thing about her was the shell carapace and the seaweed mane that trailed behind her when she moved.

The fact she was no longer bound to one spot filled Elspeth with hope. There was the prospect of her holding her, maybe taking her home to nurse and raise, perhaps even tucking her into a cot like a regular child. But there was nothing regular about Aphrodite. Her need for seawater would prohibit a normal home life. It would be more likely to nestle her into a bathtub than a crib. And then there was her diet to consider.

Elspeth stopped the train of her thoughts before they gained momentum. She didn't want to ruin this moment by worrying about how Aphrodite would fit into the world around her. It was enough that she was growing stronger, taking her first steps boldly along the shore. She watched Aphrodite amble toward her, her movements slower now as if she were fatigued. Or hungry. Elspeth knelt beside her and Aphrodite placed a stumpy oily limb on her leg.

Elspeth knew what she wanted and was happy to comply. Aphrodite deserved to be rewarded for such an achievement. Under the gaze of the driftwood man, she lifted up her sleeve, exposing the flesh of her wrist and let Aphrodite's cold, wet skin envelop her.

Elspeth found she adapted to motherhood well. She took pleasure bathing Aphrodite in the surf, plaiting her seaweed tresses. She even enjoyed the night feeds, untroubled by the lack of sleep. She could anticipate now when Aphrodite would call her, distinguishing her cry from the similar sound of the gulls. And wrapping a shawl about her shoulders she'd hasten to the shore and lift Aphrodite onto her lap. Then she'd pull up her sleeve and feel Aphrodite's cold, moist flesh coil itself around her in the way she imagined an octopus would fasten itself to its prey.

She hadn't expected to feel this kind of joy so late in life, this deep sense of contentment as she nursed Aphrodite. She wondered if all mothers felt such a bond. It didn't matter to her that it was blood instead of milk, she was feeding this nascent life with a part of herself and that was all that mattered.

The flower shop didn't even come close to this feeling, though it was the single product of her life's labour and though it had sucked out her energy and time in much the same way. It was just a shadow compared to the living thing in her arms and Elspeth felt a pang of regret that she had not arrived at motherhood earlier.

In the moonlight Aphrodite's shell-skin shone the colour of pearl. Elspeth took to identifying the seashells that made up her mantle as she rocked her: dog whelks and cockles, tellins and periwinkles. Interspersed with these empty shells, the exoskeletons of long-dead molluscs, clusters of barnacles grew in abundance and rock lice flitted along the surface, burrowing into the crevices and hollows left vacant.

Aphrodite purred in time with the lapping of the waves and Elspeth withdrew her arm. Would it just be barnacles and isopods that would crowd Aphrodite's carapace, or would she, one day sprout other more curious life forms, creatures as mysterious and strange as she was? And how would she cope, with all this life to support, crouching along the shoreline with her monstrous children on her back?

The next morning there were two men beside the boat. Elspeth rubbed her eyes and made her way closer to the window, hoping she had conjured a second driftwood man from her sleep-addled mind. But there he was, a real man, slightly shorter than her creation though dressed in matching oilskins, stooping slightly to examine the boat.

Elspeth bolted toward the door, struggling with her shoes and coat before racing out onto the beach. If he looked beneath the driftwood, what would he make of Aphrodite? He'd flee surely, perhaps report her to the authorities and they would take Aphrodite away to prod and examine. Or maybe out of revulsion or fear, he would attack her. What chance would she have, barely able to walk, let alone run from an assailant? She might retreat into the sea and perhaps disappear forever. Elspeth ran harder, with a speed and agility to her movements that belied her age. She needed to reach her child, to protect her from the man and the world he brought with him.

But as she made her way closer, she saw that he had disappeared. She scanned the scene ahead, looking for the slick, rubberised fabric, wondering briefly if she had imagined the intruder after all.

And then she saw his walking boots, sticking out from behind the boat, at the end of two narrow ankles that disappeared from view. Rounding the boat, she saw the whole hideous spectacle.

Aphrodite had pinned him to the ground, spreading her bulk across his chest. Her surface area was wider than normal as if she had elongated herself somehow, the effect being that more of her pink body was exposed beneath her shell exterior than normal. Elspeth edged closer, confused as to where Aphrodite's flesh ended and the man's began. She made the same gentle purring sound she made when Elspeth fed her.

"Aphrodite!" Elspeth said, summoning the voice she heard parents use when chastising their children in her shop. She repeated it again, more loudly this time, noticing how Aphrodite's body had spread over the man's face, perhaps obstructing his breathing. She began to consider a way to prise her off, looking about for some kind of stick or tool rather than touch her with her bare hands, possessed by some instinctive knowledge that physical contact at this moment would be precarious. Her gaze settled upon the driftwood man—his blank expression seemed to convey the same sense of bemusement she felt—when

Aphrodite relinquished her grasp and slid back to her place beside the boat.

Elspeth wished she hadn't moved because now she could see what Aphrodite had done to the man. He was bloodied and disfigured; an Aphrodite-shaped hollow where she had lain on top, the man's face and torso reduced to a fleshy, red depression. Elspeth moved forward tentatively, watching the waves lap against his body, filling the concave that was completely devoid of organs and entrails.

She stumbled back to shore and fell against the shingle. She could see Aphrodite purring contentedly beside the boat and next to that, the man's backpack bobbed back and forth with the tide.

Elspeth sat on the shore for a long time. At one point she lay back against the rocks, hardly caring if Aphrodite crept silently toward her and up onto her prostrate body as she had done with the backpacker. She studied the grey sky, whorls of black clouds swelling like the dark undercurrents of the ocean and thought of the green spectacle on the night of Aphrodite's conception.

Because in her mind, that strange light was responsible. It had compelled her into the sea, charging the water with its mysterious energy. It was inconceivable to Elspeth now that Aphrodite was merely washed in with the tide, transported from some place far or deep. No, she'd come to feel that Aphrodite was part of her. Not just because she fed her from time to time but because she had engendered her that night in the glowing water. Aphrodite was the fruit of her loins and the sea, a surrogate womb, had carried her and deposited her, newly-formed, on the shore.

Maybe that was why she experienced this feeling of disappointment more acutely. Even when Aphrodite did crawl toward her later, nuzzling her wet and bloodied body against her skin, Elspeth did not stroke her seaweed mane, nor caress her seashell skin, but lay there tight-lipped and unmoving, denying her the stories and songs she'd previously given so freely. Aphrodite reached out her slimy appendage and placed it against Elspeth's cheek, meaning perhaps to wipe away the tears.

As the radio had forecast, the weather worsened as the week progressed and Elspeth had a convenient excuse not to leave the croft-house. She watched the sea from the window, tumultuous and wild and thought of Aphrodite alone on the shore. In her more compassionate moments, she considered bringing Aphrodite out of the rain and wind and into the house but then she'd remember the backpacker's mutilated body and didn't know how she would ever forgive her.

She knew if Aphrodite didn't already have a ready supply of food—with regard to the remainder of the backpacker's body— she would have found a way to feed her, though the idea of personally nursing her as she had done, was suddenly repugnant. Likewise, though she wanted to punish Aphrodite, her protective impulse was stronger, convincing her of the need to conceal the evidence, filling the man's backpack with stones and casting it out deep into the ocean.

As for his body, it was diminishing day by day. What Aphrodite didn't eat, the sea washed away, as if both Aphrodite's mothers were complicit in covering her crime.

Elspeth had found the first few days the hardest. She had turned up the radio to drown out the sound of Aphrodite's cries. There was no mistaking her high-pitched squall for the sound of the gulls anymore, for since Aphrodite had killed the backpacker, the birds kept their distance. Where oystercatchers and seagulls used to converge on the surf, the gannets on the roof of the croft, now they avoided the beach altogether.

Lately though, either the wind was more riotous or Aphrodite called for her less. Elspeth suspected it was the latter; Aphrodite was certainly becoming more independent. Without the driftwood boat to contain her, she roamed the shore unimpeded, her movements confident and agile. Watching her progress through binoculars, Elspeth saw that she delighted in chasing crabs or collecting debris from the beach, decorating the prow of the boat with nets of kelp as if constructing a lair. At some point she had pushed the driftwood man forward, so that he fell pitifully against the boat, his oilskins gaping open to form a tarpaulin enclosure. Even within this makeshift den, when the wind and rain was particularly ferocious, Aphrodite dug herself into the sand, so that only her shell exterior was visible.

And when she disappeared beneath the earth like this, Elspeth thought of the flower shop and the seeds she planted in the rich soil, wondering if when Aphrodite re-emerged she would have grown into something else. Perhaps something more beautiful.

Elspeth woke to a scratching outside her window. She lay staring into the darkness for a long time, unsure whether she was imagining things. Just as she was ready to dismiss it, the sound resumed with renewed fervour. There was something outside in the darkness, scratching eagerly at the pane.

Curiously, Elspeth's first thoughts were of the trows from the island's folk stories before she even considered Aphrodite. She imagined the impish sprites emerging from their hollows and mounds, climbing up onto the roof and dancing wildly to plague her peace of mind. And she wondered if the original owners of the house had adhered to superstition, leaving water outside for them, sweeping the hearth on a Saturday as was the custom, to appease their troublesome natures. But as the scratching became more feverish, she realised that the monster outside her window was of her own making.

Elspeth made her way slowly to the window, thankful that she had pulled the curtains, not wanting to see Aphrodite's pearlised exterior in the moonlight. Moreover, the fact she had crawled all the way to the croft-house was alarming. Though she was becoming increasingly strong, she had never covered so much ground. And she had never left the shore. Yet here she was curled up outside Elspeth's window, drumming her shell-clad mantle against the pane.

"Go away," Elsepth called.

And softly, within the whistling of the wind she thought she heard the creature emit a deep, growling exhalation,

"Die . . . "

Elspeth edged closer, her heart beating faster.

"Die-ty", the voice repeated and Elspeth realised she was trying to say her name.

"Aphrodite," Elspeth called, as if correcting her, "go back to the shore."

And with that she heard a low shuffling, a scrapping sound against the shingle path, the sound diminishing as Aphrodite retreated into the distance.

Elspeth made her way back to bed, Aphrodite's words swimming in her head. It was miraculous, incredible that she could communicate.

Die. Die-ty. But it was the word *deity* that she thought about the longest.

At dawn, Elspeth made her way down to the beach. It had been a week since the death of the backpacker, an inordinate amount of time in Aphrodite's brief lifetime to experience solitude. But arriving at her lair, Elspeth saw that Aphrodite was not there, though the place on the shore looked more inhabited than ever before. Lifting the oilskin roof, she peered into the darkness, the ground strewn with the remains of crabs and cuttlefish. Seaweed hung from the spine of the driftwood man and entangled within it were human bones and the torn shreds of the backpacker's clothing.

Elspeth backed away, aware of the smell of decay. She had only thought of the shore bringing life, not death. What had prompted Aphrodite to build such a place, to nest among dead things? Maybe it was for comfort, a way to cope with the sudden isolation; being among the dead was better than being completely alone. Or maybe they were trophies.

Elspeth turned to make her way back, spying a protrusion

in the sand up ahead. She watched as the sand bulged upward, growing mound-like, a sandy hillock existing suddenly where none had stood before. Then she saw the flail of seaweed, the chitinous carapace before the serpentine body coiled itself out of the sand.

Aphrodite was much bigger. She no longer crawled across the sand but seemed to glide, on limbs that appeared slender and long. As she got closer, Elspeth could see tatters of the backpacker's oilskin enmeshed within her seaweed train and as she sidled up alongside her, Elspeth noted the other curious development.

She had grown hair. Thick dark hair sprouting from the edge of her seashell skin, emerging from the pink fleshy parts of her body.

Elspeth reached out a tentative hand. The backpacker's hair had been dark. There had been no other identifiable features left after Aphrodite's attack. But his hair had fanned out upon the waves, moving like seagrass through the water. Had Aphrodite appropriated his hair as she had done his clothes? How could they grow so naturally from her flesh?

Aphrodite let Elspeth rest her hand against her skin. The texture was reassuringly cold and slimy, as it always had been.

"There, there Aphrodite," Elspeth cooed.

But as she withdrew her hand she saw that the flesh of her palm had been eaten away. She clutched the gaping wound with her other hand, stumbling back bewildered.

"*Die-ty, die-ty,*" Aphrodite called as Elspeth ran from the creature on the shore.

"You were right," Elspeth's voice wavered, "I am crazy to stay here. Please come." She spoke the last words softly into the receiver, still unsure whether inviting someone else in was the right thing to do. Though Elspeth was her mother, Aphrodite was still a creature of the island and maybe an islander would be better equipped to deal with her. She listened to the beep of Donal's voice recording, longing to hear a human voice, before hanging up.

She'd bandaged her hand, applied antiseptic to the lesion, sur-prised to see that it didn't gush blood as she would have suspected from a wound of its kind. It was as if it had been cauterised at the same time the flesh had been torn, or else the blood had been sucked away. Elspeth felt faint thinking about it and sat down heavily on her chair beside the hearth.

It had taken all her energy to barricade herself inside the croft-house. All the doors were locked, the curtains pulled in case Aphrodite crept toward the window once more, to clink her seashell bulk against the pane. She'd thought about driving to the ferry in the hope that it was running. Even waiting in her car, miles from the shore would be better than being stuck inside the croft-house with Aphrodite lurking outside. But she couldn't drive with her hand the way it was and she worried about passing out at the wheel, feeling drowsy already from the cocktail of painkillers she'd taken.

Her hand still throbbed, her body broadcasting the loss of its flesh. She reached for the whisky bottle on the table and poured herself a generous measure. Beside it was the compendium of mythology, where she had read about Aphrodite's namesake. The goddess Aphrodite wasn't the only thing conceived when Uranus' genitals had been cast into the sea. From his blood had come the Furies, hideous hags with snakes for hair. Elspeth thought of the creature on the shore and of which set of sisters she resembled most. Maybe it had been foolish of her to think that her Aphro-dite was made of the stuff of gods. She should have accepted her monstrous nature from the beginning.

Elspeth rose slowly and made her way to the window. Pulling the curtain aside, she could see Aphrodite slithering across the shore, scurrying into the sand in pursuit of crabs. In the dimin-ishing light she looked even more surreal, like some mythical sea serpent from the pages of a medieval bestiary. A creature constructed from the imagination, rather than of flesh and shell.

Frankenstein had killed his she-monster, torn her apart with his bare hands in front of his first creation, fearing his monsters would procreate and fill the world with their hideous progeny. Elspeth thought of Aphrodite's body, of the living mantle on her back, wondering if she would be able to grow her own children one day. Would she be able to produce life asexually, sprouting her offspring as easily as the hair follicles she'd assimilated from the backpacker, or would she need a mate, a creature as strange as she was, to fertilise her somehow?

Elspeth felt tired. She had not thought of the future, of Aphrodite's legacy. She imagined the croft-house surrounded by an army of eerie shell creatures, crawling onto the windowsills to bang their shell-limbs against the glass, or scurrying up onto the roof to dance like the trows. All of them baying for human blood, needing to be fed.

She realised then what a mistake it had been to call Donal. How could he possibly know what to expect or how to deal with such a creature. Besides, Aphrodite was stronger and faster than she'd been since her encounter with the backpacker. Donal wouldn't stand a chance; she'd make a meal of him in no time at all.

Elspeth poured herself another whisky and drank it quickly before she could change her mind, then she went to the front door and opened it wide, welcoming the darkness in. She stood for a moment on the threshold, seeking the aurora's luminescence in the sky, a twinkle of green above the water. But it was black. On her way to the bedroom, she stopped by the kitchen and found a long, sharp knife in the drawer.

She waited a long time. Such a long time that she lay back on the bed and closed her eyes. She could see the green haze then, dancing in her mind's eye as it had done that night in the water and then just before she let herself drift into it entirely, she heard a scraping sound on the shingle path, the clinking of shell against shell that signalled Aphrodite's approach.

She had always wanted to bring Aphrodite into her world. To give her a home, a place to let her grow but now, the sound of her progress up the stone steps and into the hallway, the scratching of shell against the hardwood floor, made her uneasy. She could hear the crash of Aphrodite's body against the chair and table legs, the slick slither of her seaweed mane against the polished surfaces. And then she was purring outside her bedroom door.

"*Die. Die-ty*".

Yet she entered the room soundlessly and crawled up onto the bed with similar stealthy dexterity, so that Elspeth was almost surprised to see her shadowed outline at the foot of the bed. It was too dark to see her clearly, to make out her slippery form beneath the husk of shell. Besides, her mind was still glowing green, the green of new life, of waxy seedlings pushing their heads out of the earth. And she thought of her flower shop and the life cycle of plants.

Often asexual reproduction involved the annihilation of the parent. Daffodils and potato plants grew their replacements beneath the earth, a lateral bulb forming when the old plant died. Maybe this was the natural order of things, Elspeth thought as Aphrodite climbed up on to her. And it wasn't as if she'd be forgotten. In the same way Aphrodite had assimilated the back-packer, perhaps something of her would become reproduced in Aphrodite's malleable flesh. She would live on in her daughter, part of her monstrous inheritance, unless of course she raised the knife and aimed it beneath the rim of seashell.

The purring became more contented as Aphrodite slid up Elspeth's body, her seaweed tresses licking her skin. She could smell the sea and the iron-reek of blood as she welcomed her shell baby to her breast.

THE ATTEMPT

Rosalie Parker

SASKIA COULD SEE THAT THE ICE NEAR the shore was several centimetres thick. Pieter had told her that the lake never froze over entirely, that there was always an expanse of water at the centre which remained liquid. As he had also insisted that there were monsters in the bottom of the lake, she thought it was probably safe not to believe him.

She stepped tentatively onto the ice, her booted feet sliding a little on the slippery surface. The lake was so large that it was impossible for her to see to its centre. Ahead was a vast expanse of white. Pieter had been taken into the city for his piano lesson so she should have at least three hours, more than enough time for her attempt. It was not fair that Pieter should have the piano lessons that she wanted so badly, just because he was two years older. He wasn't even particularly enthusiastic about them, but whining and arguing for lessons had so far got her nowhere.

Pieter said that no one had ever walked across the frozen lake, that if she did then it would be a world record. Saskia was not sure if she believed him about the world record but it sounded exciting. She picked up her pace over the ice, heading towards where she thought the middle of the lake must be. It was a beautifully still, bitterly cold day—her padded coat, hat and gloves kept out the worst of the chill—the sky a translucent pale blue. After three or four minutes she turned and looked back to the shore. The buildings were far away already, small, like the toy town she and Pieter had created from their plastic building blocks, populated by tiny articulated figures. She thought she could just make out their house up on the rise, bigger than its neighbours, the red paint standing out from the ochre and yellow all around. The cold seemed to be keeping everyone inside.

Saskia marched on over the ice. When she turned round again, the houses were just specks of colour. All around her was a dull expanse of white, and Saskia began to be uncertain of which direction she should take. According to Pieter the other side of the lake was another country, so she would, strictly speaking, need a passport, but he said that the people of the country would be glad to see her so it wouldn't matter that she didn't have one. He said they would help celebrate her world record. Saskia had never been abroad and this was one of the great attractions of the attempt. Apart from showing Pieter that she could do it. She picked a spot on the horizon and headed for it.

There were bubbles of air trapped beneath the ice that expanded and contracted under the pressure of her feet. Saskia grew so entranced with watching them that she lost contact with her spot on the horizon. Still, it did not matter, as long as she was aiming in more or less the right direction. The far shore might be as wide as the one she had started from, so exactly where she landed was not important, so long as it was inhabited.

After an hour or so Saskia felt thirsty. Feeling proud of her forethought, she took out a small bottle of water from her coat pocket. After a couple of sips, she put the bottle back and extracted a chocolate bar. She ate a few squares, then wrapped up the remainder carefully. An icy breeze was now blowing from the far shore and the sky had clouded over. Saskia shivered. The town was no longer visible behind her, and she could see nothing ahead but ice.

As she strode on over the lake, Saskia thought of the little figures in the toy town back home. Her favourite was a family called Petrova, with two children, a boy and a girl. She and Pieter put them through all kinds of adventures and traumatic experiences, including a fire and an earthquake. The boy, Boris, was the hero of most of these escapades, the girl, Anna, the coper, the nurse, the cook. Saskia liked her practical strength. Pieter often pretended that he didn't really care about the Petrovas and their adventures, but he spent as much time as Saskia thinking up scenarios and acting them out. The senior Petrovas were distant figures, often away at work or outside gardening. One of the best things about the toy town was that Boris and Anna did not have to go to school.

Saskia stopped and shielded her eyes. Ahead, in the far distance, tiny black specks were appearing. She walked on at a faster pace. Her watch told her that she had been walking for an hour and a half, and although she was beginning to feel tired, she was glad that she would reach the far shore at her first attempt.

As Saskia drew closer, the wooden buildings took shape. They were dowdier than those of her own town, being mostly unpainted log cabins. There were no people to be seen. She stepped off the ice onto the frozen ground and approached the largest cabin, but when she knocked on the door, no one answered. She tried some of the other cabins, returning at last to the largest. Carefully she opened the door. Inside there were items of furniture covered in dust, a cooker and an iron bedstead. It looked as if it was a summer house that no one had visited for a long time.

Feeling somewhat crestfallen that there was no one to help her celebrate, Saskia resolved to make her way around the shore until she found an inhabited settlement. After walking for another half an hour, she realised that it was taking too long. She would not now be able to get home in time to greet Pieter and their parents on their return from the city. Indeed she would be in trouble for staying out on her own. She wished that she had left a note saying that she had gone to Maria's house.

Saskia stepped onto the ice and headed back towards the centre of the lake. After an hours' walk, although she scanned the horizon carefully, there was no trace of the cheerful colours of her town, just the endless white of the ice. Saskia drank the rest of the water from the bottle and ate all the chocolate. She was beginning to feel cold. In a few hours it would be dark.

How would she prove to Pieter that she had really walked over the lake to the far shore? She kicked herself that she hadn't brought some artefact from the cabin to show him. She could imagine his scornful face as she pleaded with him to believe her. Then she realised that even if she brought evidence he might still decide she was being untruthful. Hot shameful tears trickled down her cheeks.

Saskia was trying not to panic, but it felt as if the ice stretched on forever. When she thought it through, she realised that it was possible that she had not reached the far shore at all, but had instead cut across a segment of the lake. That would explain why it was now taking so much longer to get home—she was walking across the lake's true diameter, which would be much further than her outward journey. In any case she was lost, and there was nothing she could do except keep on walking.

After another hour, Saskia stopped and again scanned the horizon. This time she thought she could see some specks which might be buildings. After another half an hour she could see definite blocks of colour. As she drew nearer, she realised that it was not her hometown but another with a more regular layout. The houses were rectangular and built of primary coloured bricks, with flat roofs. Each house had a square of green lawn and a tarmac drive. Saskia stepped off the ice and onto the land. The town seemed familiar although she was sure she had never been there before. She headed for a prominent red house and knocked on the door. It was answered by a man in a v-necked jumper and tie.

"Hello," he said. "You look exhausted."

Saskia stumbled into the kitchen. "I'm sorry to bother you but I've walked across the lake and now I'm lost."

A woman in a flowered dress came into the kitchen. She switched on the kettle.

"I'll make you a hot drink and you can have some toast and honey," she said. "You'll feel better when you have something inside you."

The man looked down at her. "You're rather young to be out on your own. Don't worry though, we'll look after you."

The woman spooned hot chocolate powder into a mug. The kettle boiled and she poured in the hot water. Two slices of bread were placed in the toaster. "Take off your coat and boots, it's quite warm in here," she said.

Saskia did as she was told, then sipped the delicious hot chocolate. Soon she was gobbling the toast and honey. After she had finished she felt sleepy. The woman took her into the living room and encouraged her to lie down on the sofa. It wasn't long before Saskia had fallen into a dreamless sleep.

When she awoke it was dark outside and the curtains had been drawn. The room was very warm, warmer than the living room in her own house. She saw that two almost grown up children were sitting on the floor, reading books. As she sat up they turned to face her.

"Hello Saskia," said the boy. "Do you know who we are?"

"Yes," said Saskia, "you're Boris and Anna."

Anna laughed. "You see, Boris, I told you she would know."

Boris stood up. "Our parents are looking after you. They say you walked across the lake. No-one has crossed the lake on foot before. There are signs everywhere warning people not to walk on the ice."

"I was perfectly safe. I am quite small and the ice was thick enough to take my weight."

"It was very brave of you," said Anna. "Father said you were tired and cold when you got here."

"I feel better now I have slept a little," said Saskia defensively. "Pieter said I would set a world record if I crossed the lake and as I am the first person to do so then he must be right."

"Congratulations," said Boris.

At that moment Mrs Petrova came in carrying three glasses of lemonade on a tray. "This is to help celebrate your great achievement," she said, handing them round to the children. "The lake does not freeze over completely every year, so you have been lucky that you chose to make your attempt during an exceptionally cold spell."

Boris raised his glass: 'to Saskia'.

Saskia gulped down the fizzy drink. Mrs Petrova looked at the clock on the mantelpiece. "It is quite late and time for Boris and Anna to go to bed. I suggest that you should sleep again, Saskia."

Saskia suddenly gasped in dismay—"but my parents, and Pieter! They will be wondering where I am!"

"We will worry about that in the morning," said Mrs Petrova.

Saskia sank down on the sofa under the blanket and to her surprise did not wake up until half way through the next morning. She found the Petrovas in the kitchen having a late breakfast.

"Can I telephone my parents, please?"

"Mr Petrova cleared his throat. "I am afraid we're so remote and insignificant that we have not been considered for telephones," he said. The best thing is if you stay with us until Pieter realises that you are here. Don't worry. We will make sure you have enough food. You can have a bath now if you would like one."

"But I don't understand. How will Pieter know that I am here?"

"He will work it out," said Anna.

"Perhaps he will think to provide us with a telephone and then our problem will be solved," said Boris.

After her bath Saskia played board games with Boris and Anna, but her mind was elsewhere.

"I think I should leave now and try to find my way home," she said. "My parents may have called the police."

"Oh I shouldn't worry," said Boris. "Pieter will cover for you. He will think up some reason why you are not there."

Anna smiled encouragingly. "And you are not fully recovered from your exertions of yesterday."

After lunch there was a knock at the door. To Saskia's amazement, Mrs Petrova showed Pieter into the living room.

"Hello little sis!" he said cheerfully. "So you're saying you made it to the far shore?"

"I'm not just saying it, I did it!" Saskia replied crossly. "I knew you wouldn't believe me."

"Whatever," said Pieter. "*If* you say so. Only you can know. I hope you've been making notes about anything we need to provide here. A telephone is the most obvious thing. Mr Petrova is quite cross about that."

"They don't have a television or computers."

"No. I suppose we envisaged them existing in an earlier time. A time before those things were commonplace."

"You're pretty inconsistent about the things you have provided," said Boris. "We have a toaster but no television. I for one would appreciate being able to communicate with the outside world."

Anna nodded. "It would help make the down times less boring."

"Down times?" queried Saskia.

"You know," said Pieter, "when we're not playing with them."

"Where do our parents think I am?" Saskia asked Pieter.

"I told them you said you were staying the night with Maria. I've come to collect you and take you home."

"You are welcome to stay as long as you like," said Anna, politely.

"We'd better not cross the boundary for long," said Pieter. "Otherwise we may never get back."

Saskia put on her coat, hat and gloves, and after thanking Mr and Mrs Petrova, she and Pieter let themselves out of the front door. It was a cold grey day. Pieter took Saskia's hand and led her to the edge of the ice.

"We needn't walk on the lake, we can just follow the shore. It is more dangerous walking on ice, especially with two of us."

"How was your piano lesson?" asked Saskia.

"Ok, I suppose. To tell you the truth I'm getting a bit bored of the piano. I've asked Mum if I can have guitar lessons instead. She said you can take over the piano lessons if you like."

Saskia whooped for joy. "How far do we have to walk to get home?" she asked.

"I don't know," said Pieter "it took about an hour for me to get here, but then I walked over the lake."

"I really did walk across from the far shore, Pieter."

"Well then," he said, "it's something that you'll never need to do again."

THE CLOSURE

Conrad Williams

SIDDALL CAME DOWN THE CANTED ROAD in the dark and the soles of his boots slipped and skidded on the polished cobblestone tops. He was cold; his first cup of coffee was still an hour away. He had drifted north, stopping every so often for a week or so to do casual work—usually hard labour—in places that sounded as if they ought to exist in a gnarled, industrial fantasy novel: Esher, Peatling Parva, Grimpo, Slattocks. Now, something in the architecture, or maybe even the people, called to distant memories.

He thought he might be close to home, or rather, the house in which he had grown up with Jen, his older sister. After Jen moved out—she married an Argentinian and went to live on a farm in Purmamarca—and his parents died, he relocated to Birmingham and found work on building sites. He was just seventeen. He never married. He never stayed in one place long enough to make the right kind of connections. He couldn't shed the feeling that being itinerant was in some way associated with criminality, though he had never done real wrong. It flavoured the way he spoke, and moved. There was a shiftiness about him, he knew, but he could not change now. Twenty years stumbled by, a relay of trains and buses, rented accommodation, pints of heavy and the clack of pool balls, solitary walks along canal towpaths and late-night meals of battered something and chips snaffled from polystyrene trays. He felt sometimes that he was ghosting through life, that he might actually have died at some point but never noticed.

He crossed the bridge over the motorway and, as he often did if it was not raining, stopped to gaze down at the road. It appeared impossibly clean and bright, futuristic even. The few cars abroad at this hour gleamed under the streetlights as they swept by the more numerous HGVs, trying to beat the early morning rush. A gap in the traffic; silence fell, along with a rook, alighting on the hard shoulder where it swaggered over to peck at the unpacked carcass of a weeks-dead badger. Siddall moved on. He would be late at this rate.

This place was familiar to him: this field abutting the railway embankment. It called out from a shadowy corner of his mind. Did he play a football match here once? Was that it? Memories of the school minibus, which was really little more than a stretched van: jouncing around in the back of it with the chosen few selected to travel with Mr Rose—the teacher charged with looking after the football team—while the other boys had to cadge lifts off reluctant dads. Toepoke, the boys called Mr Rose, because he couldn't kick a ball properly. He stared out at them from behind John Lennon-style glasses, his thin bearded face pale but for the border where it met hair, the skin an ugly, blotched red. Mr Rose took football because there were no other male teachers and Peanut wasn't interested. Peanut was the headmaster, so called because his first initial was P (to this day Siddall had no idea what it had stood for), and his head was very round and relatively small.

Siddall glanced left and saw another street he recognised. He followed it, all thoughts of work banished from his mind under the sudden onslaught of recollections. Mr Rose wore tennis shoes on the football pitch. Mr Rose ate Mr Kipling's apple pies starting with the lid first before he scooped out the pallid contents with his little finger. Mr Rose had a voice that made everything he said sound like an accusation.

He remembered Miss Hurst, his form teacher in the last year of primary school. She drove a Mini. Large leather bag. Towards the end of the year they had started a topic called Jobs. Her voice, light and lyrical (she was American, she came from Sheboygan, Wisconsin; Siddall paused, startled by this sudden detail). *What do you want to be when you grow up?* They went around the class. Baker, like my mum. Ferry pilot, like my granddad. Policeman, fireman, teacher, astronaut. *And you, Jeffrey, what do you want to be?*

A surgeon, Miss.

He'd fallen in love with the inside of the body, spent hours poring over the copy of *Gray's Anatomy* he'd found for pennies in a charity shop box; the elegant poses of a physique that ought not to be able to arrange itself so. His mother had bought him a colouring book but instead of the usual pictures of animals and beaches and picnics, here was the body presented as a series of black and white spaces, stripped back to muscle, to nerve, to bone. He neatly coloured the arteries red and the veins blue. The lymphatic system, with its sequence of nodes and lumps, he treated to a pale green. He was fascinated by the names of these hidden, secret regions, and remembered by heart some of the sentences in that colouring book despite not really understanding them at the time. He referred to them often, like mantra.

The pharyngeal muscles are primarily concerned with deglutition.

The procedures—developed over centuries of trial and error—to repair the body became a fascination for him, from first incision to final suture, and he grew impatient to hold those perfectly balanced tools of carbon stainless steel. His mother found him a medical kit in a junk shop; it contained forceps, clamps, enamel kidney bowls and a glassine bag of reverse cutting needles. He spent long hours threading them with fishing line and practising sutures on offcuts from an indulgent butcher who was a friend of the family. Running stitches, simple interrupted stitches, running locked stitches, pulley stitches, vertical mattress stitches . . . he became expert at them all. It was a long way from the warehouses and scrapyards where he had fetched up. At the back of his mind was the strange regret that he would never get to see the peculiar arrangement of his own internal organs.

He found himself at the junction of a road—Lodge Lane— where he had lived and gone to school. He thought of the ice cream van that pulled up outside his house, and the next-door neighbours whose garden was blighted by a pair of BMWs slowly rotting into the earth. Harry Roughsedge, his best friend, had lived at number 63. Here was 12, his old house. He felt a lancing of the heart when he saw the stone wall that separated the front garden from the back. He had helped his dad build that wall back in the early 70s, when he was a toddler. It had served as a goal whenever his dad wanted to take some shots at him. So much else had changed: the front door, the fence, the garage. But there was the huge chunk of granite his parents had brought back in their car from Scotland after a family holiday to serve as a tombstone for their old cat, Ziggy. There too, the magnolia tree they had planted together on his mother's 50th birthday.

A weakness flooded him under the onslaught of memories, all the good and bad things to have happened under that roof. Aware of a face at the bedroom window—what had been his parents' window—he sidled along to the school gates, where a different kind of grief awaited him. The route through these gates and along the approach road to the school was one he had taken so many times that the view seemed permanently imprinted on his retina. He ought to have seen the diamond-link fences that cordoned off the concrete tennis courts and the distinctive shape of the Octagonal hall, where the fourth and fifth years attended assembly. Beyond that, the low blocks of the canteens and the playing fields.

There was nothing but opened ground and the stilled hulks of demolition plants. Bulldozers, crushers, hook wagons. What had been the classrooms and staff rooms and laboratories and corridors was so much wreckage piled in a far corner waiting for the lorries to take it away. He couldn't go into his old house, but he would go in here. He felt anger rising inside him. Why had this been allowed to happen?

Siddall clambered over the gate and hurried up the approach road. A hospice was being built where the tennis courts had stood. There was nobody around. He glanced at his watch and saw that his shift had started twenty minutes previously. Another job lost. It didn't matter. There would be others. The ground, carved up by the caterpillar tracks, had frozen into unforgiving ridges that he now stumbled over as he made his way up to see if the gym and the old canteen buildings might still be standing. He almost didn't see the girl. She was sitting against bags of cement, and was almost the same colour. A scarf was wrapped around her neck and mouth, but it didn't muffle the wet, phlegmy sound in her throat that caught his attention. Her eyes were large and pale blue; he couldn't see her eyebrows because of a low, straight fringe of dark brown hair. It didn't matter. He knew her. Recognition drove a spike through his thoughts, though he could not yet conjure a name.

"Hello," he said. She didn't reply immediately, but looked off to her right, towards the area he was trying to get to. She stirred and slowly drew herself upright with some difficulty as if she had been sitting down there in the cold for some time. She began to totter after him, but was unable to keep pace. Possibly she was ill. The scarf around her throat and mouth suggested a bad cold, maybe something worse. He thought of his textbooks. He thought of asthma and bronchitis and emphysema and chronic obstructive airways disease. He thought of corticosteroids and N-acetyl cysteine.

The sound of her heels scraping the uneven ground reminded him of the clatter of shoes at lunchtime when everyone raced to beat the queues in the canteens. The fear of corporal punishment chased many of those feet. Teachers could get away with all manner of brutality back then. He remembered one of the maths teachers, a Mr Nelson, who doubled up as a PE teacher when needed. He was a nasty bastard. There was some poor soul, Dobson his name might have been, who roused Nelson's ire one day for whatever reason. Nelson dragged him around the changing rooms, clouting his knees against the metal lockers, slapping his face against the tiles. You looked askance at a pupil these days and there might be legal action. He didn't know what had happened to Nelson, or Dobson for that matter. Nelson had probably retired because you weren't allowed to knuckle heads any more. Now he thought of it, he didn't know what had happened to any of the teachers from his time at the school. He dug for their names, some of them probably in the ground twenty years now: Jarvis, the music teacher; Latham, the physics teacher. Manton, who taught French. He couldn't remember the name of his form teacher for his last year. She was coming to the end of her working life then, he guessed, and she wore her hair in an old fashioned way, a tight bun with a crimped edge like a pie top. It must have taken her an age to prepare every morning. Mrs Dunbavin, was it? Dun-something, anyway.

He wondered why the school had closed in the first place, but surely the writing had been on the wall for some time. Even when he was in his final year, revising for exams he would not pass, standards and results were both falling. The annual intake had diminished year on year, despite the school being in a good catchment area. Truanting had been a problem (he'd done his own sterling work to add to the absentee list) and towards the end of his time there, he'd sometimes see the teachers doing the crossword, or leafing through a magazine in front of a class of children whose apathy was almost militant. The overriding attitude seemed to be that if the pupils weren't prepared to learn then the teachers weren't prepared to teach. It was an impasse that could only have one outcome.

"Are you okay?" he asked. He thought the girl might faint. "Do you want me to get help?" And following on from that: *too late . . . way too late.*

He wondered what she was doing here, and how she had fetched up on the old school grounds. The site must be closed off at all points to prevent trespassers, yet there must be a breach somewhere; he couldn't imagine this girl vaulting over a fence, or crawling under one for that matter.

She stared at him with those large wet eyes and a hand flew to her scarf where it trembled like that of a magician about to perform a reveal. Instead she fingered the ragged edges of the wool and shook her head slightly.

"Can't you speak?" he asked, stopping to look back at her. He thought it might be laryngitis. He thought of vocal polyps or vocal cord paralysis.

The devil was a midwife and when I was born I screamed so hard I ruptured my voice box. She kept walking and every baby step threatened to send her falling into the hardened wedges of mud.

Siddall made to laugh but he managed only to send a mouthful of spit down his chin. He felt very keenly the spur of his heart.

How could he know this girl? She was much younger than him. Maybe she just reminded him of someone he had been at school with. Someone who was now his age, working hard to put food on a table for her family.

You know. You know very well.

He stared down at the ground and watched his boots press on across the perilous terrain. Where the canteens had stood was now so much long grass. He stared at it for a long time. A fence marched off deep into what had once been the school fields, marking the boundary of a new housing estate. The only thing that remained was the three-step stone staircase that led up from the road as if swept around the corner of the Home Economics building. It looked utterly out of place now, like an ancient artefact exposed during a roadworks excavation.

The road followed an incline down to the south entrance on Clapgates Road. To the left were the shattered remains of the science labs; to the right, the gymnasiums. Seeing them again, albeit partially denuded by the claws of the excavators, unlocked memories in a rapid procession: Muzz hawking and spitting thick green phlegm (*myeloperoxidases*, he thought . . . he thought of chest infections and pneumonia) into the cracks between the science lab brick walls "to keep it from falling down"; Jacko finding a Polaroid of an erect penis in the froth of dusty nettles fringing the gymnasium courtyard; Mank being chased across the paved area in front of the headmaster's office by his fifth year peers when they found out he had a French pen pal.

The girl followed at a distance but he was always aware of her and the wet rattle of air as it chicaned through the ruin of her throat. She unnerved him. *I swallowed a mouthful of crushed glass; somebody tried to strangle me with barbed wire; as a toddler I fell on to an opened pair of scissors.* Every few minutes there was a different story, as if she was testing his resolve, or practicing lines from a grim play in which she was due to appear.

There wasn't much in the way of ambient sound to distract him from her breathing, or the fibs that spooled by. The shock of a magpie's cackle or the distant cough of an engine as it started in the cold morning, little else. It sounded a bit like the badly-maintained cart the rag-and-bone man used to steer around these streets, something creaking and groaning, all leather and waterlogged wood complaining of the pressures it was being forced to bear. He tried to ignore it, for the sake of nostalgia; he didn't want his recollections to be spoilt though he had yet to muster anything pleasant. It was hammered into you that school days were the best of your life, and maybe you believed it after a while, especially if everything afterwards was so grim. But already he was regretting his decision to come here.

He picked carefully through the rubble, forcing himself to try to remember the rooms that had stood where now there were only foundations, and half-bricks, and drifts of cement dust, forcing his mind away from the girl, and the impossibility of her. The diggers stood among them frozen in positions of attack, fangs stained by the red clay in the undersoil. The offices of the headmaster and his deputy had been here, hadn't they? Pale brick extensions to the venerable deep red of the original building. A trophy cabinet and the smells of Brasso and Windolene. Panoramic photographs of the school population. He remembered sitting in drowsy hot mathematics classes, grizzling over impenetrable equations. Mr Sankey in his fug of coffee breath and nicotine; chalk dust motes hanging in the daggers of sunlight. Staring outside and wishing the bell would go, trying to impel the second hand more quickly around the clock using the power of his mind.

What do you want to be when you grow up? He wondered about the other children in his class, and what they were doing now. He had seen a man of around twenty leaving a noodle restaurant the other night. He had been wearing a three-piece suit. No person under the age of forty ought to be wearing a waistcoat, he thought. It just didn't look right. It looked like you were going to a fancy dress party. But Siddall couldn't talk. In his life he'd worn a tie twice—a clip-on affair borrowed from a security guard acquaintance—to his parents' funerals.

What do you want to be?

His dreams of becoming a surgeon had been dashed, not because of his academic performance, although soon enough that would reveal itself as wanting, but because of an unexpected squeamishness. It had nothing to do with blood though. What had put him off was the thought of operating on limp, unresponsive bodies. A general anaesthetic was often necessary, he knew, especially where invasive surgery was concerned, but the thought of slitting someone open with a scalpel and seeing no reaction bothered him beyond words. It didn't matter how many machines were on hand to display vital life signs: in effect he would be operating on a dummy, and he knew he could not cope with that. He thought that growing up was as much about coping with the loss of such dreams, and the concomitant brutal realities, as anything else.

"What do you want to be when you grow up?" he asked, and his voice was a faint, frightened thing curdling in the morning air.

Now it was her turn to laugh. Or at least that's what he thought it was. Any alternative was too horrible to consider.

It struck him that he was very afraid, that the cold had nothing to do with the shake in his legs, or the stiffness in the skin of his face. Here he was dredging through the nonsense of his youth because he didn't want to acknowledge the dawning of a realisation that could not be possible. The girl. He remembered the girl now. Of course he did. Her name was Alison. Her name had been Alison. Did you lose your name because you died?

He heard a change in the quality of her step. A decay, as if she was somehow diminishing, perhaps because he had fully acknowledged her at last, perhaps because he had put some distance between them. He had certainly increased his pace in the last few minutes. But when he checked behind him she was still there, six feet away, as she had been since they began this long tour of the dead zones of his childhood. Their childhood.

Houses were rising where once had reached five acres of playing fields. A four-hundred metre running track had been scorched into the grass. There were half a dozen soccer pitches and a couple of rugby pitches. The goal-posts remained throughout the year. In the summer, a cricket wicket was shaved close to the ground. He had carried his bat for 56 runs one glorious summer evening. In the wind and the rain he had scored two goals in an eight-nil thrashing of their local rivals. He broke a decades-old school record when he jumped one metre forty in the high jump. The deputy headteacher had leaned in close during the assembly when he received his certificate to whisper that the irony of winning in such a discipline was not lost on him. Now there were new roads with new names and houses that all looked the same built on the ghosts of all that sporting endeavour. Where was the proof any more of what he had achieved? All the record books and trophies and framed certificates on that hallway wall. Where were they now? Were they just so much debris at the bottom of an excavator's bucket? The kiss he had stolen from Michelle Carter on the way down the steps from a geography class in the third year. Had that actually happened?

He suffered a brief disoriented moment when he couldn't be sure he was where he believed himself to be, that there had never been a school here, that he was trespassing on alien soil. But then the girl's foot crackled in a shallow, iced puddle and he saw the old school crest on her blazer, the comically large knot in her tie, the way they had all worn them back then. She was close enough now for him to see the flawless sweep of the skin on her face, and the ruptured veins that reddened her eyes.

A subconjunctival haemorrhage is blood that is located between the conjunctiva and the underlying sclera.

She was lifting her hands from her pockets now, but they were balled into fists, knuckles white against the skin, so tight he thought they might split open.

"I tried to save your life," he said.

"In doing so you ended it."

"How was I to know? If we'd stood and stared—and we all did, all except me—then you were dead anyway."

It had been an autumn day; hard winds blew dry curls of leaves and litter across the fields. Siddall had been late to the lunchtime queue. He hated not being among the first in line. It meant a plate full of cooling, staling things. It meant having to sneak on to a crammed table and feeling many pairs of eyes willing him to go elsewhere. All of the chips were gone by the time he made it round to the food. There was a tray of minced beef and a tray of mashed potato. Cold carrot coins. At least there were some Devonshire splits left for afters.

At the table (Chilts, Baggo, Cudge, Foz, Warbz, Graffy) he asked for the salt and Warbz slid it his way. Siddall positioned the cruet over his food and watched as the top fell off and a small hill cascaded on to his pool of mince. Laughter all round. He laughed too. *Good one. Bullseye.* He didn't have enough money left to buy a fresh serving. He scraped away the excess as best he could but it was ruined. He bolted his mash, intending to leave as soon as possible and eat his dessert in the playground.

Curious sound.

Cole, the laboratory assistant, was sitting at the staff table pouring water from a plastic jug into a beaker, but it wasn't that kind of gurgle. This was more . . . organic. He felt his heart leap at the fractured rhythm of it. Soon it was obscured under other noises, of panic and alarm. He turned in his chair and saw the girl, Alison?—she was in the year below him—bending as if looking for something she had dropped under the table. Her knife and fork fell from her fingers and the sound of them hitting the floor shut everyone up. She was bowed like the rod of an angler who has hooked a big fish. Into the silence flooded the sounds of her choking. It seemed such a private sound, something that nobody ought to be privy too. It was ugly and staccato and utterly breathless. Ropes of saliva hung from her distended jaws. Her skin was turning blue.

Siddall went to her as if in a dream. His decisiveness caused others, even the teacher, to stand back. He lifted her upright from behind and jammed his hand under her breastbone, gripping it with his other. He yanked his hands towards him, exerting pressure at the base of her diaphragm, jerking her off her feet in the process. He expected to hear the surprised snap of her lungs, a chunk of food to fly from her darkening lips but there was nothing now, not even the slightest squeak and snarl to suggest any procession of air in the shrinking O of her windpipe. Again he tried it. Again. But either he was performing the manoeuvre incorrectly or the morsel in her throat was stuck fast.

The significant forces involved in this procedure, even when done correctly, can cause bruising, but also more serious injuries such as fracture of the xiphoid process or ribs.

"I've called an ambulance," Cole, his face ashen, said to nobody in particular before shouldering his way out of the throng that was growing around Siddall and his stricken patient.

Siddall was aware of unblinking eyes, like a parliament of owls, watching his every move in complete silence. Alison had lost consciousness now. There might be enough oxygen in her lungs to keep her alive for another minute or so. He shrugged off his blazer and laid her down upon it. He positioned her head so that her throat was proud. With his finger he felt below her Adam's apple for a second bulge: the cricoid cartilage. He clamped his teeth on the end of his Bic Cristal and withdrew the ink tube and then the stopper at the bottom of the barrel. He held the pen in his fist, pointed end down, making sure there was about an inch of plastic showing, then he rammed this into her throat. He was vaguely aware of some people fainting. He was aware, on some level, of voices being raised. There might have been a siren in the distance. He watched blood fill the barrel of the pen and begin pulsing out of the end. He'd gone in too far; he hadn't gone in far enough. He didn't know what to do. Through it all Alison watched him with one eye open, lazy, frosted by senselessness.

Some of the problems that can occur as a result of a tracheotomy: air trapped in the pleural spaces around the lungs (pneumothorax), the presence of extraluminal air in the deeper layers of the chest (pneumomediastinum), subcutaneous emphysema, oesophageal trauma, injury to the recurrent laryngeal nerve that moves the vocal cords.

And bleeding. Don't forget bleeding.

He had stood up. His blazer was puddled with blood. The pulsing of it had ceased. He knew what that meant.

Now he felt his own breath catch in his throat as she reached out to touch him. She was colder than freezer burn. He saw horrible movement beneath the scarf as if she was still struggling with the piece of food that had killed her. The smell of cooked meat drifted to him and it was all he could do to quell his rising stomach. He wished he had not come here. What could he have hoped to achieve beyond a pang of regret? He thought a glimpse of his old school might act as some sort of tonic, but it only put him in mind of a long-lost family life that he had no hope of replicating. And of a girl he had wanted to save with a knowledge that was nothing of the sort.

The school was gone, but both of them were still bound to it. She had been the lucky one, he thought as he turned his back on the demolition site and trudged towards the exit, his fingers tingling with the memory of her body arching beneath them. She, at least, had escaped.

THE WATER KINGS

Manish Melwani

T HE FIRST TIME SANJAY SAW US WAS THE
night Dad passed. He only glimpsed us for a
second, though; he didn't quite understand what he'd
seen.

Only this: smoking on the verandah of Dad's mansion, staring across the low fence into his own neigh-
bouring villa, Sanjay had noticed the light on in his
half-renovated kitchen. And seen a strange man standing there. His head like a beak: long, curved and ocean-
green. Sanjay, numb from grief and lack of sleep, stared
as he took a drag from his cigarette. In his lungs, smoke
curled around the anemone-strands of his cilia, slowly
necrotising tissue: making him cough and retch and
avert his gaze. He looked up, but the man had vanished.

Confused, Sanjay rubbed his eyes. The man's impossible, crocodilian silhouette an afterglow; a fissure in
his mind. The light was still on next door, but the
kitchen was empty; the apparition gone. Unbidden, a
half-forgotten Hindi word from his childhood bub-
bled up through the murk: *Magar. Crocodile.*

Sanjay put the cigarette out. He walked past the
shared swimming pool and went through the gate,
the threshold between Mum and Dad's house and his

own. Dad had bought the adjacent property years ago. Sanjay had taken over its mortgage, but the renovation, like so many other things, had come to a halt with Dad's sudden illness. The villa loomed half-gutted in the night. Sacks of sand, ladders and other construction tools rested outside. Sanjay opened the door to his unfinished home, imagining reptilian shadows dripping dark water on exposed floors. Then a more pedestrian horror: Sunil Uncle, breaking into his house, parading vengefully and inexplicably with an umbrella over his head.

"Hello?" Sanjay called into the darkness. He stalked through the half-excavated living room, gaping at the house's bones. The kitchen light was on; but it was empty. No sign of intruder or umbrella.

He looked down: a puddle of water stood on the kitchen floor. Scowling, thinking of scathing words for the construction workers, he pulled a filthy towel off the sawdust-covered kitchen counter and mopped up the water. Then he switched off the light and went back to his parents' house, certain that grief and exhaustion were taking their toll on his mind.

As for us? We were still learning how to walk on land, but Sanjay could no longer see us with the light off.

Back on the verandah, he lit another cigarette, coughing again, ragged hacks that dislodged tiny flecks in his throat. Sanjay thought of Dad, two kilometres away in his hospital bed, withering from man to patient to corpse. Anil Mirchand's body rested in the embrace of three great machines that drained his kidneys and force-fed oxygen into failed lungs.

Sanjay put out the cigarette early and went to bed; recoiling as though he'd been granted a fleeting, terrifying vision of his own fate.

But he didn't sleep well. No son should, on the night of his father's death. His eyes opened to darkness and its phantoms, furniture transformed to huddled shapes. Vidya was already awake, sitting up in bed with her back to Sanjay, a shroud of blankets gathered around her as she stared out the bay windows into the humid Singapore night.

The telephone's urgent ring cut through the hum of the air conditioner. Sanjay fumbled for the receiver and put it to his ear.

"Hello?" he rasped, as Vidya turned on her bedside light, chasing the shadows back to their corners.

"Mr. Mirchand?" the nurse said in his ear. "His pulse is dropping. You should come now."

"Okay. We'll be there soon. Thank you."

He put down the phone. Vidya turned to face him, blinking in the sudden light.

"It's time," Sanjay said.

She nodded. "I'll wake Mummy. You start the car?"

Dad passed at 4.45am. The private hospital wasn't far from home, but they only just got there in time. Anil Mirchand had left the faculty of speech behind days ago, his illness shifting from a medical concern to a spiritual one. Sanjay stood by the bed with Mum and Vidya, watching the old man's pulse drop—*he hadn't been an old man until six months ago.* He held the withered hand of a man who'd once been father and mentor, watching the green spikes on the monitor and the ragged, mechanical breaths that punctuated the long silences growing further and further apart, until they finally ceased, and Sanjay found himself holding Dad's corpse-hand. Dad looked as empty and slack-jawed as he had all week, but some final essence had fled his body. The oxygen tubes rested pointlessly in his nostrils, continuing to force air into lungs that no longer needed it.

"Dad—" Sanjay began, but whatever he'd had to say was choked away. They stood in silence around the hospital bed until Mum slowly began to chant the Gayatri Mantra.

"Om bhur bhuvah svaha, tat savitur vareniyam . . ." Mum prayed again and again, hands together over her mouth, tears dappling her cheeks. They stood there like that, holding each other, red-eyed, standing vigil over the empty vessel. It was the only moment of peace Sanjay would have the entire day. Twenty minutes later, Dad's younger brother arrived. Sunil Uncle was wailing and tearful, Sanjay noted, as though he hadn't been the one to drive his older brother to the grave.

Dad's funeral consumed the entire day. They placed three obituaries in the newspaper: one from the family, a second from Saagar Raj Limited, and a third—at Sunil Uncle's insistence—from the board of directors. An unnecessary indulgence, meant to show anyone who read the paper that this dead man was an important one. But among the dead, even the rich walk barefoot, thorns and smouldering ashes in their heels.

Sunil, of course, had wanted the most expensive casket, wanted to send his Bhai off to God in a gaudy monstrosity. *Send him off like a king*, Sunil had demanded. Sunil Uncle never *spoke*. He *wheedled*, he *accused*. He made it seem like you were never doing enough. That conversation about the casket was the closest Sanjay had ever come to physically harming his uncle.

And so Sanjay stood silently, watching Sunil Uncle welcome mourners to Dad's house, hooded eyes glistening tearfully under his glasses. *Crocodile tears*, Sanjay thought, and looked away. He was sick of his uncle's face. But they were both Anil's pallbearers, and so Sanjay found himself standing next to Sunil again and again over the course of the day.

Together, Sanjay and Sunil hefted Dad's casket onto the hearse, soft merchant backs straining under its weight. Together they stood, sweaty and barefoot outside Mount Vernon Crematorium to welcome the mourners, feet burning on the hot tiles. Hello, hello. Thank you for coming. Sunil Uncle, ingratiating himself to the new Minister for Trade and Industry, Dad's old friend since donkey's years ago as Sanjay watched out of the corner of his eye. Finally, they stood together in the crematorium hall, flanking Dad's casket as the priest chanted, sprinkling rose water as family and friends adorned the body with garland after garland. Sanjay and Sunil did not speak, they did not meet eyes; they interacted with each other only at the priest's behest.

When the ceremony was over and everyone had said goodbye to Dad—though by now his body was empty as a broken ship—Sanjay, Sunil and the rest of the pallbearers picked up the coffin. In the far wall, a metal cap revealed a hungry opening, just the right shape for a casket. This hole led to a place of scorching heat; a place the living could not enter, but we were there as the casket began to burn: first wood, then flowers, and finally flesh. We lay there with Dad as he began to cook. Sanjay stood for a moment by the opening, his face flush with inhuman heat. Then the cap swung shut, and he followed the crowd outside, his bare feet filthy now, white kurta stained with sweat. The mourners still surrounded him, shaking his hand, looking into his eyes with morose expressions and consoling words that echoed forgotten in the pristine concrete halls of the dead. Sanjay wanted a cigarette. But he remembered Dad's laboured, machine-assisted breathing, and swallowed the urge.

Around him jostled old men and women with liver spots emerging from the collars of bone-white shirts and saris. They shook hands and leaned on walking sticks, speaking to each other in hushed tones. Older than Sanjay's father: his grandfather's contemporaries. *Our* contemporaries, who remember when Singapore was called Syonan-To. If only we had been allowed to grow old.

"Sanjay," Sunil murmured. He turned to see his uncle flanked by two suited men. One Indian, a young man with hair slick as oil on water. The other Australian, huge and balding, an ogre of capital.

"You know our investment bankers, no? They're helping us with the deal," Sunil said. "Ravi and ..."

" ... Chet," the big man said, extending his hand in a menacing clasp. "Sorry for your loss, mate. Your father was a *giant*. He'll be missed."

"Our condolences," Ravi said. He sounded almost like an Englishman. "Please, let us know if there's anything we can do for you in this difficult time."

"Thank you," Sanjay said.

"I imagine we'll be seeing more of each other soon," Chet said.

Sanjay's eyes narrowed, but the bankers turned and walked away, Chet's suited form towering over the crowd. He bent to whisper to his colleague.

"They are good guys," Sunil muttered. "Very kind of them to come." This was finally too much.

"Uncle," Sanjay hissed, releasing some of the venom that had been building in him since morning. "I can't believe you invited them here."

"Why, behta? They *wanted* to come. They knew your father. Even visited him in hospital."

Sanjay bit his tongue. *Why, so they could help you cheat him on his deathbed?*

"I know how difficult it is, behta," Sunil soothed. "Really. I'm here to help. We're family."

"We'll see about that," Sanjay snapped, turning and leaving to find Vidya and Mum.

Dad's old Jaguar still waited on the driveway when they returned to Mum and Dad's house, its big cat lines smothered under a grey tarp. Dad loved that car, but had to stop driving soon after his midlife crisis gave way to a medical one. Sanjay looked mournfully at the Jag as he pulled up next to it. Like Dad, the car no longer belonged to the living. Sanjay killed the engine and helped Mum out of the car. She'd been so strong, standing straight-backed through Dad's illness and death, but now when she grabbed her son's arm, she weighed him down like a dropped anchor. They staggered up the ramp that had been installed when Dad could no longer climb his own front steps.

Inside, Mum sat at the dining table and put her weary face in her palms. She'd grown so thin, the last few months, mirroring Dad so much that Sunil Uncle, who almost understood, had asked if she wanted to have a CT scan with him.

"I'm going to sleep in the guest room tonight," she said.

"You sure, Mum? Do you want me and Vidya to sleep in your room with you?"

"No. I . . . I can't sleep there tonight," she said. Her voice, so calm all day, finally broke, and out surged the flood of sorrow that had been building for months.

"Can I get you something to eat, Mummy? I think there's leftovers," Vidya offered.

They ate in silence, exhausted, as though all the energy expended in caring for Dad and sustaining him through his decline had been consigned to the fire with his body.

After putting Mum to bed, Sanjay and Vidya went upstairs. Sanjay lingered in the hallway for a moment, in front of the ancestral photographs of his grandfather and great-grandfather. He felt closer to this pantheon of ancestors, now that Dad had joined their number, and bowed his head to them.

While Vidya brushed her teeth, Sanjay sat in bed with a stack of the company's financial reports. Saagar Raj Limited owned thirteen ships, dry bulk carriers that sailed the world's arteries, as they had for nearly half a century since the War.

Sunil Uncle wanted to sell the ships, to *unburden* himself of their tonnage. Sanjay disagreed—like Dad he loved ships, but more than anything he suspected his uncle of fraud. He hated the way Sunil Uncle conducted himself, sneaking into hospital with a stack of papers for his weak, sedated brother to sign. Sanjay caught what he believed to be his uncle's sin, a single line on a shareholder's resolution worth three million dollars. Six ships for each brother, but what about the seventh? Sanjay, like Sunil, was already a rich man. But he battled his uncle over crumbs, like we did in those filthy holds, rats gnawing on fingers and toes.

"You don't have to do that right now, you know," Vidya said, emerging from the bathroom.

"What else am I supposed to do?" Sanjay asked.

"Try to rest. You need it."

"I'm going to see him tomorrow," Sanjay said. "When we scatter Dad's ashes."

"That's not an appropriate time to talk business, honey," Vidya said, climbing into bed.

"Appropriate? Sunil's been anything but *appropriate* this whole time."

"Listen . . . I don't trust him either. But you still don't know for sure."

"I don't," Sanjay conceded. "But I also don't know how *not* to bring it up."

"Just *don't*. Wait till next week. Speak to the lawyer first. It's really not the right time," Vidya said.

"He brought his *investment bankers* to the cremation today. Can you believe that?"

Vidya shook her head. "He's always been a little crazy. Be glad that he's trying to leave the company. You won't have to see him anymore."

Sanjay sighed. "Well, I'll have to see him a lot more until then."

Vidya slept well. Sanjay did not. He will never sleep well again. We watched him toss and turn, toss and turn, angle his head up to peer into the room's darkest corners, and then we went out into the hallway, to the ancestral portraits.

Ah. There he is. *L.K. Mirchand*. Dad's dad. The rot at this family's heart. Lal Krishna Mirchand, sent across the kala paani, the black water, on the eve of War to manage his father's shipping offices. We did not know him then, but we know him now. L.K., who would name his ship *Saagar Raj*, the Sea King; who would later trade that ship along with his soul, his sins congealing into crores and crores of gold.

Sanjay thinks of his grandfather as a pioneer, an empire-builder. But we remember L.K.'s guilt shining bright as a lighthouse. It called to us as we drowned, shackled in steel, hungering for the peace that was stolen from us. Robbed of hearth; of home; of sons and daughters and grandchildren. But we were trapped, unable to answer the call until finally those steel bones were cracked and we could smell the open, salty sea.

And so we set sail, not quite free, but no longer prisoners; *something else now*. We came back here, back again across the black water to Singapore. Like the hungry flower that blossomed in Dad's lungs and bones, we are part of Sanjay, entwined into this family, mixed into the brick and stone of this house bought with our bodies. We have been here since the beginning, and we will consume him, because we are so very, very famished. We have not eaten in half a century, and you, Bhai Lalchand, O Water King, you and your sons have eaten so very much.

The next morning, Sanjay drove to his uncle's house, a low-slung mansion on Singapore's East Coast. Sunil lived alone. No wife, no children. A lifelong bachelor. Sanjay waited outside the gold-trimmed gates, honking twice before Sunil emerged. Sanjay watched his uncle tread slowly up the driveway. The premature ageing had afflicted him too: his hair mostly receded, dark spots devouring his face, the hawk nose turning bulbous beneath his glasses. He walked like a breeze could knock him over.

Finally, he opened the passenger side door and got in. The two men drove in silence, each waiting for the other to speak.

"Turn right here," Sunil directed.

"I know the way."

"Listen, Sanjay . . . " Sunil began, hesitantly. "I'm done with all this. With the business."

Sanjay did not respond; he let his uncle continue his pitch as they drove. "You know me. I'm more into the numbers than the ships. I'd rather cash out, set up a small investment company. You can stay, if you *really* want. I just don't want to be in this business without your father. You know, my Bhai—"

A tide of rage surged through Sanjay, his fingers clenched the wheel. "Don't talk about my Dad," he snarled, pulling them to a stop at a signal light. In front of the car, a Chinese woman held her aged father's hand as they crossed the street together.

"He was your Dad; well; he was my *Bhai*! I've been in business with him since before you were born. You think I'm your enemy? I'm not."

"Then *why* are you trying to fleece us?"

"What? I'm not trying to fleece you, Sanjay."

"Come on, don't lie to me."

A car honked behind them. The light had turned green. "I saw the shareholder resolution you had Dad sign," Sanjay said as they accelerated. "He was on morphine. He was *dying*, for God's sake. And you got him to sign away one of the ships. Our flagship. The *Saagar Raj*. You thought you could take advantage of him. Of us."

Sunil stared at him, horrified. "No, no . . . that's not what you saw, Sanjay."

"I know what I saw. Now what am I supposed to do? Take you to court? So the papers can say we're having a family feud? So everyone can see what a *bad son* I am?"

"No, behta. We aren't selling that ship!"

"Oh, so *you're* selling everything *you* own in the company, but you're keeping *our* ship? You—"

"No!" Sunil shouted. "We're giving it away! You don't understand anything, Sanjay."

"What? Why the hell would you give it away?"

"We're selling the ship and giving the money to charity! I've set up a foundation in India. Under your father's name! And I'm giving $50,000 on top. Out of my pocket. You should do the same, since you're such a *good son*."

The words hung bitter in the recycled air between them.

"Look, Sanjay," Sunil offered, calmer now. "You think I'm crazy. But I'm not. I'm sorry your father didn't tell you about this. But we have a responsibility. *To pay our debts*." Sunil chewed on his lip and stared out the window. He *almost* understood.

They did not speak again, not until they reached the crematorium. The building had two entrances: one held auditoriums to host the living. The other held only what was left of the dead. They parked the car and met the priest in the lobby. He'd been waiting for them; keeping their place in line. Nowadays even Brahmins bow before money.

Finally, when it was their turn, Sunil Uncle, fearful he might catch a glimpse of us, said to Sanjay: "You should go in alone."

Sunil needn't have worried. We'd already had our fill. What remained of Dad waited for Sanjay on a low metal table that still radiated heat. A sea of ash; fragments of skull and hip rising like islands. Low columns in the shape of single vertebrae, like the ashen tubes Sanjay's cigarettes leave when they burn unattended.

The priest handed Sanjay the urn, and began to chant and sprinkle water as Sanjay scooped Dad into it. He thought about Dad; his voice, his grin, cracking jokes and drinking father-son whiskies over football games. But none of that existed in the end. Only ash. Soon the urn was full; the steel table empty except for sprinklings of human dust, and Sanjay's silk shirt stained with Dad's ashes.

They drove east, to the ferry terminal, past those beaches where the Japanese lined up all those Chinese men and boys. So many we knew: shopkeepers and accountants, teachers and labourers; the sand stained red as shallow water filled with blood and bullets. We remember.

At the ferry terminal, Sanjay, Sunil Uncle and the priest met the undertaker. The tall Tamil man pressed his palms together to greet the priest, his forehead already marked with crimson.

"Boat is ready?" the priest asked.

"All ready," the undertaker replied, leading them to the jetty, where a sunburnt Chinese man waved at them from his moored motorboat, hands stained with engine oil. The priest climbed aboard first, and held out his hand to help Sanjay, who clutched Dad's urn tight to his body as he stepped aboard the rocking deck. Sunil Uncle followed, refusing the priest's help, waving his arms wildly to balance himself. The undertaker undid the moorings as the boat sputtered and growled to life. The boat picked up speed, and soon they were out on the water. Sanjay breathed deep: gasoline, kelp and salty brine. He felt most free on the ocean. But the last time *we* boarded a ship, it was below deck, in chains.

Halfway into the Straits of Johor, the boatman killed the engine. The boat rocked gently; water lapped its hull. Tankers and cargo ships buoyed the horizon like floating coffins.

Sunil Uncle stood on the deck, hands on the boat's side, staring out into the horizon. Sanjay, still not understanding, wondered what would happen if he pushed his uncle overboard. Sunil pointed towards the corrugated line of ships.

"See that ship, Sanjay? That old one." In the distance floated an ancient hulk of a barge with a long, low body. A ship just like ours. We refused to mutiny, you see, unlike the oath-breakers who traded one master for another; King for Shōwa Emperor. And so it was our brothers who kicked us, beat us, forced us aboard a ship like that one. A ship owned by our countryman, but flying the flag of the Rising Sun. *Saagar Raj.*

"What about it?"

"Must be forty, fifty years old. We used to have one just like it. The first ship your grandfather bought. The first *Saagar Raj.* That's where our company name comes from. It went missing during the War. When we tracked it down in Bangladesh—"

"I know the story, Uncle."

Sunil fell silent, staring off into the horizon. The little boat rocked back and forth, and Sanjay cradled Dad's urn under his arm.

"Well," Sanjay said. "You loved the ocean, Dad. This is where you belong."

The priest chanted in Sanskrit, and Sanjay leaned over the boat's edge. Sunil held Sanjay's hip; the undertaker held his shoulder, and Sanjay felt a sudden stab of fear. Perhaps his uncle would be the one to drown *him.* But they held him tight as Sanjay emptied his father's remains into the sun-kissed sea, where they would mingle with the currents of the world's great oceans, the same currents that had blessed their family with so much fortune, and taken ours away. Ash and bone flowed from the urn, plopping gently into the water. There was so much of it. Sanjay shook the urn, until it was empty and his arms began to tremble.

"Throw the urn, also," the priest said, and Sanjay dropped it into the waves. What was left of Dad's body mixed with the waters of his family's crossing from India, a spreading cloud of bone, meat and burnt-out marrow. It all becomes ash in the end, down here in the blackest waters beneath the world, where not even ships can cross.

But we desired to taste what was left of him, and so we broke the water's surface for just a moment, and pulled what little remained of Dad down to the depths.

"Did you see that?" Sanjay asked. He'd seen it now, something sleek and dark cutting through the cloud of ash. The urn tumbled over itself, filled up with water and began to sink. Sunil, trembling, released Sanjay as he stepped back onto the deck. The undertaker pulled Sanjay up to his feet.

"Fish, probably," the priest shrugged. "Not to worry. It's good luck. The fish is the divine vehicle of Goddess Ganga, called *Makara*."

On their way back to land, the Brahmin told Sanjay about the Makara, but all he could think was that *something* had eaten Dad's ashes. And Sunil Uncle's lips were drawn tight and thin; he did not utter another word, not even when Sanjay dropped him at home.

The priest had told him to go home and shower, but Sanjay went to the office instead. Saagar Raj Limited occupied the 32nd floor of a building that overlooked the port. Sanjay, like Dad, had always loved the view. He'd inherited Dad's love for the maritime side of the business. Unlike Sunil Uncle, who saw ships as no more than the cold sums of their cargo manifests, assets to be reconciled in the accounts.

But today, instead of invigorating Sanjay, the ocean had left him empty. He sat down at Dad's desk, pushing himself back on the wheeled chair, remembered playing at being CEO when he was a boy. But boyhood was long behind him now. Adulthood, and its inheritance, weighed on him like rusty chains slipping beneath dark water. Sanjay thought about Dad who would never sit at this desk again, about Sunil Uncle and the *Saagar Raj*, about secret agreements made when he was still a child, their perpetrators made unquestionable by age, illness and respect.

And there they were, right on the desk. Dad, Sunil, and Granddad, on the deck of Granddad's yacht. Sunil was a young man in the photograph, younger than Sanjay. He wore a tight-fitting shirt and blue sunglasses, a champagne glass in his hand. Sanjay picked up the photograph, trying to understand. He glanced at the other photos on the desk; Dad and Captain Singh, head of fleet ops, together on the bridge of *Royal Durga*, sea jackets casually unzipped. There was Dad, Mum and ten-year-old Sanjay, happy and smiling. A hinged picture frame showed two old photos from a party in someone's garden, Christmas lights strung from the trees. Granddad and Grandma, smiling with drinks in their hands. In the second photograph, Granddad stood in the same garden, standing next to the former Prime Minister. *LKY & LKM*, someone had written in the corner. Sanjay smirked at the pun, and at his family's association with the powerful. But what about those of us who've been trampled and left to rot in the water? What about Risaldar Satwant Singh, Lance-Naik Mohan Nair, and the rest of the loyal lads whose soggy bodies have no urns or caskets? What about those who were devoured, cooked and eaten while the rest of us watched? We cannot blame our starving captors. They were soldiers, like us. Bound together in dharma, we forgave them their hunger as we slipped together into the sea. But you, O Water King, O soft-fleshed child of plenty? *You* cannot possibly imagine our hunger.

Sanjay searched Dad's keychain for the right key and unlocked the desk drawer. It was jammed, but he forced it open and found his father's treasures inside. The drawer smelt of moldy paper, and of flowers: the smell of priests and temples, of garlands wet and shiny, blooming from a casket.

Rummaging, he found a stack of manilla envelopes behind the box, marked in Dad's handwriting. One of them said *S.R.* Trembling, Sanjay undid its metal clasp and shook out a folded yellow paper and a rubber-banded stack of photographs. The photos depicted an ancient, beached ship, very much like the one Sunil had pointed at when they were out on the water. Who-ever took them had been staring up at its colossal hulk, and had photographed it so the name was clearly visible, fading on its rotted hull. *Saagar Raj.* The Sea King. That first, missing ship, which bequeathed its name to the family business, along with its sin. *Our ship.*

Sanjay unfolded the piece of paper: a photocopied note, written in terrible, cursive handwriting: *Mr. Mirchand, I hv found ship . . . Chittagong Yard . . . see photo . . . hv asserted yr ownership . . . badly corroded . . . not much . . . value . . . nevertheless hv negotiate . . . US$100,000 . . . shld accept . . . full credit . . . transfer . . . pls advise hw to dispose remains? kindly revert . . . Mr. Prakash.*

Mr. Prakash. Not a scrap broker Sanjay had ever heard of. He picked up the stack of photographs. Flipping through them, he saw the *Saagar Raj's* funeral. The ship beached at the breaker's yard, decaying and turning skeletal; its hull cracked open, dismembered components littering the beach. The hold was open too, its secrets strewn across sand stained red with blood and rust, where poor boys laboured, smashing fingers and snapping bones as they prepared ships for the afterlife and lined the pockets of rich men. Photo by photo, the *Saagar Raj* became an empty shell, a desecrated tomb. Scrapped for profit, peeled apart; its bones completely exposed.

And then the final photograph. A close up, inside the cargo hold. Something pale and yellow, scattered against the corroded wall.

Pls advise hw to dispose remains?

Sanjay put the photo down. His hands shook, his jaw clenched hard enough to shatter teeth. Panicking, he left Dad's office, walking down the corridor to his own. He ransacked his drawers, looking for cigarettes. Finally he found a bashed pack of Marlboros—with three left inside, thank God. Trembling, he put one in his mouth, chewing frantically on the butt. He lit it and filled the room with smoke, distracting himself with fevered drags until he started coughing. Sanjay thought about cancer, spreading like Dad's bones in the sea, like our dusty bones in the *Saagar Raj's* belly. He rubbed his neck, feeling for swollen nodules, and put the cigarette out early, fingers stained and shaking with ash and horror.

He walked back to Dad's office. The answering machine on the desk blinked orange, a new message waiting inside it. Had it always been there? Confused, Sanjay sat back down in Dad's chair and played the message. Sunil Uncle's voice filled the room, drunk and distorted.

"Anil Bhai," Sunil sighed. "I came to see you. I don't know if you could hear me. But . . . anyway, they say . . . hearing's the last thing to go. But you didn't . . . *look* like you anymore. Like you were already gone. I'm so sorry, Bhai. There's so much I wanted to say. But it's too late now. I don't know why I'm calling you. Maybe I've gone crazy. But I . . . needed to say goodbye. And to tell you something. I'm—*I'm sick, too.* What happened to you . . . it's going to happen to me. It's that ship. I'm trying to stop it. Trying to do what I can. I'll take care of everyone. Radhika. Sanjay. Vidya. I miss you, Bro . . . I-I'll see you soon. Goodbye.'"

A long pause, and then his voice returned, darker, insistent and full of revelation: *"Anil. People were eaten on that ship, did you know that?"*

The line went dead. Sanjay stared at the answering machine, wondering what else it contained. But that was it. He thought about calling his uncle. Sunil sounded crazy. Suicidal, even. He looked at the photos spread on the desk. Whatever happened on that ship was in the past, he decided. What was important was the future. The future of his family, the future of the company. And Sunil Uncle, whatever his intentions, was a threat to that future.

Angrily, Sanjay swept the photographs back into the drawer and shut it. He cradled his forehead in his hand. He would call the lawyer tomorrow. This was far too much for one day.

That night, Sanjay was afraid to sleep. He watched Vidya as her eyelids fluttered and she began to snore. He felt abandoned, left alone and haunted in the waking world. When he shut his eyes he saw corpses, skeletal bodies floating face-down in murky black puddles. He wandered through the corroded, claustrophobic tunnels of an old ship, pushing his way between walls not even wide enough to hold a body hollowed by cancer. An open container yawned at him, like the mouth of a monstrous fish.

Magar. Makara.

Corpse-hands pulled him inside and lay him on his back. Sanjay's eyes opened to darkness, a crushing weight on his chest. Next to him lay a body, pale and unmoving. He gasped—

"Hm?" Vidya responded sleepily. Sanjay forced the heavy blankets off him, and propped himself up on his elbow to look down at her. There was no corpse. Only Vidya. But imagine if he had been us, forced to turn gasping and sweating in that hold, waking from a fever dream expecting to see his wife but seeing only the man next to him, again and again. *We have been here since the beginning.*

"Nothing. Bad dream," Sanjay said, and Vidya made a small, sleepy noise. He had to urinate, but was afraid of the darkness, of putting his feet on the bedroom floor. He feared the wood had turned to water by now, and if he dipped his feet overboard he would surely sink down, down into the crushing depths. But soon the urge became too much, and he stumbled shivering towards the bathroom.

Sanjay opened the bathroom door. Through the frosted windows, the moon traced spidery shadows on the floor and wall like emaciated, grasping fingers. He wanted to turn on the light, but then he would have to venture back out into pure darkness. So he stood over the darkened toilet and urinated, feeling relief replace pressure in his over-full bladder. Out of the corner of his eye, he saw a shape caress his own in the bathroom mirror, and spun, panicking, spilling hot urine all over his feet.

But there was nothing there, nothing peering out from the reflection's dark edges.

Sanjay cursed under his breath. Of course there was nothing there. Yet as he washed his hands in the darkness, splashing clean tap water on his feet and wiping them dry with his towel, he saw them. The shapes in the mirror; impossibly compacted limbs angling out from the reflected shelves, misshapen forms of ash and shadow. He whirled around, but there was nothing.

Back in the bedroom, shivering in the air conditioner's draft, he wanted to lie down next to Vidya, to clutch her to him, but he worried the body in bed would not be hers. The shape of the blankets unsettled him; bunched-up like the hump of an ocean creature breaking the waves for just a moment. He needed fresh air, needed to feel the cool, humid night on his skin. So he left the bedroom, the eyes of his grandfather and great-grandfather watching from inside their frames. He descended the stairs, careful not to wake his mother who slept downstairs in the guest room because she would no longer sleep in the room she once shared with her husband.

Sanjay moved like a sleepwalker through a living room made hostile by shadows, a kingdom claimed by the dead in which he was no longer welcome. He pushed open the verandah door, and the moist swimming pool air bathed his skin, the chlorine smell pulling his mind firmly into the waking world. Into the present, where his past awaits him.

Sanjay walks past the old plastic chairs that Dad never saw the point in replacing and steps onto the pale tiles that surround the thirty-metre long swimming pool, lit from within so nobody will slip and fall in at night. He is careful not to look inside as he walks the length of the pool, but then he slips, wet feet sliding out from under him, his back and hips crashing onto hard ceramic.

Groaning, he rubs his aching back, damp through the t-shirt. The tiles are soaked, as though something huge had jumped into the pool, or a platoon of swimmers had emerged dripping just moments earlier. Then Sanjay looks into the water, and sees us.

We have been waiting for him. Like a spreading oil slick, like the flower blooming in his lungs. We spread and coalesce, our tendrils unfurling into the dimly-lit chlorine water like Dad's ashes in the ocean. Sanjay sees the darkness growing and uncoiling in the swimming pool, and knows it is his reckoning. We swim towards him. We come to collect the debt.

Shocked, he scrambles backwards across the slippery tiles,

onto the grass. He cannot escape us, the dark shape rearing out of the water now, taking form as we come into contact with the air. Watery talons splash onto tiles, kala paani dripping everywhere as we regurgitate ourselves out of the pool and make our landfall; a huge, reptilian shadow looming over him.

Magar. Makara.

"Please," he whispers, but we are here for him.

"You've become rich, bhai-sahib," we whisper. "So rich. But every rupee is a bite of flesh from our bodies."

Our teeth are eyeballs. Our mouth a hundred starving mouths.

"Mujhe maaf karo," Sanjay pleads in his fragmented Hindi. "Forgive me. Please."

"Nahein," we hiss. "We have waited so long to find you, Saagar Ra."

His skin is cold in the humid night. We tower over him, and he can see now that we are made of dead men, our bodies reconfigured, some partially chewed and digested, others torn to shreds to make teeth and tail and talons. Every claw a hand with ten emaciated fingers, nails broken on the walls of the hold. *People were eaten on that ship, did you know that?*

"But my father is dead," Sanjay pleads.

"Yeh unka ghar hain. Yeh aapka ghar hain," we reply. *This is his house. This is your house.*

And when the ghost of the black waters opens its mouth, Sanjay smells salt water and metallic blood and the rotting stench of shit. He sees all *our* faces, us poor betrayed comrades, starving and hollow-eyed lads, our uniforms all in tatters. He hears the buzzing of flies, and *our voices*, as we scream and moan and plead with our captors, our equally starving captors who cut us, cooked us and ate our flesh, far, far across the black waters, so that we might never again return home.

We raise our hand to his mouth and caress him like a bloodthirsty lover.

And as he is devoured in the shadow of his father's mansion, Sanjay finally understands why.

IN THE TALL GRASS

Simon Strantzas

WHEN REITER IS AWAKE, HEIKE SITS AT his side, entwines her fingers with his, sometimes strokes his face. But when he's asleep she steals out to the tall grass at the edge of the farm and finds a spot deep within it to kneel. She doesn't know what she prays to—there's nothing to believe in anymore—but she prays all the same. She prays because deep in the tall grass, far away from the house and from Reiter and from everything she knows, the world is softer and more malleable. She's closer to something she has no name for—be it God or Fate or whatever. No matter how foolish it might be, she hopes if she prays there she will be heard. Reiter will be saved and the two of them will be happy forever.

But she isn't heard and Reiter is gone by the time she returns.

He's buried in the tall grass because that's what he wanted, but she never visits him. She can't go back to where her world ended. Without him, she is untethered. Those crow's feet in the corners of her eyes eventually stretch farther across her broad face, and her red hair turns a grey like water tinged with blood. The woman in the mirror who returns her furrowed-brow glare looks as though she's forgotten everything Reiter taught her about being alive.

She doesn't notice Baum in the grass because he takes his time arriving. At first he is no more than a shoot between the seed-heavy blades, a thin reach of green that grabs hold of whatever it can to climb its way into the sun, open a lone pink flower to the light. It's during the subsequent autumns and winters and summers and springs that Baum grows and blossoms, getting larger, stronger, until he is finally able to uproot his twisted legs from the soil and find himself steady enough to move forward.

Baum emerges from the grass while Heike works on her truck, shirtsleeves folded to above her elbow. She hears the snap of a thousand twigs and turns her grease-smeared face to find Baum crying, crooked arms spread wide. The smell of new green wafts from him while light diffuses through his foliage, dappling shadows over her face.

Baum attempts to speak, to tell her he has watched her move from window to window, from door to garage; watched her sit on the back stoop in the cool evenings with only a cigarette and a mug, and watched her rub her face and the back of her neck alone in the dark. But there are no words, only a quiet and fluttering rustle. Only in this moment does Baum realize Heike could be unreachable in her sorrow. His round knots well with tears as his crooked limbs stretch farther out. The wind picks up, blows through the leaves, and Heike wordlessly puts her wrench on the truck's running board, then pulls Baum to her breast. Her heart makes a sound like knuckles on a hollow door.

There were never children between Heike and Reiter, and his clothes were given away long ago, so Heike has nothing that will fit Baum's irregular shape. She makes any alterations she can to her own old clothes using nylon thread and stiff-backed perseverance. It's not the easiest solution, or the swiftest, and Baum's small round eyes stare unblinkingly at her the entire time, but eventually Heike is able to fashion a rudimentary pair of trousers to envelope the trunks of Baum's legs, and a jigsaw shirt that makes room for the blossoming pink shoots along his grooved skin. When she is done and Baum is dressed, the noise is like the whistle of rain-soaked leaves. Baum lights up, and Heike recalls how it feels to smile.

The two sit by the dried up pond, soaking their bare feet in memories. Memories are all Heike has of Reiter—the two of them cooling off by the water, laughing and teasing one another. Sometimes she thinks she can see his weathered face reflected back in the remembered water. Other times, she can't see the reflection at all, no matter how long or hard she squints. At these moments, there is nothing in the pond but sunbaked mud, its cracks as deep as the grooves on Baum's flesh. Slowly, they spiral outward.

The farm is no place for a boy. The days are long and hard and Heike likes it that way because it keeps her from remembering Reiter. Remembering his wasting face and body and pallid skin. But Baum needs more than that. He is alive and Reiter is not and he needs to learn more than Heike can teach, see more than Heike can show.

Baum has never heard the knocking sound before and even after Heike explains it's a visitor at the door he still lumbers away to hide. The front door opens and unfamiliar voices mumble in the other room. One he believes is Heike's, but the woman is so taciturn Baum cannot be certain. The second is not familiar at all, and leaves him unhappy and apprehensive. Dry twigs break as he shifts, scratching the worn floor. Leaves fall. If he remains motionless perhaps he will fade to safety.

The tutor, Ana, is not prepared for what she finds when she turns the corner in the faltering farmhouse. She has taken odd assignments before—she hasn't had much choice; there are too few tutors so far outside the city, and yet too few students needing help to discriminate. Ana took the job with Baum because she had to, but also because the cousin she remembers most from childhood wore an oversized hearing aid and a single thick-soled boot. That boy went out of his way to treat her well and demanded nothing in return. She hopes helping other challenged students will in some small way assuage her guilt.

But when Ana turns the corner she understands this is not her cousin. This is nothing she has seen before, and for a brief moment the world is completely still, and she is staring at Baum who is staring back with round shimmering eyes, Ana convinces herself it's a joke of some sort. A hoax. A horrible statue posed in a dark house to surprise her. She glances around for her husband and her friends who will soon emerge to laugh at her discomfort. It is only at the end of that second, when the horrible statue moves and she understands it's alive and looking right into her that she gasps and turns away.

There isn't much to say after Ana flees, bags pressed against her chest, eyes darting madly, but Heike does her best to find words to comfort Baum. A rivulet of tears runs in the grooves of his face. It doesn't matter what Heike says, however. They both understand perfectly. Ana, the tutor, has done exactly what she was hired to do and more. She has taught them an unforgettable lesson.

Nothing is the same afterward. Leaves darken. Dry. Fall and crunch underfoot. Pink shoots wither. Baum becomes sullen, withdrawn. Heike does her best to talk to him, but Baum shrinks from the feel of her gnarled hands on his corrugated flesh. When he speaks, if he speaks, it's with branches thrashing and cracking in thunderous resentment. The farm is too small, its fences a prison of constricting walls. He lashes out and storms through Heike's life with wind and fury. Baum wants to escape, but where can he go where he won't be judged or mocked or shunned? Heike doesn't know. But she must do something.

The farm is so far from the city she and Reiter had to stay overnight during each of his treatments. She knows it will be the same for Baum. She has spoken to the county hospital and there is no specialist closer than Dr. Meyer. But this is what Baum wants. He wants to be normal. Through Baum's winter branches Heike can see those knotted eyes and thinks not for the first time there is something of Reiter in them.

Baum never believed he would ever see what lies beyond the tall grass, but Heike's truck sputters and pops, and the air smells as though it's on fire, and he doesn't worry about memorizing that moment because the smell will always remind him of sitting in the truck, branches scraping the bare metal cab. The farmhouse shrinks behind the grasses, then the road, then the world itself, and where Heike is taking him is filled with bright blue sky and nothing more for a long time.

Baum's angst withers when the trees come into view. Towering giants marching over the horizon, they grow with each passing moment until they eclipse the sky, laying a veil of shadows over the road and Heike's truck. Baum presses his grooved face against the window but still cannot see their dark canopy. All he sees are the hundreds of trunks woven together on each side of the road, two impenetrable walls ushering the truck toward the wavering sun bursting orange as it approaches the horizon.

They could make it to the city if they drive into the night, but Heike doesn't want to push the truck too hard. The engine needle is already creeping higher than she'd like, and the radiator is guzzling water like Reiter once his kidneys failed. Heike doesn't like thinking about his yellowing skin or cracking lips, so she turns off the highway at the first neon sign she sees. It has become night so swiftly, so completely, it's as though a switch has been thrown, which Heike hopes will keep passers-by from noticing Baum in the car as he waits for her to pay for the room. He doesn't deserve whatever strangers at a rundown motel might heap upon him.

But she needn't have worried. There is only one person who walks by. He introduces himself through the truck's grimy window as Waechter. Impossibly tall and slender, his coats are black and yet the tie he wears is the colour of summer soap bubbles. In his lapel he wears a pink flower whose petals radiate like a starburst. Waechter peers at Baum with eyes just as slippery, just as mesmerizing, that make his face look as though it has recently caught fire. The brim of Waechter's hat is large and folded and beneath it Baum can see the rows of gleaming teeth. Waechter taps a long finger on the car window, and Baum's branches tremble as he shifts in his seat. He searches for rescue but cannot find Heike.

Baum chirps nervously, the hitch in his voice like a bustle of squirrels caught in autumn branches. Waechter sizes him up while simultaneously looking past him. Then he speaks with a sonorous boom and asks Baum why he is in the car. Baum doesn't know how to respond. Is fear stifling the answer, or is there no answer at all? He is travelling with Heike westward. Branches creak.

Waechter understands. Baum is a prisoner.

Baum protests, but Waechter ignores him, taps his long finger again above the lock. Baum looks at the door, then up at the man's broad smile and slow nod. Leaves blanket the car as Baum shakes. Heike will help him, he repeats to himself. When Heike comes, she will help him.

But Heike does not help him. Heike is inside the motel office, impatient for paperwork to be completed by the stout clerk in thick glasses, wondering how her life twisted so strangely. Everything has been familiar since leaving the farm despite it being years since she's seen any of it. Every inch of road, every curve of hill on her road trip through her memories has been a reminder of how far that journey has taken her only to end up in the same place. The only difference being Baum beside her instead of Reiter. Afterward, when Heike leaves the office, room key in hand, and steps outside, she takes only two steps then stops. The truck is where she parked it, but the passenger door is open, and the solitary light from the motel flickers blue neon and illuminates the empty passenger seat inside the cab.

Cold creeps up Heike's spine, dries her mouth, disassociates her. She floats a half foot above herself, watches from the aether as her body goes on, always a few seconds delayed. She hears herself call out Baum's name, sees herself jog to the truck. There are leaves and twigs on the cab's floor, something like sap on the handles. Heike's body looks in every direction while her mind tries to understand something that's just beyond her. She calls out with more volume, moves more frantically.

The neon buzzes then clicks and light shines on the edge of the parking lot. There is a familiar rustle, and both Heike's halves turn to see the shadow of branches swaying in the periphery. No less frantic, Heike swallows her concern and approaches Baum who stands on the edge of the paved world and who stares into the darkness of the arboreal.

Heike puts her calloused hand on Baum's rough bark. She thinks of Reiter.

Baum doesn't turn, but he too thinks of Reiter. His hand is twisted into the shape of a fist. He creaks and moans and wonders where Waechter has gone. A few minutes later, Baum looks at Heike but he can't see anything, his knotted eyes engraved by the forest. Heike guides him back to the truck, then into their rented room. During the night the neon buzzes and clicks and neither Heike nor Baum are able to sleep for the thoughts rattling in their heads.

In the morning Baum is more or less himself, although quiet, and Heike does not want to push him. Instead they gather their things and drive off in the direction of the city with a burst of exhaust and the rattle of a truck unused to meeting its limits. If anyone from the motel has seen Baum, they make no effort to get a closer look. Baum looks for Waechter, but if he once was near, he has long since retreated into the woods.

And the two drive on.

The jagged cityscape rises from the horizon as the forest had, but with concrete taller than trees and lights brighter than fireflies. It looks grand and endless, but Baum finds little excitement in seeing such a vast monstrosity. There are loud and sudden noises, and the air grows harder to breathe the closer the truck gets. Baum looks at Heike and sees her aged hands turned pale as they grip the steering wheel too tightly. She turns her head a fraction and her hands and shoulders slacken. The corner of her mouth offers a smile. Reassured, Baum turns back to the window, and the sights there bend his rough bark into a frown.

It's nearly noon when the truck, overheated and thirsty, finally pulls to a stop in the small parking lot adjoining the hospital. Baum has never seen a building so large, and makes him feel insignificant. His problems, nothing in the face of the gigantic.

He puts his hand on the concrete wall to prove its real, and it's cold and rough and splinters catch on it like brambles. He can't put into words why he isn't surprised, nor explain why he pretends not to notice Heike watching.

Dr. Meyer is officed on the fifth floor. They take an elevator, and Baum cannot help inspecting every inch of the small room. It makes Heike weaken, but she says nothing and wonders again if she was wrong to hide Baum from the world. But what choice did she have? Heike does not like the city—too many reminders of Reiter in the curved streets and looming buildings. Avoidance had served her well, and would have continued to do so had Baum not needed her more than she needed herself. The understanding makes Heike stagger, but she doesn't falter. Instead, she pushes the realization aside. It won't help her where they're going.

When Heike and Baum enter, the receptionist purposely avoids reacting to Baum's corrugated face. Instead, she hands them a clipboard with a pen tied to it by a piece of frayed twine. The form must be filled out, and she asks them to sit in the waiting chairs while they do so. Heike struggles for the words to describe her relationship to Baum, afraid to write what she knows is true.

A nurse with tight brown curls leads them to a room only slightly larger than the elevator and has them wait behind the closed door. Baum is nervous and timid, but once she is gone his inquisitiveness resurfaces. Heike watches him probe the room and test the world. Baum wraps vines around drawer pulls and leafs through a stack of forms, but with each investigation he comes away disappointed and soon disinterested. Whatever he was looking for, he can't find it.

There is a clipped series of knocks on the door, and before either Heike or Baum can react Dr. Meyer enters the room. Energy crackles off him as he speaks, lightning-eyed and curious in a way that Heike doesn't trust. But she never trusts anyone who is too curious, and since Reiter's passing she trusts doctors even less. Dr. Meyer introduces himself but Heike doesn't pay much attention. She's too busy looking at Baum to see how he's reacting. Limbs shake as though there are rodents scurrying between them, the sound like a crashing river. Baum's knot-holed eyes have sunk so deep into his phloem that they are hidden. The only evidence they are there at all is the glint of light from deep within the recession of his tear-filled eyes.

Dr. Meyer reassures Baum it will be okay, but something about his manner concerns Heike. He acts like a pig waiting impatiently by the trough.

Baum nods when Dr. Meyer says he needs to run a few tests, and asks if Baum can be brave for him. He feels as though birds are nesting in his branches, their weight slight but aggravating, and knows the only way to dispel the sensation is to shakes them out. He does this obsessively three times to be sure they're gone, and when he looks up again through the rain of dry coloured leaves floating to the ground it's only Heike's smile that is no longer there.

Dr. Meyer finds it hard to contain his excitement about such an important autosomal case, and is nearly skipping as he leaves the subject in the small room, promising to be back in a moment with more information. But leaving was only to give him a moment to process the intensity of his excitement. Dr. Meyer looks at the nurse, aware of the broad smile on his face, and sees her eyes are already alight. She, too, has never seen anything like this. *Epidermodysplasia verruciformis*, in all its glory. It's a find that could, if coordinated properly, mean solving the riddle of HPV and potentially more. There is so much good they can do. When Dr. Meyer gets to his private office, he places a call to the Research University, then waits as he's transferred to the dean. Above his door hangs a framed novelty Time magazine cover with his photo, and above the headline reads: "Doctor of the Year". Dr. Meyer smiles and puts his feet up.

But in the middle of explaining his find, there's an urgent knock at Dr. Meyer's door. He puts the receiver to his chest as the nurse rushes in with the news. It's the last thing Dr. Meyer wants to hear. It takes a moment to catch up with his thoughts. He tells the dean he'll have to call him back.

Getting to the car again is more difficult than Heike had expected. There are too many people rushing through the streets, and if they make Heike feel uncomfortable and claustrophobic, she can only imagine how they are affecting Baum. There's no point in going back into the hospital—no one there is interested in helping. Heike urges Baum to hurry as she notices passers-by slowing. She can see it in their mannerisms: they are beginning to question if what they're seeing is real, and instinct is prompting them to advance. Baum notices it, too, the slow migration toward him, and he shrivels in fright, branches shaking off his last straggling leaves. Heike is helping him into the truck as the first curious gawker arrives.

What is that? he asks. Some kind of costume? And Heike won't look at Baum because if she doesn't maybe Baum won't have heard anything. But Heike hears. She hears twigs scraping the roof of her truck, back and forth the sticks worrying the old metal, and Heike grows irritated, angry. She puts her hand flat on the chest of the man trying to peer through the truck's window and shoves him. Tells him to mind his own damn business. The man corrects his twisted shirt; looks hurt and annoyed. He was just asking about the costume, for Pete's sake, and Heike teasingly imagines for a second—for less than a second, for a fraction of a second—slamming the man's teeth into his face to show him and all the approaching gawkers that they can't say these things about her son.

Baum. Her son.

The idea frightens her. She looks through the window at the trembling Baum and understands how much Reiter would have loved him, and he Reiter. Death robs so much from everyone, stopping only when there is nothing left worth taking. Heike turns, unsure if she intends to hug the man or beat him senseless, but it doesn't matter. He's already gone—back up the street to rejoin the gawkers who now keep their distance, who have decided they no longer need to see the freak—and the end of the afternoon feels closer than ever. The wheat is probably ripening at the farm as she stands on the dark asphalt of the hospital parking lot, so far from her centre, from where Reiter waits patiently for the day she will inevitably join him. She'll be there soon, she thinks. Home with Baum, home with Reiter close by. She feels better when he's near. Closer to being complete.

Baum doesn't speak as the truck pulls out of the parking lot, finds the long road toward home. He watches out the window, tendrils on the glass, as the world passes by; as the crowds on the streets thin, as office buildings become storefronts become houses. The truck crawls from the depths of looming concrete to surface on the flat landscape of grasses and rocks. And all the while, Baum doesn't speak, not even as the city fades in the rear mirror, taking with it the last of Baum's hopes. There's nothing left for him now. The roughness of the road vibrates from the tires into the cab but Baum doesn't feel it. He doesn't feel anything. Disconnected and untethered, he is starting to float away. He turns to Heike, though he's not sure if it's for help or to say goodbye. What comes out of his mouth is the long sorrowful creak of a branch about to yield from strain.

Heike looks at him, at his grey bark, at his softened grooves and ridges, and she knows she's made a mistake. She's made so many—running from Dr. Meyer, bringing Baum to the city, hiring Ana—and she wonders how far back it goes. Where did it start? Was there a single choice from which all her mistakes sprung? If she could change that one thing, maybe everything would be different. The answer comes almost immediately, and it makes her so sick she can barely form the thought.

If she'd never met Reiter. Maybe if she'd never met Reiter then . . .

She glances at Baum.

"I ever tell you about the day I first met my Reiter? He was seven; I was nine. His aunt lived in the house next to mine, so he'd sometimes visit there. Once, he was visiting because the aunt was sick, and when he was shooed outside I was already there playing. So, he joined me and we played till the sun went in. Then his aunt died and his family took him away and never came back.

"That's the story he told me a year after we married. I didn't remember it then. Don't remember it now. But it makes sense it happened like that. Reiter and me, we belonged to each other from the very beginning. No bad luck or hardship or nothing can change that. Not even him dying. Those people back there who stared at you, all the people you hide from? They don't get it. They don't get belonging. It's not about pushing away things that are different, it's about finding how things are the same. It's about finding your place. I found mine and a piece of me is still with him underground, wrapped in a sheet. Forget those people. Forget Dr. Meyer and the rest. Just worry about where you belong."

Baum stares unblinkingly at her, each bump on the road shaking his bare branches. Heike twists her hands on the wheel, frustrated the words came out wrong. She wanted them to make Baum feel better, to reassure him. They were the wrong words. But before she can fumble for the right ones, he reaches out and gently touches her hand.

The forest materializes out of aether and mist. It isn't that Heike doesn't recognize the highway as it takes them into the woods, but that the day is late and her back is hurting from the bent spring in her seat, so everything appears slightly distorted and foreign. Trees look older than they had earlier in the day, thicker and balder, and they glare down at the truck passing at their feet as though they've been expecting this return. Heike leans forward, looks up at the imperfect canopy, and considers how bizarre it is that such a sparse mesh can still snare so much light.

She has no plan beyond reaching the farm as soon as possible, driving through the night if necessary, but all of Heike's fight drains once the truck enters the thickest section of the forest. The endless shadows overtake the truck, clawing it back as the fading day stretches time to its thinnest strand. Heike feels the drag of exhaustion slowing her movements, filling her arms with sand, and she knows she won't be able to drive much farther. At least Baum is slowly shaking his stupor. Once among the endless web of trunks and brush he stirs, presses his face against the window, and looks intensely among the trees for something.

If the clerk at the motel recognizes Heike from the morning, she doesn't show it. Or, perhaps it's a different clerk at a different place. Heike cannot be sure when every motel looks like the one before. Bored, irritated without obvious reason, the pudgy woman gives Heike the key and turns away before Heike can retrieve it. Heike staggers back to the car in a race to get to bed before the sleep hurtling towards her arrives, wondering how much of what she is experiencing is real and not waking dream. The truck wavers in the lot and she feels a chill when she sees it, sees Baum's face behind the glass; his ashen, leafless face moulded with an emptiness Heike cannot define any better than she can her own.

They settle in the room for the night, speaking little to each other. Baum sits by the open window, watching the forest outside while Heike sits on the edge of the bed, staring down at the wrinkled photograph of Reiter she carries with her. Between them lays nothing but worn and dirty carpet. Eventually, exhaustion comes for Heike, but she doesn't question its source for fear of the answer. Instead she pulls the covers up to her chest and turns out the light. Baum remains in the window, so Heike watches him—his leafless branches fracturing the rectangle of sky that's cut into the room's darkness—and listens for his breathing. It's slow and steady and mirrors her own. When sleep comes, and reality softens, a moment before Heike succumbs she wonders if Baum's breathing is so familiar because it's always only been Heike's. A reflection in darkness. She rolls over before she can wonder more and the thought is gone.

There is a solitary light on the highway, illuminating a small circle of road, and those few leafed branches that reach for it. Baum watches them sway in the night breeze, dancing or beckoning, he doesn't know which. Tall and without burden, they just exist, growing forever into one another's embrace. They belong, so why doesn't he? Tears fill his grooves, travel a long way down until their momentum dissipates. He remembers his life in the tall grass, remembers how it nourished him. Now he slowly drifts away inside a cheap room, unable to feel that grass or those woods beyond the highway. Baum runs his splitting vines on the glass to clean a blemish, but it doesn't move, and he realizes the spot is something else. Something more, hidden among the trees. Baum leans forward, his trunk creaking, and witnesses the trees part like a curtain. From the void between steps Waechter. He is dressed in pink now—pink shirt, pink linen jacket and trousers, all dingy to the elbows and knees—and his legs strangely bend in the wrong direction like the legs of a goat. His toothful mouth emits no sound, but laughs all the same, his head bobbing along with it. He mouths a word Baum cannot make out but recognizes the sound. He has heard it before. It is the sound of the forest, and Waechter speaks for it as he beckons Baum onward while stepping back into the darkness between the trees, fading into the tall grass where the world is its softest and most malleable.

Heike is thrown from bed and onto her feet before she is fully awake. Somehow, it's mid-morning, and the late day and lingering grogginess induce a vertigo she can't fully tamp down. Baum is no longer at the window, but he is not in the bed, either. Heike checks the bathroom, then opens the front door. Beyond it is the gravel lot, followed by a narrow asphalt strip of highway with cars that whizz too fast. On the opposite side, the world full of trees. A thunderstorm of panic swirls inside Heike, but it's suppressed by an inchoate layer of something else—something cold that keeps it at a distance where it is unable to affect her. It is a form of shock designed to help her displace her terror and keep moving, though there's a whisper that tells Heike that it's all she will be able to feel from now on, forever and ever. It's the feeling of leaving the world behind.

The first place Heike goes to is the pond, but when she arrives there is no Baum, and there is no pond. It's as dry as the one on the farm. She looks into it, but does not see the reflections of memories, does not see Reiter or Baum or anyone else. What Heike sees is nothing. Nothing but an empty vacant hole in the ground. No, not empty, she realizes. There's something in the middle of the dry pond, something small and bulbous. She carefully gets to her knees, ignoring any pain, and throws her legs over the bank one at a time before sliding in. When she reaches the bottom, she realizes the dried mud belies the wet muck beneath, and her feet sink five slowly-filling inches. She trudges through the mud at the centre of the dried pond and finds the fibrous pod waiting for her there, small green vines clutched around it. She bends over, her back already sore from strain and picks it up.

Baum is gone as though he was never there. Heike spends the day walking through the woods, calling his name, but he never appears and the coldness never dissipates. It stays, seeping into her flesh, pricking her skin. About an hour into the tangle of trees she finds a small Redbud covered in pink blooms. Its branches hang low, and dangling from them are strips of dingy cloth like a shirt Baum once owned—though they could just as easily be pieces of something else.

When she emerges from the woods the sun's orange has leaked across the sky. Heike's throat is hoarse from calling for Baum, and mud has caked her arms and legs. She crosses the highway without a cautionary glance in either direction, and gets into her truck. She places the pod on the empty seat beside her, using the strips of torn shirt to form a nest. The truck's engine starts with a hollow, distant cough, and it jerks when she puts it in gear and drags it onto the road. Heike leaves everything she had behind, heads back to where she came from. She doesn't look at anything beyond the road, doesn't do anything but drive. There's no reason to.

It's only been three days since she was at the farm, but she barely recognizes it. It's like entering an old photograph, familiar only at a distance. Heike parks the truck and turns off the engine, and stares at the culmination of her life. She wonders: if not here, then where? She exhales, deflates, and takes the pod she remembers being much lighter into her hand. The walk into the tall grass—the grass she has not looked at, or visited, or acknowledged in years—is long, and the blades have grown to her waist. But they reach higher, catching her with barbed ends, like fingers trying to pull her close for an embrace. Heike pushes them aside, unwilling to be slowed, as she searches through the overgrowth for what she knows is there.

A lifetime has passed, but not long enough to hide where Reiter rests. She finds his marker not by sight but because she nearly trips over it. He is where she left him, beneath the small stone monument that announces his passing. Heike kneels and touches the stone with her gnarled wrinkled fingers, runs them over the carving, uses her nails to dig out those letters obscured. She cleans the stone as best as she's able while her heart knocks on her chest and the sweat loosens her glasses from the bridge of her nose. She tells Reiter everything, what's happened since he left, how Baum entered her life and how he left. She empties her heart of everything, and though she expects a number of times to cry, she does not. When she's done unburdening herself, she lifts a divot of dirt from the ground and places the seed pod underneath. Then Heike does her best to stand and tap it with the flat of her shoe.

Heike waits, looking at what lays at her feet, and somewhere inside her the clouds she did not think would break do, and a torrential thunderstorm rushes through her. It seems never-ending until it does, and when she wipes her face she finds the ground soaked and the divot of dirt has produced a small shoot that gingerly tests the sky. She sniffles, smiles, watches it as the tiny stalk reaches upward and catches the rough cotton weave of her trousers. Watches it cling, then wrap itself around her leg. She watches leaves slowly unfurl and open to the light while the shoots grow longer, thicker, stronger, intertwining with her limbs.

And she continues to watch as time splits the seams of her shoes and fibrous roots appear, then sink into the soil. Her skin hardens, her wrinkles deepen, become grooves. In her hair, shoots blossom, silky pink with yellow pistils. Soon, there is little difference between her and the tree that envelops her. Weather and sun rot her clothes while the two grow further enmeshed, and she utters a noise that sounds like the soft percussion of a hundred starlings taking flight at once. Heike's final thought is of Reiter, of that time in the sunshine, their hands locked together by the edge of the pond, and she imagines Baum with them, the son they never had, flesh and blood and smiling. Before she can smile the thought is gone, and all that remains are two trees forever twisted and entwined, inseparably anchored by a grave buried beneath the tall grass at the edge of the farm.

THE ERASED

Steve Rasnic Tem

SOME THINGS YOU REMEMBER CLEARLY, after but the merest glance: a spot passed on a journey to somewhere else, a woman who gazed long enough to make you wonder about a different life. Other things vanish for no reason, even though you hold them dear: a friend's name, a favorite souvenir, a beloved's life. Some days it feels as if none of these things ever existed at all, and you yourself, are no more tangible than smoke.

These events recur with increasing rapidity until one day you realize: this is how the world goes away.

On most days Roy could see all the way into downtown from his apartment window. Today there was a brownish haze as if some buildings might be burning. Downtown lay comatose, diminished, the taller buildings disintegrating into increasingly narrow threads until Roy could see ancient stretches of undeveloped land in between, while overhead the clouds dropped rapidly, chimneys and roofs and windows distributing into mist.

He thought he heard screams. The air was loaded with too much conversation. He kept watching, anticipating but not hoping to see streams of refugees.

He closed his eyes and did the exercise. The exercise consisted of recalling the world as it truly was: the clock-tower, that silver needle of an office building still under construction, the top of an amusement park's giant Ferris wheel, and the upper reach of the water slide, the gleeful or terrified children momentarily trapped within. And all the buildings in between, some he could recollect now and then, and the others he invariably forgot.

He was a committed realist, or tried to be. He did not get his hopes up. He did not look for the brighter side. His was a small life, easily countable, easily captured in a single photograph. He liked it that way, or at least he was acclimated to it. He'd never imagined more. He'd put himself out there early on as most people did, tried to do well in school, talked to women, applied to jobs and opportunities, and the things that came his way, came his way, and he had accepted that. He'd never married, but the jobs had been adequate, paying just enough for day to day, but not for what would come after. Unfortunately now he was living in what came after, and had to make do with what the government sent him until he, or the government, ran its course. But he was a realist, and so he managed.

He finished his juice and looked around the room. Bed and table and chair, a refrigerator, hot plate, sink, a few things left out, everything else tidied away into closet and cupboard. He liked to keep the things he could count down to ten or so, never more than fifteen. More than fifteen he felt sloppy. More than twenty meant that chaos had descended, and you were well on your way to death or at least ruin.

But where was his cereal box? It should have been by the bed to sate some middle of the night hunger. The dual use of breakfast food for snack satisfied Roy's appetite for efficiency. He suddenly had the disturbing notion that someone had slipped into his room while he was sleeping and stolen his cereal. At least he could know for certain—it was one of the advantages of having a life that was countable.

He looked into the trashcan beneath the sink and found the empty cereal box. He had no memory of having finished it—that memory had been erased. He would have to go out and buy another box, and somehow not think about how that memory had gotten away from him. It was one thing to get rid of some no longer useful recollection, yet another to have that memory stolen away.

He found the piece of paper he kept as a shopping list, a "To Do" list, for whatever needed recording so that he didn't have to count on his increasingly unreliable memory. Words had been scratched out, rewritten, and erased so many times the paper had achieved a level of transparency. When he held the paper up some words floated in the air as if stray thoughts. He could sense other things floating nearby: plans, memories, suggestions of people, hints of scenes, but he was hungry and had no time for this.

Outside, the sun burned from a definite place, high above and slightly behind his left shoulder. It seemed unusual to apprehend the sun so specifically, as if it were a lightbulb fixed in an invisible fixture. He couldn't remember having that perception before, certainly not with this much conviction. He had an impulse to weep. He wanted to raise his head and turn and look at the sun directly, but he'd always heard that was a very bad thing to do. Or was that an old wives' tale? He was old enough he could probably risk some permanent damage, but he needed his box of cereal so being struck blind wasn't part of the day's plan.

From here he had a broad view of this part of the city. Roy had seen this view almost every day since he'd turned fifty, but he hadn't always paid attention, and now it appeared broken, bits completely rubbed out or obscured by new bits. A missing building here and there, and other buildings discolored, polished, altered, the horizon line a damaged grin of aging and repaired teeth beneath a thick lip of smoky pollution. He started to reason it out, but hungry and impatient he made a dismissive wave and turned onto the next street toward the tiny local grocery.

But he apparently made a wrong turn, and was lost a scant block or two from home. He looked left and right and slowly began to recognize individual bits and pieces of buildings, a certain tree, a certain green-painted lamppost leftover from an earlier era of electrification, but there was a blurriness where things rubbed up against each other, and right in front of him there was an enormous empty hole, enclosed by one of those floppy orange plastic fences meant more for warning than security. He walked slowly to the end of the block to get his bearings, and saw the grocery store on the next street over, and then he walked back again and stood before the gigantic missing piece. He was pretty sure he knew where he was now. The huge old Victorian which had been there all his life was gone.

He peered over the edge of the pit. It was all raw dirt down there—every last bit of the house had been taken. An ancient drain pipe rose out of the center of the excavation like a severed root. There was a clanking of traffic sounds behind him, a certain metallic clatter that might have been a streetcar, but they hadn't had streetcars in the city for years. He turned around. The street was empty.

Roy flopped down onto the thin grassy patch in front of the not-house. That house had been built long before he was born. He'd heard it had first been a hospital for poor women, and then the Clarksons had lived there for generations, and Will Clarkson still did. No, *did*.

"Pity, isn't it? They must have torn it down sometime during the past two weeks."

Roy knew the fellow walking towards him, but he didn't have his name handy. He ran through his catalog of names, but some were missing, some scratched out, and only an alarmingly few had faces attached. Roy did know that the man lived in that house behind the missing one, its visible outer wall a pale gray patch of stucco unused to direct sunlight. Further down the block—he wasn't sure how far—another house began to shimmer, as if the entire structure were under water.

William. No, Willem. Roy remembered now, the only person with that name he'd ever known. Dutch, maybe. But he detected no accent.

Willem had a big brown dog with him, which Roy wanted

to call a mastiff, but which was probably something far less glamorous. But certainly descended from big breeds, practically a monster. When the dog breathed it made the air around it tremble. Suddenly the dog barked so loudly it made itself disappear.

Roy closed then opened his eyes and it was back again. It barked once more and Roy shut his eyes again—he couldn't help himself. It was as if the air in front of him had suddenly frozen, then snapped into pieces, the dog's throat a passage into some other dimension of pain.

"Duke! Quiet!" Willem shouted. "Sorry, Roy." Still, Roy didn't open his eyes. In the darkness inside his head he still lived on a quiet street lined with giant trees and the same old familiar houses. No one in that neighborhood was a monster or owned monsters.

The dog was whimpering now and Roy opened his eyes. The dog moved behind Willem as if seeking protection. "He's been jumpy lately," Willem explained. "He doesn't like change, but then, neither do I. And neither do you, from the looks of you."

"What happened? Was there a fire?"

"Nothing so dramatic. Some men and equipment came one morning, and they tore it down, hauled the pieces away. I didn't see it myself. I'm not even sure if anyone lived there anymore. The older Clarkson brother—he was the last, wasn't he? Did he die? I don't remember him dying, do you? I live right next door, but I didn't know—I had to ask around. There was just this hole, as if there had never been a house. I just never looked out those windows." He gestured vaguely toward his house. "And when I walk Duke, I usually don't walk him on this part of the block. A family of cats lived here for a while—they teased him."

Willem's hair was wild and windblown and appeared to be on fire. Roy at first thought the sun was behind it, but the sun was still high over Roy's left shoulder. It hadn't moved—some greater power had pinned it to the sky. Willem's face was dark and opaque, and Roy couldn't see the man's expression, couldn't even see his face for that matter, which was disconcerting.

"Could you move just a bit to one side, Willem?" Roy was inordinately pleased that he now had the man's name correctly. "I can't quite see your face." But he couldn't tell him his head appeared to be on fire.

The dark face barked. Roy looked for the dog, but Willem's dog had apparently wandered away.

Willem stepped aside wordlessly. Was he angry? Roy looked up—Willem's face was hard and cracked like damaged pottery. He couldn't find the man's eyes—were they closed?

"What happened to your dog?"

"My dog? I haven't had a dog since . . ."

"The big brown one. Duke."

Willem scowled unhappily. "Roy, have you been drinking? Duke died years ago."

Roy shook his head. He made a decision to forget all about the dog. "This house, it was here just the other day. Someone was living here—I saw him looking at me from that window." Roy pointed to where the window had been, then dropped his hand awkwardly. His finger had pointed at nothing but empty sky, a faint trace of smoke.

Willem stared into the not-place. "They keep tearing down old houses, putting up three or four new ones in their place. I imagine they could put six units into a lot this size. Boxes, mostly. Urban industrial. Bolt a few panels of rusted metal or polished wood on the outside and then you're done." He stepped closer to the hole and looked in. The sun suddenly shifted and shadows flowed from under the bushes and out of the sewer grates. "I'm glad my Alice didn't live to see this." Dark regions spread through the raw earth and quickly combined, heaving.

Roy stared at the leash dangling from Willem's hand. Willem made that barking sound again and then the leash was gone. "Willem?" he asked, blinking his tears away. "Do you have some water? Water is . . . we're all one hundred percent water, I believe. Our faces, the rest of us, are just dreams floating on all that water. Could I have some water, please? And some cereal? Do you have cereal?"

A screen of variegated noise filled the silence between them, but as Roy's eyes searched the street he saw nothing but parked cars. Nothing appeared to be moving, and there were no people or animals about. And yet his head still thrummed from the noise of traffic, excitement, conversations so layered they were impossible to follow. He looked around anxiously, expecting to be overcome at any moment by the press of all that life and activity. He was aware of shaking his head incessantly, Willem hovering over him looking concerned.

Willem helped Roy from the grass, hooked his arm through his and guided him as if escorting his date to a ball. They went up the slight hill, staying on the narrow sidewalk until they reached the front of Willem's house, where they turned and climbed the steps to the porch. The porch was wide and spacious and covered with dead potted plants. "I need to water those," Willem said softly, "but I always forget."

"But they're already . . ." Roy began, but stopped. The tide of noise had risen again, pushing behind him, distinctive individual voices but he still couldn't make out individual words.

Willem inserted his key, wiggled it. "Sometimes it sticks," he said. He appeared to be pushing on the door, but something was blocking its swing.

Roy turned his head. They were all gathering behind him, the mass of them—men, women, children—some of them shimmering, some less solid than smoke. He thought he recognized a few, but of course he could not remember their names. They were dressed in old clothes or none. He wondered if they actually had names anymore.

Some stumbled on the steps and sprawled. Their necks grew long and snake-like, twisting their way across the porch, their heads like hairy fingertips, touching, tasting. Eager and inescapable. But perhaps Roy misunderstood what he was seeing.

The door gave way and Willem pushed inside, Roy close behind. Roy looked down—it was like shoveling—books and a debris of mail, clothing, and trash spilled around the bottom of the advancing door. Something struck him in the face and he lost his sense of smell, but he still had the wherewithal to back up against the door and shut it against what he imagined was happening on the porch, a frenetic confusion of memory and dream.

He gazed around him. Intertwined stacks of boxes, bags, the odd bit of furniture, layers of reading material, opened and unopened mail, food cartons, clothing, hardware, bottles, kitchenware, unidentifiable cloth objects, wires and lumber and even an odd tree limb or two, material knit together and leaned together, rising high over their heads almost to the ceiling. Snagged bits of brown fur accessorized some sharp corners of rubbish. He counted three, four, six dog bowls, their contents solidified, and threaded with green.

"Follow my lead into the kitchen," Willem said beside him.

Willem stepped into what appeared to be a solid wall of collected objects, but although he struggled a bit he was able to wiggle and push his way through. Roy could see now that that section of material was less dense, and as Willem passed into it Roy could see more or less bare patches of floor beneath Willem's shoes. He was still reluctant to proceed, afraid that the entire conglomerate might shift and crush him, but he was even more apprehensive about the possibility of Willem leaving him behind, stranded. So he took the plunge. As he became enveloped in paper and dusty objects he tilted his head back in order to breathe. Behind him he could hear a rising murmur, and then a slow serpentine progression of arms and legs and necks and torsos, the backs of heads, swept over the ceiling and through the junk and trash alongside him. He did not know whether to be frightened or relieved that these figures would not show him their faces.

There was nothing substantial about any of these forms—they passed through Willem's treasures and the tiny spaces between these treasures without a resulting disturbance of any kind. They were like the dust that covered everything and filled every cubic centimeter of air: they made an unpleasant effect, and they weighed nothing. They were like a visible odor.

And as if triggered by that thought Roy's nose began to work again. Everything Roy touched, reeked. He felt trapped in the bottom of the trashcan with the worst part of the garbage. He began to cough and choke and ran into more solid and less penetrable portions of the mass of Willem's possessions.

"Willem!" he cried, before stumbling into an open space. It was the kitchen. A light bulb dangled overhead: greasy, fly-specked, buttery. The air itself had a similar beige cast, like a vintage photograph. Willem sat in a chair at a small rickety table, an apple in one hand, a deeply yellowed newspaper clutched in the other. One of those skimpily dressed young female popstars of several years ago was on the open page, beneath the banner "Entertainment."

"So this is what passes for entertainment these days," Willem said.

Roy took a breath. The stench was weaker here, but still present. "That story is from several years ago, isn't it?"

Willem examined the page heading. "So it is, but it'll do. History repeats itself, after all. Today's headline is 'We Die.' No amount of gyrating or singing, no matter how many people you shoot down from your rooftop, no matter how much money you steal from the poor, no matter what higher office you hold, you will, eventually, be erased."

Roy looked for another chair. There was none. "But they believe their names will be remembered, and their deeds, their performances. And they're right in that, actually, I believe."

"It's just a desperate grab for some small taste of immortality. People forget names, the small details of history. They do it all the time," Willem said. Voices began to issue from the debris surrounding them, first whispers then declarations then shouts, often accompanied by weeping. When Roy glanced at his surroundings he could see their faces now, and quickly turned away. Willem appeared to pay them no attention—he certainly betrayed no alarm—but he was raising his voice, as if to be heard above the din. "I have your cereal here! I've filled your *bowl*!"

Roy took the offering, raising the bowl to peer inside. The

wrinkled flakes looked more like wood chips than breakfast cereal. They were covered by the water he'd requested. There was no spoon, and he decided he wouldn't ask for one. At least it didn't smell, so he raised it to his lips and began to slurp. The flakes were stale, like bits of cardboard as they gathered in his mouth. But he allowed them in anyway. He swallowed what he could and allowed the rest to fall back into the bowl.

"How long . . ." Roy looked around at the walls of trash, avoiding the eyes scattered in the shadowed spaces. "How long have you been . . . collecting?"

"Mostly since Alice died. I'd always been interested in things, finding interesting stuff in the world. Often I would bring these things home. But when Alice lived with me there were limits, you know? Back then I couldn't keep everything. But when you're by yourself—you make your own rules. And most importantly, you don't have to explain them." An empty shoebox drifted off the top of one of the piles and fell at Willem's feet. A scurrying and a rearrangement occurred within the depths of the assemblage. "I'm partial to interesting containers," he continued. "Things that will hold other things. They mean organization, even when nothing is being organized. We all need that sense of organization, that ability to place parentheses, and a period at the end. Other things I like are things I know might be useful to someone else: a part, a knob, one piece of some ensemble. Everyone is missing something—I'd like to provide them with that missing piece someday."

"Have you ever given any of this away?"

Willem looked up at his stacks, his eyes sweeping the walls of objects. "I have to find the right people to give them to. Do you realize how difficult that is in this day and age? People just won't stop anymore to figure out what they're missing."

Roy felt the pressure in his gut, the impending disruption. "Could I please use your restroom?"

Willem stood up, reached for something in the corner behind him. "Out of order, I'm afraid. I can't get anyone in here to even look at it. So that room's just additional storage space for now.

You'll need to go into the back yard." He held out a beige grocery bag and a handful of old newspaper. He gestured toward the small door in one corner of the kitchen, by an old stove whose top was buried beneath dusty pots and pans.

Roy ignored the offered materials and shuffled over to that door. The top half was glass, permitting a view of the back yard. Immediately outside there were grocery bags, paper sacks, garbage bags stacked everywhere, several feet high and barely contained by the sagging wooden fence. Several squirrels worked feverishly at a bulging, misshapen package recently fallen, its contents spilled.

Roy left the room, forcing his way into Willem's belongings until he found a soft spot, then pushed harder, wading through what appeared to be one of everything imaginable as he attempted to find the door to the front porch. Things crashed behind him and Willem cursed and screamed in offended rage or pain, it was impossible to determine or process.

Roy was close enough to those visiting forms—the turned faces and offered lips—to hear what they were whispering, but the noise inside his head was louder than all their voices. He pushed past them as if they were no more than added bits to Willem's collection.

Some of the stacks beside the front door had collapsed around it. Roy turned the knob and dragged the door inside as far as it would go, then climbed over the obstacles and squeezed himself through the narrow opening. He fell out onto the porch and felt a sharp pain in his knee as something gave way.

Everything murmured. Everything had something to say. But Roy wouldn't look at any of them. He deliberately ignored them all. He climbed to his feet and hobbled down the steps and out onto the sidewalk. He stank. He needed to get home.

A great noise suddenly swallowed him up as if the secret engine of the world had just turned over. The air exploded around him in an ecstasy of escape. It was all he could do to hold onto his thoughts to prevent them from being completely swept off the planet.

A snow of tiny fragments powdered his head, his outstretched arms, and his hands. He brushed them off: bits of yellowed newspaper, trash. When finally he turned around he confronted the hole, the freshly raw ground, the fact that nothing remained to indicate that anything had ever existed there at all.

Roy wandered the empty streets looking for some familiar landmark. Off in the distance the conversations continued, but thank God the uncomfortably familiar forms kept their distance. When finally he found his block of course his apartment building was gone. In its place the terraced squares of freshly turned ground resembled most those peculiar South American pyramids, the ones where human sacrifices were performed, and everywhere you went you knew full well you were walking on the dead.

THE SWIMMING POOL PARTY

Robert Shearman

O NCE IN A WHILE A MEMORY OF MAX WILL
pop into her head, and she won't quite know
what to do with it. Totally unbidden, and triggered by
nothing in particular, and sometimes she won't mind,
she'll let the memory play out like a little movie. That
time, one Christmas, when they'd given Max his first
bike—it had taken Tom ages to wrap it up, and once it
was done it was just so *obvious*, the wrapping paper did
nothing to disguise what was underneath at all; "We'll
have to do it again," she'd said, "but this time we'll put
lumps and bumps in," and Tom hadn't minded, they'd
done it again, together, and in the end the present
for Max under the tree looked like nothing on earth,
and certainly nothing like a bicycle; that Christmas
morning they told him to save that present for last
though he was *itching* to open it, and he wasn't disappointed. Oh, she still remembers that exquisite look of
joy and surprise on his face when he realised Santa had
brought him the bike he wanted after all. Or—there
was that memory of when they were on holiday, where
was it, Cornwall? It was warm, anyway. And they were
all sitting out in the beer garden, Max had a lemonade.
There was a wasp. It landed on Max. They shooed it

off, and the wasp went onto the table, and Tom upturned his empty pint glass and put it on top. And Max was crying, and she was suddenly so frightened—had he been stung? Where was he stung? Would he have an allergic reaction? But he wasn't stung at all—"The poor buzzie," he kept saying, "the poor buzzie." The poor buzzie was trapped, flying around its beery prison looking for some way out, bashing its body against the sides of the glass. Max was howling now, he said, "Please let the buzzie out, it's so scared," and Tom took the glass away, and the wasp didn't sting anyone, it flew off, and Max laughed, all tears forgotten, and went back to his lemonade.

Or, of course—there was that memory, the first memory. The doctor putting Max into her arms. And her realising that it was really all over, the whole giving birth thing, and it hadn't been quite as difficult or painful as she'd feared. And Tom was grinning. And she'd spend so long privately worrying about this very moment—but when I'm actually there with it, with my own child, what happens if I don't like it? Don't want it? Can feel nothing for it? Max crying, and she crying herself with relief, that this tiny human being in her arms that had come from inside her and was a part of her was something she loved with all her heart, and she would love it forever, until the day she died.

Sometimes she's so moved by the memories that it takes her a little while to realise that nothing is wrong, nothing is lost—that it's Tom who's moved out, and Max is still there, and alive, and well, and probably playing computer games in his bedroom. And it would only take a moment to go and see him, and look at him, and give him a hug. And she might even do this. And she might not.

Max is in trouble at school again. It isn't his fault. (Oh, it is never his fault.) She shouldn't be too concerned, but would she mind coming in some time and having a little chat with the head of year? This Tuesday? Wonderful.

The head of year, a decidedly ugly woman called Mrs Trent, invites her to sit down, and asks her if she'd like a cup of tea.

Max is being bullied. Yes, that little spate of bullying that had taken place in the spring term had been dealt with; this was a different spate of bullying altogether. Mrs Trent is just wondering if something at home is the matter. She knows there's been problems, Max isn't very forthcoming, but . . . Would she like some sugar? Here, she'll pass the sugar. There you are.

"He still sees his father every other weekend," she says. "That's quite a lot. That's more than some kids get when their fathers live at home."

"How long has it been since you and your husband separated?" asks Mrs Trent. She tells her. "And was it amicable?" Are they every amicable, really?

"We just worry," says Mrs Trent. "Because Max is a good boy. But we just think. That with the *amount* of bullying he gets. We just wonder. Is he in some way *inviting* it?"

Of course he's inviting it, she thinks. He's weak. He's weak, just like his father is. He's one of life's fuckups. You can see it written all over his face. Like his father, he's never going to be anyone, or achieve anything. It's like he's got a sign on his back saying 'Kick Hard Here'. What she says is, "What do you mean?"

Mrs Trent gives a cautious smile. "Max doesn't seem to have any friends. Not a single friend at all. Does he have friends at home?"

She thinks, I want the bullies to go after him. I want them to hurt him. Maybe it'll knock some sense into him, make him grow up a bit. Is it wrong that I take the side of the bullies over my own child? Of course it is. This is the position he puts me in. He makes me into a bad mother. He makes me into a bad person. The little shit. She says, "He has friends. He has *me*."

Mrs Trent doesn't seem very convinced by that. That cautious smile looks even more watery. She wonders if Mrs Trent has children of her own. She guesses that she doesn't.

What they agree is, they'll both monitor Max more carefully from now on. In the classroom, and at home. Because maybe there's nothing to be worried about. But no one wants this to become a situation anyone *has* to worry about. It all feels rather inconclusive, and she supposes Mrs Trent thinks the same, and she realises that Mrs Trent probably only called this meeting because it was part of her job, she doesn't really care what happens to her weak little son either. They shake hands.

Max is waiting for his mother on a bench in the corridor outside. He gets up when he sees her, "Well then," she says. She knows she'll have to come up with something better than that eventually. But right now it's the best that she's got.

"Are you cross with me?" he asks.

"No."

To prove she's not cross, on the way home she takes him to MacDonald's as a treat. She watches him as he joylessly dips French fries into a little tub of barbeque sauce, the sauce drips onto the table. "Any good?" she says, and he nods. Then she takes him home.

"Is there something you want to talk about?" she asks, and it's right before his bedtime, and she supposes she ought to have asked earlier, but she's asking him *now*, isn't she? He shrugs, and it's such an ugly little gesture. Then he drags his heels upstairs to his bedroom and closes the door. And she thinks: remember the bike. Remember the wasp. Remember when he came out of you, shiny and brand new.

She recognises it as the exact same shrug Tom gives her a couple of days later when he comes to pick up Max for the weekend. She thinks she should tell him what had happened at school, about the teacher's concern their son has no one to play with; and there it is, that shrug, that's where Max has got it from. She should have known.

"I'm sure he's okay," says Tom.

"And that's it, is it? That you're sure he's okay?"

The shrug.

"What will you boys be getting up to this weekend?" She wonders if Tom is trying to grow a moustache or if he simply hasn't shaved. But there's no stubble on his chin, so he's shaving the chin, and that means he's deliberately not shaving under his nose. Probably. She wonders whether it's to impress some other woman. Probably.

"I don't think we'll *do* anything," says Tom. "We'll just hang. We'll just chill. You know? Hey, superstar,"—for Max has now appeared, and Tom has started calling him 'superstar', and she guesses Tom's picked that up from a TV show—"hey, you got your bag, you got your things? I was just telling your mum, we'll just hang and chill this weekend, okay?"

She bends down to give Max a hug. She doesn't really need to bend, he's nearly as tall as she is now, she hopes the bending to hug him makes the act look more endearing. "You be a good boy for your dad, yeah?" He grunts, he hugs back. She doesn't know why they're hugging, she supposes it's mostly for Tom's benefit.

"And, you know, don't worry," says Tom. "It's part of growing up. Being a boy. I know. I was a boy once!"

"Yes," she says to that.

"And you," he says suddenly, "You have a good weekend too. You're okay, you're doing okay?"

"I'm fine."

"Good," he says. "Good. Well. Bye, then." She never knows whether he's going to try for a hug himself or not. Three months ago he'd knocked on the door, he'd been in tears. His girlfriend had thrown him out, and she could have seen *that* coming, she was practically half his age. ("Two thirds!" he'd protested. "She's two thirds my age!") "I've made such a terrible mistake," he said, "you are the love of my life! I wish you could find some way to forgive me." "But I do forgive you," she'd said, and she did, for the silly affair, at least, she did—"I do forgive you, which is why I'm not punching you in your fucking face." And she'd closed the door on him. He's never mentioned the incident since, and sometimes when he comes round to pick up Max he seems hurt and snippy, bristling with passive aggression, sometimes he just bounces about and makes jokes like they're cool sophisticated adults and it's easy and it's fun to ignore all the betrayal and all the waste. In the last three months he's never tried for a hug, but she knows it'll happen, one of these days it's coming.

And that's it, Max's gone, now starts her little fortnightly break. She gets Max on Saturday mornings, and he'll be back for Sunday evening, but otherwise she has practically the whole weekend to herself. She feels lighter already. And she feels guilty too. What will she do with her new won freedom? She doesn't know. She never knows. Maybe she'll do some shopping this afternoon, maybe she'll tidy Max's room. She goes into the kitchen and has some cold cuts from the fridge, there doesn't seem much point cooking when it's only for her.

A week or so later she asks Max, "Are things any better at school?" and Max manages a smile and says thank you, everything now is fine. That's just two days before he comes home with his face bruised and bleeding. Max insists it's nothing, but she sees red— she demands to speak to Mrs Trent about the matter, but for some reason Mrs Trent is now so much busier and cannot see any parents at all about anything, maybe phone ahead and see if she's available next week? And for three whole afternoons she pulls a sickie at work, and she sits in her car outside the play-ground, and watches the children when they are let out to play, and she doesn't get out of the car for fear that Max will see her, but she sees *him*—and she watches all the kids, and wonders which of them are hurting her son, and what she will do when she finds out. Will she climb the fence and go and protect her boy? Will she find the bully and track him down and beat him herself? What she won't do—what she doesn't need to do—she won't ask the bully *why*.

The invitation comes in the post. It's addressed to Max, but it's also addressed to her, in parenthesis—it says, 'To Maxwell Wil-liamson! (and also to Mrs Williamson!!); either way, she doesn't feel bad about opening it first. 'It's Nicky's Birthday!' the card says inside. 'Come And Celebrate At Our Swimming Pool Party! (bring trunks). And there's a little picture of a smiling fish, presumably because fish can swim, even if they rarely do so in chlorinated water. The envelope is scented, and that's an odd choice of stationery for a boy, she supposes the invitations were sent out by Nicky's mother.

She shows Max the invitation when he gets home. "Who's Nicky?" she asks.

"Just someone at school."

"Is he a friend of yours?"

"He's not even in my class."

"Do you want to go to his party?"

Shrug.

"You'd better go, mister." Lately she's been calling him 'mister' whenever she wants to sounds stern—she doesn't know why, maybe *she* picked it up from a TV show. "The school says you need some friends, mister. You're going to that party."

The party is the coming Sunday. That's a weekend Max is supposed to spend with Tom; she phones Tom and asks him to reschedule. Tom whinges about it, he says he's already got plans the following week. So she says it's up to him then—Tom can be the one to take their son to his best friend's birthday party if he wants, she's more than happy not to have to bother with it. Tom agrees to reschedule after all.

"Shall we get Nicky a birthday present? Shall we go shopping for a birthday present? What do you think Nicky might like?" Max says he has no idea. He's barely spoken to Nicky, he says, he doesn't know why Nicky's invited him, Nicky must have invited *everyone*. She supposes that is probably true—but she reminds herself Nicky's mother went to the effort of sending a postal invitation, and finding their address to do so, it can't be as random as all that. On the Saturday they go out to buy Nicky a present, all she knows is he must like the water, she buys him an inflatable Donald Duck for the pool—she also buys a card, which she'll get Max to sign—and she buys Max some new swimming trunks.

Sunday morning, and it's raining. Not the gentle sort either—it falls as mean sharp strips, no one would want to be out in this.

"What a shame," she says. Max brightens—does that mean he won't have to go to the party after all? She is having none of that. She tells him to get into the car, and he's sulking now, positively sulking, he's twelve-years-old and he should know better. He slams the car door and won't speak to her all the way there. She brings the birthday present and the birthday card, and she brings Max's swimming trunks too, just in case. The rain is thick and nasty as they drive, but as they reach the other side of town the weather starts to lift, and once they reach Nicky's house the clouds are gone and the sun is shining hot and warm, it's a beautiful summer's day.

"Come on," she says. "And for Christ's sake, smile a bit."

They ring the doorbell, and a little boy answers, neatly dressed, and beaming happily. "Nicky?" she asks, and he says—"Yes, yes!" He says to Max, "Maxwell, it is *so* very good of you to come." And he offers her his hand, "Mrs Williamson, my mother will be thrilled that you're here. Please, come through, both of you. Everyone's out back in the garden!"

There must be about twenty children standing by the swimming pool, all of them boys, all of them in their bathing costumes. She thought there would be more of them, and she feels a weird thrill of pride for her son—now he's the twenty-first most wanted child at the party, and not, as she had feared, the hundredth. The water in the pool looks so blue and warm, it looks good enough to sleep in, good enough to drink. She says to Nicky, but why aren't you all swimming? And Nicky looks genuinely shocked and says, "We wouldn't start until Maxwell got here! That would be rude!"

The boys don't seem impatient or annoyed that Max has kept them waiting; they smile, a couple of them standing by the far end of the pool wave in greeting.

"Well," she says to Max. "Do you want to run along and play?"

Max says, "I don't know these boys."

"What do you mean?"

"They're not at my school. I don't know any of them."

"Don't worry, Max," says Nicky. "These are my friends, and that means they're your friends too. I'll introduce you, and we're going to have such fun! Did you bring your trunks? You did? Let's go inside and get changed. I haven't got changed either yet; I waited for you." And he holds out his hand, and that seems such a peculiar thing—but Nicky is smiling so warmly, there is no malice in it, or sarcasm, or even just dutiful politeness—and when Max hesitates for a moment Nicky doesn't take offence, he smiles even more widely and gives his outstretched hand a little flutter of encouragement. And Max takes it. And they hurry indoors.

She feels suddenly awkward now, left all alone, alone except for the twenty little boys all staring at her. "Hello," she says, but they don't reply. She becomes aware that she is still holding a birthday card and a birthday present with Disney wrapping; she puts them down upon the poolside table.

And then, suddenly—"I'm sorry to have kept you waiting, what *must* you think of me!" Nicky's mother is not a prepossessing woman. She's short, and a little plump, and she doesn't wear any makeup; her hair is sort of brown and tied into an efficient bob. And yet it's curious—there's nothing drab about her, she looks comforting, she looks *mumsy*. And Max's mum feels a short stab of jealousy that anyone can look as mumsy as that, the kindly mother of children's books and fairy tales, the mother she'd hoped she'd be for Max. A stab of jealousy, just for a moment, then it's gone.

"Thank you for inviting us," she says to her. "Max is *so* excited!"

"I hope you're excited too," says Nicky's mum, "Just a little bit! The invitation was for both of you! You will stay?"

"Oh. Because my car is outside . . ."

"Please. Have a glass of wine."

"And I'll have to drive back."

"Not for hours yet. Please. Everyone else stayed. Please."

"Oh, yes, Mrs Williamson, you must stay! Everyone's welcome to my party!" Because Nicky is outside again, and he has brought Max with him.

Both boys are in swimming trunks. And it occurs to her that she hasn't seen Max's bare body, not in years. She'd always supposed that he was rather a plain boy, the way he carries himself as he slouches about the house made her think he was running to fat. But that isn't fair. He's not fat. There's a bit of extra flesh, maybe, but it looks sweet and ripe. The skin isn't quite smooth—there are a few scab marks where Max has no doubt scratched away spots—and there's a little downy fur on his chest that can't yet decide whether it wants to be hair or not. But she's surprised by her son—he looks good, he looks attractive.

He is not as attractive as Nicky, standing beside him, and showing off muscles and tanned skin. But that's fine, that's not a slur on Max, she rather suspects that in the years to come no one will compete with Nicky.

"Please stay," Nicky says one more time.

"Yes, all right."

"You're staying?"

"Yes."

"Good."

"We got you a card and a present. They're on the table."

"Thank you. Well, Maxwell! Are you ready for the pool?"

"Yes," says Max.

"Oh, watch this," says Nicky's mother. "This is good, you'll like this."

The boys all take their positions around the perimeter of the pool. Nicky leads Max to the edge; he shows him where to stand, next to him. Max looks apprehensive, but Nicky touches him on the shoulder and smiles; Max looks reassured. Then, at the other side of the pool, one of the boys raises his arms high above his head, tilts his body, and dives in. And as he dives, the boy next to him raises his arms likewise, diving as well. It's like watching domino toppling, she thinks, as the actions of one boy precipitate the actions of the next—or, no, more like one of those old black and white Hollywood musicals, weren't there lots of movies like that once upon a time? Because it feels perfectly choreographed, each boy hitting the water a matter of seconds after the last one has jumped, and entering it so cleanly, there's barely a splash.

And she's frightened for Max now, as the Mexican wave of

diving boys fans its way around the poolside to where he stands waiting. Don't fuck it up now, she thinks. Don't fuck it up. Three boys to go, two boys, Nicky himself. Max jumps. He doesn't dive, he jumps. His splash is loud and explosive and throws water over the side. He fucks it up.

"I'm sorry," she says. "Max's not much of a swimmer."

"Oh, but he's charming," says Nicky's mother. "And he'll learn." She taps at her arm lightly with a fingernail. "Come inside. Swimming for the children, and for the grown ups there's wine and cigarettes and fresh fruit."

"Don't you think we should watch them?"

"Oh, we'll watch them. Indoors." That tap with the fingernail again, and then she turns and leaves. Max's mum follows her.

"Oh, this is a nice house," she says. "I like your house, it's nice, isn't it?' In truth, it's as unprepossessing as its owner—but it also feels homely, and warm, it feels *safe*. "Have you lived here long, Mrs . . . ?" She remembers, ridiculously, she has no idea what this woman's name is. "Are you new to the area?"

"Have some wine," says Nicky's mother.

"Well, a glass of white, maybe."

"I'm sorry, I only have red." And she does sound sorry too. "But I think you'll like it, it's very good." She pours two glasses of red; she's right, it's smooth. "And a cigarette?"

"Oh, no, I've given up."

"So have I! Many times!" Laughter. And out from a plain wooden box on the table two cigarettes, and they are the whitest Max's mother has ever seen. She knows as she accepts a light that it's a mistake, she hasn't smoked in years—how long, not since Max was born, she gave up when she was pregnant! She used to enjoy smoking, that's something else Max has taken away from her. She prepares to cough. The cigarette is just as smooth as the wine. She recognises the smell, where does she know that from? It smells like the scent on the birthday invitation.

And she stands there, drinking and puffing away, and on she babbles. "So, do you live here all alone, Mrs . . . ? I mean, with Nicky, all alone. Is there a Mr . . . ?"

"How is Maxwell getting on at school?"

"Oh. You know."

"Tell me."

"Good at some subjects. Bad at others! You know!"

"Yes."

She's somehow finished her glass. She's poured another one.

"He's not an unkind boy," she says. "He never was. There's nothing *wrong* with him. I think. I just wish. I just wish he could be a bit more *likeable*."

"Likeable, yes."

"The way your son is likeable. Nicky, I mean, he's obviously very likeable."

"Nicky has always had a certain charm."

"You see, you're lucky! If it is luck. I don't know, maybe likeable is something you can work at. Maybe being *better* is just something you can make yourself be. I don't know. I just look at Max sometimes and think . . . You had such *promise*. Right at the beginning. Right when you were born. And then you just got worse and worse. What's that about? Like something went wrong, and I never noticed, and I didn't fix it in time, and now it's too late. But maybe it'll sort itself out! Kids. They grow up so fast, don't they?"

"They grow up just as quickly as it takes."

"Yes. Sorry. Of course. Yes. Do you think? Do you think we should check up on them?"

"Nicky's very responsible. But we'll check on them. Come upstairs. We can see better from there."

In the bedroom there is a sliding door that leads onto a thin little balcony. There are two chairs out there, and a table. On the table there are fresh cigarettes, fresh wine. There is a basket of strawberries. "Sit down," says Nicky's mother. "Make yourself at home." From the balcony they can both clearly see the pool, and hear the squeals of pleasure as the children splash about in it. Max sees his mother, waves up at her. He is smiling. It is good to see him smile.

"I like to watch them from above," says Nicky's mother. She

has a pair of binoculars. Surely she doesn't need binoculars; the boys are only a few feet away? She peers at the children through them; she helps herself to strawberries as she does so.

It suddenly occurs to Max's mum: "Where are the other mothers?"

"There are no other mothers."

"But, I thought you said . . ."

"It's just me. And you." Nicky's mother takes the binoculars from her face and gives such a lovely smile. "And all my lovely children."

Max's mother thinks the smoke in her mouth tastes soft and warming, it tickles her nostrils as she puffs it out her nose, it tickles her tongue as she puffs through her mouth. Both ways are good, both are nice. "Try the binoculars," she is told, and so she does—she is startled at first by how close the boys in the pool now seem to her, she can see the very pores on their skin, she can see every sweet blemish. They're so close they're just flesh and hair, she can't tell them apart any more. "Try the strawberries too, they taste better with the binoculars," and that seems silly, but somehow it's true.

"I'm sorry," she finds herself saying. "For what I said. I'm sorry."

Maybe she was expecting some sort of reassurance. "Well," says Nicky's mother, "we're all sorry, aren't we?"

Nicky claps his hands, and all his fellows stop what they're doing. He's got a new game for them to play.

Nicky's mother says suddenly, "I mean, what about Jesus?"

She doesn't know what she means by that.

"Jesus turned out well, didn't he?" says Nicky's mother. "Or so some say. And he got off to a promising start. The stable was a bit uncomfortable, but the Nativity, and all the attention of the Nativity, kings coming to pay homage, angels, shepherds, stars leading the way. Well, maybe not so much the shepherds. But that's a great start for a little boy in a desert. And then what? The Bible doesn't tell us. It passes over his childhood in silence. Nothing for years. The next time we pick up the story, Jesus is a grown man, he's suddenly out there preaching, telling parables and healing the sick. At last! his parents would have thought. At last, he's finally making a name for himself. Because all that early promise seemed just squandered, you know? Get off your arse and *do* something with your life!"

For some reason, Max's mother finds all this very funny, and she laughs and laughs. Nicky's mother smiles at her curiously. Nicky's mother then says, "Do you think you're the first mother who couldn't love her child?"

"What?" And suddenly she feels so cold. "What?"

"The children are having such fun," says her new friend. "Look."

Max's mother watches. "But what are they doing?"

"One of Nicky's favourites. And he's so good at it! They're playing the Drowning Game."

The rules to the Drowning Game are very simple. A boy dives under the water. He stays there for as long as possible. Whilst he does so, the other boys stand around the poolside in a circle and clap and chant.

"Shouldn't we help them?" she says.

"I think they're playing it very well without us, don't you think?" And so it seems. They watch in silence as one child stays beneath the water for four minutes, the next very nearly five. They pass the binoculars back and forth, they smoke and drink and eat strawberries.

"Ah," says Nicky's mother. "Let's now see whether your son is better than any of mine."

Max turns to look up at the balcony. He calls out to his mother, but she can't hear what he says above the chanting. She waves at him, she tries to get him to stop. He seems to misunderstand— he waves too, he grins, he gives her a thumbs up. He gets into the pool. He looks so frail and lonely now he's in there on his own. He takes a deep breath, then pops his head under.

"But of course Jesus had a childhood," says Nicky's mother. "Whether the Bible chooses to ignore it or not. And some of the stories got out."

She watches the surface of the water. There is not a ripple on it. And she can't help it, she steals a look at her watch.

"The stories aren't very nice ones. Maybe that's why the Bible didn't want them? Jesus killing children who so much as bump into him, blinding the parents who complain. I suppose you can't blame him. Having all those great powers, must be very confusing for an infant."

She checks her watch. A full ninety seconds has passed.

"This is my favourite story. Is it true or not? Who can tell? Jesus liked to play with his friends from school. One day he thought that the most fun would be to play on the moon. It was a crescent moon that evening and it was so close, he knew if he jumped high enough from the cliff he could reach it. And so he did. There he was, now he was the man in the moon, sitting back within that crescent as if it were a comfy chair. Come and join me, he called to his friends. Come and jump. Don't be frightened. Don't you trust me?"

Three minutes now. She tries to get out of her chair. She has to get down to the pool. She can't. Nicky's mother has got her arm. Nicky's mother has a story to tell.

"The children all fell to their deaths. Their little bodies smashed to pieces at the bottom of the cliff. Jesus was angry about that. He wanted his friends! If he didn't have friends, who could he play his games with? Who did he have left to impress? So he brought them all back from the dead, every last one of them."

Five minutes. Max's beaten the high score now. He's beaten the target Nicky set. Surely they'll let him come to the surface now? Surely they'll stop their chanting, their cat calling, their hallelujahs and hosannas?

"Their bodies were broken, of course. And they couldn't speak any more. But what of that? He didn't need friends who could speak. His parents were angry. They knew he had to be stopped. The father spoke to him. Hey, superstar. We can't go around killing our friends and resurrecting them, can we? Then where would we all be? All right? Promise you won't do it again. But fathers are so weak, aren't they? They may love the child, but it's easy to love something when it's not been inside of you eating away for nine months. It's down to the mother, always, to discipline it. It's the mother who knows it, understands it, and can be disgusted by it."

Eight minutes. Even the children look worried now. They've stopped clapping. They've stopped their songs. All except Nicky, he sings his heart out, and how his eyes gleam.

"It's left to the mother. As always. She says, you let those children die right now. You put an end to this, or it's straight to bed with a smacked bottom. How Jesus sulks! He threatens her. He'll drown her. He'll curse her. *She'll* never die, she'll just suffer, she'll be made to walk the earth forever. But he does what he is told. The children collapse. Their hearts all burst at once, and their faces look so grateful, they fall to the ground and there they rot."

And now—yes—she sees Max's body. And for a moment she thinks it's just the corpse bobbing to the surface, and it'll be full and bloated—but no, no, up he comes, and he's laughing, he's splashing out of the water in triumph! Nine minutes twenty! Nine minutes twenty, and all the boys by the side of the pool are clapping him on the back, and none of them with greater gusto that Nicky, and Max looks so proud.

She wants to cry out she's proud of him too. She wants to cry out she loves him. She wants him to know he's her little champion.

"The point I'm making," says Nicky's mother. "Is there a point? The point I'm making. If your child is a somebody, or if your child is a nobody. If they have potential, or are a waste of space. If they're Jesus themselves. If they're Jesus. Then there's still only so much a mother can do with them. We're screwed either way."

She gets to her feet. She claps her hands, just the once, and all her children fall silent, and look up to her. Max too, all the children wait to do whatever she says.

"Nicky," she says. "That's enough now. Time we all put our playthings away." Nicky's face clouds over. He looks like he'll throw a tantrum. His mouth twists, and he suddenly looks so ugly. But his mother is having none of it. She stands her ground. He gives in.

Once again, all the boys take their places around the perimeter of the swimming pool. Max takes his place too. Maybe he thinks they're all going to dive in like last time. Maybe he thinks it'll all be some Busby Berkeley number, and that he'll get it right this time. And maybe, given the chance, he would.

The first child doesn't dive. He merely steps into the water, and on contact he dissolves, the remains of his body look thick and granular in the water.

Nicky's mother watches with her binoculars as each of her children step into the pool and break apart like fine sand. She eats a strawberry. She licks her lips.

It does not take long before it's Max's turn. He looks up. He is smiling. He is happy.

"No," says his mother.

"No?" says the woman.

"Yes," she replies. It comes out in a whisper.

Max seems to take longer to dissolve, but maybe she's biased, maybe he's no more special than any of the other kids.

The swimming pool now seems thick and meaty, like gravy.

Nicky is the last to go in. He refuses to look at his mother, and as he drops down into oblivion with a petulant splash, he's still having his sulk.

Max's mother doesn't know what to say. She puts down her wine glass, she stubs out her cigarette.

The woman turns to her, gently taking her chin by her hand. Kisses her, just once, very softly, on the lips. And says:

"Listen to me. You are not the only mother who cannot love her child. It is all right. It is all right. And this can be your home now, for as long as you like. This can be your home, forever."

And the woman goes on, "This bedroom is yours. Enjoy." And leaves her, with a balcony to watch the setting sun from, and some wine to finish, and all of the cigarettes, and all of the delicious strawberries.

She lies in bed. She half expects the woman will come and join her. She half hopes she will. She doesn't. So, in the very dead of night, she gets up. She feels a little giddy. She cannot tell whether she is drunk or not, maybe she's in shock, maybe she's just very tired. She goes downstairs. She thinks the doors might be locked, but they aren't, she's free to leave at any time. She finds a discarded bottle of wine, she pours out the dregs, and rinses it clean from the tap. Then into the garden she goes. It is dark, and the swimming pool looks dark too, you'd think it was just water in there if you didn't know better. She stops down by the poolside, right at the point where Max went in—it was here, wasn't it, or hereabouts? She holds the wine bottle under the surface, and lets the water run in. and the water runs over her hands too, and it feels like grit. The bottle is full. She'll take it home. It is the best she can do.

She sees, too, the birthday card and the birthday present, both unopened, still standing on the table where she left them. On a whim she takes the inflatable Donald Duck in its Disney wrapping paper. She doesn't bother with the birthday card.

She drives home, holding the bottle careful between her legs, being sure not to spill a drop.

She goes up to Max's bedroom. The bedroom is a mess, it's always a mess. Max hasn't even made the bed. She makes the bed for him, she smooths down the sheets and straightens the pillows. It looks nice. Then—she takes the bottle. She doesn't know what to do with it. In the light it looks like dirty water—mostly clear, but there are bits of grime floating about in it, you wouldn't dare drink it. She knows it isn't Max, but bits of it are probably Max, aren't they, most likely? She pours it slowly over the bed—the length of it, from the pillow on which Max's head would lie, down to where his feet would reach. The water just seems to rest on the surface, it doesn't soak through. She bends close to it. It smells sweet.

She doesn't know why on earth she took the Donald Duck, and leaves it on his bedside table.

In the morning she checks on the damp patch on Max's bed, and she thinks that something is growing there.

She goes to the supermarket and she buys lots of bottles of red wine, and lots of packs of cigarettes. But no matter what grape she drinks, what brand she smokes, she finds nothing as smooth or as satisfying as what she tasted at Nicky's party.

She calls work to tell them she's sick. She calls school too. Tells them Max isn't well enough to come in for a while, and no one seems to care.

One morning she drinks too much wine and smokes too many cigarettes and pukes them all out, and, sadly, she realises enough is enough, and she'll never find that happiness again, and puts the rest in the bin.

Is she too old to have another child? She might be. Online it suggests she is 'on the turn'. What does that mean? What a thing, to be on the turn. She wishes she hadn't thrown away all the wine and fags.

The smell from Max's bedroom is still sweet, but there's a meaty tang to it too.

And once in a while a memory of Max pops into her head, and she doesn't know what the fuck to do with it. That Christmas with his bike. And Tom took ages to wrap it up, and it did nothing to disguise what it was at all, the wheels, the handlebars, it was just so bloody obvious. She said to Tom, "I bloody told you not to leave it till last thing on Christmas Eve! Now what are we going to do?" She thinks she cried. Tom told her not to worry—it didn't matter—he'd wrap it up again. And it was *fun*, she wasn't expecting that, to be kneeling together under the Christmas tree, and be trying to bend the wrapping out of shape, put in all these little lumps and bumps so that no one could tell what was really hiding underneath. And in the morning—in the morning, Max got up early, it was Christmas day and he came into their room and he jumped on their bed, he couldn't wait any longer! What it was to be so excited by something, she had forgotten what it was like! She and Tom both groaned, but Tom said, let's just hang onto this because he'll grow up fast, it won't last forever—and how strange it was that Tom said something *wise*. They went downstairs to the Christmas tree. What on earth had Santa left him? What was that strange misshapen thing? Max wanted to open it right away, but no, they said, leave that one till last. Let that be the special one. And Max liked his other presents just fine, the board game, the anorak, the book of fairy tales from his grandma—but he couldn't wait to tear into that bicycle! Off came the wrapping paper, and he made a whooping noise as he tore into it, and Tom whooped too, and she joined in—there they were, all whooping! And there was the bike. A sudden flash like panic. What if all the build-up was for nothing? What if it was the wrong bike? What if he'd gone off bikes altogether? Kids could be so fickle. Max stared at the bike. Then he ran to it, and he *hugged* it, as if it were a new friend. As if it were his best friend in the world. And then he turned around, and he threw his arms around his father, thank you, thank you, he said—and he hugged his mum too. Thank you, it's perfect. And his face. The joy. The surprise. It was exquisite. And yet. And yet, as the memory pops into her head. As it plays there, like a movie, totally unbidden, and triggered by nothing in particular. She can't quite recall the face. She can't recall what it really looked like.

She has no idea what to feed the creature that is growing on Max's bed, so leaves it odds and sods from the fridge, and it takes what it wants and leaves the rest. It isn't really Max, she knows that—but there's Max in it. She's pretty sure she can identify bits of him, here and there.

Tom phones to ask whether he should pick up Max the usual time on Saturday. "I don't see why not," she says.

She answers the door to him. "Hello, hello!" he says. "How are you? You all right? Where's my superstar?" He's in a bouncy mood, that'll make it easier.

The moustache is full grown now, and when she kisses him, she feels it bristle, she can taste the sweat that's got caught in the hairs. "I've missed you," she says.

He looks properly poleaxed, he looks like he's having a stroke. She'd be laughing if this weren't so important. "I've missed you too."

"Come on," she says, and she takes his hand, and pulls him in over the threshold, "Come on."

"Where's Max?"

"He's in his bedroom. Don't worry about him. Come *on*."

They go upstairs. Tom hasn't been upstairs in nearly a year; he's never been allowed to stray further than the hallway and the downstairs toilet. Even now, he still isn't sure he's got permission to enter what used to be their bedroom. She smiles at him, pulls open the door.

"Wow," he says.

There are candles everywhere and there's soft lighting, and she's found something pretty to drape over the sheets, she thinks it might be a scarf or something, but it looks nice. There's a bottle of wine on the dressing table. "Do you want some?" she asks. "Get you in the mood?"

She can see he's already in the mood, he's been that way ever since the kiss on the doorstep. And she supposes she should be a little flattered by that, but really, does he have to be this easy? He makes one last attempt to sound responsible. "But what about Max? I mean, is he . . . ?"

"I told you," she says. "Don't you worry about him for now." She lies down upon the bed.

He pours himself some wine. He asks whether she wants. She doesn't, no, not any more.

She takes off her clothes, it doesn't take her long, she is ready. He takes his off too. Seeing his naked body for the first time in ages, she still feels a rush of the over-familiar. There's nothing new to be gleaned here. Well, she thinks, that's Max's genes right there.

He says, "I've missed you. Look. I wasn't prepared. I haven't brought any protection? Do you have any protection?"

"Oh, come on, Tom," she says. "You think I can still get pregnant at my age?"

"I don't know," he says.

"I'm still on the pill. Of course I'm still on the pill. Hurry up, and get inside me. I've missed you so much."

He's on top of her, he's excited, it doesn't take long.

He rolls off her. "Thank you," he says.

"That's perfectly all right."

"I love you."

They lie there for a bit. She wonders, if she says nothing at all, whether that will make him get up sooner. She starts to count the seconds go by in her head. It's the like the Drowning Game. How long till Tom gives up and breaks to the surface?

He gets up. He drains his glass of wine. She watches him, he's so sweaty and limp. "Listen," he says. "Listen." She raises her eyebrows, just to show that she's listening. "That was . . . I don't know what that was. But I should tell you. I'm with someone. It's early days, but I like her." So, the moustache *was* for a girl, what funny taste she must have. "And I don't know. I mean, is this just a thing? Or is this something?"

It's almost amusing. She says, "It's just a thing, Tom."

"Right. Because it doesn't have to be."

"No."

"I mean, I'd break up with her. If you'd like."

"No," she says. "That really won't be necessary."

"Right," he says. "Right." And he puts on his clothes.

She actually feels sorry for him. Up to the point where, now dressed, he stoops over her awkwardly, and tries to give her a kiss. She turns her head away.

"I'll go and find Max then," he says. "He's in his room? I'll go and find him." And he tries to give her a sort of smile, and then thinks better of it, and he leaves.

Now he's gone, at last he's gone. She can put up her hand to her belly, she can stroke it and nuzzle it, and she likes to think how soon—please God, soon—the belly might grow, it'll warp and distend. She gives her body a playful little shake, and she fancies she can hear new life sloshing around inside. And she listens out to hear what sort of scream will come from Max's bedroom.

WE CAN WALK IT OFF
COME THE MORNING

Malcolm Devlin

A S FAR AS STANDING STONES WERE concerned, the one they found that New Year's Day
was both impressive and disappointing. Planted deep
in the middle of a sheltered field on the eastern flank
on the hill, there was an undeniable scale to it. It was a
good fifteen feet of stark grey granite, eight foot wide
and eight foot deep, reaching up out of the mud like
a pointing finger. Despite this, there remained something industrial about it, something prosaic. Its faces
were too smooth, its edges too defined, it felt crudely
at odds with the soft and sodden landscape that surrounded it.

"Is that it?" Jack said. He sounded disappointed but
also resigned. It was unreasonable to be angry when
they had been promised no more than a point on the
map. Still, it was anticlimactic. It was just a stone,
standing in a field, brusquely surprised anyone should
have searched for it at all.

Aleyna didn't answer. She approached the stone,
and regarded it with the reverence she assumed such a
monument must deserve. The shape of it was certainly
monolithic: its uppermost edge a dark, straight line
against the unvaried grey of the sky. As an afterthought,

remembering something her father once said about how she would press her palms against the ragged barks of trees when she had been a child, she slipped her hand from her glove so she could feel the texture of the stone without impediment. For some reason, she expected there to be an inexplicable warmth to it: some mechanical hum to set it apart from the muted chill of the afternoon, but it was cold beneath her fingertips, made stark and frigid by the rain and the wind. The texture was barely perceptible beneath the growing numbness of her hands. A gentle lunar landscape of shallow contours but no more than that. She stepped back again, disappointed more with her own perception than with the stone itself.

Jack waded back into view.

"I read book once, when I was a kid," he said. "And in it, there was this stone up on the moor somewhere and if you walked around it three times, it would summon up a rabble of little goblins who would chase you down and stab you with spears."

"So don't walk around it three times." Aleyna took another step back. The field was heavy with the rain and if she didn't keep moving, she had the sense she might sink into the mud and never move again. *A hell of a way to start the year.*

Jack lifted one boot, planted it back then lifted the next. He looked absurd, like he was treading grapes in wellington boots. "Thing is," he said, "I know the moor the book was talking about. And they've built a road around it now. All the way around it like an island. So whenever I pass by that way, I always wonder if driving around it would count as walking around the stone? Or do you have to be right up close? Maybe distance itself didn't matter at all. Because these days, there must be thousands of commuters going one way or another around this thing, and at some point they'll have to have gone round it three times, right? Maybe not all at once, but eventually, right? Thousands of them. So do they all get chased? Do the goblins come out and go: 'Fuck me, traffic's bad today,' and then just get on with it anyway?"

He joined her in front of the stone, reaching out to it with his gloved hand.

"I can just imagine them. All broken and dying at the side of the road. These armies of goblins throwing themselves into the traffic and getting killed like all the foxes and deer and badgers. Goblin road kill. What chance does something from a fairy tale stand against a rush-hour's worth of Transit vans?"

Aleyna laughed despite herself. "Well, I don't fancy my chances outrunning anything in this," she said.

Water pooled around the base of the stone and even in the grey light, she could see the faint green of the grass beneath it, rocking in a gentle current like pondweed.

She glanced back down the field where they had come and saw how the edges were now completely lost in the fog.

"We should go back," she said.

Jack nodded.

"Might be able to catch the others up," he said. "Tell them what they missed."

He plunged his hands into his pockets and jutted out his elbow, inviting Aleyna to take his arm. She rolled her eyes before complying. He leaned over to kiss her but she pushed him back with her free hand. He felt stubborn and solid, not quite standing-stone solid, but immovable in his own way.

"If they see us—," she said.

"They'll have damn good eyesight," Jack said.

They set off down the field, heading back to the corner from where they had entered. The mud was marshy underfoot, the standing water rushing in to fill the heavy footprints they left behind. Joined together, the going was awkward, but neither saw fit to go it alone.

"So what do we tell them?" Jack said.

"We'll tell them we saw the standing stone," Aleyna said. It had been the whole point of the expedition after all. They'd poured over the map at the kitchen table searching for something to mark the day, something to clear their heads after all the drink from the night before. It had been Kevin who had spotted the monument, marked in blackletter script in the middle of an otherwise unpromising looking pasture. The walk had been longer than anyone had anticipated, following the narrow, minor roads up the hills, which rose deceptively steeply on the opposite side of the main road from the cottage they had hired. While it wasn't exactly raining, the clouds had lowered to envelope the landscape and the air they walked through felt dense with poised moisture. It lingered before them, allowing them to drench themselves just by moving through it.

Lou had given up first, complaining of a headache and the likelihood she might wind up sick as well. Kevin had gone with her, measuring his own gallantry against Jack's like they were drawing straws. Turning back down the path, the two had diminished into the blankness and Aleyna had watched them go, a faint notch of panic opening up within her. They disappeared with such a gentle precision it looked like the climactic scene fading out at the end of a film and she had to fight the urge to run down the path after them to make sure they were still there.

"We'll tell them it was magnificent," Jack said. "A secret Stonehenge, lost from view in the beautiful *Oirish* landscape."

The accent made Aleyna wince. Jack might have looked local, but he certainly didn't sound it.

"They won't believe us," she said.

"They will. We'll tell them that when we stood in the middle of the circle, the stones made the wind sound like it was singing to us."

"There isn't any wind."

"Then maybe the stones themselves were singing to us."

"You're full of shit."

"So's this field, and yet here we are."

"Jack." She broke away from him so she could vault the stile, casting him a dark look as she did so.

He grinned at her. The rain had plastered his fringe to his forehead, making him look younger. He had his holiday beard on: a week's growth of red whiskers that gave him a pleasant and scruffy nonchalance she couldn't quite square with the clean-shaven and office-suited Jack she was more familiar with.

"Kidding," he said. "I'm just loathe to admit they might have been right about turning back."

"We could just say it was nice," Aleyna said.

Jack shook his head, clambering over the stile after her. "There's no magic in *nice*," he said.

The path down the hill was mostly gravel, ground deep into the mud. Hazy shapes of demarcated farmland ascended in steep embankments on either side, knotted cords of hedgerows and low stone walls frayed into the whiteness. They walked onwards and the dogged clouds followed them, water running freely down the path in a steady stream.

Aleyna's coat had long since soaked through, it was woolen and heavy and completely the wrong sort of thing to wear for a walk of this nature, but then the weather hadn't seemed quite so miserable when they'd started out from the cottage and by the time they were halfway up the hill, it would have been far too much of a fuss to ask to go back for something more sensible. Worse still, it would only have cemented the second thoughts about the enterprise that Lou had already started to entertain.

Jack started whistling through his teeth. The tune almost recognizable, but out of reach until he spoke again.

"Do you think these are the actual Cork and Kerry mountains?" he said. "I always figured they were different things. Like the guy was walking through one and then the other. It never really occurred to me the county border might run through them."

He didn't wait for an answer, he just carried on whistling as before, but something struck Aleyna about what he had said.

It felt appropriate they should be walking along a border in the hazy, hung-over gap between the years, having left one behind and yet not quite committed to the next.

"Borderlands," she spoke the word aloud, and while Jack didn't reply, Aleyna smiled to herself as though there was something satisfying, something *spell-like* about the phrase.

The cottage was by the sea, half way down the Beara Peninsula. They'd spent the best part of the previous day jammed alongside each other in the rental car; Lou and Jack had taken it in turns to drive the coast road, passing through a succession of tiny communities pinned to the edge of the Cork landscape.

"Michael Collins country," Jack had said as the road twisted through the rocky outcrops. He pointed out signs to Clonakilty as they passed, and gestured to where he thought Bealnablath should be through the rear view mirror.

Aleyna hadn't risen to his guidebook wisdom. There was more to history than just the coordinates marking where something began and where something ended, it was the tangle in-between that resonated. She leaned against the window, watching the landscape roll past them. There was a beauty to it but it felt stark to her, a similar untamed rawness that she imagined of the sea.

They'd spent the night of New Year's Eve in the cottage, eschewing the local bars to drink together undisturbed. It had felt strangely decadent, taking all that effort of flying somewhere new just to ignore it and drink indoors like they so often did back home. They were the last of their circle of friends to succumb to the designated responsibilities of adulthood. They didn't have kids, they didn't have dogs and only Jack could claim to have a mortgage. Everyone else had peeled away as their thirties had eroded, their youthful priorities gently realigned to adult expectation, social calendars hijacked by nappies and inoculations and schools and savings schemes. Aleyna had looked around at the four of them who were left and allowed herself the private suspicion that given the choice, they may not have been the friends she would have chosen to be marooned with.

Even so, they had a shared purpose for the evening. They worked their way through the wine and rum and whisky they'd stocked up with at the local shop, they'd smoked the weed that Jack had smuggled through the flight, packed tightly in a talcum powder tin and still smelling slightly of roses and old ladies. Although Kevin had tried to intervene, they had dined on the sort of junk food that holidays make acceptable: Pizzas and crisps and those sugary cakes that come off a production line in neatly sealed plastic. They watched midnight arrive on the local television station and they had stepped outside in the rain to toast the New Year. They had come all that distance, but they could have been anywhere really. Time found them, ticked them off and moved on, the passing year's departure both momentous and anticlimactic. They stayed up until four in the morning, drinking and smoking and playing cards.

The following afternoon, the sky had remained grey, but the hills looked sharp and distinct and the landscape surrounding them seemed brighter and more alive after the rainfall. The greens and browns and yellows were richly saturated like raw and unmixed paints applied in great round swatches to a fresh blank canvas. There was a beauty to it certainly, but more than that, there was the promise of something verdant, something vital and alive.

"Is this the way we came?" Jack said.

The landscape had evened out as they descended the hill, the path rising a little so the embankments shallowed and hazy moorland stretched upwards on their right, and downwards on their left. The views on both sides were foreshortened by the mist, but there was a sense of unbounded space nonetheless, a hint of the infinite, hidden just out of view.

"Yes," Aleyna said. "I think so."

"Okay, then." Jack kicked a loose pebble and watched it skitter ahead of them, coming to rest in the middle of the path, splitting the current of water into a pair of plaited streams. Perhaps unconsciously, he quickened his pace as though impatient to reach it again. "Has the fog got worse?" He held his arm in front of him as though it might help him judge.

"A bit, maybe."

He glanced back up the path at her, squinting with concern.

"Listen," he said. "I know it's probably too late, but do you want to swap jackets? That old thing is going to give you hypothermia or something."

That old thing.

He started unzipping his Karimoor overcoat, slow enough she could stop him before he was done.

"It's fine," she said when he was past half way. "Doubt mine would fit you anyway."

She smiled.

"But I'm fine," she said again. "It's not cold, it's just wet." *And horrible*, she would have added, but she didn't want to say it out loud in case it might make things feel worse. It wasn't that bad. Not really. And the cottage wasn't far away, and if Kevin had got there already, he'd have the fire lit . . .

"Well, if you change your mind." Jack zipped his coat back up again and hunched into it. "Sorry I didn't think of it earlier. We're getting way too old for expeditions like this."

"Speak for yourself."

"Hangovers make me feel older."

"Don't drink so much then. We had lots of fruit juice. Coke."

"Fruit juice makes me feel like a kid. How are you feeling?"

"I didn't drink as much as you did."

It was true, but only just true. It had been a long time since drinking had felt so illicit to her. Back then it had been the last fluttering ends of her childhood faith nagging at her with stern disapproval, but this was different and felt more transgressive in its way.

Before they'd arrived, Aleyna had promised herself she wasn't going to drink at all, but once plump-little Mrs Leachy had unlocked the cottage and briskly shown them around, Aleyna had accepted a glass of prosecco from Jack without a thought. After that, she found herself engaged in a game. If Kevin offered her a new drink she would refuse, but if Jack did, she would accept. Three glasses of wine in and she remembered how Jack didn't really ask. He just leaned in and topped up her glass when he judged it to be low. She had smiled. She had polished off everything he had given her. It would be his fault either way.

They passed a row of three small houses, low slung rooftops and whitewashed walls; each had the appearance of being buried half way into the hillside. A fourth house at the end of the row looked unfinished and a wide aperture in one wall was masked by a canvas sheet that the wind had loosened so it flapped and snapped at them like a chained dog as they passed.

"Where is everyone?" Jack said. "Everywhere looks deserted."

"They probably think only idiots would go out for a walk in weather like this. Mad dogs and Englishmen."

"Which of those am I?" he said, turning back to her.

"Mad Englishman."

"Half-English."

"No-one's half-English. When you're brought up in England, it blots out everything else." She tapped the side of her head. "Shadow of the Empire, fitted as standard."

He snorted, glancing up at her as though he was gauging a retort, but then he looked away again, losing his nerve as he always did. "They all looked empty," he said instead. "Every house we passed looked empty. No lights, no movement."

"They're all sleeping in. Nursing their heads like normal people."

"Even so."

"It's fine."

Perhaps she sounded more confident than she felt, because before they rounded the corner, she glanced back. The houses didn't seem so empty to her, in fact she was struck by the clear impression that there really was someone there in the unfinished house at the end of the row, standing just out of sight behind the flapping canvas, watching them pass.

Figures moving through the fog, she thought, imagining the homeowners glimpsing their forms emerging from the whiteness like spectres. No wonder everyone had their doors firmly closed.

"Holiday homes, maybe," she said.

Jack winced, staring ahead unfocussed.

"My mum used to come to these parts in the holidays," he said.

"Back in the fifties, sixties. Near enough anyway. Had cousins round near Bantry, but best I can tell, she spent most of her time being shuffled from one relative to another over the holidays. She said she remembered seeing kids around these parts walking into school barefoot, holding their shoes to save the wear on them."

He shook his head.

"Seems crazy it should be all holiday homes now. Doesn't seem right."

Aleyna touched him on the shoulder and he stopped in surprise.

She leaned forward and kissed him. His lips were edged with a fierce cold, but there was warmth in there too and her hunger for it both surprised and embarrassed her.

It was his turn to gently push her away.

"They could be just ahead of us," he said.

Aleyna shook her head, but her look remained uncertain. "They'll be home by now. Lighting a fire. Putting the kettle on."

Jack laughed. "They won't be moving that fast. If we pick up the pace we'll likely catch up with them before we get back."

"They're not that slow."

"Lou is, trust me. And if she's complaining—and by god, she will be complaining—it'll slow her down further."

"You should be nicer to her."

"I'm a gentleman with her."

"But behind her back . . . ?"

"In the fog . . ."

They kissed again, longer, deeper, until Aleyna broke away, sensing some distant movement beyond Jack's shoulder, a flickering motion like a bird, perhaps, or an animal. She looked back the way they had come, hidden now by the whiteness that had closed behind them like a curtain. Again, she had the distinct sense there was someone there, just out of sight, barely invisible.

"Could they be behind us, maybe?" she said.

"Only if they took a wrong turn." Jack turned to see where she was looking.

Aleyna called into the fog. "Kev?" she said. "Lou?"

The words felt stunted, abrupt. Cast into the whiteness, they didn't sound like names to her at all.

"There's no-one there." Jack turned back to her, his hand came up to her cheek but she flinched away.

"That last junction," she said. "Maybe they went straight when they should have turned left? Maybe they backtracked when they realized their mistake?"

"There's no-one there," Jack said. "If we carry on, we can catch up with them. Hey." Again, his hand was at her cheek, but its gear had changed: this wasn't seduction, it was concern. "Look at me," he said.

He looked at her, serious as a father.

"You stare into that fog," he said, "you're going to see whatever you think you're seeing. Doesn't mean it's really there, though. Trick of the eye. It's full of shit."

"I didn't see anything," Aleyna said. It was mostly true but still discomforting.

"Come on, you're cold and soaked through." She felt his hand on her shoulder, pushing, *steering* her back down the path. "Let's get you back to that fire. I'm sorry for delaying us at all."

"Such a gentleman."

"Only to your face."

"Asshole."

"Cow."

The path gave way to a tarmac road that descended gradually, zigzagging between the farmland on the left and right. There were drainage ditches on either side, but the roadway was crosshatched with sparkling rivulets of water, chasing their way downwards.

The air felt thicker, denser, and from somewhere, Aleyna imagined a faint smell of wood smoke drifting across on an intermittent breeze.

"You know what this reminds me of?" Jack said.

Aleyna shook her head, but didn't look at him, moving would only move her coat and it already felt colder and heavier around her. She could feel the dampness had soaked through to the lining and the wool of the jersey she wore beneath. It felt to her like cool fingertips tracing down her arms, hooking around her chest from behind.

"Volumetric fog," Jack said.

"You're waiting for me to ask what that is, aren't you?"

"That game Kevin and I worked on back in the late nineties. It was called Something Invasion, Mutant Invasion? Mutoids? Shit, I don't know, I've tried to block it out. It was one of those third person shooters, trying to cash in on GoldenEye on the N64. Only it was *awful*. You were walking around this planet, shooting insurgents—you were invading the whole planet single-handed, you know how those computer game plots used to be—and it looked terrible. Crap textures, low poly count. Terrible.

"But the thing with that sort of game is that you're only shown the landscape your character could see. Nothing else really existed, the hills were all hollow. And even more-so than other games of its type, it was completely unstable. There was this weird sense that without warning, the player might break free from the point of view and the illusion would fold up just like that. You'd turn around and there'd be nothing there at all. Just blackness."

He stared out into the fog, his grin only loosely pinned into place.

"The hills were hollow," he said again, thoughtful. "Anyway, the system was so slow, we could barely show any of the land-scape at all, and if we did, everything just ground to a halt like you were wading through treacle.

"So time was short and we cut corners. We cranked up the volumetric fog to hide the fact the scenery was popping-up in the distance and being redrawn when you turned around."

"What happened?"

"Everyone hated it. Went straight to the bargain bin in Wool-worths. Remember Woolworths?"

They walked on in silence for a while.

They had all worked together once. Aleyna had arrived,

youthful and enthusiastic from some Lancashire backstreet, flushed with the colors and variety of the capital. The company was one of those little start-ups that grew too fast, too bright and too eager. Before they knew what was happening, before their feet even touched the ground, the company was already gone, snapped up by a bigger fish, scattered to the winds. But the four of them circled each other still, the same workplaces, the same bars. Constantly cycling, over and over and over.

"Is that why you stopped writing the games yourself?" Aleyna said after a while. She'd heard versions of the story before, different variants with different villains as though whoever asked got someone else to blame.

Jack sighed.

"I wasn't even supposed to write most of that one. In one way, I fucked things up by compromising, in another, I saved the day by actually finishing the bloody thing." He shrugged. "In the future, I figured I'd leave the coding to the Kevins of the world."

Aleyna stopped.

"Be nicer," she said.

"That's not what I meant," Jack said. "I mean he's better at that sort of thing than I am. I bluff my way through, he absolutely gets it. I'm better at the other stuff. Managing, getting funding, *talking* to people, you know? I'm good at that."

"Sure. You're doing a bang up job."

"You know what I mean. Kevin's smart. The man's an artist. But if he didn't have me watching his back people would be fucking him over at every turn."

They walked onwards in silence. Aleyna didn't write code, she wrote copy. Back then she had written documentation and manuals, newsletters that no-one read. These days, she worked freelance for a catalogue company spending her hours coming up with different ways to describe the same things: A dozen ways to say *carry cot*; one hundred ways to say *push chair*; one thousand ways to say *child, baby, bairn*. She tabulated her work in spreadsheets that from a distance didn't look so different from the pages of code that Kevin would trawl through. Editing, debugging, refining, releasing. The day-to-day dance was familiar to both of them.

On their right, Aleyna and Jack passed the gate to a farm and like the other buildings they had seen, it was a dark and cold looking place. The farmhouse, a low building at the far end of a muddy concrete forecourt, had a melancholy quality accentuated by the collection of faded plastic children's toys gathered outside. A pink slide pointed downwards to a slick of grey puddle, a squinting swing set with frayed ropes, a rocking horse left on its side. The place felt too empty, too quiet to be fully real. The barn opening out on the yard was a rusted skeleton, crowded with neglected machinery, all spikes and blades, bundled and forgotten like rolls of barbed wire.

"What time is it?" Aleyna said.

Jack shrugged.

"I left my phone in the cottage," he said. "Looked like it was on the blink this morning anyway. No signal, nothing." He shot her a glance and tried to look reassuring. "Probably nearly three or so," he said.

"So late?"

"We started late." He grinned. "When we said last night how we could walk it off come the morning, I think we were all thinking we'd actually *see* the morning. Why? What time did you think it was?"

Aleyna turned, looking back up the path. She felt very conscious about how their voices carried. Somewhere, she could hear the gentle hiss of the sea, the clatter and turn of pebbles in a distant tide, but otherwise, it was quiet and still. She found warmth in the way Jack talked, but at the same time, it felt too loud, too impolite. It drew attention in a way that made her uncomfortable.

"I don't know," she said. "To be honest, I'm not even sure what day it is."

Jack laughed.

"Trick question," he said.

"I don't know," Aleyna said again. "It should be New Year's

Day, but how would we know? We haven't seen anyone else. We could have slept for days for all I know. Months. We woke up and it's like the world has been emptied while we were asleep."

Jack didn't reply, but Aleyna felt his eyes on her, she felt he was studying her, looking for a sign she was joking, a hook on which he could hang a smart remark. Instead, he turned away again and sighed.

"Do not partake of the food they give you," he said, his tone affected as though he was quoting something from memory.

"Excuse me?"

"Faeries. If they offer you food and you eat it, you'd become trapped in their world and subject to their whims. Don't look at me like that, I read it somewhere. In a book. So it must be true."

"I haven't eaten any faerie food," Aleyna said, amused despite herself.

"You had one of those scones Mrs O'Landlady left out for us."

"*Mrs Leachy* is not a faerie."

Jack shrugged. "How would we know?"

"I doubt faeries make scones."

Jack looked skeptical.

"I wish they would," he said. "I'm getting hungry."

They walked onwards in silence for a spell and Aleyna hugged her coat tight around her as though she could squeeze more comfort from it, even though the dampness had infiltrated it entirely. Kevin had bought it for her and it seemed so extravagant that she assumed he was apologizing for something he had yet to confess to. He had never been particularly good with choosing gifts for her. On their first Christmas together, he had bought her a second-hand paperback copy of The Siege of Krishnapor, confessing as he did so that it had only cost him two-fifty from one of the vendors under Waterloo Bridge, and that he only bought it because he liked the cover. He made up for it with his cooking, to which he applied the same level of attention he spent on his code. If he was an engineer in the kitchen rather than an artist, there was passion there too: he saw processes and subroutines, his ingredients subjected to functions and iterative loops, but there was love stirred in with each, binding everything together at a level deeper than chemistry.

Aleyna had grown up with good food, but Kevin's recipes still had the ability to take her by surprise. She hated to imagine how much greyer her life would be without his cooking, without him.

The coat was beautiful and clearly more expensive than he could afford. She'd brought it with her to Ireland to demonstrate how much she appreciated it, but now as it hung heavy and misshapen on her and she wondered if she had ruined it by wearing it for the walk.

"What do you think they're doing right now?" she said.

"Who?"

"Who do you think?"

"Maybe they're back in the cottage after all. Fire lit, feet up."

"Holding hands?"

"Kissing. Fucking."

Beside them, the stone wall they'd been following for the past hundred yards gave way to a three-wire fence bordering a broad field that disappeared uphill into whiteness. At its distant edges, Aleyna thought she saw movement again, something dark against the mist. Looking closer, she saw there were several shapes there, too dark to be seagulls, they could have been crows. They moved with a clumsy flapping motion that suggested wings, but at a distance, their size was troubling. Perhaps it was only a trick of perspective, but there was something about them that felt too big for common birds, and the way they moved unsettled her: they stumbled and flustered and flapped about like the loose tarpaulin on the empty house. They rolled and blustered chaotically as they edged slowly down the field towards the fence.

"Lou's probably asleep by now," Jack said, his attention elsewhere. "All tucked up and content to have that cramped little bed to herself. She barely slept at all last night. Tossing and turning all the time, it's a miracle she got as far as she did on the walk."

"Let's move quicker then." Aleyna said.

Jack looked at her, concerned.

"Alright," he said, and he reached out to take her hand.

She didn't look back as they hurried down the road together and Jack didn't speak, making their flight feel more urgent.

She hadn't been paying attention to their surroundings as the four of them had begun their walk, she'd been talking to Lou, the two of them had been planting one foot in front of the other with little attention spared for the passing landscape.

It always used to bother her that she only knew Lou because of Jack and Kevin. To begin with, she was never entirely sure if she liked her or just felt she should accommodate her for Jack's sake, but time had brought them closer, sanding down the residual prickliness between them and leaving them with a mutual respect that they were both still there despite everything. Aleyna had never been confident when it came to friend maintenance and working from home as a freelancer had whittled her list of face-to-face colleagues down to the bone. She was grateful she had Lou there, somewhere in the background. An almost-friend was sometimes good enough.

Lou had met Jack when the company had been bought out way back when. She had been the one hired to project manage the transition, breaking the start-up apart to salvage what worked and throw everything else out. Jack, she kept for herself, not in a mercenary move, but an unexpected development, unaccounted for but worked around. That was how Lou worked. Her life was scheduled in Gant charts and dependency diagrams. She had been the one to organize the New Year's holiday but the walk had never been part of the plan. Little wonder she'd turned back so soon.

The path felt alien to Aleyna, and while the fog had thickened since their outward journey, the road itself was new to her, the hedges and walls and fences on either side were unfamiliar; the potholes in the tarmac seemed fresh.

She stopped abruptly, forcing Jack to tug at her arm in surprise.

"What is it?" he said.

"This isn't the way we came."

He looked about him, flustered.

"It has to be," he said. "There's no other way we could have gone."

"It's wrong," Aleyna said. "We didn't come this way."

Jack sighed.

"We could go back," he said.

"No." She pulled out the map from her coat pocket and started unfolding it. But it was too big, too unwieldy. Lines and shapes and endless place names. Already she felt the paper softening in the mist.

"Listen." Jack squinted into the fog. "The sea's that way, you can hear it. If we carry on downhill, we'll get to the main road eventually, and we can just walk along it to get to the cottage. We can't be far."

"Fuck," Aleyna said. The word sounded misshapen when she said it, like the previous night's drinking, it felt like something she should have been giving up. The map was defeating her. She crumpled it thoughtlessly, searching its hieroglyphics for the cottage, the path, the standing stone. But she couldn't engage with it, not entirely. The geography swam before her and all the labels conspired to say the same thing in different ways. A hundred places she had never heard of, a thousand places she never thought to see.

"Come on." Jack rested his hand on the map, a gentle gesture and one that surprised her by its calmness. It occurred to her how she felt at ease in his presence in a way she didn't feel with Kevin. It wasn't a relaxing feeling, there was always a nub of sickly tension that she was doing something she shouldn't, but it felt *comfortable* in some other, inexplicable way, like two pieces from different jigsaws fitting together snugly even if the picture made no sense.

"I'm sorry," she said.

"It's okay." He smiled. "Let's go back."

He took the map off her and started folding it. She saw immediately he was doing it wrong, fold against fold, it bunched awkwardly in his hands, but she didn't say anything.

They set off again, downward, seaward, deep into the white.

Aleyna glanced back over her shoulder, the way from which they had come looking near the same as they path they had chosen to continue down. There was no sign of movement that she could see. No shapes, no shadows, no flapping wings.

Jack reached up and pressed his hands to his head.

"My mum would appreciate this," he said.

"The walk?"

"The fact I have a hangover. She'd say it was penance. Some sort of purgatorial state the drunk have to pass through before they earn sobriety. She'd say all that to me like she was quoting scripture, but she'd be laughing at the same time." He grimaced. "Catholics," he said. "It's all about what you deserve with them. Sadistic fuckers the lot of them."

Aleyna could only imagine what her mother would say if she knew her only daughter had been drinking. She certainly wouldn't laugh, she wouldn't give speeches either. She'd just remain silent in that way of hers, leaving the room when Aleyna would come in.

"Hey," Jack said. He had stopped in the path some paces behind her, standing by the low stone wall, staring into the field angling down to their left. He turned back to her, grinning. "Look," he said.

At the end of the field, the sun was shining. A hazy amber disc suspended low in the spread of grey, punching through where the clouds had weakened. The field beneath it was oddly beautiful, even and muddied, the day's moisture hung on the too-early shoots of greenery, forming a glittering path to the far side. Aleyna could see a wire fence in the distance, on the other side of which was the angular ghost of a low building, a telegraph pole, a skeleton tree.

"It's the road," Jack said. "That's the place just a few hundred yards up from the cottage, which means we're over that way somewhere." He gestured airily, back and to the left.

"So we are on the wrong road," Aleyna said.

"I don't know," Jack said. "This one probably connects eventually."

They stood together, side-by-side at the wall, and neither said anything for what felt like hours. As they watched, the sun sunk imperceptibly lower and the path of light it cast broadened.

Aleyna sighed. "We should cut across." One of them had to say it. "We should climb over the wall and just . . . just walk across."

She sensed Jack had turned to look at her but she didn't meet his eyes.

"Farmer might have a gun," he said. "Might not take kindly to us traipsing over his neatly ploughed field."

"Farmer is probably as hung-over as you are."

"True."

Again, silence and again, it was Aleyna who spoke first.

"I just want to go home," she said.

She felt Jack's hand on her shoulder.

"Come on then," he said.

The field was wet underfoot, a film of standing water reflected the subtle pleats of the clouds, but the ground itself, while spongy, was firm enough. They walked together in silence, Jack a few paces ahead and Aleyna happy to tail behind. As they walked, the mist seemed to loosen around them and the sun brightened to the extent that Aleyna could feel a trace of its warmth on her forehead and cheeks.

Ahead of them, the line of the road slowly began to come into sharper focus and Aleyna could make out the shape of the building they had seen more clearly. It was a hunched little cottage with its back to the road, a single, tiny square window hanging tight under the roofline. They had passed it on their way uphill, and while then it had struck her as a lonely looking place, now there was a warmth to it that felt compulsive.

Jack stopped to shake the mud off his boots.

"Christ," he said. "It's like . . . it's like fucking porridge."

He kicked at nothing, long legged and gangly and while small sods of mud spun off his feet, the rest remained clenched around the soles and the uppers, thick and dense and solidifying.

"It's not worth it," Aleyna said. "You'll only get more."

"It's the more I'm worried about." Another kick, this one almost unbalanced him. She caught him and laughed but he shook her off and plunged on ahead.

The mud was sticking to her shoes as well. It felt first like she had something in her shoe and then like she was standing on something, a rock or a tussock, something uneven that threatened to upend her. More than anything, she could feel the weight of it. She could feel the weight of the landscape, pulling at her and slowing her pace.

"I need a stick or something," Jack was saying. "Do you have a pen? Or some keys?"

"Just keep going."

"How about the map? Give me the map."

"Jack."

But she understood his impatience with it, and when his back was turned again, she set her own feet down at angles, as though she could push off the excess mud against the ground itself, but it just clung to the sides of her shoes, making them thicker and heavier still.

Her legs ached, but still she persevered.

They approached the center of the field, but Aleyna had to look back to see where they had come from to be certain. The road ahead of them looked barely closer than it had been when they had first climbed over the wall. It was clearer, true, but no nearer. Behind her, the path they had come from also seemed too far away. It was a distant blurry line in the mist, another hint of something boundless and infinite.

It reminded her, inexplicably, of a holiday she and Kevin had taken years before to the west coast of Australia. They'd visited a beach with signs warning of riptides to the north. Aleyna had been frightened by the prospect of being caught by the currents and dragged out to sea and yet there had been kids splashing about the waves regardless, some barely toddlers, waddling about the surf in inflatable armbands. Their parents were lying on the beach, oblivious under paperbacks and beer bottles. Aleyna and

Kevin hadn't stayed long. He was trying to do work but the sun bleached out his laptop screen, she found herself counting and recounting other people's children, terrified not just that one of them might get swept out on the horizon, but that she might be the one expected to follow, just because she had been the one paying attention.

Now the field felt bigger to Aleyna than it had been before, it felt sea-like, oceanic, tangled with hidden currents. It was a vertiginous thought and she stopped so abruptly and her heavy feet stumbled so she almost pitched forward into the mud.

And then I'd never get up, she thought.

What a way to start the year.

Jack was still moving onwards. He looked like a string puppet, each foot raised comically high in turn, his shoulders angling first one way then the other, his arms flailing for balance. One foot, two feet. He looked so determined, like a child learning to walk for the first time.

She wondered what would happen if she let him keep walking. Maybe he would disappear into the fog like Kevin and Lou had. Maybe the field would keep stretching and stretching to accommodate the distance between them.

"Jack," she said. She only spoke quietly, but he turned in surprise as though she had been beside him after all.

"What is it?"

He glanced around him, then without even a thought, started picking his way back to her. One foot, two foot. He looked pleased with himself, as though he had traded his dignity for a way to master himself.

"There's something I need to tell you," Aleyna said, taking herself by surprise. She hadn't intended to say anything at all. Not to Jack, not to Kevin, not to anyone. She smiled at him instead as he reached her, and he put out a hand, maybe to comfort her, maybe to support himself.

"It's alright," he said. "We just have to power through. We'll only get stuck if we let it."

She looked down at their feet, facing each other like dance

partners. For a moment she wondered if it was all too late anyway. She wondered if she would ever be able to move again. She felt that the mud was drawing her downwards. In her shoes, her feet were as cold as stone, water had pooled around them, green shoots rocking like pondweed.

"Jack," she said and there was something about the way she spoke that made him pull her close and hold her.

Across the outer edges of the field, there was the ghost of something moving. Dark shapes flickered and flapped around the grey-white fringes. Aleyna watched them over Jack's shoulder, she saw how they approached: circling, fluttering, stumbling, surrounding them.

"We should go back," she said.

THE CENACLE

Robert Levy

THE WIDOW WAITS FOR THE SERVICE TO be over. The incomprehensible liturgy of atonal Hebrew gutturals, millennia of meaning resonant for so many but not her. She'd never learned the language of her ancestors, never considered that her supposed faith might lend her any comfort until now. Her husband's coffin thirteen feet away and sunk six more, the pine box lowered south from the light of a sun invisible behind dreary February clouds. She can't face the hole so she stares down at her feet in the mud-dirtied snow, stockinged legs like sticks beneath her long coat. Everyone in black, from her stepdaughter to the rabbi to the cemetery attendants and scattered among the Brooklyn gravestones, the land blotted out by the unyielding blizzard that had buried the city in its own white grave. Even still the snow swirls.

She waits for them all to leave. From her awkward brothers to her overattentive coworkers, she nods as they go, each one in turn, moving on to the luncheon, then later *shiva*, and finally to a peaceful sleep she herself could never bear. She is an *onen*, in a state of mourning beyond reach. "I'll be along, I'll be along," she says, "I just need some time to myself." A deception. She wants no time alone, not ever. What she wants is her husband back.

Her husband's daughter, born of his previous marriage, is the hardest goodbye. "Why did he have to die?" the girl sobs, her wet face pressed against the widow's breast; the girl's mother keeps a safe distance, frozen beneath a denuded elm far from the plot. "Everyone dies, my love," the widow replies, and strokes the ten-year-old's strawberry hair, her wedding ring snagging in the girl's tangled mess of curls. "Only some go sooner than later."

She waits until the sun sinks behind the horizon of distant buildings before she admits to herself that she's too cold to remain here forever, that eventually the attendants will return to usher her from the premises, tell her she can return in the morning, some widows do, day after day after day. Darkening sky and she moves from the gravesite at last, shuffles through the snow until she's back at the road that snakes through the cemetery in one long and intricate seam.

She steps onto the path, and movement catches her attention: a dark shadow in the distance, hunched and shuffling along a mausoleum-dotted hillock overlooking the snow-caked grounds. The figure progresses slowly across the landscape, shreds of gauzy black cloth flapping like clerical vestments in the wind as it reaches with sickled arms to touch upon each tombstone as if blind and feeling the way forward. The stranger stops and cocks an ear to the side, nose threading the air, a bloodhound seeking a scent.

The widow is chilled by a bitter wind. She lifts the neck of her coat against it, the furred collar tugged up to her eyes as the figure turns toward her and lifts a hand in acknowledgment, the scraps of what seems to be a shawl shifting in the breeze. An elderly woman by the looks of it, hunched in a manner that suggests a kyphotic spine bent by defect or age.

The stranger turns and lowers her head once more before soldiering on, trudging through the scattered stones and disappearing around the side of a large rotunded mausoleum. The widow waits. But when the stranger fails to appear she makes her way up the hill, drawn to the crypt as if toward an answer to an unspoken but persistent question. Her shoes brown with mud as she slides against the wet earth, the still falling snow. She rights herself, and she climbs, until she reaches the twin doors that announce the entrance to the crypt.

The braided door handles have been wiped clean of frost, and she takes hold of their cold iron and pulls. Softly at first, but then she puts her weight into it, leaning back as she yanks until the doors groan open, just wide enough to pass. Within the slash of muted light an interior wall is visible—much deeper inside than she'd expected, given the vault's outward dimensions—and it's only upon entering the antechamber and daring to ease the doors shut in her wake that she makes out the dim illuminations of candleflame flickering farther inside the crypt. That, and the pleasing smell of cedar smoke, as well as the vague susurrations of voices, just as they fall silent.

She takes care not to trip upon the raised step leading into the main rotunda of the tomb, and she treads forward, broaching the arched entryway as she comes to a halt beneath the rose marble lintel.

Seated in an approximation of a semicircle are two women, one quite old and another young, along with an elderly man. Lit only by votive candles burning upon the crypt's every ledge, the three are dressed in funereal black and huddled about a raised granite slab. Upon the stone surface are a further arrangement of votives, pale wax dripping and pooling into gray swirls along the floor of the rounded tomb.

"Hello, dear," the old woman says from her place between the others, eyes bright in the candle flame as she draws her shawl with a wrinkled hand, brown fingers sparkling with gold and azure rings. "Would you like to join us? We're just having a spot of dinner before it gets too late." The hunched woman casts a hand across the stone block: inside the circle of candles a pile of smoked fowl is laid out, picked at with tiny bones jutting from charred skin upon a bed of unidentifiable berries and roots. The widow knows she should be repulsed but her stomach lurches for a moment like a dog jerked on a chain, and she's shocked by her sudden hunger.

"Who are you?" she asks. "What are you doing in here?"

"What are *you* doing in here?" the old man says, his voice a scratched-vinyl rasp. "We're in this together, aren't we?" He gestures for her to sit. She stares down at her feet and the puddle of melted snow they've left upon the flagstone, and she regrets not stamping the ice off them before entering.

"Come," the old woman says, "don't be shy," and so the widow lowers herself onto the near side of the slab. "Excellent, excellent. Happy to see you're joining us here today. We're always looking for a decent fourth."

"Bridge numbers," the old man says. "I tried teaching them rummy, but there's really no convincing these two."

The old woman laughs, then covers her mouth. "Sorry. Bad joke, I'm afraid. We're not really much for bridge."

"What are you, then?" the widow asks, and turns to face the young woman, who remains quiet and still.

"Ah," the old woman says. "Well. I suppose we're many things, of course, no person being just *one* thing. But mostly, we're the ones left behind."

"Left behind by who?"

Even as the widow asks the question, however, she knows. For what is she now, but left behind herself? The young woman's light blue eyes swell with such alarming compassion that it makes her want to weep in recognition.

"How long have you been here?" the widow asks.

"Some time, now," the old woman replies. "After a while, you lose count of the days. You just . . . stay." Her expectant face shines, incandescent in the flickering candlelight reflected upon the granite slab. "You'll stay, won't you?"

"I . . . don't think so." The widow makes no move to leave, however. Shadows dance about the curved walls as dusk's last light evaporates beyond the surprising warmth of the stone shelter. "I have to go."

"There's nothing for you out there," the old woman says. "Not anymore."

"I have a stepdaughter," the widow says. "I have friends."

"We'll be your friends now. We'll be your family too."

"I should go."

"We're the only ones who can care for you."

"I should go."

"We're the only ones that can know you."

"Let her go already!" the old man barks, spittle flung from the corner of his mouth as he waves her away. "Let her see for herself what it's like out there, now."

They fall silent. The widow begins to back away from them and toward the doors, but makes it no farther than the step leading to the anteroom when she stills, all the while her eyes on theirs. She has a stepdaughter; she has friends; she drinks two cups of coffee in the morning as she does the crossword with a ballpoint pen. But she had a husband, then. So none of that could now be so.

"Perhaps I will stay," the widow says. "For a little while."

The old woman smiles. "Good," she says, and nods in eager approval. "Good."

So she stays. For a few minutes, and then for an hour, for the evening and then overnight, sleeping beside them beneath an oilskin tarpaulin on the cold and damp flagstones that pave the floor of the crypt. They wake her at dawn and lead her to the evergreen hedges abutting the high flat stone of the cemetery walls to collect chokeberries, which grow there in red clotted bunches, a gift of winter. They show her how they use barbed wire as snares to catch sparrows and pigeons, starlings and other birds too stupid or slow to fly south for the winter. She keeps expecting someone to come looking for her—her family, her friends, the police—but no one ever does.

She spends the day with them, and then another night, another morning and a new day, spent occupied with the daily business of acquiring food, of learning from the others the customs and rules of their strange and insular world. They melt frost in marble cisterns and drink from ornamental urns, the accoutrements of the dead refashioned for the needs of the living. But isn't it all for the living? The widow casts her eyes across the snow-blanketed graves. The coffins and tombstones, the ritual pyres and monumental obelisks . . . What do the dead care, anymore?

Most wonderful of all, there's no need for the widow to speak of her husband, for any of them to speak of their husbands, or the old man of his wife. It's enough for them to be together in their grief. Their simple companionship abates the pain of her loss more than she would have ever thought possible.

Early on the morning of the third day, they finish stealing candles from the small chapel near the gates when they come upon a pair of parka-clad workers digging a fresh grave on the south side of the cemetery. The widow, exposed to them in the bright light of day, scuttles behind the obscuring limbs of a weeping willow, but the others continue undaunted along the path toward the mausoleum that is their home. The gravediggers fail to acknowledge them, and after some time she realizes that the workers take no notice of them whatsoever.

"Why don't they see us?" she asks the others once she's caught up with them.

The old woman shrugs. "They don't want to see us, I suppose. It's too . . . difficult for them."

"They don't have any skin in the game," the old man says, and hocks a dark yellow loogie into the thick paste of snow. "They might as well work at a bank."

"Once the funeral is over, they move on. Everyone does. But not us." The old woman smiles her bright warm smile, but this time there's something sorrowful in it, which feels just right.

By the seventh day, the end of *shiva*, the widow rarely thinks of the life that awaits her at her former home, doesn't even remember more than a vague outline of what she ever did with her time. Where did I work? she wonders. Was it at an office building? Or was it some kind of school? By the ninth day it's like walking through a waking dream: she no longer recalls her stepdaughter's age, or the color of her hair, and soon the girl's name is lost to her altogether, along with the general features of her face. All she remembers now is her husband, and she clings to his memory like a talisman, a lantern in the dark of night. It's all she has left to hold.

She knows it's because of her new friends. They understand her, in a way others are unable, and she knows this to be true because she understands them the same way. The widow knows that by staying with them—by haunting the hallowed grounds of the cemetery and living off what grows here, and alights here, and is fed by the flesh and marrow of the departed—that she needn't move on, not ever. Because some people never do.

By the tenth day in the cemetery, however, the pain of her husband's absence returns unabated. It surges like a cresting wave and crashes over her, bringing her back to that awful phone call, that moment that ushered her unwillingly into the midnight realm of unmitigated despair. I can't breathe, she thinks, I'll never breathe again, and she runs the familiar distance from the crypt down the hill to the family plot, where her husband's grave, as with the rest, is buried in white. Her chapped pink hands dig at the wet ground, her tears pocking the snow. It's only once she's made her way to the hard dirt below that she stops to wonder whether she's trying to dig her husband out of his resting place or make a grave for herself to crawl into, where she can lie down and pull the earth around her like a shroud. Even the accusation of her stepdaughter's face begins to return, the dark almond eyes the girl shared with her father, the single dimple in her right cheek. She has abandoned her husband's daughter, as she herself has been abandoned. She wants to die.

And what truth this is! As true as the aim of the steering column that had impaled her husband in his twisted metal cage, the one they needed the Jaws of Life to free him from, though there would be no life for him, not anymore. Twelve days gone since the phone call from the police, the race to the hospital to bear witness to his mangled body, her knuckles white against the steering wheel of her own car as she tried to wish it undone the way she had wished Tinkerbell back to life as a little girl, one among many at a crowded matinee clapping her hands at the screen so hard she was sure her numbed fingers would bleed.

Has it been only twelve days? Impossible. Surely it has been months. Twelve days? No. She couldn't do this. No. She could not. Never.

"You can," the old woman says at her side, all three of them here now, her friends. "You will."

"How?" The widow wipes away tears and peers down at the pathetic little pit she's carved. "How can I keep from wanting it to be over, every second of every hour?"

The old woman looks to the man, who slowly nods, just once, his head drooping so that his pallid chin touches the immaculate Windsor knot in his tweed necktie. He looks to the young woman, who nods once herself, the air crisping with electric tension.

"We have a trick that helps." The old woman steps closer, her stale breath carried on the wind. "Would you like us to show you?"

That night after their rounds they trail back inside the crypt, back to the central round chamber, the widow entering last of all. The young woman lights the arrangement of ledge candles, one after the next, as the temple-like room takes on the eerie half-flame of a winter hearth. The old man clears their last meal's detritus from the granite slab to help the old woman as she lowers herself down upon the tomb.

The old man and the young woman gather on either side of her prone form, the pair tugging back the old woman's tatty black shawl. They unbutton her blouse and lower it, unfasten her nude-colored brassiere and shimmy it out from beneath her, peeling off the rest of her mourning attire until she is naked upon the slab. The old woman crosses her arms over her breasts and closes her eyes, as if she herself is laid out in death's final repose.

All along the woman's body are painted intricate black circles. Of varying size and shape, the patterns run up and down her sides in erratic intervals, appearing to spot her the way a leopard's coat is spotted, dark swirls patching her sagging and distended skin.

Mesmerized, the widow steps forward. Inches away now, and she can see at last that they aren't inked-on designs, but are in fact suppurated wounds, the size of bite marks. Just as soon as she realizes this fact a festering smell hits her, and she staggers back gasping from the slab.

"What is this?" the widow asks, and covers her nose and mouth with a trembling hand.

"This," the old man says, "is the trick."

The widow stares at the young woman, who remains silent as ever, only nodding gravely as she lowers herself to her knees beside the older woman's prostrate figure. Without taking her eyes off the widow, the young woman lifts the older woman's arm, brings it to her mouth, and sinks her teeth into its spongy flesh, the aged brown parchment of skin bruising and bleeding a deeper shade of red.

"My God," the widow whispers. "Why?"

"This is our sacrament," the old woman says from the slab, eyes still shut though her parted lips quiver as if jolted by an electric current. "This is the holy of holy, the flesh that binds us together."

"Take of her," the old man says, so close his rotted breath masks the scent of the old woman's wounds. "Take of her flesh and blood, so that you may strengthen grief's resolve. It's the only way, now."

"I . . . can't. I can't." She wipes away tears and retreats for the doors, wedges her chaffed fingers into the narrow space between them and wrenches them open, ready to flee into the darkness. No one tries to stop her.

But looking out at the pale tombstones that litter the dim

night like scattered teeth, she hesitates. It's because she knows she cannot face the outside world, not anymore. She cannot face anyone who had ever known her before. She needs to be with her own kind, now.

The widow eases the doors shut, a whinnying grind of iron on stone as she turns back to face them. A thrill prickles her skin, an admixture of terror and fascination as she walks the length of the antechamber and back inside the domed sepulcher, where they wait for her in their strange tableau.

She lowers herself beside the slab. "Show me how it's done."

The young woman wipes her mouth and points with a blood-flecked finger at the old woman's free arm. The widow lifts it, bringing the hand toward her. The smell of the old woman's lesions is gone now, replaced by that of snuffed-out candles, as well as a holier scent, sandalwood, perhaps. The widow finds an unblemished section of skin along the inside of the old woman's papery wrist, brings it to her lips, and sinks her teeth into the flesh.

The taste is revolting, and also extraordinary; it reminds her of her first taste of tomato, of being a young girl and plucking one from her grandmother's garden vines, sliding its tough membrane across her lips before biting down. How surprising the spurting of its contents, the strong perfumy taste of lifeblood and liquefied meat, and she retches now as she did then.

But even as she raises her head from where she is sick beside the slab and stares up at them—the looming old man, the wide-eyed young woman, the mutilated older one whose death mask of a face remains still, save the tears spilling from her closed eyes—even as she wants to scream and run from them and die from anguish and sorrow and the guilt of abandoning her step-daughter, she knows that she will not.

She will not scream. She will not run away. She will stay, and she will eat. And she will live. Without her stepdaughter, who is better off without the burden of the widow's annihilative grief. She will live without her husband. But for him. For him.

"Think of him as you eat of me," the old woman whispers, her eyes still closed tight. "Think of him, and the pain begins to slip away, like braised meat off the bone."

The widow grimaces, a trickle of blood leaking from the corner of her mouth as she swallows back a bit of fleshy gristle, the taste of it like tomato skin. She lowers her skull to the old woman's arm, and bites down again, more.

This she could do. Yes. She could. Forever, even. Yes.

On the seventeenth day, they take of the old man. Of his chalky white skin and sinewy flesh, his tough hide and enlarged veins, a thin cord of muscle snagging in the widow's teeth before she manages to swallow it down. He doesn't remain still the way the old woman had, but rather hums and rocks from side to side as the three women feed upon him, their shadows expanding and contracting against the curved walls of the crypt like their own set of dark wounds. "Think of him as you eat of me," the old man whispers and groans, the scent of sandalwood permeating the musty air. "Think of him. Think of him."

And so she does. Of her husband's coppery thick beard and wire-rim spectacles, his swollen gut that he used to take in his two large hands and cradle as if it were a baby. The old man's blooded flesh travels fast through her system, and she feels a calm she hasn't known in memory.

On the twenty-fourth day, they eat of the young woman. She whimpers as the old woman suckles at her thigh, her little hands pressed over her mouth as if trying to keep something down herself. The widow feels a tremor of unease. But didn't she see for herself how the young woman had given herself over? Submission is a precept of faith, the old woman had said, what the widow's own people would call a *mitzvah*, or even *tikkun olam*. Think of him, she reminds herself, and crouches beside the old man to taste of the young woman's bony shoulder, the meat soft beneath its warm baste of blood. Think of him. And she does.

The thirtieth day arrives. The end of *shloshim*, the traditional period of mourning, the one her mother had practiced, and her mother's mother before her. Back from the chokeberry shrubs she walks weaving through the maze of gravestones, the snow reduced to patches, the sun bright overhead with a faint blossoming scent in the air. Spring is on its way to Gravesend Cemetery at last.

Just as she reaches the turnoff to the crypt, she catches the unmistakable sound of liturgy on the wind, and she slows, a small service taking place on the other side of the road. A Greek one, she believes, the priest droning on in his own devotional recitations, the way her rabbi had in his. A few dozen mourners are arranged around the priest, around the square hole dug into the earth and framed by too-bright AstroTurf meant to conceal the fresh grave dirt scattered upon the soft ground. None of them see her standing there. Not the priest or the cemetery workers, the mourners or even the dead. She is but a ghost among them, something so raw and terrible the brain stutters upon sight of her, the eye failing to alight before it quickly flits away.

But then one of them looks up, and she starts: a salt-and-pepper-haired man not terribly much older than herself, but with the prematurely aged face and shocked hollow expression of a widower. His glazed eyes narrow and blink, and they stare at each other, the world falling silent of prayer. I see you, she thinks, and nods slowly before she moves on. I see you. She wonders if he'll be lucky enough to find his way to the crypt, or if the outside world will force him into its plastic and deadening embrace, all platitudes and hopeful falsities. Sometimes it's better not to be seen.

She smells the incense the moment she opens the doors to the crypt, that same perfumy scent that seemed to arise from nowhere each time they took of one another. It was as if the very act had caused some unaccountable pheromone to be secreted from beneath the skin, either the consumer or the consumed. Today, she thinks. It must be the day for me to submit to them, so that their own pain might be eased in turn. Today.

But when she passes through the narrow antechamber and enters the main room of the crypt, she's surprised to see the granite slab is already taken. A large figure lies upon it, swathed crown to toe in a *tachrichim*, which reminds the widow of nothing so much as a last-minute Halloween costume, someone playing at being a ghost.

The others are gathered around the slab, their eyes upon her, watchful. You see me, she thinks, and steps forward to join them.

"Go on," the old man says, and chins toward the head of the shrouded figure. Who else has joined us, then? It never occurred to her before that there would ever be five of them. The widow leans over, and begins to unwrap the dressing.

Even before she has the linen undone, she knows. But still she must see to be sure. She pulls down the folds of the shroud to find his coppery red hair, and only a bit more, only a bit, his skin a dead and dark shade of charcoal around the sunken pits of black and unidentifiable matter where her husband's eyes once were, but no longer are. She finds she cannot breathe.

"You must take of him." The old woman's voice is like a rock hurled against the widow's breast. "To be bound to him forever. The way you've been bound to us."

"This is the night feast," the old man says, "the feast of last partings. The final sacrament of the oldest funerary rites, passed down but occulted from one culture to the next. We have set the table in the sacred space, so that you too might become a part of greater things. This is our gift to you, in the manner we have been gifted by others."

"No." The widow pulls the cloth back over her husband's too-bright hair. "No. I won't do it. Not to him." She looks to the young woman, who only bows her head, whether in prayer or shame it's unclear.

"There must be a feast," the old woman says. "And there must be one tonight." The kindness gone from her wizened face, she rears up from the floor and takes hold of the shroud in two clawlike hands and begins to tug it away. The widow pulls her husband toward herself, and the old woman pulls him back, the corpse rocking between them as if undecided.

She finally reaches over the slab and shoves the old woman, who stumbles against the wall of the crypt, toppling a shelf of candles, the shroud still grasped in one fist. The uncovered body goes with her. It tumbles from the back of the slab, only the briefest glimpse of its hideous decomposition as it falls mercifully into the shadows with a dull thunk.

The widow hurries toward the doors. The old man and young woman are soon upon her, however, dragging her back by her hair and wrestling her toward the slab as they pull away her long coat, her own shroud of winter these past thirty days. The old man thrusts her down onto the cold granite, her head slamming against it so hard she blacks out.

But not for long enough. She awakens moments later to a nighttime sea of imagined stars, dancing about her mind. There is a disturbing sensation of icy breath across her naked belly, followed by an acute stabbing upon her inner thigh, where they're already beginning to take.

"Move over, move over," the old man mutters in the near dark. The three are backlit now, the candlelight and shadow a long distant dream; everything looks darker from the slab.

"Give it here," the old woman says. "You're not doing it right!" The woman takes the widow's hand, sinks her sharp teeth into the soft white flesh of her arm and the widow cries out, the worst pain she's ever learned. No, not the worst: even this blinding curtain of agony pales next to that phone call, a month gone. It's still not enough. So that's what she thinks of, the phone call that ended her old life. That and the back of her husband's freckled and sunburnt neck, his wavy red hair as he runs laughing from her and down to the sea on some past and distant shore. Sand whips all around them as she hurries and fails to keep pace, his sunhatted daughter trailing behind them both, a bright yellow bucket dragged in her wake.

The old woman grunts as she chaws her way up the bloodied and spasming arm, and the widow's own mouth goes agape. She forces herself back to the greater pain, her loss a worried scab that's been prized open anew. They take of her, and they think of lost loves, and it should be enough for them all. She will survive this.

Think of him.

"Help me! Help!" she screams, and the old man hurries to mount her, bends leering over her and lowers his skull in an open-mouthed kiss. He finds her tongue and fastens his brittle teeth to it, blood spattering his glasses and rushing down both their throats as he silences her. Her tongue severed now, the old man turns his head to spit it slippery and wet against the curved wall of the crypt. The old woman scrambles after it, a starved dog after a scrap of meat, the widow gurgling in protestation as she continues to drink of her own blood. Now she knows why the young woman never speaks.

Help me!

She screams in silence, as they continue to devour her.

Think of him.

A distant shore, a laugh. It should be enough.

His face!

She sees him, again.

His face!

At last, she smiles.

SLIMIKINS

Charles Wilkinson

G ILES SHOOTER STIFLED A GASP OF astonishment when he saw Noel Hillup's hands, which were utterly out of proportion with the rest of the boy's body. The elongated thumbs and forefingers tapered towards the end, as if they belonged to a much taller person; the pale colour and sheen of the skin was at odds with the yellowish flesh of the forearms exposed beneath the cuffs. The nails had a dull white gleam. A nickname he'd given another child, so many years before, came back to him.

The minute hand on the wall clock reached a quarter past the hour.

"You may begin now."

Noel picked up the pencil in his right hand and turned his attention to the Wechsler Intelligence Test. The fingers of his left hand, so still as to seem nerveless, were spread out, seemingly stuck to the paper. Shooter tried to suppress the thought it might be necessary to peel them off, digit by digit, sucker by sucker. His consulting room was at the top of the building; all he could see were tiny flecks of snow falling from the padded grey sky.

It had been a tiresome morning. Nothing of

importance had occurred; merely a series of maddening incidents: an appointment cancelled; his secretary unexpectedly off sick; then, minutes before the late arrival of the Hillups, his wife persuading the switchboard to put her call through.

"When are you coming home?"

"I told you. I'm working all day."

"So four o'clock. You'll be home by then."

"Not necessarily. It depends if I'm running late."

"So I'm to deal with him by myself. Without any support whatsoever?"

"Just ignore him. He'll soon go away. You know that."

She was about to dictate a shopping list when he cut her off: "Sorry. A patient's just arrived. I'll speak to you later."

Why had he said "patient"? To lend his calling gravitas, a way of implying he was about to deal with a serious professional matter? The succession of children with dyslexia, attention deficit disorders and handwriting difficulties often had pressing problems, but none amounting to a medical emergency. He'd opened the door to reveal a dumpy woman with discontented features gripping the hand of an undersized, sallow-skinned child.

"Mrs Hillup and Noel?"

As the mother unburdened herself on the shortcomings of the boy's school, Shooter somehow succeeded in persuading her to complete the necessary paperwork. The boy remained standing at a safe distance from the adults. His long oval face, with a receding chin and a small mouth, was set above sloping shoulders; light blue eyes protruded expressionlessly. He held both hands behind his back: the posture of an old man. It was winter, but he wore no jacket; merely a white shirt a size too small for him and a striped tie; in contrast, his grey shorts were baggy and shapeless. Shooter had shuddered, as if he'd uncovered something unpleasant in a black bin-liner.

He now glanced down at the note he had made of the start time and then leant back in his swivel chair. Outside, it was still snowing. The boy had not yet seen fit to start writing. As he observed him, Shooter felt a shiver of professional disquiet. He was running late and had not spent sufficient time putting the boy at ease, asking him about his hobbies and favourite subjects. Was it that he wanted to get him out of the office as soon as possible? The snowflakes were larger. He knew that under a microscope they would reveal patterns, each one startlingly delicate and beautiful in its individual complexity. But he could only think how they would soon settle in a great white mass, deforming the streets and the park in which he had planned to walk during his lunch hour.

When he awoke at three o'clock in the morning, Giles Shooter remembered he had been dreaming about winter. The image of a snowdrift, somehow connected to the empty space on the double bed where his wife used to sleep, started to recede. He switched on the side lamp: his blankets on the floor; the wind rippling the curtains. Then as he swung his legs out of bed and moved towards the window, a scene from thirty years ago presented itself from the back of his memory, where it had been perfectly preserved: the last day of his inglorious teaching career:

He's by himself on the muddy playing fields at the back of the school: a bedraggled figure in a track suit; Mr Shooter to the twelve-year-olds whose game of football he's just supervised; a master too unpopular for the accolade of a nickname. After a week of snow and ice, a slight thaw has supposedly rendered the pitches playable. Giles's game consists of the least glamorous of the senior sides—the 3rd and 4th XIs. They play on a sloping tract of land, the part of the fields most exposed to the lacerating east winds. It's the Michaelmas Term. The upper goal still blackened by November's bonfire; the bottom of the pitch, where the drainage is at it poorest, is sodden and slimy with worm casts. A small pit filled with water has replaced the centre spot, but the white lines marked in January are no longer discernible.

The game was the worst he has refereed all season: so one-sided that the goalkeeper at the bonfire end was making mud pies streaked with charcoal; the backs refused to move up with play and stood, hunched with cold, in the area. But the battle by the bottom goalmouth had been fought with fearful intensity: sliding tackles gashed the mud and ripped out the few blades of grass on the wings; players surrounding the ball lashed out without regard to the laws of the game. A centre back hopped away, clutching his knee. Pushing and shoving. Vile imprecations. Something was wrong with Giles's whistle, which emitted only a barely audible dry rattle. He glanced at his watch: ten more minutes. With a furious scream, he brought the game to a halt.

Now he's waiting on the touchline. It is almost quiet. The cries from the other matches are weirdly remote, carried away on the wind. On the other side of the fence, the furrows in the farmer's field are striped with snow. In the nearby copse, a solitary rook caws and flaps away over the dark churned pitch. Giles has sent his game on a run: along the gravel path, then through the woods that mark the limits of the school grounds, across the front lawn, then back past the swimming pool to the playing fields. It is three minutes since they have galloped off and at this moment a monstrous thought occurs to him: he hasn't sent Andrew Ollaby with them, surely?

Shooter rented the consulting room when working at home became impossible. After seeing an advertisement in the local paper, he drove out to a part of the town he'd never visited before: an estate with light industrial buildings, a red-brick factory converted into arts and crafts studios, storage units and office space. The block in which he worked was the highest on the estate. If the architect hadn't placed the windows so far up the wall, Shooter would have had a fine view; instead, he had a simple prospect of snowflakes, the white dots falling slower than on the previous day. As he watched, he tried to work out which ones were furthest from him. He couldn't tell whether his sense of perspective was faulty: one moment it was as if the flakes were drifting on a level plane; the next, there was a sense of distance, the spaces between them.

His computer screen was black. He tapped a key and the unfinished report on Noel Hillup reappeared. The unnatural length of the boy's fingers suggested he had Beale's disease and yet this had not been mentioned by the mother or the school. Would it be best to shelve the report until contact had been made with the boy's medical practitioner? He sighed. *Why do you call him Slimikins, sir? He doesn't like it.* One thing was certain: Noel's hands had brought back the memories.

A knock on the door followed by the worried white face of his secretary.

"Your wife's on the line, Mr Shooter. Shall I put her through?"

He put his hands together to form a contemplative spire. He had appointments later in the day and wasn't making much progress with the report. Could Beale's disease affect a child's cognitive development? He wasn't sure.

"I'll take the call."

The snow in the frames of the left-hand window appeared to be falling slightly faster than in the right. Was this to do with his perception of events or some subtlety in the wind?

"Yes, dear."

"He's back. And do you know what he's doing?"

"Well . . . no. Obviously not."

"He's sitting in the chair in the living-room. The best one. I'm calling the police."

"Please, dear. You simply mustn't do that. Do you understand?"

"Why ever not! I've told him to go away, but he doesn't pay the slightest bit of attention."

"This is not a police matter. You can take it from me."

"I'm sorry, Giles. But it's simply not right . . . "

"Listen!" he hissed. "He will go away. He always does in the end."

Silence, black and miserable at the end of the line.

"All right," he said, relenting a little. "I tell you what: if he's still there at lunch time, give me another ring. How's that?"

"Well, I suppose. . . ."

"Fine! And whatever you do, don't contact the police."

He put the phone down. The right-hand window was slightly longer and narrower than the left. Until now he had always thought of them as identical. Was that true? There were burning white points of memory and then the glazed black gaps between them. A month ago at a conference, he'd been introduced to a colleague who had the same slightly unusual surname as a boy he'd taught during the one year and unfinished term he'd spent as a schoolmaster. He realised he'd not thought of the boy for thirty years. When he tried to visualise him, he could only bring to mind a slight figure with brown hair: the features refused to coalesce, the shape of the nose shifted, the colour of the eyes changed; even the sense of an expression, a scowl or smile, had vanished. Yet some of what occurred at that time returned to him with appalling exactitude. The only way to bury the memory was to consider it first from his point of view and then reconstruct the evening, its every incident and angle. By returning to it, again and again, asking every question, he would finally drain the tragedy of significance, deprive it of that buoyancy that made it rise, white and terrible to the surface, time after time. Only then could he commit it to recollection's deepest waters.

Unable to find proper football boots, Shooter had put on old pair of trainers. Now he's stopped refereeing, he's aware of his soaked woollen socks and damp striped shirt clammy on his cooling chest. The first red-faced runners are coming up the hill towards him. As soon as he shouts and signals to go straight to the changing-rooms, he remembers he should have asked about Ollaby. He searches for his whistle, but it has fallen through a hole in his tracksuit. Was the boy playing? He's unable to summon up a recent image of him on the pitch: a delicate spindleshanks of a child with pale red hair and cream white skin, usually to be seen loitering on the wing or giggling with the goalkeeper. There was no one on the off-games list and Ollaby had not given him a note from Matron. He tried to picture them running off. Surely the boy would have been visible somewhere near the back, his head bobbing above his thin shoulders as he lolloped along, his spindly arms flailing. "Andrew Ollaby is on no account to undertake strenuous exercise." The note in Matron's black copperplate has been pinned to the Staff Room notice board for as long as Shooter has been at the school. Of course, it is perfectly possible the boy has been shirking somewhere: in the stationery cupboard, if it's been left unlocked again, or one of the darker recesses of the changing rooms. Now the runners are jogging back to the pitch in groups.

—*Have any of you seen Ollaby?*

—*Ollaby, sir? He wasn't with us.*

—*He's not supposed to do cross-country, sir . . . is Ollaby.*

—*I know that. But was he playing football earlier?*

—*Football, sir? Was that what it was? I thought it was . . .*

—*That's quite enough. This is a serious matter.*

They glance at each other: small eyes concocting the correct answer. Or perhaps they are genuinely uncertain.

"I think he was, sir."

"That's not good enough. Either he was or he wasn't."

"I saw him. Definite," says someone rubbing blue hands together, desperate to be dismissed.

He waves them away. Most the games are heading for the changing rooms and his runners are joining them, rather than report back to the pitch: only an overweight straggler lumbers towards him.

—*Are you the last one in?*

—*Yes, sir.*

—*What about Ollaby?*

—*Oh, I think he dropped out. He was with me in the woods . . . then I lost sight of him.*

Shooter runs back to the changing rooms. Through the grey fug from the showers, he can see the master on duty pointing accusingly at items of discarded games kit.

—*Has Ollaby been through yet?*

—*No, his clothes are still on his peg. If he's one of yours tell him to get a shift on, will you? I want to get out of here.*

Shooter turns and heads back to the games fields. It's darkening now: the cloud blemished blue-grey; the red-pink seepage of sunlight on the horizon; the woods in the distance thickening with the approach of dusk. The 3rd XI pitch is a glistening black wound. Yellow lights are on in the classrooms. In ten minutes, the bell will go for the first of the last two lessons of the day.

It is beginning to snow. Yet there is a slim figure coming from the direction of the dark mass of the woods towards him: the arms move, as if repeatedly clutching at handholds; the legs are so stick-thin that at moments they disappear in the murk, leaving the frail body and blur of a head to float in the air. Shooter runs toward him, through fiercely shining snow-specks.

Andrew!

No reply but there is something about the swaying head: the boy is unmistakeably Ollaby. He's wearing his white gym vest rather than his football shirt, which he must have discarded in the woods. The wind has picked up; the snow's heavier: driving across the fields in cold flakes, burning for a second on Shooter's hot face. The boy is moving faster now, as if there's something stronger than a mere gale on his back. Then he's standing in front of Shooter, his breath ragged and terrible, worse than the tide's grate on shingle.

The five-minute warning bell for lessons. The pattering quick feet and shrill cries of boys running along paths to the classrooms. Shooter is going to be late unless he appears in his tracksuit, which is not allowed. Ollaby too will not be on time.

—I'm sorry, Andrew. I didn't intend to send you on a run; you should have had the common sense to see me before joining the others. The bell's gone. Just try to get to your lesson as soon as you can.

As Shooter runs towards the school building, he hears the strenuous breathing of Ollaby running just behind his shoulder: a rasp, counterpointed by coughing, the windpipe wheezing, the rattle of phlegm on the thin chest. For a second, he wonders how the boy can keep up, but then the sounds recede. He does not turn round—and soon he is inside, striding alone down the corridor.

Defying the forecasts, an unaccountably warmer winter's day: the vanquished snow turned to slush, a pale brown-pink where salt and grit mixed; the cloud cover wrapped up and put away, revealing a depth of blue not glimpsed for weeks; stark branches somehow softer in the sunshine, as if they might bud at any moment. Shooter walked across the estate and cut through the park to the café-bistro where he lunched if his appointments diary was light. A modern place, minimally furnished with teak chairs and tables that were all straight lines; a floor of varnished hardwood; the blank white walls that did nothing to absorb the echoing footsteps. By one o'clock it would usually be filled with young professionals pitching business proposals or taking calls while club sandwiches sat ignored next to carafes of iced water. On Fridays, the mood was sometimes more festive if big deals had been done: senior management with swept-back wings of grey hair and plush pink faces above dark suits and crested ties.

But today it was unexpectedly quiet: a few regulars grouped around the high tables by the windows; a woman with her back to him at the rear of the restaurant. Shooter took his normal alcove table and watched the passers-by, lightly clad for late November; the same time of year as the fateful football match—the first in a chain of events culminating in his dismissal and a change of career.

A waiter, whom he'd never seen before, came out to take his order. It was odd how often they changed. Somehow it added to the impersonality of the place, the lack of warmth Shooter found so congenial. In a way his dismissal, although inconvenient at the time, had not been unwelcome. An agreement had been reached: a term's wages on condition he vacated his job and accommodation immediately. Generous—in the circumstances. Of course, he'd begun to realise he wasn't suited to teaching: his temper was quick; he found too many of his pupils repellent, even though he was to some extent intrigued by the condition of childhood. Returning to university to re-qualify had been expensive but worth it: in his new profession however odious a child and its parents might prove, he never had to put up with them for long.

His drink arrived at the same time as a commotion on the other side of the restaurant: a plate dropped on the floor; a woman's sharp voice reprimanding; childish protestations of innocence and explanation. The waiter scurried off. As the woman stood up, he saw her face in profile—Mrs Hillup. Noel was now under the table, his abnormally long white fingers salvaging cutlery from what looked like the curried fish casserole with rice. For a moment, Shooter was unable to imagine what could have brought them to the restaurant to invade one of his rare moments of relaxation. Then he remembered: they were due to see him second appointment after lunch. Fortunately the waiter returning distracted them. Shooter was just about to move to the innermost seat in the alcove, when his secretary rushed through the entrance and run-walked straight to his table. He was scarcely able to credit the sudden convergence of his personal and professional lives.

"What is it?" he snapped, *sotto voce* so as not to attract the attention of the Hillups.

"It's your wife, Mr Shooter . . ."

"I've told you I am on no account to be disturbed." How often had he explained to the secretary that the strange men his wife saw at home were symptoms of her condition and no cause for alarm? "I don't care if she says there is an army of . . ."

"She didn't phone; it was the police."

"Good lord! What's happened?"

"She's perfectly safe . . . but under arrest. The call was from the Station."

As he hurried coatless out of the restaurant and into the cold day, his bill unpaid, he caught a glimpse of the Hillups, open-mouthed, and the waiter turning towards him, one arm raised.

As Shooter sits in his single room in the teachers' accommodation block correcting exercise books he will never return in person, he does not know it is the last evening of his teaching life. The lessons have finished; the day boys are being signed off by the duty master before going home. Ollaby is missing.

Shooter has corrected the first six essays on the top of the pile. They are all very bad. It would appear he has taught them nothing. He gets up from his armchair and pours himself a small whiskey, to which he adds a splash of water. Outside, the snow continues to fall, although only the largest flakes are discernible through the black squares of the windows. He sits down again, takes a sip of the whiskey and picks up his red biro. As he underlines a grammatical error, the boy, whose footsteps Shooter has just heard crunching along the path below his window, has reached the deputy headmaster's house with a message: Ollaby is nowhere to be found; his mother is waiting in the front hall.

The pile of marked exercise books on the striped counterpane of Shooter's bed grows. He glances at his watch: another three quarters of an hour to go before staff supper. He may as well try to finish the set before then. Without warning, his biro dries up, leaving nothing more than inkless indentations on the page. He searches his jacket and trouser pockets without result, before remembering there is a perfectly functioning felt-tipped pen in his desk. As he levers himself up, he hears voices: a boy and the deputy head, their tones agitated and querulous. Shooter strains to listen but catches only the occasional word: "mother" and "everywhere"—meaningless without a context? He quickly overcomes a moment of icy dread; it is nothing to do with him. He returns and opens another exercise book.

It is established that Ollaby attended neither of his last two lessons. Boys and staff have assumed he is with his woodwind tutor or Matron. Now registers and timetables are consulted; peripatetic teachers and the boy's father are phoned. Ollaby is often absent, away for reasons musical or medical. But this time there is no record. The headmaster's wife arrives to reassure Mrs Ollaby, who is taken to the drawing room and offered a cup of tea.

A sharp knock on Shooter's door, which opens as he responds. The cold air from the corridor and the headmaster come in.

—Andrew Ollaby's vanished. I'm told he was on your game. That correct, Shooter?

—Yes, headmaster.

—Did he turn up?"

—Yes. "

—The duty master says he didn't come into the changing rooms.

—Andrew was the last one in.

—Did you see him through?"

—No, I was running late. The first bell had gone.

—So you don't really know where he went, do you?

—He was running behind me—and towards the changing rooms. I remember that quite clearly.

—Well, since you're the last person to see him, Shooter, you'd better help us now. We're searching the grounds.

As the headmaster leaves, slamming the door behind him, Shooter picks up another exercise book. He is not to be ordered around so peremptorily; only when he has finished the task in hand will he join the others. He glances at the name on the cover: Andrew Ollaby.

As Shooter reads, pausing to underline spelling mistakes and add comments in the margin, the deputy headmaster, most of the boarding staff and several senior boys are scouring the playing fields, the copse, the front gardens, as well as the rough ground behind the science laboratories and the tennis courts. As Shooter finishes writing his comment, which is longer and more encouraging than usual, at the foot of the essay, the deputy headmaster and two monitors, armed with torches, reach the spot in the woods, where Andrew Ollaby lies face down and breathless at last, his long delicate legs awry, the back of his head already covered by a layer of snow.

Once they were outside, Shooter told his secretary to go back into the restaurant and inform the Hillups their appointment had been cancelled. He glanced both ways and then ran across the road. There was still no snow falling, but the limpid blue sky reminded him of Arctic waters; a few ice floes of cloud dissolved in thermals far above. He soon reached the park, where he pulled out his mobile phone. In summer, every bench would be occupied, but it was cold enough now to deter the hardiest picnickers and office workers with packed lunches. He sat down and dialled the number his secretary had given him. Mrs Shooter, he discovered, has been detained for wasting police time. On four occasions she's contacted the station to complain of mysterious intruders, who had always unaccountably vanished by the time assistance arrived. Shooter explained: his wife's memory was dis-ordered; the medication no longer effective; a measurable degree of cognitive loss. Then more recently new symptoms: ethereal visitors or sometimes a sense that her house was not her own. His apologies. A difficult month; two of her carers on holiday at the same time; a need for further support. And yes, he would be grateful if an officer could drive her home.

A duty of care, that's what we have. Shooter had left his car in a side street not far from his office. One of the early symptoms of his wife's condition was being unable to recall which level of the multi-storey car park she'd parked the Honda only to discover she'd left it outside the hotel where they were staying. *In the circumstances, it would be best if you leave at once.* The headmaster's voice. *Of course, you have a right of appeal to the Governors.*

Fortuitously the car keys were at the office. With the roads clear, he experienced a frisson of unfamiliarity on reaching the by-pass in half the usual time. *Personally I can't think of a better example of professional negligence than sending a child with a hole in his heart on a cross-country run.* A dual carriageway for five miles: he must concentrate. No slush on the roads, but the hard shoulders corrugated with dirty snow. He wondered whether a WPC would be with his wife when he got home. Making her a cup of tea. *What really surprises me, Shooter, are the string of lies you told me last night; all which you still maintain, in spite of the evidence to the contrary, are true.* He slowed down, signalled and turned off the motorway. *So what am I to say to Ollaby's parents? That he reported to you on the playing fields and then ran back into the woods to die?*

Already Shooter has arrived: the detached house with bay windows where he'd lived with his wife for twenty years. No police car parked on the gravel drive and so presumably no WPC to reproach him for leaving his wife alone. He unlocked the door and at once she emerged from the sitting-room, which in recent months she'd shared with assorted phantoms of her imagination.

"Thank heavens you're back. I've had another intruder."

In spite of her condition, she remained superlatively well-attired: a blue dress bought from Liberty's of London; an antique brooch pinned to her breast; her make-up carefully applied; the grey waves of her plentiful hair tinted and permed. Only a year older than Shooter, she'd not lost the air of authority that had made her a commanding figure in the bridge club. It was easy to understand why her mental competence was not always immediately questioned.

"I think you'll find, dear," said Shooter, resting a hand gently on her arm, "that if we both go back to the sitting-room your gentleman visitor will have left."

"But it's not a man. That's what I told them; much good that it did me. It's a boy?

"What sort of a boy?"

"Well, not a very small boy, but even so far too young to be wandering around by himself in other people's houses. He's in your study, right now. Up to heavens knows what!"

Shooter walked quickly down the corridor and into his study. Inside, it was snowing—and dark. He reached for the switch but couldn't find it. For a moment, there was nothing but the flakes, so clear he could see their asymmetrical crystal patterns as one by one they were blown across the fields of darkness, sparkling individually for an instant in front of his microscope eye. Then his sight began to adjust: the filing cabinets with their soft moon-metal gleam; the shape of the bookshelf; his desk and the hump of a swivel chair.

Was it snowing in here because his wife had left a window open? Certainly some strange luminosity was flowing in the curtains. The must from old books and boxfiles has been replaced by the tang of ice and the scent of wet black leaves. Perhaps an intruder had forced an entry. He'd never believed in his wife's visitors. Yet now there was a shape in the corner, something growing there or discarded? Clothes to be taken to the charity shop? A head on the top of the pile; then slowly the rest of the body snaked upwards, turning taller, thinner, paler. Marfan's disease. Then Ollaby's face, level with his, ice-flakes spinning in dark sockets; once again, the terrible breath issuing from the cracked mouth. But now he was loftier than he'd ever been in life: an up rush of wild white clothes and spiralling limbs, soaring to the ceiling. Oh Slimikins! Then Shooter remembered the question he'd forgotten to ask, which had been worried at since the retreat of the glaciers: *what is it like to die, alone in the woods, in the snow and the dark?*

THE VOICE OF THE PEOPLE

Alison Moore

O N THE DAY OF THE PROTEST, GLENDA decided to drive out to the retail park to buy weedkiller. She was just setting out, getting into third gear, when a pigeon dawdling in the road caused her to brake hard. The pigeon seemed oblivious, even when Glenda's two-tonne car was virtually on top of it. Perhaps the car actually was on top of it, because having stopped dead, Glenda could not see the pigeon anywhere. She was just about to get out to look beneath her wheels when she saw the pigeon wandering to the side of the road. She watched its strangely sluggish progress, and then drove on, towards the edge of the village.

The garden was really Dougie's responsibility, but work was taking it out of him these days. On his day off, he just lay on the sofa, with the cat asleep on top of him, or sometimes the cat fell asleep on the carpet or in the lengthening grass, wherever it happened to be. Dougie himself did not really sleep, he just lay there, with no energy for Glenda, or for his projects: at the far end of the overgrown garden, a half-dug pond had been abandoned; and the second-hand furniture that he had bought to spruce up was gathering dust in the spare room. The last piece he had done was the little table on which their telephone stood: he had spent weeks sanding and then staining and varnishing it, although Glenda hated it, the darkness of its wood, and its rickety, skeletal legs.

She had just got onto a faster stretch of road leading out of the village when another pigeon staggered out in front of her car, not even flinching away from the vehicle as she skimmed past. She wondered what was wrong with these pigeons; they were like zombies.

It was not just Dougie; it seemed to be everyone who worked at that factory. They had all lost their pep. No one in the village liked the factory, although the men needed the jobs; it employed hundreds of them. It was an ugly, stony-faced building, ruining what had been a nice stretch of riverside, at a spot where the locals used to swim—some still did, but not many. The women had been worrying about the factory's emissions, about what exactly was going into the air. Sometimes the smoke that went into the clouds looked yellow. And was anything going into the river, anything that should not be? Dougie used to fish there, but he did not do that anymore. And there was that terrible smell, which had to be coming from the factory.

At the bend, where the road turned away from the river, there was a pigeon, flattened against the tarmac. Its grey wings were splayed around its crushed body. Its underbelly was turned up to face the sky, to face the wheels of the oncoming traffic. These pigeons reminded Glenda of the summer outbreak of flying ants, which did not fly off at the flap of a hand as houseflies did; or they reminded her of the houseflies themselves, the listlessness that came over them at the end of the summer, leaving them too slow to avoid the swatter. But she had never before noticed the phenomenon in birds or other creatures.

Glenda had written the council a letter, which the other women had signed. The letter asked questions about those emissions; it suggested that the factory might be affecting the health of the workers; it requested a thorough investigation and the suspension of operations pending the results. The men had not signed the letter. The letter had been forwarded to a secretary who would liaise with the relevant committee; it was then, after somebody's holiday, to be discussed at a forthcoming meeting. Not having heard anything for a while, Glenda had left messages on a council answerphone. In the meantime, the women were going to go on a protest march. "We never used to take things lying down," Glenda had said to the women. "When we were students, we used to march." They used to go down to London, on coaches; they had marched through the capital in their thousands, to force things to change. "We *should*," the women had said in response. "We *should* do that." Since then, they had been meeting every Wednesday morning at Fiona's house. Fiona had provided refreshments while they made placards, nailing boards to wooden sticks and painting slogans on them—WE WANT ANSWERS!—slogans that they would shout as they marched. They had photocopied flyers to put through people's letterboxes. They had notified the local paper.

Glenda glanced at the dashboard clock. It was almost noon; they were due to meet to start the protest at one o'clock. They would march down Union Street to the river, right down to the factory. They would stand outside that grim building and stamp their feet and shout, make some noise. Someone would have to respond; something would have to be done.

She pulled into the car park of the Do-It-Yourself store, disturbing a couple of birds, which flapped up into the air and flew away. She parked near the entrance and went inside the store. As she entered the gardening section, she recognised a neighbour who was standing looking at the lawnmowers. Glenda said hello. She could not think of her neighbour's name. The woman continued to stare at a lawnmower, and Glenda thought that she had not heard her, but then the woman said, "I've been here for hours. I just can't decide."

"Are you coming on the protest?" asked Glenda.

"I just can't decide," said the woman.

Glenda turned away and picked up a spray-gun bottle of ready-to-use weedkiller. She took it over to the till, where the cashier was sharing a joke with a man who had bought paint in a shade called "Nursery". The colour looked putrid to Glenda. The man turned away and the cashier looked at Glenda and said, "Are you all right?"

"I'm fine," said Glenda, lifting her free hand and touching her face. "It's just a rash." She handed over the weedkiller.

"Two pounds," said the cashier.

Glenda looked at the silver and copper in her purse. She could not be bothered to count out the coins. She handed over a note and waited for her change, and then stood struggling with the zip of her purse. She took her weedkiller and moved towards the exit, aware of the cashier watching her as she walked away.

She strapped the weedkiller into the passenger seat, as if it were a child. She did not want it sliding around, busting open, weedkiller going everywhere. She drove home slowly, carefully.

It was after one o'clock when she returned to the outskirts of the village, where she found Fiona sitting on the kerb, with a placard on the pavement beside her. Glenda came to a stop and wound down her window. She said to Fiona, "Have they gone already?"

Fiona raised her eyes. "Who?"

"The other women," said Glenda. "Have they started the march?"

"No one else has turned up," said Fiona.

"Oh," said Glenda. "Well, I have to take the car home, then I'm going to walk back down here and join you. Even if it's just the two of us, we can still march down to the factory. We can still make some noise." She drove home, passing a car that was so badly parked it looked as if it had just been abandoned mid-manoeuvre, and stopping to move a child's bike that had been left lying across the road. She backed her car into a kerbside space and took the weedkiller inside. She put on some sunscreen and checked her appearance in the mirror. She was wearing the olive-green eyeliner that Dougie had once said brought alive her copper-coloured eyes, but now she wondered if it was just making her look a bit ill. She put down some food for the cat.

By the time she got back down to the corner with her placard, Fiona was no longer there. Glenda thought about going to the factory anyway, on her own, but she did not really think she had the energy.

When Glenda got home again, she filled a glass with water from the tap, and drank it standing at the sink. It was past lunchtime, but she was not hungry, and there was still food in the cat's bowl from before. She went through to the lounge and sat down in an armchair, next to the second-hand table with the phone on it. She had disliked that table, she thought, but now she could not really see what was wrong with it; she did not have any strong feelings about it either way. Next to the phone were her phone numbers. There was the number for the council—she would have to call them again at some point, about that letter she had sent to them. And there was Fiona's number—she ought to call her; she ought to call everyone. The protest would have to be rescheduled. The numbers seemed to blur; she must be tired. She switched on the TV and watched the afternoon programmes. She was still sitting there when Dougie came in from the factory. He lay down on the sofa.

"Have you seen the cat?" asked Glenda.

"Uh-uh," said Dougie.

In between TV programmes, Glenda said, "I'm going to go up to bed," but she did not actually move for a while.

Eventually, she got to the bathroom and picked up her toothbrush. She looked at herself in the mirror. It felt like being stared at by a stranger. Her eyes were the colour of dull pennies. She left the bathroom and got into bed. She looked at her book but she felt that she just wanted to sleep. She realised that she had somehow not cleaned her teeth after all. She thought about her unbrushed teeth rotting in the night, but she did not get up again; she just left them.

A week and a half later, Glenda found the cat beneath the back wheel of her car, against the kerb. It must not have moved out of the way when Glenda was parking. She had not been any-where since the previous weekend, when she went to fetch that weedkiller.

She stood at the kerb, trying to remember what she had come outside for. There was no point driving over to Fiona's house: the group had dissolved.

Glenda's placard was still propped against the front wall. She picked it up, looking at the faded lettering: WE WANT ANSWERS! Had she written that? It did not sound like her, like something she would say. Perhaps she had got somebody else's placard by mistake. She stood on the pavement, near the kerb. She could see the factory chimney in the distance, down by the river, belching its mustard smoke into the sky. Dougie would be taking his lunch break soon. She could walk down there and try to see him, see if he was feeling any better. If she found, on the way, that she did not want to keep carrying the placard, which may or may not have been hers, she could just leave it somewhere.

She stepped into the road, with the sign hanging down, the message (WE WANT ANSWERS!) dangling in the gutter. She moved out into the road, slowly, as if she were stepping through the mud at the edge of the river, mud in which Dougie had seen fish lying belly up.

She did have a sense of the size and weight of the vehicle that was coming towards her. She was not oblivious to the juggernaut that was bearing down on her. But it felt more peripheral, more distant, than it was. She was moving forward, looking towards the far side of the road, but with no great sense of urgency.

CURB DAY

Rebecca Kuder

EACH YEAR IN MAY, WE MUST HAUL A ghastly number of items to the curb. It's mandatory. For years now. We don't even question it anymore.

They start collecting the third Friday at dawn. They start at a different house each year. No one knows how they choose. We have to be ready. We have to produce. They measure what we put out.

I hate the scramble. Stacks and boxes and cabinets to paddle through. I need to touch each scrap, have a conversation before discarding. I promised myself I would start early this year: the bottom of the house, because that's where time and gravity rule the world of accumulation. In the basement last Thursday, I unfurled three new bags, thinking it would be easier to add scraps as I found them. Into one bag I tossed parts of several broken coffeemakers full of mealy dust, a chipped mixing bowl, two ancient light fixtures that will never shine again, and reams of disintegrating-rubber-band-wrapped greeting cards from when I was a child and forced by Mother to write too many thank you notes (those whimsical bunnies, kittens, now greeting no one).

Despite all this gathering, I still need more.

On the basement shelves last Friday, I found a box marked *fragile*. Grandmother's handwriting. As I opened it, the box fluttered apart. Inside I found stained lace curtains used as padding. I unwrapped them and extracted the first treasure: a Depression glass refrigerator dish. Grandmother kept butter in it. For nearly thirty minutes, I held the dish. Its lid is chipped. I don't use it, clearly. Into the trash bag nest it went, with the padding. In a rush of energy, I opened another box and found several bottles of Dickinson's Witch Hazel. One still had a lick of amber in the bottom. I held this bottle even longer than the butter dish. Finally, I opened the bottle, its corroded metal lid snowing bits of rust on my lap, and inhaled. Grandmother ... long-dead ... setting her hair, cotton balls of witch hazel baptizing strands of silver, twirling hair and pinning the pin curl clips ... Next, her ancient Noxzema jar, with a layer of cracked white glazing at the bottom. The things that she touched and used. The invisible backdrop to her days. The second bag would wait. I stopped to fix lunch.

The light fixture and butter dish bag waits at the foot of the basement steps. I've been tripping over it since I left it there last week. The object (trash bag) becomes an action (trip), becomes more and also less than what it actually is. The bag is no longer a bag. What it actually *is* shifts, is another way of putting it.

All this tripping over bags. You would think I'd just stop going down there, but the yearly collection won't allow me to avoid a single corner of this gaping house. So much for starting early. Before I bring *that* bag to the curb I will have to peer inside again and confirm I can jettison the contents. Must double-check. Starting early only makes more work.

I had a visit from the local government. They knocked at the door, said they want us to produce at least a third, *one whole third more* than last year. Hard to fathom how. Last year was brutal.

Last year I put out three bags and still earned a caution notice. But the more we produce, so they claim, the safer we are, and the less they will bother us. The less they will come knocking at the door, faces full of cheer, plastic-framed mouths buttering us as if we are warm toast. *Oh, excuse me, but in searching our records, we find that historically, you haven't put out enough. Our records indicate that last year, you didn't seem to be in earnest. This is your complimentary warning. We assume you plan to endure?* Words spoken in that tone of buttering, nothing in writing. I have looked in several of the mirrors recently. Behold, I am not warm toast. I am human. The plastic butter-ghosts stood on my porch with their knives to spread spread spread buttered requests and warnings, as if all we live for is to lug out some ever-increasing amount. Each year there is math, and each year the only thing that accumulates is my unwanting. Now, a fourth bag?

No one objects or complains. And with what we've seen, why should we? We follow rules and drag, drag it all to the curb. But I worry there might be something in those bags that I will need again. Some wire, some lace. Can't some of it stay in my house? Deciding what to expel is excruciating. I spent yesterday hunting an appliance until I remembered I had bagged it last year; it's gone. How will it be possible to find enough?

I have been moving up and down flights of stairs all morning. Up, down. I go to the basement. Groping through the butter dish bag, something sharp bites my hand, rips the bag. The flimsy membrane of the bag won't hold it. Why do I always buy such cheap bags? Mr. Warner next door—his bags are ridiculously sturdy. No one on our street produces like Mr. Warner does. He walks from house to curb carrying two at a time, off the ground. No dragging, not for Mr. Warner. An optimist. Yesterday I heard him whistling! Something from the '50s. Those bags of his are big enough to hold a dog's carcass, a wet one. A wet dog's carcass, I tell you. I tell you I'm going to *take* one of his bags. He puts them out days ahead, no fear of anyone taking one or two; he has so many. I would hide one or two fat ones in my basement for next year. I would.

It's going to be tight this year. Yes, I admit I have trouble letting go. But even if I didn't. The noise in my house is quieter when scraps and layers remain undisturbed. With my scraps intact it's a warmer house; my walls are safer; I can exhale. Sometimes I can relax. You might not believe this but when I keep scraps, the house exhales and sometimes relaxes. Without the scraps, the wind comes through, even on a warm day. Those scraps are all that is keeping me safe.

But they said *one third more* and my hand is bleeding. Damn that sharpness, which has now squirmed to the bottom of the frail bag. And the bag is leaking. Just now I dragged it up from the basement to the parlor and was followed by a glistening trail, something a slug would leave behind. Bile, it's more like bile than the iridescence of a slug. No slug glitter. Just gut glitter. I can smell it. I bet you can, too.

Why won't they allow us to put out casings or gears? I have plenty of those. Of course I have the old windows, but they are uncharacteristically firm: they will not take old windows. No, the plastic mouth-frames say *no*, and say it so kindly, with thick, buttery shine, *no, none of that, sorry dear, we don't deal in that.* It's Curb Day, I say, so who cares? Come the third Friday it will all get eaten by the machines anyway. What's the difference? They never answer that one.

This afternoon, Mr. Warner whistled out another two bags, show tunes, and now two more bags before nightfall! He must have skipped dinner. Where does he get all his contents? That last bag, I swear, is the shape of a commode. Hulking as if it's waiting for a fight. What else can I pry from my house to lug out there?

Before it's really dark I should go ask Mr. Warner where he gets those extraordinary bags. He probably buys them in bulk. He must have a couple of empty bags for a neighbor, but he's never shown a shred of sunshine my way, so why should I expect it this week, of all times? No, it's each for themselves right now.

Survival. My puny pile will make his pile look better, more correct. And to ask him, I'd have to crawl across the house and turn on the water, make myself ready to present.

I used to admire him so much, though I never told him. Should have done.

Yesterday I tried to go ask, but he was out all day, likely at the bag store. He was likely thinking ahead. But I go at things the right way; I *examine* the scraps. Take my time. He must have found some shortcut. There's no way he could do it all, do it properly, and have so much to put out. I have a theory he's been rooting through the alley. I have a theory he has something buried back there, waiting to fill bags. I have a theory he puts his stale food in there. Food is prohibited. Everyone knows that.

I am not going to the attic unless I have to. I can't breathe in the attic. It is thick and humid like stepping into someone's mouth.

Curse this third Thursday, bright and shiny like a slap in the face. Me with only the one bag and no more scraps to sort. I need at least four. Four! It will be impossible to avoid the attic.

The attic door is sticking. Who did that, was it the humidity and the old scraps pasting themselves in the crack? At midnight, I violate whatever is holding the door shut, yank it open and go up to find the one box I've avoided all year. I look everywhere up there in that mouth. In the layers of stacks I find plenty I must keep, but cannot find that box.

I rake the entire house; I look inside the walls. With only seven hours until dawn, I lean into bed and cough out a breath, exhale. It hurts my lungs; even the air is against me. Something, a fin beneath the mattress, jabs my side. I roll over and peel back the bedding, the heavy lumps of mattress. It's the box. She's there after all.

This box holds what remains of my mother. I really cannot put her out there, not this year.

I should not say that Mr. Warner has never shown me any sunshine. He came to my door one day with a stack of things. Months ago now, but he did come. He knocked. I had been watching, so I knew it was he. (I have that window on the top floor. If he had looked up he might have seen me. There are a lot of hatboxes in that window, but I rigged a place to watch when I need to.) When I answered the door, he was so polite, so upright, as if the only thing on his conscience was whatever propelled him toward my porch.

I tried to act surprised in the way we are supposed to do. Not seeing each other, fortresses keeping to ourselves, upholding the social contract as if he could have been anyone and not my neighbor of twenty-seven years. As if he hadn't been over there combing his tidy yard when my Joe left me, as if he didn't see any of that. *Oh, yes? May I help you?* I said to Mr. Warner, as if I didn't know and hadn't studied the (perfect/ineffable/imponderable) drape of his trousers.

He looked at me and for a moment he smiled. Finally he said *sorry to bother you, but your mail was delivered to my box*. Some of my orders, a pile of things I was waiting for and had forgotten to expect, so many items coming and going, so many scraps, too many to remember.

He could have kept my orders for the collections. He didn't have to bring them to me. But he handed me the stack and left.

Mr. Warner lives alone, now. Mr. Warner and his multitude of upright bags. Like a brood! If I had that many bags, maybe I would walk around with that straight a back, such a straight back. When he came to my door months ago I felt he had broken my skin. Months ago and I still feel it. He had never been to my porch before, never breached my front walk. He had always stayed on his side of the fence with yard work, his side so tidy, but there must be frayed edges somewhere; no one is that clean. I don't like to think of him on my porch, the time he spent there standing so upright, the crooked boards beneath his feet.

———

When the municipality first announced the Collection Program, they held a meeting for the town. So many years ago. Strange and almost sweet to think back. The meeting was well attended: hundreds of us went to the town hall because it was back before Distraction and Apathy. Mr. Warner was there early, and so was I, and a handful of others. Joe was already gone by then. Mr. Warner has always been upright, one of those scrubbed people who look shinier than the rest of us. At the meeting, Mr. Warner asked questions about volume and purpose, about usage. The dignitary who officiated wasn't very forthcoming, so Mr. Warner had to shift how he asked questions. He became more direct. There was a look of glee on Mr. Warner's face as he asked his questions.

If I'm honest, I'd say I thought him fabulous back then. I'd even say I felt an affinity, a peculiar crush on him. His skin so shiny and clear, how his lips moved when he asked questions. When the dignitary spoke, Mr. Warner wrote more questions on index cards, scribbling as the dignitary described the Collection Program. Every mote of dust surrounding his body was dancing, itchy and ready to learn, ready to follow the instructions if only they were clear enough.

The dignitaries probably didn't care what people thought of the Program. Our town never specialized in clarity. It has always been a place of blur and innuendo, a place where you could get around just about any obstacle by thinking it through and finding ambiguity. But Mr. Warner demanded clarity. Mr. Warner wanted specifics, to understand the requirements, dimensions, and scope, essentially: how many bags would keep him, or anyone, alive. His whole posture demanded to know, and when these relatively new dignitaries announced the Program, it was as if a thing awoke in Mr. Warner, a beast with a need for order. As if this meeting liberated something that had been hiding in his spine.

He also asked what would be done with the Collections. On the stage there were uncomfortable shiftings in seats when he asked about that. I myself had been wondering and hoping someone would ask. Of the hundreds gathered in a sea of awkward yellow folding chairs, Mr. Warner was the only one who wrote questions on index cards, and asked them. I was proud he was my neighbor, at the time. Now it's all mixed up and muddy: my cheap and leaking bags and his sturdy and incontrovertible bags, if that's the word I want. It's all tangled ropes.

I don't sleep much at this time of year. When I do, it's accidental, the human body crashing against the need to emerge from under water so it can keep beating its heart. Pitter pat. How things in my cheap plastic bags do, and don't. Perry won't pitter-pat anymore, hasn't for years. Poor Perry. Perry was a songbird, was a song, so long ago, Perry such a pretty bird, didn't ask to be frozen like that, poor Perry. I will go and find Perry. Not a good true just end for that winged creature, not the best epilogue, but I must find all I have and give it over, can't give my box of Mother up, not this year, and this other winged creature, the one I sometimes fancy myself to be, must live. Perry is the way. Perry will save me, will keep *me* from being stuffed into one of those bags. My own are too cheap, but Mr. Warner's heavier bags would fit me, would carry me off the ground to the curb, elbows and all, and if I don't take Perry out there, poor little popsicle, it will be me. I have time now, before dawn, time to pickaxe Perry from his protective ice layer, poor little song, poor little mite who might have been a song forever. What's wrong with a forever song? I can't leave him for whoever would find me.

They never answered Mr. Warner about what happens with the collections, what they *do* with the collections, but I don't want to find out this year, not yet, not me in the bags, not yet.

Briefly: At the meeting, Mr. Warner was not satisfied with their answers. That honeyed, naive first year, when we were all adapting. Most people put out whatever they could. Not much different from the weekly trash collection. We had no idea of the consequences, just that it was mandatory. They called it a Pilot.

Mr. Warner, who had asked so many questions, lodged a small protest that first year. He simply put out nothing.

The second year, when Mr. Warner again put out nothing, they came on the third Saturday. I watched it all.

They came from a long car. Two men got out and came to his porch and talked to Mr. Warner for a few minutes. Then another man in a green suit emerged from the long car and walked to the porch, past Mr. Warner and straight into his house. Five minutes later the green man came back out, arm in arm with Mr. Warner's wife. She was wearing a floral dress. Everyone but Mr. Warner got into the long car and it drove away. Since then, Mr. Warner brings out the bags.

When I'm asleep I have plenty I could take out. When I'm asleep, often I have an entire wing or floor of a house that I inhabit. A wing or floor I'm just discovering. Sometimes three vast floors of well-organized belongings, or furniture, or boating equipment. Things that I have no use for, nor attachment to, not even, in particular, *my* things. Maybe I should go to sleep now. If I could have one of those dreams now, it would be grand, because I could stuff into a bag and drag any number of things to the curb, and wouldn't Mr. Warner be shocked and possibly impressed, come morning? A dream of an unencountered wing, tonight, would certainly save my life.

Just now I thought I heard something clunk in the west part of the attic. It could be anything; my imagination has whole warehouses of question marks stored inside. It's full of those clunks that happen whenever you aren't looking, whenever you stop listening. Just now it sounded like ice, like being trapped somewhere cold like inside a chunk of ice and that makes me think of Perry again, poor Perry. It's been a lifetime since he sang anything. After Perry died, my father froze him. My grandmother's bird.

Father got Perry for Grandmother, to cheer her in the final months. She named the bird for that man who used to sing even and steady, nothing upsetting or foul in his songs, just beautiful, bland, scrap-less notes. The bird sang in the cage by her bed in the dining room after she couldn't manage the stairs, and then sang in the cage in the hospital when she went there. I never heard him sing in the hospital. I never saw her dining room bed. I was not around until after she died. Too far away, or something. From Father I inherited Grandmother's house, full of her items, his items, scraps that keep the wind outside. From Father I inherited Mother. Everything was frozen by time, in that way we are all of us covered and surrounded by frozen things—a chair made seventy years ago, a piece of sheet music, *They go wild, simply wild, over me*, sang my aged aunt, Grandmother's younger sister, recalling the days when she was a flapper. The manic face on the man on the *wild, simply wild*, sheet music that now hangs on my wall is a bit like the face on my father. They go wild (simply wild) over me is a bit like the bird in the cage in the hospital, doing the only thing it really knows how to do. I inherited a frozen song.

Perry in a layer of ice in a plastic bag must be in the freezer, still. No cage now except death and that ice. I am going to walk down to the freezer and look. I am. It might be possible to make my quota if I can find the dead bird that should have been buried years ago. And maybe they won't notice I've included an item that breaks the rules—*no carcasses*. They are a little vague on the rules, but I've always assumed that meant nothing you've eaten the best of, leg of lamb and so on. Nothing gnawed. Frozen canary might fly, as it were, especially if I wait until the first stretch of morning and Perry stays frozen.

Light will arrive soon. I can make it, if I stay awake long enough to chip away the ice that has certainly grown around the plastic bag that holds the songbird . . . maybe it's just as well he's no longer alive and singing. Grandmother died long ago and can no longer hear the thing warble in that soothing, uncontroversial way, and maybe Perry can help *me* now.

The ice will help, more bulk.

They won't notice the debatable carcass. Perry is not really what I think of as a carcass, anyway. Such a light thing, even with the ice, a thing of so little substance. A song gone on the wind. Mr. Warner can whistle and carry to the curb all he wants. I have Perry. I know I'll find him there in the cold; I know I'll have time to chip it all away if I start now.

ENGINES OF THE OCEAN

Christopher Slatsky

CORA, DEAREST . . .

On first receiving the letter, Cordelia chalked it up to a simple postal error. Her father had died long ago, and the note she'd sent thanking him for the birthday present had no reason to come back to her decades later. There wasn't an explanation as to why the envelope had been opened then sealed shut again.

Whoever had resealed the flap had done so quite expertly, the intrusion nearly undetectable. Cordelia would have blamed the odd occurrence on a postal employee's curiosity, then subsequent attempt to cover their act, if she hadn't seen written in blue ink at the bottom of the paper beneath a fold-crease now loosely held together by fibers:

Cora dearest, I still have your salt in my hair.

She wasn't sure how to proceed, if at all, until recognizing the swooping curves and loops of the letters as her father's handwriting.

The forgery was perfect. Why anyone decided to make such an effort and follow through on the hoax all these years later was baffling. And how had the sender known to perfume the paper with the moist, salty scent of her father's private room?

That room in the basement. The stuff of childhood terrors. She'd never actually entered it, only glimpsed the brick-lined interior on those rare occasions the door had been left ajar. The unpleasant scent of the space was forever in her memory. A sweaty residue—or was it more like the ocean?

The room had always been off-limits. It was where her father wrote his ideas down, sketching various machine designs as a hobby. A frustrated engineer, relegated to a field service technician position for the city's water department, she'd never seen any of his finished projects actually operating. The weird machines of unknown function never made it from the page to fruition, and nothing ever led to a promotion or increased income.

While Cordelia's mother had always been the doting, familial type, her father was a loner. Always hidden behind that door in his study, working at all hours so frequently that Cordelia and her brothers made jokes about him being a serial killer. The secret room became an abattoir where he disposed of his victims. Or maybe he was a mad scientist, building underground engines to take over the world. The children's gruesome imaginations ran rampant.

But Cordelia knew better. She remembered her father spending time with her, playing tag in the yard, listening to him read her favorite books. Their frequent trips to the beach were particularly memorable. She'd been awed by the power and immensity of the ocean. The mind was an unreliable thing, all too often preserving dark moments while neglecting the joyful. There was some light in between the cracks of a dreary childhood, and most were illuminated by their adventures at the ocean.

Cordelia decided to take the long drive back to her old home to satiate her curiosity. Maybe this would quell any remaining vestiges of childhood nostalgia. She didn't expect to find anything of consequence, much less evidence of ghosts writing letters from beyond the grave. But it was as good an excuse as any to visit the neighborhood she hadn't seen in so long.

The 10-hour drive to Oak Field was uneventful. The town had been hard hit by the recession. All of the shops she drove past were empty. Blank windows with the occasional FOR LEASE sign interrupted the monotony.

She passed the Klein Theater where she'd seen her first film unaccompanied by any adult. The front of the building was boarded up, the side appeared to have collapsed due to fire damage. The small parking lot was weed covered, parking lines faded and barely distinguishable.

But she was surprised to see that the corner grocery story was still operating. The front door was open, screen door shut with a handwritten OPEN sign taped to it from the inside. Cordelia had spent many an afternoon loitering here, drinking Cherry Cokes and dropping quarters into the *Meteor Madness* video game that was obsolete even when she was a teenager.

Nobody greeted her on entering. The cash register was unattended. A curtained off area behind the counter led to the employee's break room.

The interior was a relic from a bygone age: cereal boxes with mascots retired from the company's marketing were still on the shelves. All of the magazines on the rack were dated 30-years ago. Even the old *Meteor Madness* video game was in the corner, the screen flickering with pixelated chaos. Flavors of sodas that were no longer bottled filled the refrigerator in the back. The store was immaculate, free of dust or grime. A cold bottle of Cherry Coke in hand, she headed to the front to pay.

She rang the silver bell on the counter next to a jar of pickled eggs. She didn't want to think about how long the rubbery snacks must have been soaking in there.

Minutes later, she rang again. Something made a noise in the back, but it must have been the refrigerator's fan turning on. "Hello?" Cordelia called out anyway.

Nobody answered behind the curtain. Resigned, she left the correct amount of cash on the counter, dropped the drink into her purse, and left. As she reached the car, her phone rang.

The number was from a lifetime ago.

She'd called it countless times from school to let her father know she was ready to be picked up after volleyball practice. Called it more times than she could remember from Janice's house, to ask her parents if she could stay the night.

She touched IGNORE. She'd only imagined the call was from her old home. She'd transposed the numbers, shuffled them around from disparate particles of memories. A wrong number.

Walking to the house from the convenience store would have been a nice nostalgic stroll, but was also out of the question—the sun was setting and the streetlights weren't on yet. The sidewalk held too many shadows, offering the potential to hide someone. The nearby houses didn't have any lights on either, though people had to be home since most had cars parked in front.

An unusual white crust on their hoods and wheels made Cordelia suspect the vehicles hadn't been driven in quite some time. Opening her own car door, she felt crystals scrape against fingertips. It was too gloomy to make out what it was, but the substance was granular and rough. Tentatively, she touched her tongue.

She tasted salt.

Everything was layered in a fine dusting of the mineral. Something to do with the soil salinity, flushed out by neglected sewage systems, or improper irrigation perhaps? She took a long drink of her Cherry Coke, rinsed her mouth out, spat the liquid on the asphalt. Cordelia imagined she heard a rumbling, as if great engines under the earth's salted crust were churning to life.

She drove down the darkening street to her childhood residence.

Pulling up to the curb, she noticed an unusual atmospheric phenomena playing out in the sky. Bloated sheets of silver mist rolled overhead like a brackish spill. The house was coated in a white rime, though it was far too warm for ice to have formed.

The home still looked like a cream-colored layer cake, the crown molding a delicate filigree like piped frosting. The colors were vivid, and there was no weathering damage visible. Someone must have bought the place after her father died—she wasn't sure about the details.

It looked as if nobody had lived here in the years since; while the house had been maintained, the driveway was pitted, and the weeds jutting from the cracks made her doubt anyone had parked here in quite some time. A house left vacant for decades made little sense.

The sun had lowered further, but the streetlights were still dead. Their malfunction emphasized the emptiness of the neighborhood. Cordelia couldn't hear any traffic from the main road two streets over. It used to be so loud when she'd play in the front yard as a kid.

The lawn was low dry yellow grass, speckled with tiny white bits. A rectangle of blackness caught her attention. The concrete lid covering the water meter was gone.

Those meters terrified her as far back as she could remember. The purpose of those clockwork machines in the ground eluded any rational explanation—or so 6-year old Cordelia insisted. She'd been absolutely certain the meters were buried on the lawns so they would be easier to access from *below*. Her mother's explanation that they were how the city determined water usage and billed accordingly had never been an acceptable answer.

Their subterraneous purpose was a mystery. Her father's playful claim that meters monitored the neighborhood criss-crossed with catacombs filled her with anxiety. He'd said this with a wink, but simply entertaining the possibility that devices worked their oily machinations at all hours to measure the rising waters and their mysterious tides was traumatizing.

She once lifted the concrete lid of a meter and bashed a brick against the glass cover inside. The glass shattered, the meter buzzed angrily, but the dials continued to turn, documenting their strange unfathomable course. She was certain that vandalizing the machine meant the equipment beneath would fail, allowing the oceans to rise, the gutters to overflow with water. Her neighborhood submerged in vast seas.

The lock on the side door to the garage was corroded, the wood frame soft with age. A heavy shove and it swung open and she was inside the old place. The garage was empty, but the door leading to the living room was unlocked.

Little had changed inside. The exact same wallpaper pattern that always made her think of fluttering eyelashes. The very sofa in which she'd spent many a Saturday morning watching cartoons. The ancient TV was still on the same nightstand, though the crack in its screen meant it was probably no longer working, even if the electricity were operational. The curtains were the same fabric and color, the carpet powdered with salt but recognizably original. Even the rotary dial phone was intact. The receiver was on the hook, though it wasn't possible to tell if anyone had touched it to call her. Everything was preserved.

Hadn't her mother taken the furniture with them when they'd moved? It was so long ago and she was so little when everything happened the memories were conflicted and fragmentary. Cordelia couldn't fathom why so many of the house's old trappings remained.

A thin covering of fine salt particulates on the coffee table quivered from air currents as she moved. Flecks of pale grit on the walls, furniture, and floor sparkled. The air was soupy like brine.

Cordelia looked into each room, closet, and entryway. Of course there was nobody here. For one brief moment she thought she'd best call her brother in case anything happened here, even though ghosts weren't real. And if there existed anything that deserved to be called such, they'd be insubstantial, composed of enough matter for light to bounce off of, but little else. A phantom wouldn't be able to touch, strangle or make a phone call. Spirits were just history projected against nostalgia.

Entering her old bedroom, she found it empty. The wallpaper near the defunct light switch was peeling at chest level. Beneath a layer of white powder was written CORA age 6. A dash mark showed her height at the time. She pulled away the curling flakes to reveal a series of numbers and marks descending down the wall to the age of 2. The only reminder of who she used to be.

A short flight of steps crunchy with white granules led down to the basement. She faced the door to her father's study. The door was covered in powdery splotches that may have been hand prints if she wasn't certain the place was uninhabited. The knob turned freely, but the door was jammed, or something was blocking it on the other side.

She remembered her mother telling her that dad wasn't well, and prolonged care after brain death wasn't in his best interest. At the time, Cordelia was so young she didn't fully understand why her parent was essentially no longer her father. The thought bothered her so much she refused to visit him in the hospital, throwing such a fierce tantrum in the lobby a nurse said she'd watch her while the rest of the family went in. It was long ago, and any repercussions from her absence had dissipated like ripples from a single grain thrown into the ocean.

Cordelia explained away her shame over the years: he'd fallen into a coma; her visiting would have been all but meaningless even if he could have comprehended his daughter's presence. A contraption pointlessly functioning because nobody had the courage to switch it off. When he did pass away, he took any and all reasons as to why he'd decided to retreat to his private room on feeling the stirrings of a blood clot in his head.

And Cordelia was certain he'd made that choice. He may have died from a stroke, but she'd no doubts he'd felt that black eyed dog nipping at his heels while retreating into his personal space for the last time. Returning to the scene of her father's tragedy should have been emotionally resonant, but she felt only a flake of the guilt she'd expected.

After heading back upstairs, she walked into the dining room. A pristine picture of the house formed in her mind, but long ago, when everything was bright and immaculate from her mother's persistent housekeeping. She'd always cherished talking to her parents here at the table. They'd discuss school; what she wanted for dinner; their favorite TV shows; made the same silly jokes they'd always made to each other. All while sitting at that familiar antique oak dining room table shipped from Poland at great expense.

If she closed her eyes, Cordelia could see them again. She gazed at their faces lovingly, marveled at the familiarity of their presence. The way her father moved his hands when talking, the way her mother's gray hair curled at the temples. If she concentrated, she could hear the parakeet they kept in a small blue cage in the living room, chirping and fluttering in its confines. She smelled potpourri bundled in a wooden bowl and a lavender scent blown in on a breeze through an open window.

Cordelia could picture the yard out back as it used to be; bright green behind the sliding glass doors. The pomegranate tree used to be full of fruit, the trellis built by her dad's hand covered in ivy. Roses once grew; the stone birdbath once active with aviary life.

They'd play out here, her dad chasing her around a lawn that felt enormous to a child. He'd throw her little body into the air, always catching her just before she hit the ground.

Cordelia wished she could tell her father how much she missed him. Even in her memory he seemed delicate, as if he were propped up in a chair and a touch would collapse his body into inert bits and pieces.

It was an odd recovered memory, but she remembered glimpsing something unfamiliar in the back yard. A drainage pipe poking out of the ground, the metal surface scaly with rust. A distant moaning emanated from the pipe.

There was nothing visible from where she now stood, but she distinctly recalled the dinner plate-sized opening to the pipe had been covered with mesh to prevent wildlife from entering. And it hadn't been a moan, but the sound of waves from deep down. Another thought came to her, something more aggressive than nostalgia. An old dream perhaps, or several dreams, more vision than reminiscence.

Something had once moved behind her. She'd glanced back to see the pomegranate tree fallen over. Its prodigious, leafy branches blocking the entrance back into the house. The upturned roots had gouged a deep depression in the ground. Cordelia thought she may have peered over the rim of the hole to see a large brick-lined room below with several brick-lined passages trailing off into darkness. The sound and smell of the salty sea drifted from within.

The memory gripped Cordelia with such intensity she could still hear the ocean nestled in her ears, like the moist beginnings of an earache. But she was here, in the present, the table solid beneath her hands and her parents no longer part of her life. She stood, her handprints remained behind in grainy salt particles over the wood's polished veneer.

She looked through the sliding glass doors into the backyard. The pomegranate tree was intact, but there was no hole in the ground, and the lawn was dirt. The sun had nearly fully set, the scant remaining light emphasizing the salt spread across the yard. Her memory hadn't been particularly frightening, just troubling, like hearing the tinkle of broken glass in an unoccupied room late at night. Only the crisp dome of the sun was visible now, the sky nearly sown with stars.

Turning from the sliding glass doors, she walked down a short hall into her brothers' shared bedroom. It was slightly *off*, something missing that didn't quite match what she'd once known. The rational part of her brain knew her old home never looked exactly like this—her memory must have created as close an approximation as possible, yet realized it hadn't quite managed to recreate the details perfectly. She'd fallen into the uncanny valley of sentiment, a childhood imperfectly replicated.

Her parent's room was unchanged. The bed was still here, though the blankets were missing. The shape of what Cordelia assumed was a body was stained onto the mattress, presumably in sweat. Fine crystals of salt glittered inside the outline. The figure was too thin to be either of her parents.

The hutch displaying her mother's ceramic collection remained, the little figurines unmoved in all this time. The sensation of returning home, decades after her father's death, was all rather bittersweet. But an air of distress persisted. None of this made sense.

She picked up a journal on the nightstand. The first page read,

> *On some distant wedding anniversary, I remembered you handing me a book made out of silk, each thin page covered with painstakingly ornate handwriting. But I wasn't sure if this had actually happened or if I'd merely wanted it to be true. I don't have any silk books in my collection.*

It may have been her father's handwriting. Cordelia wasn't sure.

She heard someone moving around in the back yard. Racing to the sliding glass doors, she saw the suggestion of a pale face fall from the pomegranate tree, then roll to the other end of the yard.

Once outside, she was convinced that what she'd seen must have been a flurry of salt tumbled on the wind. She cast her phone's light beam around. The pomegranate tree's leaves were green, but the little remaining fruit had split, oozing a resinous sap swarming with gnats. Globules of the syrup had gathered on the ground. The phone's light shone upon the piles like rubies.

The fence defining the property was mostly intact, though a few patches of weathered holes allowed a glimpse into the neighbor's back yard. Cordelia leaned down to peer through. What the phone light could reach revealed that the area around the swimming pool was a dirt lot.

The pool was filled with salt.

A sound at the stone birdbath caught her attention. Shining her light on it showed the slimy water was squirming with tadpoles gathered around a U-shaped object, like sperm around an ovum. She blew on the water to part the animals. The tadpoles moved enough for her to see they were clustered around a rusty orthodontic retainer.

Flakes of salt fell gently from the sky. She hurried back inside.

A noise, as of something crumbling apart as it moved, came from the basement. She rushed to the steps.

Whatever had been preventing the door from budging must have fallen away; this time, it opened with no difficulty.

Her father's private room was smaller than she'd expected, only furnished with an office desk and chair. One corner of the desk was piled chest high with papers. The room reeked of the ocean air. So many memories came cascading back she was momentarily breathless.

Something shuffled in the shadows at the back of the room, sounding as if it had difficulty maintaining its shape. Cordelia thought of a broken hourglass, spilling its bulk across the floor.

She poked the phone light's beam into the darker recesses. There was nothing there but a brick wall, crumbly segments on the floor here and there.

The layer of salt on the desk had been recently disturbed. She shook the paper on top of the pile, looked it over, then another. Each bore a sketch her father had been working on, with a date recorded at the bottom. She rifled through several more, increasingly reluctant, though compelled to look at each and every one of his concepts drawn over the years.

The pages had been scrawled in an amateur's hand. The clumsy drawings of an intellectually deficient child.

She noticed a sheet on the floor beneath the desk. Shaking the salty residue off revealed blue words clearly written by her father:

> *Salted with fire, they seem to show*
> *How spirits lost in endless woe*
> *May undecaying live.*

The room was increasingly dank. What must have been faulty pipes in the ceiling failed to keep strands of salt water from splashing in increments. The wet touched Cordelia's skin. Salt granules spackled her clothes and hair.

This was where her father had thought his last thoughts. Perhaps he'd retreated here to capture a perfect moment, freeze time at the only instance he'd ever been happy, in here, working on his ideas that were nothing more than scrawls of nonsense. But what moment of his life had seemed more bearable than previous moments? By himself, building useless engines in this room? Away from her?

Cordelia realized the depths of her sorrow. Too many years had gone by to make amends of any sort, but she felt the weight of grief, the burden that comes from absence.

The room was small, but she was suddenly confused by its layout. She couldn't remember where the door was. Taking a step towards a wall, she knew she'd made a mistake, so she turned to face another wall. She found herself before an endless progression of brick corridors that hadn't been there before. A pale crust glittered on the bricks and floor.

Deep down the corridors came the gentle sound of waves lapping at an unseen shore. Machinery churned within damp niches. Backing away, she bumped her calf against an obstacle. She squatted and gripped it to get her bearings.

She held a pipe poking out of the floor. Lowering her face to the grate-covered opening, she breathed deeply of the ocean air. It was increasingly difficult to see. There was too much salt on her face. A shuffling, laborious gait moved towards her.

Something ashen appeared. A crystallized thing preserved in a ghastly semblance of life. Cordelia suddenly lost sight of it, her eyelids lowering from the accumulation of salt.

Someone spoke, but Cordelia couldn't understand over the roar of the ocean. Hands gently touched her face. She tried to pull away, but they caught her with such certainty she knew she'd never hit the ground.

Gritty arms held her with waning strength. She returned the embrace so tightly pieces of the body crumbled away. There was so much salt in the air now. The engines ran faster, pumping more spray into the room, though quieter, more efficiently. Cordelia could now hear the figure whispering,

Cora dearest.

Now that they were together again, maybe they'd be able to visit the ocean once more. Maybe she'd be light enough to lift above his head and twirl until she was dizzy and exuberant like she used to be.

But Cordelia knew she was too big now, and her father was too long gone to do much more than hold her while she fought back tears with profuse apologies.

They needed to get away from this room, back to the rest of their home that had miraculously sustained itself all this time. But the gleaming lattices of salt were already too bright, and her father was far too dilapidated to sustain himself.

Who would repair the water meters when they eventually break down? The panicky thought came to Cordelia with such despair she could only accept the inevitable with quiet grace.

Her father's minerals dissolved in her blood, particles collected on her skin. The lantern of her world was shuttered, the flame within snuffed out by the pinch of an unseen hand.

The murmur of the ocean continued to flow out of the pipe from far below.

SUN DOGS

Laura Mauro

IT HADN'T RAINED IN CLOSE TO SEVEN weeks the night I met you. The rain-barrels were down to the last silty dregs, the skies stubborn in their pale blue clarity. I wasn't even certain the car would start; it chugged to life on the third attempt, emitting a choked gurgle like a throat full of sand. My sole back-up plan: an ageing Chevy Cavalier, tyres balding, paintwork leprous, a quarter-tank of gas which might not even get me the whole way to Wildrose.

My parents had been preppers; I should've known better. Boxes of ammo next to the bread in the pantry, towering crates of bottled water in the basement. Rucksacks in the hall closet piled with emergency supplies—should the End Days catch us unawares—and a framed cross-stitch on the wall: "Failure to Prepare Is Preparing to Fail." Pastel colours, delicate bluebell border; a portent of doom, handcrafted with love.

I left at dusk. The sky was a cut mouth bleeding out onto the western mountains. It seemed there was not a single soul out on the highway that night except for me. If the Chevy broke down, I'd be screwed; cell phone reception was null this far out into the desert, and hadn't that been the entire point in the first place?

Going solo on the edge of civilisation: the complete amputation of my former life, gangrenous with regrets.

I had a foil blanket in the trunk, a protein bar in the glovebox. Half a bottle of water in the foot-well. Not good enough. I kept an eye on the fuel gauge as I drove, foot light on the gas. There was a gas station at Wildrose, a general store and a gift shop. A campsite out back full of shiny-white RVs, gleaming despite the dust. Desert adventure for kindergartners. A thought came to me in my mother's voice, criticism from beyond the grave: *at least they have water.*

The way station was just visible on the horizon, a halo of light lingering over the scrub and above it, a fat, pale moon. Not the blood-red moon of my childhood terrors, heralding the arrival of the End Days—peeling back the curtains, peering up at the sky through parted fingers, because you could never tell when it might happen, and you would have to be Ready when it did.

The asphalt gleamed black in the headlights. Something ducked out of the road, into the sparse cover of the scrub. I saw it in the rear-view mirror; bright eyes sparked momentarily, the shadow of some slender creature crouched just off the roadside. Kit fox, maybe, or bobcat. I turned back to the road.

A man stepped out in front of the car.

I hit the brakes hard. The car arced wildly; my hands were tight on the wheel, my eyes squeezed shut, awaiting the impact, the crunch of bone against metal. When I opened them, the car was still, and the man was intact, staring at me with wide-eyed surprise in the middle of the road. I unbuckled the seatbelt with trembling fingers, aware now of how sore my sternum felt, how fast my heart was beating. Slowly, I stepped out of the car.

The man took a step forward. Clutched tight in his hands was a hunting rifle. .204 Ruger, walnut stock. *Approach with caution.* He had a canteen of water at his hip, heavy-duty boots, scuffed and well worn. He scanned me. "Are you hurt?"

My ribs ached with each exhalation, muscles contracting over bruised bone. "I'm fine," I said. His shoulders were loose, his fingers slack on the gun. No obvious signs of hostility, but I was a lone female on an empty highway, and I was unarmed. I could almost hear my daddy rolling in his grave. "You ought to take care if you're coming out here in the dark. I could've killed you." I swallowed hard, tasting sour adrenaline. "I could've killed us both."

The seashore hiss of cicadas filled the momentary silence. "I'm sorry," he said, after a time. He wasn't looking at me. His eyes were focused on some point beyond the car, out towards the darkened scrub, dust-pale in the moonlight. I wondered what he was looking for. "Are you alone?" Eyes locked on mine now, a bright, lunatic urgency. I looked quickly over my shoulder, judging the distance to the car. "It's not safe to be alone out here," he said, "especially at night. There're some vicious creatures around. You got a gun?"

"Yes."

"Keep it loaded. Carry it with you." Staring back out at the roadside now, finger inching closer to the safety catch. His paranoia made my skin itch, as though it were contagious. "A kid got killed up at the campsite yesterday. Some kind of animal got him. You'd best take care."

"I've lived out here for some time now," I said, mindful of how he held the rifle, how intently he scanned the horizon. My muscles were tight, my breathing a little too quick. "I can handle animals just fine."

He snorted. "They're getting bolder. People feed them like they're pets. Try to get pictures with them, if you can believe it. They've forgotten to be afraid of humans and they ain't keeping their distance like they used to." He stepped off the road, into the sand. I flexed my fingers, loosening too-taut ligaments. I thought about asking what he was doing here, alone on the highway; what he was looking for out in the scrub. I caught the sudden glint of his rifle scope as he turned, the muscular heft of him illuminated in the headlights, and I thought better of questioning him.

The car had come to rest at an angle, bisecting the highway. I slipped into the driver's seat and locked the door behind me. The man was a little way off the road and moving further, cautious steps like a hunter flushing out a deer, gun raised and ready.

This time, the engine started on the first try. I hit reverse, pulled the car around; wheels ground on gravel. I peered over my shoulder as the car reversed.

And then I saw you, cowering in the back seat; skin and bone and blood, torn blue jeans and a man's leather jacket; I bit back a cry of surprise, staring in rapt horror at the bright blood pooling on the seat beneath you, finger-smeared over your face like war paint. You looked up at me, eyes wide, finger pressed urgently to your lips, and I could sense your terror so acutely I could almost feel it; a shot of panicked adrenaline straight to the heart.

I had no water and precious little fuel, but I swung the car round. He couldn't fail to notice the change in direction, but I paid him no mind as I hit the gas. If I drove fast enough, he'd never know where I'd taken you. If the fuel held out, we might even get there in one piece.

"It's going to be okay," I told you, though I had no idea if it really would. You pressed your face into the worn fabric of the back seat, exhausted; your limbs were slack, your eyes closed. It looked as though you were dying. The thought terrified me, not because I cared about you, but because, although I could shoot and skin and gut a deer without so much as flinching, I had never in my life watched a human being die.

The wheels ate up the distance. Above, the night gathered like a bruise. I wondered what had happened to you. How you came to be out there, all alone in the desert, and whether it was you the man had been chasing in the dark.

The car ran dry a quarter mile from home. I had to carry you the rest of the way, first on my back, then in my arms when you at last fell unconscious. My bruised ribs ached with the weight of you. Your skin was hot, as though you'd baked a while in the sun; you felt empty in my arms, exsanguinated, breathing shallow. Helpless. I thought about leaving you there. Taking you a way off the road, out into the dunes, so that when death came for you—inevitably, I thought, cradling your bird-hollow bones—the coyotes and hawks might pick your remains clean. But home was close, and your heart still beat, and I thought *we've come this far. Only a little further now.*

Home was a brick and timber shack built on land that had once been my father's. He in turn had bought the land for next to nothing from a man who'd run a campsite there in the early 90's. It was where my dad had always intended to 'bug out' to when the End Days came. As it turned out, heart failure came first. He hadn't prepared for that eventuality.

I didn't want you in my home. You have to understand that. Those last hundred metres to the house were beset with doubt. I couldn't have left you bleeding by the roadside, entirely at the mercy of an armed stranger; I knew the ways men could hurt women, how inclined they were towards it when the power balance shifted in their favour. I could've taken you to Wildrose, made you someone else's problem, but if he had been chasing you—and my instincts were screaming that he had—then he would surely think to look for you there. I can't honestly say why I took you with me except that in all my years, I had never seen anyone look quite so afraid as you had in that moment.

You stirred when I laid you out on the couch, mumbling something unintelligible. I peeled off your jacket, pulling limp arms through worn sleeves. Your limbs were slender but your muscles were tight as cord beneath the skin, the lean physique of a long-distance runner. I wondered when you'd eaten last. Adjacent to your right shoulder was a puckered hole, a glistening crater of flesh and bloody, matted shirt.

I cradled your head against my chest as I lifted you up, hoping to find an exit wound. Whoever had shot you had done so from a high angle, standing above you; the exit wound was lower down, suggesting a diagonal trajectory. Clean margins. One hand cupped the back of your skull as I traced the radius. I pried at the shredded edges of your shirt, peeling it gently away from the wound. Your muscles tensed; if you weren't so weak you might have fought me.

"It's okay," I murmured absently. Your dark hair was thick

beneath my fingers, the matted pelt of a wild thing. "You're safe now."

Slowly, you relaxed, allowing me to peel away the fabric. There was blood on the couch, a faint scrim of dirt. Your lips moved against my skin, barely a whisper. It sounded like 'thank you'.

You slept while I cleaned your wound and stitched the edges together—not a beautiful job, but good enough. I washed my hands, aware that I had only half a bottle of water left, no fuel, no way back to Wildrose. My nearest neighbours were two miles away. I didn't want to leave you alone, but that half bottle wasn't going to stretch much further. I didn't know when you'd last eaten or drank. You'd need water far more than I would when you woke.

I sat on the porch and lit a cigarette; I blew smoke into the breeze, watching it dissipate. It was long past midnight and my bones felt heavy beneath the skin, my eyes weary; I hated the idea of sleeping only yards away from a stranger. I'd lived alone for years, long before I even considered relocating to the desert. I'd never been close to my brother as a child; my school reports bluntly stated that I did not play well with others.

The lunatic cry of a coyote cut through the night. The sky was starless, the moon obscured behind a thin veil of cloud. I'd smoked almost down to my fingers. When the sun rose, I would set out with my hat in my hands and ask the Burnetts for water. They'd be quietly scornful, but I could swallow that, and they wouldn't deny me.

I stubbed the cigarette out on the step and came back inside. You watched me approach, and I saw how you cringed away from me—the simultaneous drawing inward of all your muscles, humble as a beaten dog. I hated you for that; I hated that pang of sympathy, that sharp, sudden ache in my heart.

"I'm not gonna hurt you," I said. I sat down opposite. The foldout chair creaked under my weight. You flinched. "I promise you that. But you can't stop here for long."

Your eyes were wary beneath your sweat-tangled hair. You knotted your hands in the blanket, thick with dirt beneath the nails, black crescents on bony fingers. "I don't want to," you replied, curt. Your voice was water on gravel.

"Is there anyone you want me to call? I don't have a phone here, but there's a family nearby who do."

You shook your head and looked away, staring sullenly at the curtains. It occurred to me then that you might be as unaccustomed to the company of other people as I was.

"All right. Well, as soon as the sun comes up I'm heading out. I won't be gone long; I just need to beg a little fuel and some water from the neighbours. I'm running bone dry."

"It's going to rain."

I laughed at that. "They've been saying that for weeks and I haven't seen so much as a drop."

You laid your head back on the pillow. "It's going to rain," you said, quietly now, a voice on the precipice of sleep. Your eyes were closed. "Not now, but soon. Can't you smell it?"

The air smelled of stale cigarette smoke, the ripe rust stink of blood. "I won't be gone long," I said. "An hour, maybe. I don't usually get visitors but I'll lock the door just in case. You'll be safe here 'til I get back. You should rest until then."

I rose from my chair. You were already asleep, or perhaps you were pretending. I imagined you were watching me as I left, peering through barely-parted lids. It was difficult to tell in the dark. I pulled the front door shut as I passed through the hall, turning the lock with a barely audible pop. I hadn't locked my door in years. I resented you for this sudden uncertainty.

The bedroom window framed a nascent sunrise; rose gold blooming slowly outward. I lay back on the bed, fighting sleep. You were at the periphery of my vision, utterly still. You might have been dead, and in that moment I might not have minded.

I laced my hands behind my skull and waited for morning.

You were asleep when I left. I decided against locking the door behind me; it felt like imprisonment, shutting you inside that tiny house in the gathering heat of the day. And part of me hoped you'd be gone by the time I returned. That you'd wake up to an unlocked door and smell freedom.

It was barely six AM and already the chill of the night had dissipated, a thick heat building behind the blanket of cloud overhead. I set out with a five-litre bottle under one arm, a jerry can in my free hand. The Burnetts lived out towards the hills. They'd been out here a long time, had raised and home-schooled their kids and were now alone, enjoying the solitude of their retirement. The kids moved to San Francisco, got jobs in tech startups and organic bakeries and never came back to visit. I imagined they must still dream about sand; hear the whisper of the wind along the dunes even in the depths of sleep.

The Burnetts' home was brick-built, a chimera made from parts scavenged over the best part of a decade and extended over and over, a tumorous mass expanding slowly into the scrub. They tolerated my presence; I was far enough away and suitably unobtrusive, not even a smudge on their wide blue horizon. I did not intrude upon their isolation.

Peggy was in the yard as I approached. High-waisted blue jeans slung on motherly hips, skin the shade and texture of old hide. "What brings you up here so early, Sadie?" She'd affected a perfect neutrality, but she glanced briefly down at the water bottle under my arm the way a rich man might glance at a beggar's bowl.

"Real sorry to trouble you, Peggy," I said. Humility was not my strong suit, but the shame that bowed my head was genuine. I had, after all, failed to prepare. I explained the situation without once mentioning you; as I spoke, the contortions of her face and haughty arch of her eyebrow reminded me so much of my mother it almost hurt. *Serves you right*, I imagined her saying, mouth twisted in spite. *You'll die of thirst, lazy girl. The Rapture will catch you with your pants down and your engine dry, and then you'll be sorry.*

She didn't. She listened, and did not say a word until I was done. And when I was, she beckoned me wordlessly to the back of the house. Six blue water barrels sat lined up in the shade. A far larger rain barrel was just visible beyond the curve of the far wall.

"Don't tell Dan about this," Peggy said, taking the water bottle from me. I heard her knees creak as she squatted. I thought about offering to help and knew she'd be offended. "Lord knows he means well. He's a big believer in tough love, you know? Says it's a harsh world out there and young folks have got to learn to fend for themselves, 'cause it's only gonna get harsher." Water spilled out of the tap, into the bottle. I realised then just how parched my throat was. "No doubt he's right, but that don't mean you can't lend a hand every now and again. It's about compassion, ain't it? That's what it's all about in the end." She shut off the tap, screwed the cap onto the bottle. A spattering of droplets fell from the tap, sinking without trace into the dust. Peggy stood, grimacing as her knees stretched out. "Smart girl like you, you'll do better next time, won't you?"

"I will, Peggy. Thank you."

"There's a little gas in the shed out back. Dan won't notice it's gone. Mostly it's me who drives these days, you know, since my boys moved away." She smiled then, and there was sorrow in the crease of her eyes, the starburst of wrinkles etched into her face. "Do you see much of your mother, Sadie?"

I blinked. In the two years since I'd shacked up in the desert Peggy had never once asked me anything about my life before. I thought about all the tinned food my mama had sent me over the years, always on the brink of expiration, piling up in the spare bedroom of my San Diego apartment because old habits died hard. "She passed away," I said. "Eight years ago."

"Oh." She looked down at her feet. Then, with sudden brightness: "Well, let me get you that gasoline. I'm sure you've got better things to be doing than standing around, listening to me harp on."

I stood in the shade as she went to the shed, gait slow and careful. I wondered if she might be lonely out here, with only wild beasts and a taciturn husband for company; whether perhaps the blissful isolation the Burnetts had worked so hard for was everything they'd built it up to be.

By the time I got back the sun was up high, and you were gone.

You'd folded the blanket and left it atop the pillow, streaked rust-brown with dried blood. It was the only sign you'd ever been there, and even that seemed vague, as though that carefully folded bundle might have been my own doing. I picked it up. The scent of you clung to the blanket: sweat, faintly sour but not entirely unpleasant. The sharp, animal smell of your hair. I realised I was a little worried about you—out there, exposed to the rising heat, weak and fatigued. The wound was still fresh. It might fester, the stitches might split, anything might happen to you and I had abandoned you. I swallowed down guilt as I put the blanket in the wash basket. I knew nothing about you except that someone had hurt you, and that you had been afraid, and that I had let you go. I hadn't even asked your name.

I set the water bottle down in a pool of shade outside the house. Inside, I fished out a yellow legal pad from the stash under the couch; there was a half-written article scrawled in upward slanting script, and a deadline for the end of the week. I'd hand-write articles and drive over the state border into Nevada, where Jackie Emery would lend me the use of his computer and internet connection for five bucks an hour. A few articles a month would keep me in fuel and supplies. I'd come to live the kind of pared-down, uncomplicated life my parents might have considered too sparse and therefore doomed, ultimately, to fail.

Pen hovered over paper. Through drooping eyes, my handwriting warped into inscrutable hieroglyphs, marks without form or meaning. I hadn't slept in over twenty-four hours and my eyes were heavy with grit. Just a nap, I told myself, curling up on the couch. The cushions smelled of warm, old dust, and faintly of you. Empirical evidence of your invasion, a stranger's presence yet to be erased. Strange, then, that I didn't seem to mind.

A jaundiced afternoon light cast the room in shades of faded bruise. I'd slept longer than I'd intended. My damaged ribs seemed to groan as I stretched out. A glance at the clock on the windowsill revealed that despite the gloom it was just past three o'clock.

Outside, the sky sweltered behind still clouds. The water bottle was warm to the touch. I poured a little out, washing the sweat from my face and neck; cool water wound a slow path down my spine, coursing down my arms. There was no breeze, no movement; it seemed that the world had stopped without warning and curled in on itself, interminably paused, waiting for something terrible. There was only the mechanical whirr of cicadas in the long grass, the air as still and silent as a held breath.

The first raindrop hit the ground hard, like a thrown penny.

And then the rain came, violently, and all at once. I found myself soaked and winded; the curves and concavities of my face became a waterfall, hair clinging to my face like black kelp, the shock of water in my nostrils, my open mouth. A premature twilight fell and in that sudden darkness I saw you. You were a silhouette against the deluge, growing darker, gaining corporeal form; you were unhurried as you tracked barefoot across the gleaming hardpan, dangling something unseen in your left hand.

I finally found the wherewithal to retreat into the house. My boots left great puddles on the linoleum as I shoved into the tiny shower room, retrieving the only two towels I owned. When I returned you were at the doorway, expectant but still, as though awaiting an invite. In your sodden state you seemed very small, as though the meat of you had been washed away; as though beneath it you had only ever been an imitation of a girl, fashioned from wire and draped in skin. Your smile was almost shy as you handed me your prize—a pair of skinned jackrabbits, rose-quartz flesh wet and glistening.

"I was right," you said, pointing to the sky. Your wounded shoulder drooped. You must have been in pain, but your face betrayed no hint of weakness; your lips retained a hint of a smile, a feral Mona Lisa.

"What's your name?" I asked.

"June."

Your name conjured up vibrant wildflower meadows, a cobalt sky reflected in a smooth, still lake. A Pacific Northwest spring. "As in the month?"

You smiled again, baring bone-white teeth. "As in the month. But I was born in November."

"Come inside," I said. "You'll drown out here."

So you did.

I didn't want you in my home. Except that somewhere along the way—pulling needle and thread through your open skin, perhaps, or your quiet belligerence, when you were hurt and afraid but still defiant—somewhere in among all of it I felt myself beginning to relent; a palpable sense that something inside of me had opened a little, exposing a glimpse of viscera, the hint of a rib. I hadn't wanted you there, but there you were anyway, my borrowed t-shirt hanging loose from your shoulders, wound cleaned and freshly bandaged. Your hair hung half-dried and leonine: dark honey shot through with silver, though you could surely be no older than twenty-five.

"A boy got killed up in Wildrose," I said.

You stared at the rain running down the window, silver rivulets like molten metal. "I heard an animal tore his throat out."

"Do you believe that?"

You turned your head. Your confusion was tempered with a narrow-eyed wariness; an inherent mistrust of the path I might be leading you down. "Shouldn't I?"

I sighed. "I know that man shot you, June. And he would've killed you if I hadn't found you first. What kind of a man hurts a woman the way he did? What kind of man hunts a woman down like an animal? You think someone like that would flinch at harming a child?"

I saw the flinch in your limbs, the way you folded in on yourself; I saw the defiance bleed slowly from you and felt an answering ache in my chest. "Don't," you murmured. "Please."

"What happened to you?" I wanted to grab you by the shoulders and shake you until the answers tumbled out. I wanted to hold you and soothe your ragged nerves. "It's your business, June, I know that, and maybe I don't have the right to ask questions of you. But I've never seen a person look as scared as you did that night."

"Okay." You had the look of a hunted thing, hunched and ready to bolt, but there was steel in the rigid set of your spine. "Ask me one question. Just one. But then you have to drop it, okay? Because I don't want to talk about this anymore. I want it to go away."

You're in my house, I thought. *If you're in danger then I might be too. I deserve to know.* Rain clattered relentlessly against the windows, washing away seven weeks of dust. Pouring into the rain barrels, better late than never. I should have felt trapped in that small room, forced by the elements into your sullen vicinity; I should have resented every inch of space your body occupied. "Why you?"

You smiled then, though there was no joy in it; you drew your knees up, planting bare feet on the couch cushions. A hint of slender ankle, of downy dark-gold hair. "Because he thought I was somebody else," you said. The rain thrummed like an arrhythmia against the roof shingles. You closed your eyes and said nothing more.

Every morning I woke to find you gone. You were meticulous in your absence; the couch cushions were carefully rearranged, the blankets folded and replaced in the hall closet. You moved like a ghost, silent despite the creaking floorboards; the sun would rise, and you would already be gone.

In the first few days I would linger at the windows, squinting through the heat haze at distorted shapes; I would sit smoking on the porch as the sun crawled across the sky, watching shadows shift and lengthen. I didn't know if you would come back, at least in those first days; I found myself luxuriating in the space you left behind, glad of the silence but aware, unexpectedly, that something vital was missing. I would look up from my work and expect to feel your eyes on me; I would listen out for the hiss of your feet on dusty floorboards and hear only silence.

You returned as quietly as you left. The sun would slink behind the distant mountains and you would emerge from the deep shadows as though you'd been born there. I never saw you coming, no matter how long and how carefully I watched for you. You came in on the evening breeze, smiling that clever half-smile and you would pause at the door, an odd formality, waiting for me to invite you in. I always did.

I never asked you where you'd been.

We sat side by side on the porch, the air redolent with the musty wet-weather scent of the creosote bushes. Against a spilled-ink sky sat a spattered multitude of stars, their light guttering like faraway candles. I told you I could navigate using the stars as guidance; that it was one of the first things my father taught me as a young girl, my earliest lessons in preparedness.

I pointed up. "You locate the North Star," I said, plucking your hand from your lap. I guided your outstretched finger to where the North Star sat, bright and lonely. "You see? That's Polaris. And just across from there—those stars—that's the Big Dipper."

"The Great Bear," you said, and pulled my hand along with yours as you traced the shape in the sky, a wide, faltering oblong. "She's monstrous, bigger than any bear you've ever seen. And those four stars—" punctuating each one with the tip of your finger, as though they were mere yards away "—those are pissed-off mother coyotes chasing her across the sky. My mom told me that. She said that in those days, food was scarce, and the bear had grown so hungry that she would dig up coyote dens to eat the pups. And even though the coyotes were weak and hungry and scared to death of that bear, they vowed that they would fight to protect their babies. So when the Great Bear came sniffing around, they joined together, these four fierce coyote mothers, and they chased her. They chased her for so long and so far that when they stopped to catch their breath, they realised they'd run right up into the sky."

"I've never heard it told like that before."

"It was my mom's version." You drew your hands to your chest, long fingers forming a lattice across your heart. "My dumbass sisters never listened to her stories."

"You don't get on with your family?"

"My mom died. My sisters . . . we don't see eye to eye. I guess I don't like the way they live."

I let out a snort of bitter laughter. "I know how that feels."

"I listened to all my mom's stories. I liked that we saw the stars differently to everyone else. And I guess now . . ." you were dazzling in the dark, eyes like Baltic amber set into the pale bronze of your skin; you were a small and perfect sun, and I was willingly subsumed by your gravity. "I guess you do too, don't you?"

I smiled. I felt like you'd given me something of yourself then, a small gift by which I might begin know you. I looked up at the Great Bear, at the four coyote mothers chasing her in perpetuity through the heavens, and wondered who you were, where you'd been all this time, why you kept coming back to me.

The men came a few days later. They arrived in a rust-coloured station wagon, kicking up plumes of dust behind them like the tail of a comet. I stood out on the porch as they pulled up, piling out of the car in a tangle of identical plaid limbs and khaki vests.

I straightened my back, set my shoulders square. I didn't know any of them, though I had a vague sense that I'd seen one or two before—perhaps out at Wildrose, working the gas pumps or the campsite. Three of them, each with a rifle at their hip. Men on the hunt.

A tall, thin man stepped forward. "Afternoon ma'am." He tipped his cap, an antiquated notion of politeness. Beneath it, a sparse rim of sandy hair traced an oasis of sun-pink skin. "You live out here by yourself?"

"Yes, I do." None of them were the man who'd shot you, but I was wary all the same. Men like that, they travelled in packs, associated closely with one another; they wore their guns like membership badges. I didn't like the nature of his question, the way all three of them ran their eyes the length of my body, assessing me as though I were a prize sow. "Can I ask what it is you want?"

"Sorry to disturb you, miss," the second man said, with a wide-eyed humbleness I knew was feigned. My palms itched. I wished I'd brought my gun out with me. I wished I'd never have to touch the damn thing again. "Only there's been a situation down at the campsite. Some sort of animal going round hurting folk. Rabid, maybe. Killed a couple kids . . ."

"A couple?"

"Yes miss. Little girl got killed yesterday afternoon. Wandered out a little ways into the desert. Her momma never even knew she was gone 'til it was too late. Anyway, Bryson at the store said there was someone lived on her own out in the desert. He asked us to check on you, make sure you're able to protect yourself."

"I'm able," I said.

"We've seen coyotes heading out in this direction," the thin man said. "Could be there's a pack of them somewhere nearby. You'd best take care . . ."

"They *say* it's an animal," the third man said suddenly. "But nobody's got a lick of proof. Nobody's *seen* an animal do any-thing." His companions stared at him for a moment, uncertain how they ought to proceed; clearly, this was not the agreed story. "There's a lot of transients round here, is all I'm saying. It's damn near impossible to keep track of who's coming and going. You could do anything and nobody'd know so much as your name. You want my advice, ma'am, you'd be best off watching out for strangers."

I'm a grown woman, I thought, staring at the three of them, the earnest way they presented themselves; guns respectfully lowered, pink-cheeked and sweating like pigs beneath their heavy khakis. They thought me soft, I realised. They thought it a fluke that I'd survived this long. "I'll be careful," I told them. There was no acid in my voice; I burned with the desire to tell them to get the hell off my land, but I resisted. Better not to upset three armed men. "Thank you. I appreciate your good intentions. But you don't need to check up on me again. I've been looking after myself for a long time."

They scanned the distance as they piled back into the car, checking for motion, for shadows beneath the desert sun. I watched them leave, heading back the way they'd come, the car a bloodspot on the horizon. And I thought, *better a pack of beasts than a pack of men with guns.*

I didn't tell you about the men, but you knew anyway. You were quiet when you came back; you did not join me on the porch to smoke and stargaze, but curled up silent on the couch, blanket drawn over your head so that I could see only a vaguely human-shaped lump lying very still against the cushions.

The cloud cover was thick that night, the air heavy, foretelling rain. A dry wind had picked up, casting fistfuls of sand like a spiteful child. And I didn't feel safe out there on my own, staring into a distance whose edges I could not discern; in which anyone or anything might be hiding. I shucked off my shoes in the hallway, locked the door behind me. As I passed by the couch my fingers brushed the crest of the blanket, where I supposed your face might be.

"I don't know you very well, June, but for what it's worth, I know you've got a good heart. I can feel that much." I drew my hand away, honouring the privacy of your cocoon. "I know they have you mistaken. I just wanted you to know that."

Sometime in the night I felt you crawl into the bed beside me, slow but determined in your audacity. I lay perfectly still as you slipped beneath the sheet, each movement cautious; I sensed the breath held in your lungs as you curled a hand around my arm, your knees pressed gently behind my own. I felt the tension of your muscles: apprehensive, but bold enough to persevere. I turned to face you, pulling you closer with great care. I feared I might crush you with the slightest movement. Your ribcage was sharp against my abdomen, the planes and angles of you a stark contrast to my softness, my roundness.

"Be careful out there tomorrow," I said, as though this sudden easy intimacy were normal. "There're men with guns sniffing around."

Your mouth pressed against mine. You had glass shards for teeth, wire for bones; your lips tasted like copper. My father's voice distant in my mind: *it is an abomination for a man to lay with another man.* I traced the braille of your spine with the tips of my fingers. *Joke's on you, dad,* I thought. *Neither of us are men.*

"Sadie, Sadie," you whispered, singsong. "Oh, Sadie, don't you know? I was born careful. I've been careful all my life."

Every day I feared your absence less and less; you were like the tide, receding into the gloaming, returning again as the sun set. I had not planned for the eventuality that, someday, you might not come back; curiously, I had no desire to prepare for it. It was as though after a life spent preparing fastidiously for a future that might never come, I had finally learned to absorb the present; you had taught me, somehow, that the sum total of my existence could not be pared down to numbers on a spreadsheet: how many tins, how many bullets, how fast I could run, how many weeks I might survive.

Sadie, you sang. I loved the way my name sounded in your mouth, the warm gravel of your voice lilting. *I was born careful.* Born lucky too, perhaps, because those men never found you, though I saw them on the road once or twice. They would nod, in greeting or in solidarity, and I would nod back, though I would sooner have driven on without acknowledgement.

"Can you run?" you asked me one night, perhaps a week after the men had stopped by. You were wrapped in a knitted blanket;

a sharp breeze swept in from the mountains, a familiar whistling in the eaves, heralding the very beginnings of winter.

A cigarette stub glowed between the tips of my fingers, heat licking at the calluses. "When I was ten," I said, propping myself up against the headboard, "I was so physically fit I could do five hundred push-ups in one session. I could run a mile in six minutes. I'd even go to bed with my sneakers on in case the world went to shit in the middle of the night and I'd have to run for my life."

"That's kind of fucked up."

"Yeah," I said. "Yeah, it is."

"But how about now?" You indicated the dying cigarette at my lips; you glossed over the heaviness of my thighs, the thickness of my waist, though they must have crossed your mind. "Could you run now? If you had to, I mean?"

The question sat heavy on my tongue, forbidden but always present. A ghost between us. Your face was drawn, eyes wide and anxious and beautiful. "June," I said, crushing the remnants of my cigarette between thumb and forefinger. Ash scattered the bedsheet, a thin grey snowfall. "What is it they think you've done?"

There came a strangled cry from outside, the sound of an animal caught unaware; the back of my neck prickled. We both turned our heads, staring out of the window at the darkened scrub. "Not what I've done," you murmured. "What I am."

"I don't understand."

"Listen." Your hands clasped my face, urgent. "I need you to know that what you see, right here—this is the truth. This is what's real. Do you believe me?"

You were so close I could see myself reflected in the black of your pupils. "June-"

"Whatever else I may be. Whatever anyone says. This—" You drew my head gently towards you; your lips were velvet against my forehead, your teeth hard behind them. "—all of this. I swear, Sadie. I'd give everything away just to keep this."

Everything you were to me had been pieced together; you were a loose-stitched patchwork of intuition, of little stories and guess-work. And I loved you, somehow, despite your insubstantiality; you cast no shadow, left no footprints, but the warmth of your body and the salt taste of your skin mattered far more. I wrapped my arms around you, the curve of your skull delicate beneath my chin. Your hair smelled like gasoline. I wondered where you'd been. "I see you, June," I said, after a time. "I believe you."

"It's not their fault." Barely audible. "My poor sisters. They're so hungry."

I smoothed your hair back, glancing down at your face. "Your sisters?" I asked, but you said nothing more. Your eyes were closed, your mouth a slack, sleepy line. Perhaps you'd been dreaming aloud.

The bed sagged a little under our combined weight; I lay quietly, listening to your breathing deepen; my beloved stranger, dreaming strange, sunlit dreams. I held your bones close and let my eyes slip shut.

I will always remember the look on your face when I saw you standing there, neck stretched, pulse throbbing in that vital spot beneath your jaw; the edge of a knife pressed against your throat just hard enough to break the skin. The man's grip tight on your arm, fingers buried deep in your flesh. I will always remember the spark in your eye: not fear but fury, acute as any knife-edge. It was barely dawn. I stood helpless, desperate to tear you from his grip but unarmed, unprepared.

"I said you ought to be careful." The .204 Ruger hung from his left shoulder; his right hand held the knife against your carotid. "Said there were vicious animals out there. Do you have the faintest clue what you've let into your home?"

"What I know is none of your goddamn business." I'd woken to the sound of shattering glass, a door being kicked in; your scream still echoed in my skull, ricocheting back and forth. I thought I'd lost you. I knew I still might. "I don't know where you get off hurting women—"

He spat. "She ain't a woman. Ain't even a person. What, she never told you?" Lips pulled back, a rictus sneer. His free hand yanked a clump of your hair, snapping your head sharply back; you let out a pained yelp. "Never even told your friend here the truth? What you and your bitch sisters have *done?*"

"Let her alone—"

"Watch," he said, brow knotted in disgust. "You just watch."

I could do nothing else. I watched as he dragged you by the hair, pulled you towards the shattered window, your bare feet dancing over broken glass; you shrank away from the sunlight, writhing wildly in his grip, and for the briefest of moments his balance faltered. Barely a second, but it was enough. Your teeth tore into his thick white throat; your fingers anchored in his hair, pulling him down, dragging him through the open doorway and onto the porch. He fought, but you were terrible in your persistence; his fingers spasmed, clutching ineffectually at your hair, your face. The knife clattered to the floor. In the darkness you were a girl, a furious girl with blood spilling like water from your mouth; in the sunlight I saw the truth. You were a thin, ragged animal, a starving coyote tearing the throat of a grown man as easy as paper. As you moved through that sun-dappled room you were liquid: shadow-girl, sun-dog; your pelt shone russet in the warm light, your skin smooth in the shade. Hot blood streamed from crimson lips, glistened on sharp ivory teeth, changing and warping as the sun rose, illuminating the truth of you.

At last, he slumped to the ground, and he did not move again.

In a pool of shade you stood up, all torn feet and trembling legs. You wiped your mouth with the back of your hand, streaking gore down your face, into your hair. I imagined I could hear the railroad clatter of your heart.

"Do you see me, Sadie?"

You were wild-eyed and trembling, but you were not afraid. You were a world away from the frightened, wounded girl I'd met outside Wildrose. You held your palms out to me. *This is what's real:* you, sleeping in my arms; your legs wrapped around mine, skin slick with sweat, your lips grazing my jaw. The sound of my name in your mouth. I swallowed, thick-throated. "I see you," I said.

There came the low hum of a car engine approaching. I turned. The rust-red station wagon was coming up the dirt road.

"Run with me," you said.

And we ran. You weaved through the shadows, into the light; you were a girl on torn feet, a swift coyote with the wind in your pelt. The hardpan stung my bare soles, the sun hot already at my back; my lungs burned with the effort and still there was such a long way to go. We had no plan, no destination, and perhaps we would fail, but for now we would run, and it seemed to me—breathless, exhilarated—that nothing in my life had been as pure, as perfect as this singular moment of freedom.

ROOT-LIGHT

Michael Wehunt

I. APPROACHING PRAYER

In a sudden breeze the poet watches three dandelion spores break their tethers. They drift out for a
moment like trivial monoliths. He is sick and must
die somewhere, so he has chosen a place that might
be sick with poetry. But he holds back the moment of
arrival, watching these dying small things. The air cold
and thin as the edge of a butter knife, too toothless to
carry the spores over the remnants of black rainwater,
so they fall and drink there. The poet has come much
farther, four hours down the beige highways into the
dim flat country, away from his mountains, into weary
forest, to Furlough House.

This is how he begins things, by plucking and
seeking, pulling the obvious metaphors from nature.
This is why he stopped his car before the bend that will
likely show him the house. Got out and watched the
trees deepening further into their winter motif down
the gravel drive, let the dandelion catch his eye as it
lost its young. What hair he has left stands briefly in
the wind. Pain twists low in his gut. His legs ache. The
bones he has been wrapped around for so long feel

heavy enough to simply lower them down here in the same dirty puddle as the drowning seeds.

Instead the poet turns in a slow circle, the bare fading pines and oaks scratching the purpled sky, a spearmint tang in the air, and thinks—*But*. He admits, *You're only thinking of other poets, of Mary Oliver, next you'll look for rain, a yellow thread, and God. You did not come here for tree bark and prayer and the scalloped edges of cloudbanks. The house is where the new words are. The last words, please let them be.*

Still he admires the trees, whose shadows lurch softening across the gravel, the failing sunlight confetti caught lower and lower in their branches as he stands gazing, procrastinator, wool-gatherer. A weighted and vast stillness out here. The first grains of dark sift down and he enjoys this, too, the slow curtain. He cannot escape it.

James Dickey, now, would have turned this grim wild into a feather that cut through the meat of what this all means, the choice, the way the poet has at last turned to embrace the cancer. Dickey's voice would reek of vegetation and gun oil and flash a final sun-glare into his swollen tired eyes, and Lord it would have heft.

But he is neither Oliver nor Dickey. He is not half of one. He is Corddry Smith, only that, and after seventy-three years it must be enough. Death has paid him notice, and now comes clawing, crawling from his intestines, metastasizing whatever sacs its fingers grasp inside of him. Death is not an idea but a presence now, pinned to him more certainly than a spore. Which is to say, which is to prod himself, the house is the whole point, and he returns to his creaking Volvo and eases it toward the curve in the trees.

Furlough House rises into view—or it seems to rise, somehow, cupped in a bowl as it is. The poet lets the gravel drag his car to a stop and for a handful of moments tries to picture the house in a bell of spring riot, because the place might simply burst in the green throat of May. Picturing it is a difficult effort. In November, this November, it's just an atrophied thing uprooted from some other ideal and laid into this Carolina nook. A long colonial house, the color of old blood, with twelve large windows in the front, lidless eyes without the dignity of shutters. Drab shingles. The whole of it held inside a shallow valley ringed with spruce sentinels, every one dead, everything gray but for the walls of the house and the great oak shading its right side.

This tree stands inside the bowl, a monument of roaring health and the only green for acres. A crowded monstrous thing with naked and muscled limbs, some like trunks in their own right, with seven tire swings suspended like ballast from the two lowest limbs. Some of the tires sway on their stout ropes, as though only just vacated. A dead kite peeks from the grass near the tree. A pair of vivid pink and white beach balls give the patchy yard a surreal tint—he can't imagine children staying here, but Corddry can see no other instruments of leisure or rest around the house. The brief porch has no rocking chairs. Nothing to use for contemplation of the vague slope and its arc of watchful crone trees, of the imminent reason for one's presence here.

"And my House in communion, washed in gone wine," he murmurs, tasting the words and threading them out slowly, but doesn't bother wasting space in his pocket book. "Would I wish for rain or would it soak?" Tepid as twice-steeped tea. He has always written badly when his heart is in knots. When another lover spurned him. When the lover that mattered died two hundred miles from him in a hospital bed the poet never laid eyes on. In those moments he used to imagine his eyes growing into deep holes that had seen too much of all that lay ahead again. The old routine. Yet now the horizon is readable in its nearness, its abruptness. He will not again win the National Book Award. 1979 smolders far behind in the brighter ashes. The poet only wishes for the last handful of new words. He has no time to purify them by fire, but they could be kindled on a page. Something to shelter against the single paragraph his obituary will be shoehorned into. No surviving family. No partners. Showed great promise once.

The Volvo eases down the gentle slope. Here the gravel widens into a square. There are no cars, no garage, only a tall windowless wall serving no utilitarian purpose for the house, paint flaking like an aged fresco. He gets out of the car with his overnight bag, pats the breast of his coat for his slim book.

Around the front of the house, his eyes averted from those staring tires, and the quiet is broken as he steps up onto the porch. Low voices. The owner, a Mr. Hessel, didn't mention any guests. But the poet feels no pique. Anders, a mythology man Corddry has half-known since their teaching days at Dartmouth, told him this place is a kind of hospice in which a friend of his cousin had apparently "gathered his last thoughts." There is a room here, and a bottle with an eyedropper full of "a good death" perched upon a table, that affords one a soft, guiltless shuffle off the coil. Hessel confirmed this in an evasive but acquiescent way. An end to the pain, and the striking through of that word—*suicide*—that might otherwise mar the one paragraph of eulogy in the paper. He can be interred with a kernel of pride.

But the words he feels he can write here—he has no way to know why he at once felt the assurance, the galvanization, he simply did from that single vague conversation with Anders—those are the true reason he's come. The idea, from the first, felt like removing the bookmark from himself, where he has always fallen open to the pages of his thirties, well-thumbed, his spine lightly broken.

Cobwebs lace the quartered window in the front door. He turns the brass knob and steps into a high-ceilinged space flush with warmth. This main room seems to claim the bulk of the house, and it hasn't been cleaned in some time. Part of him registers the low fire in the grate, the uneven row of various animal skulls along one of the oak walls, the downward slant of the ceiling. Too many sofas and stuffed chairs stand upon the vast area rug on the floor.

The rest of him takes in the group of people sitting in a waiting line on two of the sofas. The sofas each tilt a bit toward the other, suggesting an arrowhead that directs Corddry toward them, and the tone of everything changes. He feels it as a pressure in his ears, like driving into the mountains after a long time away from home, a headache, a swelling of the dust motes in the last blades of light falling through the parted curtains over the windows.

"Hello, dear," an elderly woman says, "it's approaching evening prayer."

Not merely elderly but deeply old, wrinkles like crevasses and dried riverbeds, a shamanic, photojournalistic old. She and two other women and three men watch him, the deer and bird and, he thinks, wolf skulls like thought balloons above their heads. They are siblings or have simply withered into a sameness, equally old, shrunken as prunes, skin stretched thin as butcher paper.

"And now a full house," one of the men says. "Take your coat off, stay with us! You can tell us some limericks." The others chuckle, five toothsome grins slipping behind knotted hands.

"Yes, mister," a second woman says, her voice reedy and accented with what his little experience insists is northern England. "We'll have soup here shortly, after we say our prayers. I know how to make a good soup!"

"And you can make us a good sap!" says another man, and they all giggle behind their hands again.

Limericks? Sap? They are mocking the poet. But the warmth, the rosy breath of the room carries the sweet smell of wood smoke. Sweat springs from his face and brings the pain spreading back into his knees. The poet removes his coat, drapes it over the back of a wingchair, and sits facing the other guests. On the single table between them is a deep red apple, a single bite removed like a shocked mouth, its flesh white with the faintest tinge of yellow oxidation.

One of the elderly folks clears a throat and the poet looks up. Only now from this lower angle does he notice the odd positioning of the women's hands, fingers laced over their bellies from which woolen robes suddenly fall away. Those bellies are globes, fully swollen with pregnancy. There must be inflatable balls, watermelons, some sort of prank under those elastic shirts, even with the outward nudge of navel in the center of each, like the aroused nipple of a breast.

"I should," the poet murmurs, and stops. His eyes trail from one distended belly to the next. He should what? He realizes he doesn't know. Leave, this is the sensible thing. But his head swims, small pieces of light fizzle around the edges of his vision, and he finds himself finishing his thought, "I should really unpack my things."

He has no indication that they hear him. He feels he has ceased to be in the room, so he stands and follows himself out. Their heads have bowed in prayer, as though to dictate the string of unpausing words from their narrow mouths.

2. LOW VOICES, OUT LOUD

His room—or the room he has fled to—has one small lamp on the bedside table, a wax-shaded thing that produces perhaps a single tallow candle's worth of light. For the past hour Corddry has fidgeted, cowered on the lumpy bed, gazing out the narrow uncurtained window. The beastlike oak squats beyond it, the tire swings deaf wind chimes. Up the slope is only an indistinct night.

He cannot hole up in here. Tonight this room would make a regrettable coffin. His stomach quivers and grumbles. Hunger is rarer these days, and he welcomes it when it comes, the way it feels like middle age. A bowl of their soup, a conversation with Mr. Hessel once he tracks him down, and he can either drive away or keep to his own end after a day of reflection and writing. Strange ancient siblings be damned. It is going on eight-thirty, but he hardly sleeps before midnight anymore, and never very deeply. His joints saw with discomfort through the night, underneath the more profound pain in his guts, those teeth that have in recent months begun to chew at his insides with real fervor.

But outside the room are the low voices, and he cannot face the drone of their interminable prayer. He sits a little longer, discovering his mind full of Daniel here at the end. It has been, he supposes, since the word "terminal" came into play. There is no bottle on the table, nothing in the room with skull and crossbones. The walls are old and bare. Spartan, austere, there are many words he finds but none of them fits the quiet despair he feels in this room. He hopes this despair isn't the crystallization of an excuse, a want for a cleaner postcard ending. He hopes Daniel hasn't filled his imagination for any lesser reasons. Or simply because of the way AIDS took him.

He last held Daniel in 1993, and Daniel last had him six years before that. Those years stretch long enough that a simple nostalgia can manage the longing. Daniel is now akin to the memory of true appetite. His lover's body wasted away into a protracted death, and the poet will not have that for himself. There is an honor in there, somewhere. He is counting on it.

"Daniel, a grave whose grass I never knelt upon, the way all things tend toward silence," he says, pulling his book over and uncapping his pen. He once wrote a poem on another, more recent man's chest with this pen. He hopes it was about something ephemeral. "Out loud, the way we would ask ourselves who dragged us from the lake," he writes. And the words begin to come, as easy as this. A cloud of dense silence gathers as he scratches at the Moleskine pages.

He is lost, dinner forgotten until he hears a voice say through the door, "Want your soup, mister?"

A female voice, the same English one from before, but now the accent is so clearly fake that he can't believe he didn't hear it the first time. These other guests, the very fact of three fully pregnant women in their nineties have impossibly dropped out of his mind. "I'm not feeling well," he calls, "I'm sorry."

"I'll leave it here by the door, then, poor old man." He hears a thick grunt, a clunk of something against the floor, and pictures the woman bending over that great fleshy globe. It is several minutes before he dares creep to the door, opens it to find a wide and yellow porcelain bowl sitting there, warm but not hot to the touch. The poet closes himself back up in the room. He doesn't want to bless the doorknob for having a lock but does it anyway. The smell the soup gives off is a wild green miasma that clears his sinuses. The hunger sweeps back to the surface and he sips at it. Vegetable stock, and spicy as hell. His stomach is just going to have to deal with it.

He writes a little more, him and Daniel standing in the grave, worms leaking out of rich soil, trying the words aloud to frame their cadences, until a heavy, musty drowsiness takes him, swift enough to be nearly unnoted. The bar of light under the door filling up a piece at a time, the scuff of shoes crowding around it.

3. WHEN WILL HE LET YOU, WHEN WILL HE COME?

Corddry wakes and his book slips to the floor. The pen clatters after it and under the night table, upon which the lamp still sheds its tallow light. He hears voices but in the sleep fog they are pitched too low, garbled. "Want him to play with us," a man's voice says, and the words are repeated more slowly by others, almost in a song. "Make him play with us." "He has to." "It's almost time for the root."

He scrubs his face with his hands, stands and moves toward the door. A new voice speaks from its other side just as he bends to press his ear against the wood: "Come out now, poet." He shrinks back, realizing the first voices might not have come from beyond the door. "We know you're trying to die on us."

He spins in the small space, hearing more of them, "Make him play," a grunted "God, it's *deep*"—what was in the soup he drank? His eyes fall on the window, the oak rearing outside, and below it, rocking toward and away from him in lazy motion, are four of the elderly guests perched on the tire swings. Their faces are obscured moons wisped with white hair. Corddry steps to the window and boxes his hands around his eyes, peers through and at the two women seated on tires, their own hands making slings beneath their heavy burdens. Their bellies seem to swell with each upward forward arc. They see him watching and wave.

The third old woman abruptly appears and presses her face against the window, grinning, motioning Corddry outside. Behind the woman two of her companions begin chasing each other around the tree, weaving in and out of the tire swings, setting them to spin.

"Go away, please!" Corddry shouts. The strain in his throat from the words doubles him over in a coughing fit. He lets his knees unhinge and he drops back onto the bed. Buries his face in his hands and squeezes his eyes shut.

The doorknob rattles twice. "Who is Daniel?" the voice says from the door. "When will he let you?"

"When will he come?" Corddry whispers, finishing the title of his first chapbook, published in 1971, his christening as a "Rimbaud for post-Free Love America." And he bought into it from the start, nothing more so than the debauchery. A trail of wine bottles and dirtier things clanking from San Francisco to Montreal to the seams of Greenwich Village. But his blood stayed clean through all of it. Everything goes out of him suddenly on this bed, the fear, the disorientation, the cancer itself, for all he knows. The narrow mattress could swallow him. He only feels hollow and very tired.

"Just leave me be," he murmurs, curling into himself, "I came here to be alone. I came here to do one thing."

From the window, muffled, another voice, "Guess he doesn't want to play tonight." Fists thump against the house, fading toward the front door. Soon the silence has wadded itself back into the room like cotton balls into prescription bottles, the ones he pushed away from himself, left back in Roanoke. His pen remains under the night table. His book waits, open, somewhere on the floor.

4. THE YOUNGEST THING HERE

And there is the poet Louise Glück, born eleven days after Corddry Smith, making them siblings of a sort. She haunts him most. Although he won a major award long before her Pulitzer and other immortalities, her poems have always sent him into bleak rages of jealousy. In the title piece of *The Wild Iris*, the very book that cast her impenetrably higher than he could ever throw, she wrote of being buried alive, and of a door at the end of suffering.

Corddry wakes the next morning, in weeping pain, with her words in his mouth and soil in his bed. "The stiff earth," as she called it, lies in crumbs upon his scalp, in the creases of the sheets. It clings in the parted cleft of his lips, tasting of stale minerals. He wishes he had brought his phone, that he hadn't doubted his resolve, but even now, who would he call? Only the proprietor, Mr. Hessel, and this would be only to enquire about the bottle with the eyedropper. Furlough House's patented "good death."

He wants that bottle. And he will try to write a little more. Those lines from yesterday evening—something he thinks he might call "Your Unearthed Coffin"—are the start of something good, maybe special, better than anything he's written in fifteen years, surely.

The main room is empty, animate with the sense of dust still settling after being disturbed. Breaths left behind to break apart into atoms, vibrations of words whispered about the poet. A lump of rot sits on the table, a riot of mold, and after a moment he recognizes the indention in it as the surprised open gape of the apple that was there the night before. Weeks have passed, if one takes this apple and disregards the remainder of the universe.

A deep spiny pain flowers in his gut. He closes his eyes, opens them with a fiercer resolve to find a phone. But the main room, extending a good hundred and fifty feet from his bedroom door, has none. He walks to the other end and opens doors, peers into messy, incongruous bedrooms with dolls and plastic robots strewn among twisted clothes, every wall alive with mildew, but the house continues to yield nothing until he reaches the square kitchen at the east end of the house. This, too, is dimmed by uncleanliness, but there are no cockroaches, no smells of spoiled food. Simply the same wilting age that seems to have coated the house like a sudden film.

One of the old women is squatting on the floor there as

though to piss, but what rills toward Corddry from between her legs is a creek of blood that reeks of copper. Her straining, sweaty face is close to as red. "The root's taking strong hold this time," she gasps at him. There is no affectation of an English accent there now.

He stands frozen and stares at her far past the reach of decorum before managing, "Can I—I'll find a towel."

"Don't mind it, it's got to run," she says. "It's awful close now." And she screams, tipping her head to the ceiling so the tendons in her neck stand out like collarbones. He seems to see the tip of something reach out from her behind the sodden hem of her hiked cream skirt. Just when he can stand it no longer, she falls quiet and flops down on her rear, the skirt blessedly concealing her to the knees.

"I saw what you wrote," she says, panting, looking up at him between damp wings of dark hair. "Is that a poem in that book? I didn't understand some of those words."

"Yes," Corddry says. It is all he can think to say.

"But I liked where you said that about the grave and all things tending toward quiet. It's true, when you think about it. Those trees up there. A room with nobody in it. Fruit when you take a bite of it, or when you take it from its place. We die so fast. Maybe your pretty words slow it down." She smiles, suddenly bashful, and looks down at the blood-smeared floor.

"It was 'silence,' not 'quiet,' but thank you." He clears a blockage from his throat. "If you don't mind, I'm trying to reach Mr. Hessel."

"Who?" She giggles.

"Mr. Hessel, the owner of this place."

"He doesn't ever come." She's still looking at the floor, dragging a finger idly through the blood, drawing an inexplicable cat with it, Corddry is nearly sure. "He's just the mouth that brings us food from out there. He tends to the tree. But we can get your nectar if you want it."

"Nectar? Is that what you call it?" He is getting a fever—it creeps out of his collar and flares on his bald scalp—and cannot think of other things he should ask. "Yes, please, I came a long way for that bottle."

"I can smell the rot in you. It hurts, it's started to hurt a lot more, hasn't it, and you want it gone. But we never give the bottle right away. We give you root soup. That's so you can get strong and think about what you want to do. And you want to write in your little book, don't you ever?"

"Yes, but—"

"What if you could write a whole book everybody would love, love, love?" At this she throws her arms wide above her head and closes them in a clap. "Something that everybody would remember forever and always?"

"I—" His vision is fuzzing around the edges again. "What is your name?"

"Willa. It's one of my favorites. You know, you can win that pluster you want so bad."

"Pluster?"

"That prize your sister won. I like her words too. There's some root in them."

Dear Christ, she means *Pulitzer*. She's reading his mind. Movement catches his eye through the window. The others are outside, chasing and wrestling and turning cartwheels. He can just see one of the women hanging from the massive oak at the far left of his angle of vision, using her legs to swing herself in large arcs. Things that should shatter their brittle bones to cornmeal. A tree that seems to flourish like nothing here does.

"Please bring the bottle to me, would you?" he says, and turns away. A great clenching in his gut stops him just inside the short hallway. He doubles over and coughs hard enough to bloom red stars in his eyes. His throat burns. Yellowish tissue streaks across the floor, ropy like the pith of a clementine.

He takes an extra moment to scrutinize the main room. Half an era has passed since his arrival, a neglected stink of time, the curtains disintegrating and spotted black around the windows. The chairs and sofas heavy with dust and discoloration. On the mildewed table is a charcoal smear where the apple sat long ago.

I am the youngest thing here, the poet thinks, and retires to his room.

5. IN THE SHAKING LIGHT

But the words come again, in a lush verdant spillage that is nearly an agony to him, though far sweeter than the creeping blight of the cancer and its brood of metastases. He nearly feels regret, that he's come here to die and given himself the will to go on. But he refuses the regret and the will at the same time and listens to just the words that fall from him. One poem is finished and the next has four stanzas that hum in the little bedroom.

The age that has infected the house does not reach here, and his surroundings cuddle him. There comes a firmness to his joints, knitted around the pain. His writing hand hardly cramps. He pauses to watch the leaves stir on the hale oak outside his window, now absent of the elderly guests as evening lowers its slip. Somewhere the sun drips away.

Yes, he does feel that he could write a book here. A collection of at least thirty elegies to the things he has seen, and to Daniel, or at least to the ideal of him, soaked in the kerosene of HIV and his own illness. Was Daniel his one love? It is a difficult thing to turn away from, yet it was so long ago. These could be an old man's pangs. An old man's predictable hindsight.

He begins to get hungry again, truly ravenous in that younger way, and stands. From below the house, shrieks rise with him. Corddry thinks of a dial tone, the overlaying of registers. Amplified, threaded with animal wetness, the sounds make his sinuses compress. His hand falls on the doorknob, the cold brass-plated metal shocking his skin. And as everything seems to be paired in the tremble of these moments, he hears a hand fall on the other end of the knob.

"Stay with us," a voice says through the hollow wood, naked and congested. One of the men. "Take care of us. Be the light here."

"I'm dying," he says. "Please, that's all I need to take care of."

"Not yet," the voice says, stretching the words. "Come down to the root cellar. We won't hurt you. You'll see. You can make poems about it. And, okay, the bottle of nectar is down there, if you really do want it."

Footsteps stomp away and Corddry follows them. The whole of the main room has now gone the spoiled black of a tumor. The ancient man is already far ahead of the old man, loping on all fours like a rabbit, back legs driving him forward into the kitchen. The poet attempts a burst of speed, braces himself for a coughing fit that doesn't quite come. The kitchen is coated in decay, the streaks of Willa's blood years ago becoming part of the cracked linoleum. A door hangs open in the back, exposing a downward sloping darkness.

He places his foot on the first step, and finds the next easier, a burden slipping away from him like a yoke. His skin prickles and tastes the cool air. The poet smells a sharp green stench, rich living earth. He thinks of candles in the shaking light. Hears the shrieks of the women, in stereo, the same huffing breaths before the next. The light gives him a gesture; it waves him down and onto the dirt floor of the cellar, his vision clouding with pin-pricks as it did before. He feels himself changing into something, but still inimitably himself.

The cellar squats beyond the rush of time rotting the main house. It holds nothing within it but the six old guests—residents—*Children, let's call them what they somehow are,* he thinks—and three great twining roots. Earthen walls lined with flickering sconces, and the vast knotted appendages thick as the poet's legs reaching through the top of the easternmost side toward the fallen sun. Down to the three women, who lie on their backs with legs spread. Corddry cannot quite bring himself to look away, instead sees the men crouched before the parted apertures, each with a root draped over his shoulder as they receive the blood-slicked infants into their primed arms.

It is not seeing the roots inserted between the women's legs that causes Corddry to turn, his gut heaving with nothing but a film of soup to bring up through his throat. It is the choreography of it. He hangs his head and hears the screams continue, a thread of high thin wails joining them, that dial tone again. A moment after he realizes he has lain, or fallen, down upon the packed dirt of the floor, he opens his eyes to three more babies emerging, he sees the men gray as ash or as the roots of the monolithic oak of this house. Their arms crack open and their faces split, crumbling into shaved bark as they stagger toward the wall and try to insert themselves into the soil. The second of each set of twins falls to the ground between its mothers' legs. The mothers are silenced. Alone the six new creatures mewl on.

6. THE RINGS OF A TREE

"You'll be our light now." A dirt-filled voice, and somewhere else, the sharp reeds of keening infants. A pressure on his shoulder, coiled under his armpit and across his chest. Daylight comes strong through the window. In it the poet sees a blur of woman bending over him with tendrils of leafless vines where her iron-white hair was. Brown acorns in eye sockets, or a fever dream. Teeth to shred through his breastbone in a moment. Where is the good death? He is back in the narrow bedroom, the empty walls, a membrane of glare coating his vision. No bottle on the bedside table.

"Everything you ever read is here with you," Willa says, and covers the crowded teeth behind a mossy hand. "Everything that ever touched you. Write your book. Dying's here but you won't like how we really are." The corners of her mouth smile and she laughs and looks away. There is no blood on the floor to draw in now, but she is no longer shy. "Sorry to say there wasn't ever a bottle you could drink to die. Mr. Hessel, he lies for us about that, even though there's a root of truth down in it. But just for you, I named one of us Daniel. I do like your poems."

Corddry lifts himself onto his elbows, squeezes clarity back into his eyes so that he can see the woman whose face has aged

beyond years. Faint circles echo out from her nose, concentric—
The rings of a tree, the poet thinks, and says, "Daniel?"

"These old bodies are going now into the roots," she says. "We
feed the tree and you feed us and we feed the tree. And start
again. That's how we flower and rot with age right off the vine.
That's how we go on, until one day we might stick and get to
grow up slow. I think I wouldn't mind not being a child."

"Please, why can't you just leave me alone?" The poet feels a
thickening in his gut, a knot of hunger, an alien tightness as
though everything is sewn up properly inside of him. But his
head is full of daylight. It is so soft and tired.

"You found your words, didn't you, and it's made your sap
sweet. You'll suckle us babes, bit by bit, until we're grown again,
and we'll grow full with child again. Or until your sap is too
polluted. Someone else will come looking for a good death." She
moves toward the door and Corddry watches her break apart.
Pieces of skin flake like veins of bark. Topsoil spills in a powder
from the crevices as she staggers out of the room.

He slips from the bed, stands on the memory of strength once
in his legs, stops his open mouth from shouting after her about
the bottle. He hears her run down the hall toward the cellar. His
book is on the bed, the pen clipped to its back cover. Standing
there he tries to remember all the poets, their words on death
and eager, leaching life. They dim and dissolve. He thinks of
Glück and Rilke and Oliver and Dickey. He can nearly grasp
a title, "Root-light," from the last, but there is something else
tethered to it, something that has never been to do with him,
never had a home with his heart, and he sits back down. Picks up
the book and feels the waiting texture of its pages, the pebbled
false leather of its covers.

He hears no newborn cries. The quiet in the house has grown
to profundity, so he writes idle words until the words reach out
to this profundity and pull the quiet into them. He writes of
things seething beneath the dirt. The things are his past and his
lovers and the night he stood on a stage and wept from the spotlight and the award placed into his strong unlined hands. In the

dark, after the spotlight, a man with a forgotten name twined around him and pushed into him and he cried out.

But he feels the words leaving him. On the page they are not quite his own. Through the half-open door, the poet sees furniture gleaming with rebirth, the walls clean as though fresh from the sawmill and the carpenter. And down the length of the house, in the kitchen, a door is thrown open and the clatter of footsteps come running with young voices chasing them. The spores break free of their tethers and caterwaul into the main room. The poet leaps forward and slams and locks the door, upon which tiny fists rain with round lisped shouts of "Mister! Mister!" and "Play with us!"

He says nothing. He writes the words "Root-Light" at the top of a new page and sits there for hours. Three of the children— which one is Willa?—gather outside the window, taking it in turns to sit on the tire swings and keep watch over the poet. The sun is slowly sucked into the west again until the words will no longer come.

By morning, the fists against the door and the window are heavier. Still the words leave him, and the tastes of his lovers' skins leave him. He can only narrate himself. The children remain in their patience,

Already the lisps are fading
    From their pleas and imprecations,
The gentle promises pulsing in the twins' hunger,
        the six voices.
Already the poet feels his blood singing to them, vocal with
        compulsion
    And sticky with sap.
He presses the pen, he pushes the black ink around, but the
        words have left the page.

THE TRIPLETS

Harmony Neal

T HEIR MOTHERS HAD BEEN CAREFUL TO conceive the girls under the same blue moon. Kaylee's mother had heard from her sister-in-law, who had heard from her tennis partner, who had heard from her hairdresser that there was an old Chinese or Japanese or possibly Cherokee legend that girl children conceived under a blue moon would be born exceptionally beautiful. They figured the story unlikely, but what could it hurt? Each woman had seduced her husband in identical red lace teddies under identical suede capes in the barely autumn air on plush microfiber throws put down under the moon in not-quite remote areas in the same municipal park. The tale supposedly went that the perfect conceptions could only be had out of doors, with the woman on top, her body perfectly silhouetted and bathed in the silver light of the knowing moon. Each husband wondered what had come over his wife, and each never suspected that two other men were being simultaneously treated to identical fellatio performed by similar women who had all read the same recycled article in that month's *Cosmo*. Each husband culminated in the similar orgasms had by circumcised men, and in that way, three girl children were conceived by three women with similar goals.

The girls were all born during the first week of June, which the mothers found to be an ideal time for girl children to be born since you could wrap their heads in satin scrunchy bows and not have to worry about too much heat escaping. They crammed their daughters' feet into tiny strappy sandals and paid $10 apiece each week to keep their toenails polished in the fashionable colors of the season. Crystal's mother also wanted to do the girls' fingernails, but their joint pediatrician suggested that since babies put everything in their mouths, including their fingers, this was not a good plan. The same pediatrician didn't really want the mothers to have the girls' toenails painted either, for the same reason, but each woman exclaimed no daughter of hers would ever dream of placing a toe in her mouth, regardless of what the writers at *Cosmo* might suggest on the topic.

The women hired identical Slavic nannies for the girls, a rare find of triplets, and congratulated each other that though the young women were not unattractive, their dour expressions, unplucked eyebrows, and jeans-and-t-shirts wardrobes would simultaneously make the mothers look better and keep the nannies focused on what mattered, which was the upkeep of the mothers' children and homes. They hoped the nannies were lesbians, and something about the way they didn't shave suggested this might be so, though of course, none of the mothers asked and none of the nannies ever said a thing to the mothers that wasn't the response to a command.

The three daughters also looked very similar, though they had small differences: after all, a truly beautiful woman is unique in her own beauty while hitting the major markers spot on. All three had pale eyes since all three mothers had judiciously only dated men with pale eyes and light hair, and were, of course, married to men with pale eyes and light to medium hair. The mothers hated biology, the way hair normally darkens and loses its luster in adulthood and skin loses its vibrancy and elasticity—unless the necessary precautions are taken, which all of the mothers took with their hair and skin and breasts. Only Lila's mother had gotten a single stretch mark during her pregnancy, through carelessly neglecting her preventative routine one weekend, but she'd had that corrected within two weeks of Lila leaving the womb.

The infant girls had intuited what was expected of them by the time they could hold their heads straight on their wobbly necks. They smiled and cooed and cutely patted peoples' faces when within reach. They accepted the itchiness of lace tights and the pressure of too-tight shoes. They learned to appreciate the stinging pull of hair being yanked and molded and dominated. They giggled, but never guffawed, learning early to always feign delighted surprise, but never be too surprised by anything.

In this way, they also learned to accept their due of fawning and smiles and compliments that dripped or gushed from adult mouths, like a slow honey or a rushing rapid. They knew their place in the universe, their role, and they were comfortable enough with it, having given little thought to the possibility that there were other places, other roles that girls like them might take, different landscapes and horizons, different shapes of existence.

There was only one thing the girls did that secretly disappointed their mothers, and that was their refusal to maintain a cold indifference toward their nannies. In public, the girls adopted the appropriate air of the attended to being taken care of by their marginally compensated attendees, but in off-camera moments, when the girls didn't know their mothers were nearby, the mothers witnessed small demonstrations of tenderness between their daughters and their help. Once, Kaylee's mother declared she'd even seen a hug between Manya and Kaylee, but Lila and Crystal's mothers assured Kaylee's mother that such was impossible since Slavic women were known to lack anything resembling warmth.

Naturally, the beautiful daughters were very popular at school and other little girls wanted to sit with them during lunch and breaks and be their reading partners and science buddies, even though as early as kindergarten the girls were known as "the triplets" and no principal had power to separate them into different classrooms and no teacher could likewise split them, no matter her reasons for wanting pairs instead of threes. No one could deny the girls had something of a magical power. Even when their mothers weren't in the wings, demanding their daughters receive their due, no one wanted to deny the girls anything.

Their primary caregivers were, of course, their nannies, who lived in small guest bedrooms in the backs of their respective houses on the first floor, out of the way in rooms they were to spend as little time in as possible. Manya, Maryia, and Marusya kept to themselves. They did their jobs, and did them well. They met when they could, understanding the necessity of family in a hostile place full of technicolor people eating technicolor food and living technicolor lives. Had they not elected to each care for one of the triplets, they wouldn't have been able to see each other at all, but since the girls were in the same dance, art, and manners classes, they saw each other regularly, retreating to back aisles and hallways to speak to each other in low voices in words incomprehensible to those around them.

Mostly, they saved money and bided their time. Their mistresses did not know much about them, not even which country they came from. They certainly did not understand that these women had chosen their names, abandoning their given names at the border of their homeland. Their mistresses neither knew nor cared that the women came from a land where the death rate had outstripped the birthrate, where hunger and desire were ways of life. They hadn't even bothered to notice that the women they'd hired were girls themselves.

The triplets shot up from infants through toddlers through elementary kids through middle school. None of them ever seemed to go through an awkward stage where the proportions of her face or body went a little off. They stayed perfect, perfect, beautiful little creatures. Perhaps they were a bit more reserved when the lights weren't shining on them than their mothers may have wished. Certainly, their mothers didn't want banshees for daughters, but the girls never raised their voices, never demanded their own way, never demanded anything.

Manya, Maryia, and Marusya surprised themselves with the genuine care and concern they felt for their stoic charges. They hated the women who paid them a pittance for work they should have done themselves, but they found their hatred could not touch the girls given over to their care. They grumbled about the frilly clothes and silly hairstyles and perfumed lotions and dance classes and quarterly portrait sittings, but they loved the girls and wanted to see them happy.

Kaylee, Crystal, and Lila did everything expected of them and little unexpected until their twelfth birthday, which was to be celebrated together, as it had been every year since their birth, on a day near, but not exactly on, any of their respective birthdays. Typically, the girls participated in identical activities (but never anything that could be considered a "sport," since none of the women wanted a sporty girl: they weren't even allowed to learn tennis), but in the world of music, they had each been assigned their own instrument at the age of 8. Kaylee's mother had insisted on the piano, since she swore her daughter had the longest and most graceful fingers. Lila's mother had wanted piano for Lila, who might have the slightest case of allergies or asthma and couldn't possibly play an instrument that used the breath, but she conceded that her daughter's fingers were slightly shorter than Kaylee's, though mostly she conceded to not piano because if both girls played piano, one was certain to be better, and she could not risk this advantage to Kaylee over Lila. So Lila learned the violin, which had pleased her mother until she saw the marks the violin left on her daughter's chin, but by then it was too late to switch since Lila would have been far behind the learning curve, so her mother bought a series of luxurious chin rests and convinced herself that the semi-permanent tilt of her daughter's head made her seem a little confused at all times, which could be nothing but a plus in the pursuit of a suitable husband, since wealthy men demand witless women.

Crystal's mother had missed the day at the spa when the

others decided on instruments. She was enraged since piano and violin were also her first two choices, but she said nothing since the reason she'd missed that spa day was that she had been recovering from a certain elective surgery about which she didn't want the other two women to know. Upon hearing the news and being asked which instrument her own daughter would play, Crystal's mother discharged her ice shard laugh and declared that of course Crystal would play the flute, there was no question, and she already had a person finding out which flute was the best.

This was how the triplets came to be a musical trio and how each of their houses developed a soundproof room in which each girl spent more time practicing her instrument than her mother could have predicted, which was a serious source of pride and concern in each woman. And since the mothers had no real appreciation of music themselves, and since they paid no attention to what the girls learned or what music they practiced, none of them knew that their nannies had spent part of their hard earned wages to purchase certain music from their homeland for the girls to play.

The only unexpected thing that the girls did before their twelfth birthday, was that when asked what she wanted for her birthday, each girl responded that she only wanted to perform a song with her trio. Since it was the first time any of the girls had really requested anything, each mother was taken aback. None of them had any idea what the girls sounded like when they played. The girls had been receiving private lessons, solo and as a trio, for four years, but the mothers had assumed it took much longer to play an instrument decently and had never allowed their daughters to participate in any recitals, much to their music teacher's angst and despair. Besides the obvious job of turning their girls into perfect paradigms of womanhood, the mothers took seriously their charge to avoid any and all embarrassment, which could taint their daughters and follow them through their lives like shadows plucking at their limbs.

The mothers agreed to the performance anyway, since how could they deny their daughters their single request? They were now very interested in hearing their daughters play. The daughters smiled their practiced coquettish smiles and said it should be a surprise, after all, the mothers had waited this long, what was one more week? The mothers each tried to sneak up on their respective daughter's practicing, but the contractors had done too good a job and the practice rooms were truly soundproof. They tried to sneak by the trios' weekly rehearsal, but when they showed up to the music space and heard half a dozen children squeaking and squawking on their instruments—because somehow the nannies had confused music practice with dance practice on the calendars—a chill ran down each mother's perfectly cracked and decompressed spine, because what if their daughters' sounded the same?

Fearing the worst, the mothers went directly to their personal shoppers and acquired the most tasteful and "in" outfits possible for their daughters for the event (and for themselves, of course) banking on the magic of beauty and the keenness of the eyes to erase any unpleasant sounds picked up by the ears of the hundred or so people who would be present for the triplets' celebration.

The mothers had no way to know that on the other side of town, Manya, Maryia, and Marusya were also choosing clothes for the girls' big day. The chosen clothes were special gifts to mark the last year of childhood in the girls, which was well-known to be the 12th year, even if a technicolor country might deny as much while doing everything in its might to turn girls into women by age ten. In their own country they had seen children turned to whores, but not in the manner they witnessed everywhere in their new land of endless opportunity. They often joked about this among themselves and nodded and spit in ways that people in the new land did not recognize as laughter.

On each girl's actual birthday, she woke in the morning to sweet milky coffee and pastries and fruits and buttered potatoes and pickled herring and varenyky with various fillings, savory and sweet, and a slew of other delicious treats. Each nanny looked down on her charge lovingly and recited a series of well wishes for the following year. Manya wished for Kaylee all the love a life could hold, good health, much laughter and warmth, piano songs to make her cry, a special boy or girl, a long life, the best fruits, fulfilling work, and protection from things that wanted to harm her. (Here Manya was thinking of Kaylee's silly mother.) Maryia wished Crystal health, a long life, good friends, a loving family (she said this with no hint of irony since she was thinking of herself, the other girls, her sisters, and Crystal's future husband and children, not Crystal's ridiculous mother and blind father), satisfying work, a comfortable home, dexterous fingers and lips and mighty lungs for her flute playing, wealth, happy days, and children with beautiful souls. Marusya wished for Lila a strong back, a quick wit, thick and serious eyebrows, the love of a good dog, the right soul for a violinist without the devil's hand, a healthy body, a clear mind, and the sort of spiritual wisdom that comes through hard work. As each woman recited her expansive list, she looked into her girl's eyes, holding her hands and stroking her hair, and she did not abbreviate her list in the manner of native English speakers, but instead said fully each time, "I wish for you x. I wish for you y. I wish for you z." By the time each nanny was done, each girl was in joyous tears of despair at being loved so well and fully and being known so well and fully by another person in this great, cluttered world.

On the afternoon of their 12th birthday, which was the day after the last girl had had her real birthday, since their mothers agreed that it should be after and not during or before, because that would mean each girl had at least a day shaved off her actual age each year, the cumulative effects of which were assumed to be much greater than simple math allows, the triplets each found laid out on their cotton-colored beds two outfit choices for the day. One outfit, curated right down to a pair of thong panties, which the girls found frightening and absurd, was a series of expensive items procured by their mothers' personal shoppers especially for the occasion. In addition to the clothes were fancy envelopes for a spa day that included "daughter's first waxing" services. These piles took up half the bed, but each girl instinctively moved toward her pillows where there were white shirts and skirts, embroidered in bright reds and oranges and trimmed in white lace. On the floor they found matching red boots and shuddered to see the mini sparkling heels at the other end of the bed.

Their nannies knocked and entered to find their girls decked out in their festive costumes. Smiling, they expertly pulled the girls' hair back and added the final touch of flowers and ribbons that each had made herself for her girl for the occasion. The triplets glowed. None wanted to visit the spa, so the six went instead to a park to dance, then to the practice room to rehearse the music for the celebration.

The mothers were none the wiser. They were at the spa and assumed their girls were too. They never thought to inquire, occupied as they were amongst themselves and their bodies and images and also their quiet concerns that their girls' might develop moles or lose their thigh gaps. They'd agreed upon the various personal trainers and dieticians and guards (if necessary) they might employ in the unfortunate circumstance that one or more of the girls might start to lose her figure. They discussed possible skin disasters with their estheticians and signed their daughters up for biweekly treatments through their eighteenth birthdays. There was some debate about which year was best to begin Botox as a preventative measure, but the estheticians insisted they couldn't possibly begin before the girls were sixteen, which made the mothers frown, not that anyone noticed since their foreheads and cheeks stayed smooth.

The mothers arrived to the rooms of the rented hotel ten minutes early to ensure the caterers and decorators and various other employees were properly doing their jobs. Everything was as it should be except they saw no sign of their daughters, who they assumed were backstage getting ready for the recital. Kaylee's mother grabbed a vanillatini from the nearest waiter since it was now after 1pm. Crystal and Lila's mothers sipped champagne from delicate flutes, shooting ugly looks at Kaylee's mother. All were worried about this very important day and how their daughters would look and be received. Children and adults began filling the white folding chairs lined up in the garden, directly in front of the small white stage that was ready with the piano and microphones.

At exactly 2 pm, the girls walked onstage and all three women gasped from their positions at the back of the crowd. Each chided herself for being so unaware of junior's fashion that season, and none could figure out how such quaint peasant clothes could possibly be in, down to those ugly, ugly boots. The hemlines were atrocious, falling down past the knees. The flowers and ribbons seemed the worst touch, reminiscent of decades gone by that the mothers had been sure would never resurface. Each made a note to herself to fire her personal shopper. As the girls took their positions, Kaylee's mother hissed "haaaaaair."

It was true, each girl had a fine blond down on her legs that glittered like gold in the sunlight. The mothers darted glares toward the large speakers in front of the stage, behind which they expected the three nannies to be inconspicuously huddled.

Lila waved her bow in a few short flicks of her wrist, and the music started. First Kaylee twinkled out a few notes on the piano, then Crystal twinkled in on her flute, then Lila joined with the same twinkling sounds on her violin. The music had a light and whimsical quality of a sort the mothers had never heard before. It seemed to shimmer in the air around the girls, who smiled into their instruments and swayed, eyes gently closed, looking so much like young angels, like little girls. The music seemed a prayer or celebration, with a note of longing murmuring under the surface.

The mothers were each transported somewhere else, some time ago, to younger versions of themselves they had locked away. They each felt brimming with possibility and curiosity, as if life wasn't laid out, as if there weren't a set of rules they had to follow. They lost themselves in the song, not looking at their daughters or trying to gauge the response of the audience. They each closed their eyes and breathed in the summer air and smiled smiles that reached all the way to their eyes, not giving a damn about wrinkles.

With their eyes closed, the mothers failed to notice that the other members of the audience likewise had their eyes closed, all gently swaying where they sat or stood. No one noticed the nannies take the stage, each garbed in outfits to match their charges, true reds and oranges and yellows that looked young on the girls, yet appeared almost fierce on the nannies, as if they were not exactly engulfed, but rather enwrapped or perhaps buoyed by flames. They performed a slow, graceful dance as a trio, coming together, then breaking away, spinning when the music picked up, flowing with sinuous arms and elegant tilts of head. Had anyone's eyes been open, they would have become entranced, had they not already been entranced by the ethereal music.

Once the girls' song was done, sleepy eyes throughout the audience cracked open, unsure what world they might only now be discovering. They'd barely had time to expel dreamy breaths and register the presence of the nannies onstage before Marusya spoke softly yet firmly into one of the microphones, "And now for our gift for our girls." Maryia placed an oboe between her lips as Manya lifted a French horn to her own. They began playing, Manya producing long then short tones of longing, Maryia's oboe slithering around the middle register. Moments later, Marusya's soprano came clear and strong, crooning and accusing in a language no one in the audience knew.

The girls swayed on stage, their arms linked behind each other's backs. The audience found themselves holding their breath, mesmerized. Each person felt a gentle tugging in their chest, an insistent longing. The charm and whimsy of the girls' song was displaced by something raw, urgent. They found themselves wishing they could check their pockets for the cure, the thing that was missing. Something was missing. That was clear. The members of the audience felt stuck in place, frozen. They could not so much as scratch an itch.

The music slowed.

The girls swayed and bobbed in their tight circle of three that took center stage. The nannies encircled the girls with their own bodies, a ring of flame, instruments and voice facing out, a wall protecting the delicate creatures contained within. Marusya hit a final, slow trebling note that rose over the sustained breath of Manya's horn. Maryia's oboe darted around their tones, tying a knot inside a knot.

Later, some audience members claimed there had been a fire. Others said a shimmering puff of smoke or a swirling mass like a tornado. Some suggested a gaseous attack; others claimed the party must have witnessed an event of incomprehensible horror. Everyone knew they were forgetting something very important. The mothers became internationally famous, pleading, begging, with wet eyes and trembling lips: someone, bring our daughters back. They had professional dressers, stylists, and personal assistants for their TV and radio tours. Late at night, each woman sat alone in her hotel room, lit only by the moon's insubstantial beams. They clawed at themselves, at their arms, stomachs, cleavage, digging for the missing thing they could no longer abide.

The only ones who never spoke of what had happened were the children who'd been there, whose eyes no longer focused on adults, but instead, drifted far away, watching the luminous grass as it grew or the erratic birds as they ate and danced and played, wandering each night to the knowing silver moon in all her different phases. They hummed or whistled a foreign tune and smiled the secret smiles of children everywhere.

DISPOSSESSION

Nicholas Royle

THREE MONTHS AGO I MOVED TO A NEW place and, while my new flat more than meets my needs, I'm finding that the old one is increasingly on my mind. I can't dismiss this as nostalgia, because I really wasn't ever happy there, but I can't stop thinking about the old place. The other night I even dreamed about it.

For a number of reasons, I was glad to move. I was moving from a rented studio, which was too small for me to have my children to stay, into a three-bedroom flat that I was buying. My children, who had never used the keys I had had cut for them for the old place, would get a bedroom each, which they would use two nights a week and alternate weekends, according to the agreement with my ex, and I would be able to get the rest of my stuff out of storage.

The flat is on the top floor of a three-storey development dating from the 1950s. There are a number of blocks, each comprising six or ten or a dozen flats, separated by communal gardens. I've filled the flat with cheap units and shelved my books according to size, doubling up where possible. I don't need to know how to find particular titles. I haven't read a book in two years. Yet I can't bring myself to give them away. I've bought new clothes for the children and these are stored in drawers in their respective bedrooms.

My son's bedroom is situated at the back of the flat, his windows offering a view across a courtyard to the rear of another block. You get the same view from the bathroom, if you open the frosted windows, and the kitchen, which is where I keep my binoculars, in an eye-level cupboard to the right of the sink. The flat opposite mine has been empty for a week, the soft outlines of shampoo bottles removed from the bathroom window ledge. Two days ago I watched a man painting woodwork in the kitchen. Since then, nothing.

After I moved, I would occasionally walk past my old place on the way to the shops, but, at first, I barely gave it a second glance. Then one day the letting agents rang me to say that the new tenant was having difficulties with the phone company and would I be kind enough to give them my old number, so they could give it to her and she could tell the phone company what it was. It seemed a funny way round to do things, but I looked it up. A couple of days later they called again, wanting to know if I had had broadband installed in the old flat without encountering any major difficulties. I said that I had and I named the provider.

The thing about the letting agents was that we had parted on bad terms. They had complained about the state of the flat when I moved out and surrendered my keys. Citing patches of peeling paint on the walls, soot on the ceiling and stubborn stains on the carpet, they had refused to return my deposit in its entirety and had informed me of their intention to deduct certain amounts, which were itemised on a memo that came attached to a tetchy email. I challenged their proposal, pointing out that the paint had peeled from the walls only where it had been behind furniture, which suggested to me that either damp or poor decorating was to blame. Also, although I had not told them this, when I had emptied the flat, I had gone round covering up the nail holes in the walls with TippEx. I hadn't anticipated any problems with the refunding of the deposit.

After an exchange of unfriendly emails, they agreed to reduce by a half the amount they intended to charge for cleaning and redecorating. I felt by that point that I had no choice but to give in.

So, when the agents started phoning me with regard to the difficulties the new tenant was experiencing, I didn't particularly welcome the contact. I felt like offering to be put directly in touch with her.

But it got me thinking and it reminded me of how I'd felt when I had just moved in, two years earlier. The flat had been unfurnished, superficially clean, but I had found myself wanting there to be some kind of trace left by the previous tenant, some clue to his or her identity. I didn't feel that he or she could be held accountable for the curtain rail that became detached from its fittings if you opened the curtain too far on one side, or for the lumpy lino in the kitchen. I found the trace I was looking for in the wardrobe cupboard in the hall. In it I found a number of empty hangers from mid-range high street fashion stores, some marked 14, others 16. I imagined a young woman, her weight fluctuating over the months or years that she lived there. I wondered what she might have looked like. I wondered where she might have gone. I wondered if she ever gave a thought to the place she had left behind.

I was grateful for her clothes hangers, having brought few with me from the house I had shared with my ex. I remember the estate agent who showed me round. It takes special skill to show someone round a studio flat. But this studio was the best of a fairly bad bunch that I had viewed over the previous week. I remember looking at him when he had shown me a smaller one, where the kitchen was so small the position of the cooker prevented two of the cupboard doors from being opened.

The landlord will remove the cooker if you don't want it, the estate agent said.

I said nothing in response to this.

It will get harder to find a good place in the New Year, he said.

Why's that, I asked?

Because couples struggle through Christmas together, he explained, and realise they can't do it any more. Come January the men are out looking for flats.

I studied the expression on his face—scorn? Despair?—and tried to work out if he, too, was living in a rented studio. He hadn't once looked me in the eye.

I took the next flat he showed me—the studio with the clothes hangers whose previous owner had, I imagined, jumped from size 14 to size 16 as she had become unhappier, alone in the flat and perhaps alone in the world, and then back to 14 once she had made up her mind to move out.

I put up a picture in my daughter's room. A framed collage of images of butterflies cut out of magazines that she made in Year 9. I also have a go at fixing the window blind, which has been catching on one side. I open the top drawer of her chest of drawers and look through her tights and socks and underwear. I take out a pair of tights and hold them to my nose—they smell only of fabric softener—then drop them on the floor.

In my son's room, I go through his football shirts. I take one out and unfold it on his bed.

The intercom buzzes and I go to the door to pick up.

Post, says a voice.

I press the button and hear the door open down below in the communal hallway. I wait until I hear it shut again and then open my door and go down to see if there's anything for me or if, as is usually the case, I was simply the only one at home to let in the postman. In my pigeonhole I find a padded envelope.

In the kitchen I put the package down on the table while I get out bread, chopping board and bread knife, and cheese from the fridge, and make myself a sandwich. While I eat this, I open the padded envelope to reveal a proof copy of a forthcoming novel. I take the book into the living room and find room for it on a shelf full of similar-sized books. My eye briefly lingers on the spines of the books. Novels, short story collections, a non-fiction book about the night, an anthology of sea stories. An academic study of a certain school of French literature. A book about underground films. All they have in common is size.

In the old flat, there had been room for no more than two bookcases. I had taken books relating to what I was working on at the time, plus a couple of series for teenagers that I was in the process of collecting. I had bought one or two of those titles originally, second-hand, for my son, as I had enjoyed them at his age, but he had lost interest in reading, so I had carried on buying them, from charity shops and second-hand bookshops, partly out of nostalgia and partly out of a dimly understood need to collect them on my son's behalf, even though he had no interest in them.

Sometimes I would hear voices in the old flat. The first time I heard them, I couldn't figure out where they were coming from. My first thought was from beyond the wall behind my bed, but when I worked out that that was outside—and my flat was at the top of the converted house—I ruled that out. Then I thought I could hear them better if I approached the wall where my desk was, but I pretty soon ruled that out, too. I only figured it out by accident. I opened the door to the boiler cupboard to get the vacuum cleaner out and there I heard voices. I realised they were the same voices, still quite muffled, but I could hear them better in the boiler cupboard than anywhere else in the flat. So, from that point on, I kept the vacuum cleaner under my desk, leaving enough room in the boiler cupboard for me to stand in there and close the door behind me.

One of my then neighbours—either the woman in her forties from the floor below or the younger woman from the flat just down the half-landing from mine—was talking to a man. They sounded like a couple. The conversations were banal, but I found the cadences of their speech, the rhythms of their dialogue, soothing, lulling. I could spend up to an hour in there at a time, sometimes longer.

I'm in the kitchen bending down in front of the washing machine, loading it with my few items of laundry. I shake powder into the tray, then add conditioner, and close everything up. I pause a moment before pressing the start button. My knees pop as I stand up. I go to my bedroom and have a quick look around, but it doesn't appear as if I have missed anything. In my daughter's room I pick up a pair of tights from the floor and there's a football shirt on my son's bed that could do with a wash. Back in the kitchen I open the machine, add these items, slam the door and set it going.

I stand up again and look out of the window. The windows opposite are bathed in wintry sunlight. In the ground-floor flat directly across from mine—two below the empty flat—a young man and a woman are standing in the kitchen facing each other. His upper body is leaning forward, while she backs off slightly. He points, jabbing at the air between them, his shirt buttoned at the cuff. But he is the one who leaves the room. She remains where she is, rocking slightly to and fro, then turns on her heel towards the sink and the window. She rests her hands on the edge of the sink. I lower the binoculars for a moment to check that my kitchen light isn't switched on and when I lift them back up again she is pouring herself a glass of water from the tap.

In the kitchen of our family house, the four of us had sat down at the kitchen table. My wife and I—was she already my ex? Effectively, yes. I had told her. We had talked. It had been a few weeks—my ex and our two children.

I heard myself saying banal and unspeakable things.

Everything else will stay the same, I finished.

I stressed this point. We both did, my ex backing me up for the sake of the children.

My daughter looked faintly embarrassed, while my son's expression darkened quickly. I had never seen such a swift and dramatic transformation in a person's face. Something fluttered inside my chest. Desperate hopes revealed as vain. The worst that could happen, now happening. I was destroying my life and possibly theirs. My son got up and walked out of the room.

The washing machine signals the end of its cycle with a high-pitched beep. I open the door and pull the wet clothes out and drop them into the basket. I drape shirts, T-shirts and my son's football top on hangers and hang these on door handles around the flat, a 14 here, a 16 there. Smaller items, including my daughter's tights, I fold neatly over the radiators.

Job done, I pull out my phone and look at it. I realise I'm frowning.

I text my ex, reminding her it's a Thursday and I'm wondering where the children are.

She doesn't reply.

I call her.

What do you want?

It's Thursday, I say.

Don't, she says. Just stop it.

She hangs up.

I go into the children's rooms. They are very tidy. Really very tidy.

I find myself back in the kitchen looking at the flats opposite. The top flat is still empty. The middle flat is in darkness. In the kitchen of the ground-floor flat a single glass sits on the worktop.

I look around my own kitchen. The bread left out, going stale. The bread board. The bread knife.

I turn to the kitchen drawers and open the second one down. I rummage around and come up with the keys I'd had cut for the children and hadn't handed in to the letting agents.

I walk over to the old flat, the contents of my bag rattling with each step. I look up at the window, which is dark. Maybe she is out in one of the local bars or restaurants, or at work, or studying in a university library, or away for a spell. I press the buzzer and wait for a response, which doesn't come. I use my key to gain entry. The entrance hall looks the same. I see some junk mail addressed to me lying on the floor beneath the pigeonholes and I leave it there as I head for the stairs. On the half-landings I pass doors that were once familiar to me. A television can be heard behind one of them; cooking smells emanate from another. When I reach the top of the building I stand with my ear to my door. It still feels like my door. The key turns in the lock and I enter.

The flat is warm. She can't be far away. It doesn't look like it did in my dream; the bed is smaller, but it's in the same place. She has a cheap white desk where I used to have my sofa and coffee table. Her TV is where my desk was.

I hear footsteps on the stairs, a key in the lock. I cross the ten feet to the boiler cupboard in the time it takes her to open the door, and while she is closing the door to the flat I close the door to the boiler cupboard behind me.

I hear her moving around, even above the suddenly deafening sound of my heartbeat. I can also hear voices coming from behind the boiler. In my dream there had been a large window in the kitchen allowing access to a grassy slope. I had jumped from tussock to tussock, feeling buoyant and free.

I close my hands around the contents of my bag and try to listen only to the voices.

Malcolm Devlin's stories have appeared in various publications including *Black Static, Interzone* and the Undertow Publications anthology *Aickman's Heirs*. His first collection, *You Will Grow Into Them*, is due to be published by Unsung Stories in June 2017.

Brian Evenson is the author of a dozen books of fiction, most recently the novella *The Warren* (Tor.com) and story collection *A Collapse of Horses* (Coffee House Press). His story collection *Windeye* and his novel *Immobility* were both finalists for a Shirley Jackson Award. His novel *Last Days* won the American Library Association's award for Best Horror Novel of 2009. His novel *The Open Curtain* was a finalist for an Edgar Award and an International Horror Guild Award. Other books include *The Wavering Knife* (which won the IHG Award for best story collection), *Dark Property* , and *Altmann's Tongue* . He is the recipient of three O. Henry Prizes as well as an NEA fellowship.His work has been translated into French, Greek, Italian, Japanese, Slovenian, and Spanish. He teaches at CalArts and lives in Los Angeles.

Michael Kelly is the editor of *Shadows & Tall Trees*, and the Series Editor for the *Year's Best Weird Fiction*. His fiction has appeared in *Black Static*, *The Mammoth Book of Best New Horror*, and *Weird Fiction Review*, among many others. As an editor he's been a finalist for the World Fantasy Award, the Shirley Jackson Award, and the British Fantasy Society Award.

Rebecca Kuder's story, "Rabbit, Cat, Girl," appeared in *Year's Best Weird Fiction*, vol. 3. Her essays have appeared in *The Manifest Station*, *Jaded Ibis Press*, *Lunch Ticket*, and *The Rumpus*. She lives in Yellow Springs, Ohio, with her husband, the writer Robert Freeman Wexler, and their daughter. Rebecca blogs at www. rebeccakuder.com.

V. H. Leslie's stories have appeared in a range of publications including, *Black Static*, *Interzone*, *Shadows & Tall Trees* and *Strange Tales* IV and have been reprinted in a range of 'Year's Best' anthologies. Her short story collection *Skein and Bone* from Undertow Books was a finalist for both the British Fantasy and World Fantasy Awards for Best Collection. Leslie was also a finalist for the 2014 Shirley Jackson Award for her novelette, 'The Quiet Room' and she won the 2013 International Lightship First Chapter Prize. She has also been awarded Fellowships at Hawthornden Castle and the Saari Institute in Finland, where she was researching Nordic water myths for her PhD. Her non-fiction has appeared in *The English Review*, *Emag*, *Thresholds*, *This is Horror* and is forthcoming in *History Today*. Her debut novel, *Bodies of Water* was released this year from Salt Publishing.

Robert Levy is an author of stories, screenplays and plays whose work has been seen Off-Broadway. A Harvard graduate subsequently trained as a forensic psychologist, his first novel *The Glittering World* was a finalist for both the Lambda Literary Award and the Shirley Jackson Award. Shorter work has appeared in *Shadows & Tall Trees*, *Black Static*, *Strange Aeons*, *Autumn Cthulhu*, *The Madness of Dr. Caligari*, and *The Best Horror of the Year,* among others. A Brooklyn native, Robert is currently at work on a number of projects in various media and can be found at TheRobertLevy.com.

Laura Mauro was born in London and now lives in Essex, largely against her will. Her short stories have appeared in *Shadows & Tall Trees*, *Black Static*, and a variety of anthologies. By day, she works as a medical laboratory technician. In her spare time, she writes strange stories, collects tattoos and probably spends too much time in front of the Playstation. She is very pleased to be appearing in *Shadows & Tall Trees* again.

Manish Melwani is a Singaporean writer of science fiction, fantasy and horror. He attended the Clarion Writers' Workshop in 2014, and currently lives in New York City, where he's completing a masters thesis in science fiction and postcolonial studies. His story "The Tigers of Bengal" can be read in *Lontar: The Journal of Southeast Asian Speculative Fiction*. That tale, and this one, are part of a forthcoming collection of Singapore ghost stories. You'll find him where the waters are darkest, or online at www.manishmelwani.com

Alison Moore's first novel, *The Lighthouse,* won the McKitterick Prize and was shortlisted for the Man Booker Prize and the National Book Awards. Reviewing her latest novel, *Death and the Seaside*, Nina Allan referred to her as "one of the most gifted and interesting writers of weird fiction in Britain today." Her short stories have been included in *Best British Short Stories* and *Best British Horror* anthologies and collected in *The Pre-War House and Other Stories*.

Harmony Neal lives in the USA and had to put her writing on hold to try to protect her local community from HATE. She hopes to continue her writing work as soon as she's gotten her new organization, Northfield United in Love, up and running.

Her essays and stories have been published in or are forth-coming from *The Fantasist*, *Interzone*, *Black Static*, *Eleven Eleven*, *Psychopomp*, *Gulf Coast*, *Nashville Review*, *The Gettysburg Review*, and *Paper Darts*, among others. You can find links to more of her writing here: harmonyisawitch.com

Rosalie Parker is a writer, publisher and film-maker who runs Tartarus Press with her partner R.B. Russell. Her first collection of short stories, *The Old Knowledge and Other Strange Tales* (2010, reprinted 2012) was published by The Swan River Press. A second collection, *Damage*, was published by PS Publishing in 2016. Rosalie lives and works in North Yorkshire, UK, in the wilds of the Yorkshire Dales National Park.

Before earning her MFA from Vermont College of Fine Arts, M. Rickert worked as kindergarten teacher, coffee shop barista, Disneyland balloon vendor, and personnel assistant in Sequoia National Park. Her first novel, *The Memory Garden*, was published in 2014, and won the Locus award. She is the winner of the Crawford Award, World Fantasy Award, and Shirley Jackson Award. She has also lost several awards for which she was nominated, including the Nebula, Bram Stoker, International Horror Guild, Sturgeon and British Science Fiction Award. Her newest collection, *You Have Never Been Here* was published by Small Beer Press in November, 2015. A certified yoga instructor, she teaches Bhakti yoga in Grafton, Wisconsin. For more information visit her website at www.mrickert.net

Steve Rasnic Tem's last novel, *Blood Kin* (Solaris, 2014) won the Bram Stoker Award. His new novel, *UBO* (Solaris, Super Secret Recordsuary 2017) is a dark science fictional tale about violence and its origins, featuring such historical viewpoint characters as Jack the Ripper, Stalin, and Heinrich Himmler. He is also a past winner of the World Fantasy and British Fantasy Awards. Recently a collection of the best of his uncollected horror—*Out of the Dark: A Storybook of Horrors*—was published by Centipede

Press. A handbook on writing, *Yours To Tell: Dialogues on the Art & Practice of Writing*, written with his late wife Melanie, will appear soon from Apex Books. Visit the Tem home on the web at: www.m-s-tem.com

Nicholas Royle is the author of seven novels, including *Counterparts, Antwerp, Regicide* and *First Novel*, and a short story collection, *Mortality*. He has won three British Fantasy Awards. He has edited twenty anthologies and is series editor of *Best British Short Stories* (Salt). A senior lecturer in creative writing at the Manchester Writing School at Manchester Metropolitan University and head judge of the annual Manchester Fiction Prize, he also runs Nightjar Press, publishing signed limited-edition chapbooks, and is an editor at Salt Publishing. His latest publication is *In Camera* (Negative Press London), a collaboration with artist David Gledhill.

Robert Shearman has written five short story collections, and between them they have won the World Fantasy Award, the Shirley Jackson Award, the Edge Hill Readers Prize, and three British Fantasy Awards. His plays for the theatre have won the Sunday Times Playwriting Award, the World Drama Trust Award, and the Guinness Award for Ingenuity in association with the Royal National Theatre. He is a regular writer for BBC Radio, and his own interactive drama series *The Chain Gang* has won two Sony Awards. But he is probably best known for his work on *Doctor Who*, bringing back the Daleks for the BAFTA winning first series in an episode nominated for a Hugo.

Christopher Slatsky's stories have appeared in *The Year's Best Weird Fiction* vol. 3, the *Lovecraft eZine, Nightscript* vol. 2, *Strange Aeons Magazine, Lost Signals*, and elsewhere. His debut collection *Alectryomancer and Other Weird Tales* (Dunhams Manor Press) was released summer of 2015. He currently resides in the Los Angeles area.

Simon Strantzas is the author of *Burnt Black Suns* (Hippocampus Press, 2014), *Nightingale Songs* (Dark Regions Press, 2011), *Cold to the Touch* (Tartarus Press, 2009), and *Beneath the Surface* (Humdrumming, 2008), as well as the editor of *Aickman's Heirs* (Undertow Publications, 2015), a finalist for both the World Fantasy and British Fantasy Awards, and the winner of the Shirley Jackson Award. He also edited *Shadows Edge* (Gray Friar Press, 2013), is the guest editor of *The Year's Best Weird Fiction*, Vol. 3 (Undertow Publications, 2016), and is co-founder and Associate Editor of the non-fiction journal, *Thinking Horror*. His writing has been reprinted in *Best New Horror*, *The Best Horror of the Year*, *The Year's Best Weird Fiction* and *The Year's Best Dark Fantasy & Horror*, and published in venues such as *Cemetery Dance*, *Postscripts*, and the *Black Wings* series. His short story, "Pinholes in Black Muslin", was a finalist for the British Fantasy Award, and his collection, *Burnt Black Suns*, a finalist for the Shirley Jackson Award. He lives with his wife in Toronto, Canada.

Michael Wehunt lives in the lost city of Atlanta, where he wishes he had more time to read. Robert Aickman fidgets next to Flannery O'Connor on his favorite bookshelf. His fiction has appeared in such lovely homes as *Cemetery Dance*, *Aickman's Heirs*, *The Dark*, *Electric Literature*, *The Year's Best Dark Fantasy & Horror*, and *Year's Best Weird Fiction*. His debut collection, *Greener Pastures*, was published in 2016 by Shock Totem. You can find him online at www.michaelwehunt.com.

Charles Wilkinson's publications include *The Pain Tree and Other Stories* (London Magazine Editions, 2000). His stories have appeared in *Best Short Stories 1990* (Heinemann), *Best English Short Stories 2* (W.W. Norton, USA), *Best British Short Stories 2015* (Salt) and in genre magazines/anthologies such as *Black Static, Supernatural Tales, Horror Without Victims* (Megazanthus Press), *Theaker's Quarterly Fiction, Phantom Drift* (USA*), Bourbon Penn* (USA), *Shadows & Tall Trees* (Canada), *Nightscript* (USA) and *Best Weird Fiction 2015* (Undertow Books, Canada).

His collection of strange tales and weird fiction, *A Twist in the Eye*, is now out from Egaeus Press. He lives in Powys, Wales.

Conrad Williams is the author of nine novels: *Head Injuries, London Revenant, The Unblemished, One, Decay Inevitable, Loss of Separation, Dust and Desire, Sonata of the Dead* and *Hell is Empty*. His short fiction is collected in *Use Once then Destroy* and *Born with Teeth*. He has won the British Fantasy award, the International Guild award and the Littlewood Arc prize. He lives in Manchester with his wife and three sons and is currently working on a haunted house novel and an interactive video game. He tweets as @salavaria and you can find more information at www.conradwilliams.net.

9 780995 094932